D1607924

ABANDONED

DECEPTION AND DELIVERANCE

A LIVELY DEADMARSH NOVEL BOOK FOUR

KATIE BERRY

ENTER TO WIN!

Visit Katieberry.ca and join my newsletter to become a Katie Berry Books Insider. By simply sharing your email address*, you will be entered into the monthly draws! That's right, draws, plural.

Each month there will be two draws, one for a free copy of one of my audiobooks from Audiobooks.com, and the other, a free autographed copy of one of my paperbacks delivered right to one lucky winner's doorstep. There will be other contests, chapter previews, short stories, and more coming soon, so don't miss out!

Become a Katie Berry Books Insider today at:

https://katieberry.ca/become-a-katie-berry-books-insider-and-win/

*Your email address will not be sold, traded, or given away. It will be kept strictly confidential and will only be used by Katie Berry Books to notify you of new content, contests, and prize notifications.

INTRODUCTION

Well, here we are, the final book in this, Lively Deadmarsh's first adventure. I hope you have enjoyed reading it as much as I did writing it. Altogether, this novel has been a journey of about five years for me. Throughout its creation, it has kept me going each and every day. I live and love to write. And being able to focus on this singular task has provided me stability and sanity in a crazy and tumultuous world.

It started, as most tales do, with a 'what if' question. Always a fan of dark and spooky places, I thought an abandoned hotel with a huge mystery seemed like a good place to start. And as I mentioned at the beginning of this series, I have always been fascinated by mass disappearances and vanishings. So, I thought, why not combine the two! What you now hold in your hand is the culmination of that idea and many others that came to me as I wrote it.

With that, I will let you go and wander the halls of the Sinclair a final time. I hope you experience some more thrills and chills along the way, and I'll see you again at the novel's end with a few additional thoughts.

-Katie Berry
July 15th, 2022

ACKNOWLEDGEMENTS

Very special thanks to Paulina and Jenna Mae. Your encouragement, assistance and friendship mean so much. Thank you both for everything.

For all my amazing readers, everywhere, always.

"Sometimes, the things you don't know can be even scarier than those you do."

-Author unknown

CHAPTER ONE

December 29th, 2021 1605 hours

The door leading to the Executive Gaming Lounge lay just up ahead, and thankfully, it was open. Minerva concentrated on putting one foot in front of the other and not looking back as she fled down the third-floor corridor. Behind her, the rustling of the painted wolf grew louder and louder as it drew closer and closer. Her mind was moving in a million different directions as she tried to think of something that could stop the impossible nightmare rapidly approaching at her back.

Minerva spun and slammed the turret door shut just as the painted wolf reached the threshold behind her. It collided with the thick oak, crumpling loudly, and she started to smile, preparing to let out a whoop of delight. And then she looked down.

Most of the doors in the Sinclair Hotel had a slight gap between the bottom of their thick wood and the floor. The door leading to the gaming lounge was no different, as Minerva now discovered to her horror.

Two claw-tipped paws scrabbled against the turret's hardwood floor as the painted wolf wriggled its crumpled body underneath the door's edge. Though only canvas, somehow, its claws seemed just as sharp as the real thing, and they dug into the foyer floor, leaving razor-thin furrows in the wood.

With a grimace, Minerva imagined what those claws might do if they made contact with her flesh. She tried to step on the paws with her leather boots' hard, angular heels, but her actions seemed to have minimal effect, and the animal continued to slither underneath the door. Panic in her eyes, Minerva looked desperately for another solution nearby.

To one side of the entrance, a decorative suit of armour stood guard in front of a large tapestry, a shield in one hand, a broadsword in the other. With a grunt, Minerva freed the sword from the armour's grasp. She turned back, alarmed to see that the creature was now more than halfway underneath the door, its painted head thrashing back and forth as it tried to snap at her legs with its canvas teeth.

Minerva hefted the ancient weapon as high as she could, feeling its comforting weight for a brief moment and relishing the burn in her shoulders; then, she stabbed the steel shaft down into the wooden flooring with all of her might, directly into the centre of the painted wolf's back.

Surprisingly, this had an effect, and the creature seemed to spasm in pain, making a sound unlike any wolf she'd ever heard. Rather than a howl, it was a rattling, breathless hiss as if a paper grocery bag filled with rattlesnakes were slithering underneath the door instead of this improbable beast. The animal struggled for a moment longer as if in anguish, but then it stilled, the hilt of the steel sword shining above its inert form like a cross at the head of a grave.

Minerva moved to the edge of the spiralling stone steps leading up to the lounge, then paused and looked back. She was half-expecting to see the creature jiggle or jerk again, but it remained motionless as though the sword had pierced its canvas heart. Not convinced it was dead since it could never have been alive in the first place, she was at least satisfied it was immobilised for the moment. But as she began the climb to the gaming lounge above, she kept one ear tuned for rustling at her back, just in case.

At the top of the stairs, the door to the lounge was closed, and she couldn't remember if she'd left it open or not. Looking to its bottom edge, she was thankful the gap between the door and the floor was a bit thinner here than at the turret's base. A beautiful, embroidered carpet runner lay just inside the entrance. Minerva rolled it up and placed it against the bottom of the door, hopeful it would keep the wolf at bay if it managed to tear itself loose below.

Things appeared normal enough in the Executive Gaming Lounge. Through the narrow, high windows that dotted the room, the last of the day's light faded to a dark and tempestuous grey as the winter storm continued to rage beyond. To one side of the entrance, the silverback gorilla pounded away on its chest as usual. Though stuffed many decades before, it still appeared as if ready to grab an unsuspecting American Tourister suitcase from a baggage check somewhere and begin to beat the hell out of it.

Moving through the room, she looked toward the video games and felt relieved to see the tiger crouched near the Ms. Pac-man arcade unit as it had been before. After her recent experience with the animated artwork down below, the last thing she wanted was to see any of these stuffed animals moving about of their own volition. Thankfully, no rustling, creaking or thumping occurred as she strode with anticipation toward the model room stairs. If the ebony box was capable of what she thought, she might be well on her way to bringing everyone home once more—at least, that was her hope.

The circular room's harsh, white spotlights made the shadows on the miniature hotel's surface so dark and deep that they appeared to have solidity. Lights shone brilliantly through the myriad of small windows that dotted the model's exterior, furthering its illusion of life. The slightly burnt smell still lingered in the air from when Lively had disappeared, and Minerva wondered if some wiring was perhaps shorting out somewhere inside.

Lively's gloves were still sitting on top of one of the model's parapets. She pulled them on, recalling the last contact she'd had with the box through the thick, dark leather. She crouched slightly and reached her hand tentatively toward the main doors. Taking a breath, she steeled herself and was not disappointed with what occurred when she touched the tiny doorknob.

Though she knew the model was powerful from her earlier contact, it now seemed even more potent than she recalled. Pulling the doors open, flashes of guests enjoying themselves streamed through her head. People laughing, eating and dancing, and other images of things not quite as pleasant— people screaming, crying and dying. But amidst all this, there was something else, a warm, fuzzy feeling, and she suspected what it was—Lively. It was the same thing she always felt when they hugged, and she felt sure that she sensed it now from within the model.

Peering through the doors, she felt as if she were the giant she'd heard thumping toward her suite the other night. She half-expected to see the small figurines moving about inside, but unlike her expectations, none of them appeared alive at this point, and she was grateful for that.

Minerva closed the tiny doors with a small sigh and began to feel along the edge of the building's eaves, where Lively said he'd found the switch that opened the model's halves. It wasn't easy with the thick gloves on her hands, but she loathed taking them off, unwilling to touch the building without their protective insulation.

Just when she'd about given up in her search, she felt a slight depression underneath one of her fingertips. A small, satisfied smile came to her lips, and she said, "There you are!" She pressed a little harder and was rewarded with a soft click.

Giving a small grunt, Minerva pushed on one side of the model, and it creaked slowly open in the middle. Once she had it halfway, she stopped and then moved to stand in the V between the halves. All around her, miniature figures posed in various positions as they went about their activities inside the hotel. Eyes wide as she took it all in, she gasped in wonder when she peered into the ballroom. The sizeable space was filled with little partygoers in decorative white face masks engaged in a formal ball. Just as in the actual ballroom downstairs, a small banner read, 'Happy New Year 1982'.

Minerva crouched to look more closely at several figures seated around one central table, a little larger than the others. A man in a black tux with reddish-brown hair sat next to an auburn-haired woman in a red gown. To their left, a thin man in a bowler hat took a drink from a tiny glass. Another man wearing a black tux was on the couple's right, and he had hair the same dark-blonde colour as Lively's.

Though she felt the urge to touch the figurines, she didn't know what would happen if she made contact with any of them. Were they just manifestations created by this hotel as it toyed with her, or were they much more than that? Would the act of her fingers touching any of these Lilliputians somehow negatively affect the person it represented, a person trapped somewhere within this hotel's very walls? She shook her head, finding herself temporarily lost in existential thought.

The metal panel covering the gold room was hanging open, and the ebony box lay exposed. It looked for all the world like the black heart of the hotel, one she almost expected to begin pulsating as it filled not only this model but the resort itself with its powerful dark energy.

But how did this box get up here in the first place? She recalled Lively saying someone would have to have moved it since it was last spotted in the grand ballroom in 1981, but who? Her previous contact with the box still fresh in her mind, Minerva knew that even with Lively's gloves, she couldn't just grab it and pull it out of the model. Whoever had moved it up here must be a person that was somehow inured to its immense power, and they had worked either wittingly or unwittingly to help this hotel with its transportation of the ebony box.

Knowing she needed additional protection for her hands, Minerva descended to the Executive Gaming Lounge in search of an insulator. She hoped a trip down to the bar would serve to provide her with what she needed.

Things seemed normal enough when she arrived at the bottom of the stairs, or at least, as normal as things ever got around here. Keeping her eyes open for any shenanigans from the stuffed sentries, she moved to the bar. An oval, sterling silver serving tray was waiting for her on top of the gleaming mahogany. It had a low lip running around its edge and handles on both ends. Almost exactly what she was looking for. She was still fascinated how this hotel seemed to know what people wanted, almost before they wanted it.

Moving behind the bar, she crouched down with the tray and rummaged around for a moment. When she stood, the tray contained a small stack of white serving towels. She planned to wear the gloves as she wrapped the towels around the box and then carry it back downstairs on the silver tray. With the additional layers of insulation, she hoped she would be okay.

Minerva stepped out from behind the bar and paused before moving to the stairs. She'd suddenly recalled the damage done to the model room's door by the tiger as it had tried to get in at Lively. A feeling of unease crept down her spine as the thought entered her mind. She looked to the stuffies with a slight frown, wondering if they were still in the same spots as when she'd descended from the model room moments ago.

The gorilla stood near the main entrance, and the polar bear guarded the model room stairs as before. But where was the cat? Hadn't it been over near the Ms. Pac-Man machine earlier? Where had it gone? Was it now lying in wait behind the pool table or the poker table, just waiting to pounce on her as she passed? Moving slowly, Minerva reached the bottom of the staircase after what seemed a very long time, due in part to her trying to look in every direction at once, but there had been no sign of the cat. She breathed a slight sigh of relief but realised she wouldn't feel safe until the door to the model room lay closed at her back.

While climbing the stairs, Minerva glanced over her shoulder every few steps to verify nothing was creeping up behind her. Fortunately, her return to the top of the turret stairs was uneventful.

When she stepped through into the model room itself, she saw things were now anything but ordinary. Sitting between the open V of the model's halves, the Siberian tiger patiently awaited her return.

CHAPTER TWO

December 31st, 1981 2002 hours

Lively closed his mouth with a crack when he realised it had been hanging open as if he were some sort of slack-jawed yokel at the county fair. He was stunned, unable to believe what he'd just witnessed, not to mention what he'd just heard come out of Edward Sinclair's mouth, and he felt almost ready to ask the man to repeat himself. Nearby, the partygoers danced to the sweet music of the Glenn Millers as if mesmerised, none of them paying any attention to the conversation playing out at the main dining table.

Growing up, Lively and Minerva had been told that their mother had died during childbirth and that she had never divulged their father's name. In light of who he was, Lively supposed that was a pretty good reason why they'd never been told. Still, he was speechless and didn't know what to say to Sinclair, who now sat looking at him expectantly, a slight smirk on his lips.

Eyes wide, Selene looked to Lively then back to Edward, her expression one of shock and disbelief. It appeared as if she had no idea who the handsome man she'd been flirting with was, and she asked, "Son? How can this fully grown man be your son, Edward? You look younger than he does!"

"Gee, thanks," Lively said.

Sinclair looked from Lively to Selene, the slight smirk still playing across his lips as if savouring his next revelation. With a slight tilt of his head, he said, "He's not just my son, Selene. He's our son."

Selene's hands flew to her chest, and she said, "What? How can that be? My son and daughter died in childbirth!"

"Did they?" Edward asked, one eyebrow raised.

Shaking her head, Selene said, "Well, I don't know for sure since I was under general anaesthetic during the cesarean, but that's what the doctor told me afterward!"

With a patient smile, Edward said, "That's what I paid him to tell you, dear."

Selene shook her head in disbelief. "What? How can this man be my son? Even if both twins survived, they wouldn't even be one year old right now!"

Edward laughed softly and said, "Yes, it was unfortunate that such obfuscation was necessary, but due to the plans that were in motion, it seemed the most prudent course of action at the time."

"Selene," Lively said, "what year is it?"

"Why, it's 1981, of course! For the next few hours at least."

Shaking his head, Lively said, "No, in reality, it's 2021 right now."

It was now Selene's turn to have her jaw drop open. "What?" She shook her head and said, "I don't understand."

"Neither do I," Lively added. "The only thing I know for sure is that you, along with everyone else in this ballroom, have been here at this resort celebrating New Year's Eve for the last forty years."

"You're crazy! I arrived here only yesterday."

"That was over fourteen thousand yesterdays ago, my dear," Edward placated, patting Selene's hand gently.

Pulling her hand out from under Edward's with a jerk, Selene said, "I think you're all insane!"

Edward shook his head. "Don't worry, all will be explained." He nodded to Bald Beefy, and the man moved next to Lively. Sinclair continued, "Why don't we adjourn to the royal suite for a few minutes, and we can have a more in-depth discussion up there?" He stood, as did Schreck, who held out his arm to help Selene to her feet. Sinclair finished, saying, "We seem to be missing one of our entourage at the moment. Thank you for your assistance, Max."

Schreck flashed a craggy-toothed grin and said, "I'm sure he'll turn up eventually. Isn't that right, Mr. DeMille?"

Lively was going to say something about bad pennies usually turning up when a vice-like hand grasped his shoulder. A flash of annoyance coursed through him, and he shrugged the large man's hand off as he stood. He turned to the bald bodyguard and looked him in the eye. "I'd recommend you keep your little touchy-feely fingers to yourself, my friend, or you're liable to lose one."

The hulking man said nothing and only scowled more intensely through his mask at Lively. However, he kept his hands to himself and didn't try to manhandle him any further.

***

The royal suite was immaculate. Near the window stood what looked to be the same blue spruce that had magically appeared in this same suite on Christmas Eve 2021. Lively was sitting on an overstuffed white leather sofa with Selene to his right and Max Schreck to his left. They had removed their masks upon leaving the ballroom, and he was glad to have it off his face. For whatever reason, it made his nose itch. Nearby, the bald behemoth stood at attention, presumably in case Lively were to get suddenly energetic and assault Edward, then bolt from the room or something unexpected like that.

Edward was at the small bar next to the snack rack, mixing drinks for everyone. He finished up and carried the libations over on a small silver tray to serve his guests; another Tom Collins for Selene, a snifter of brandy for Schreck and a bottle of Moosehead for Lively.

As Lively took his beer, Edward said, "Though it is swill for the masses, I will allow it here, just for you, Son." He placed the tray onto a small end table and sat down in the chair next to it, then removed his own double-olive martini as he joined his guests.

"Thanks... Dad." Lively was still having a hard time comprehending that the man sitting in the King Louis XIV armchair opposite him was actually his father. The irony was not lost on him that just a few days before, he'd been pining to meet the mother he'd never known. And now, all of a sudden, he not only got to meet his mother but his father as well. And not just any father, but none other than Edward Sinclair himself. What were the odds, he wondered, as he regarded Sinclair and took a sip of his beer.

Selene watched this conversation between Lively and Edward, obviously still struggling with things herself, no doubt in part to having several startling revelations thrust upon her over the last hour. Her brow furrowing in confusion, she looked to Lively and said, "So let me get this straight. You are my son." Lively nodded. Looking over to Edward, Selene continued, "Who you told me had died in childbirth." Sinclair made a slightly pained expression as if sorry for the lie. With a glance back to Lively, Selene finished, saying, "And now, you're telling me I've been somehow trapped in this hotel for forty years, and yet I haven't aged a day? How is this possible?"

With a shake of his head and a shrug of his shoulders, Lively looked over to Edward and said, "I'm not the guy to ask about that, am I, Dad?"

Edward sipped his drink, looking at them both over the rim of his martini glass, obviously still enjoying the moment. He placed it on the table, then sat back and crossed his legs. "Ah, yes. A small matter of time. While it's true that I had a hand in this, I also had some assistance." He nodded toward Schreck and said, "Max, why don't you jump in here for a second."

"Yes, I would imagine a small bit of explanation is in order, isn't that right, Edward?"

Sinclair nodded and said, "Absolutely."

Schreck placed his brandy glass on the table and proceeded to remove his thin, tan-coloured gloves, one finger at a time. Given the centre stage, the thin man seemed to be revelling in the spotlight. When he'd finished, he picked his snifter back up and took a lingering sip before speaking. He stood and turned to Lively and Selene so that he could look down on them and said, "Time is the enemy of progress."

Picking up her Tom Collins, Selene added, "And acting careers."

Schreck nodded and gave a toothy little smile, saying, "Quite so. But regarding progress and the ceaseless march of time, some advancements need more time to culminate than others."

"How so?" Lively asked as he began to peel the label from the corner of his Moosehead bottle.

"Over the millennia, some of the greatest advancements in humankind have occurred through the insights and discoveries of one single person, or sometimes, perhaps a small handful of people. But sadly, almost all of these advancements have been constrained by time."

Lively was paying complete attention to everything occurring around him at the moment but wanted to play things as if he were a little more inattentive than he actually was, just to keep up appearances. Tearing a strip from his stubby brown bottle's label, he asked Schreck, "And you took time out of the equation?"

"In a way. With our limited lifespan upon this planet, it constricts the progress that one person can make, of course," Schreck replied. "Were it not for that, the potential for things that could be accomplished in this world and beyond, is enormous."

A slight knock came at the door to the suite, and the bald bodyguard moved to answer it. On slightly wobbly legs, Blonde Beefy entered the room. He looked sheepishly to Sinclair and Schreck and moved to the other end of the couch. He stood opposite his bald-headed doppelgänger, allowing himself a final glower at Lively before standing at attention with his hands folded in front.

"Speaking of worlds beyond." Lively looked briefly at each of the massive bodyguards.

"Yes, that was one of the other things we wanted to solve. Not just the problem of time, but the issue of ready and willing manpower suitable to our needs as well," Edward said.

"All the help you could ever need, and only a universe away," Lively observed.

Edward smiled broadly and said, "Something like that," then took another sip of his drink.

"And what of the people here?" Selene asked, shaking her head sadly. "How can you justify holding myself, and all of the people in the ballroom hostage for all these years?"

"Oh, they're not all hostages, my dear," Edward said.

Lively looked up from his bottle and said, "I suspected as much. And I'll wager some of them are actively engaged in your little operation up here, isn't that right, Edward?"

"Why yes," Sinclair nodded. "But not very many. Most of them are like your mother here, what we call the forgotten." He looked to Selene sadly and added, "They're completely oblivious to what occurs here each and every night and their involvement in it. However, a select few have paid handsomely to be part of what is happening here in our little kingdom."

Lively contemplated Edward's comment for a brief moment. The man considered this his little kingdom, which was appropriate, considering he lived in a castle, or at least part of one. He wondered if, in keeping with the man's aspirations, Edward considered himself the king. This brought to mind his little experiment out the window of his suite and grey fog beyond its window. Taking another sip of Moosehead, Lively asked, "And where, exactly, is here?""

"Why we're at the Sinclair Resort Hotel, of course!" Edward raised both his arms grandly and gestured about the room.

"Well, for some reason, it doesn't look like you can go very far from your little kingdom," Lively said. "I tried a test out the window of my suite earlier, and there doesn't seem to be anything beyond this resort's walls except grey mist."

Sinclair nodded and said, "Yes, that's an unfortunate side effect of our little process."

"And what exactly is that process?" Selene asked, cocking her head as she posed the question.

Looking to both Lively and Selene, Schreck answered, saying, "In order not to bore laypeople like yourselves, suffice it to say we are utilising several divergent technologies to bring all of this about thanks to years of tireless research on both of our parts. Isn't that right, Edward?"

Sinclair stood and said, "Indeed it is. But that's enough for the moment, Max." He looked from Schreck to Selene and smiled, adding, "Right now, I'd like you to take Selene back to the ballroom for a moment. I have a few things I'd like my son to see." He moved to Selene and bent down to give her a small kiss saying, "I'll see you soon, my dear."

Selene didn't respond, turning her face at the last moment, and Edward ended up kissing the side of her cheek instead.

With a frown, Sinclair said in a low voice, "We'll talk more of this later."

Schreck bowed slightly and offered his arm to Selene, who accepted it reluctantly and stood. As she was ushered toward the exit, she gave Lively a questioning look. He tried to give her a reassuring smile in return but wasn't sure if he succeeded.

With a beefy bodyguard on either side, Edward turned to Lively, saying, "I need to show you something." Not waiting for a response, he turned and entered the bedroom, moving past the circular bed toward the ensuite bathroom.

Not sure where all this was going, Lively stood and called out, "That's okay, Dad! You go do your thing in there, and I'll wait out here with the boys."

"Oh, don't you worry, I won't be doing anything in there without you, Son." Edward walked through into the bathroom, and then both bodyguards moved menacingly toward Lively.

Looking from one mammoth man to the other, Lively said, "Well, I guess if you're going to insist..." And so, with a Beefy Boy in front and behind, he joined his father in the ensuite bathroom.

CHAPTER THREE

December 31st, 1981 2040 hours

Ricky Rosenstein closed Lively's copy of the Big Book of Busting and shook his head. So many things had happened here, culminating in the disappearance of which he seemed part. He thought of Lively DeMille for a moment. Was he who he said he was? A man from the future? If this book were to be believed, that would certainly seem to be the case.

Standing, Ricky paced back and forth as he mulled over what had happened to him since meeting DeMille. His mind was awhirl with what the man had told him, and everything he'd read in the book clutched in his hands. Was it possible that he'd been here in this hotel for almost forty years? If so, that meant he was nearly seventy-five years old! Well, he certainly didn't feel it, that was for sure.

Rosenstein paced his way into the bathroom and studied himself in the mirror. Why hadn't he aged if he had been here for that length of time? The thought of himself going through what he had earlier this evening, over fourteen-thousand times, made his stomach shrivel into a small hard ball. He would have expected his fringe of carrot-coloured hair to have turned white from fear by now after so many repetitions of such a horrific event. Just thinking of all that gave him a queasy feeling in the pit of his stomach, which was a strange sensation for him; usually, it was hunger down there, not a sense of overwhelming dread.

What would happen at midnight tonight? He presumed some sort of a reset would occur, and then everything would start all over. Would he then find himself in the Executive Gaming Lounge upstairs playing Ms. Pac-Man again, just like he had, day after day, year after year, for the past forty years? Though he'd enjoyed the initial part of his smorging, the thought of ever being abducted and duct-taped again was almost too much to bear, and he vowed to do whatever he could to make sure it happened no more.

Ricky racked his brain, trying to remember how many nights he'd stayed at this hotel. He'd arrived a couple of days ago from the east, having been in Toronto securing additional distribution channels for his line of personal computers. He was pretty sure it had only been two days. Naturally, part of him still wondered if DeMille was lying to him and was actually part of what was happening here? Not a rich man by any means, he did well enough for himself. Maybe it was just an elaborate con job to fleece him out of some of his money?

However, Lively had mentioned the concept of déjà vu, and the more Ricky thought about it, the more he seemed to recall that feeling of reliving certain events repeatedly. In fact, he'd had it happen a couple of times so far today, once before meeting DeMille and then again when he'd been sitting down to watch Stripes with a turkey leg in each hand.

Of course, that had been just before his entire world had taken a left turn into the Twilight Zone. He was surprised that being abducted, duct-taped and then transferred to a mysterious room in the basement so many times hadn't been something that would have seemed familiar to him, at least on one or two occasions. However, he'd recently read research showing a causal relationship between occurrences of emotional, psychological and/or physical distress and resultant memory loss in some of the victims. Some postulated it might be the mind's way of temporarily coping with whatever had occurred, while others thought it could be permanent, especially if there were ancillary brain injury or other disturbing events accompanying the trauma. Ricky had no idea what other disturbing events or trauma had occurred to him over the years, and he shuddered at the thought of things still unknown.

Less traumatic was the thought of eating the same smorgasbord meal countless times for almost four decades on a daily basis. This place had some seriously good eats, so at least he knew he'd had some joy. He turned sideways and looked at himself in the mirror. If he'd been partaking of that same mountain of food he usually allowed himself when holidaying here, he figured he was doing all right. He turned this way and that in front of the mirror. He certainly didn't seem any rounder than he remembered being. But now he wondered about the food. Was it drugged? Was that what caused the forgetfulness? Or was this apparent daily amnesia just from this looping of time? But if that were the case, how come some of the people around here were seemingly unaffected by it?

His head spinning, Ricky returned to the bedroom, picked up the telephone handset next to the bed, and sat down with a sigh. He dialled the number for an outside line and tried calling his answering machine at home in North Vancouver. The call resulted in only dead air. He shook his head, still unwilling to accept what was becoming painfully obvious, that Lively DeMille might be telling the truth. He dialled another outside line and tried his office at the warehouse where he operated much of his business. Though expecting the machine to pick up there, he discovered the same result as before, only a slight hissing noise on the line and nothing more.

Ricky looked thoughtfully at the large cloth-covered mirror on the wall, then looked to the bar fridge and his stomach rumbled. He'd been disappointed earlier to discover that the snacks in DeMille's 'fully-loaded' bar fridge consisted of some domestic beer, several packs of Old Dutch beef sticks and a jar of Planter's dry-roasted peanuts. They'd hardly been satisfying. Apart from the smaller rooms, meagre bar fridges were one of the other reasons why he never stayed on the second floor when he visited.

Because of that disappointment, he'd gone on a quest to get some real food from his portable in-room smorgasbord via the underworld passageways. His disappointment had been extreme upon discovering the stainless-steel seductress had been removed from the suite after his abduction, and all that remained had been a greasy turkey drumstick on the couch. His stomach growled loudly as it remembered the sad sight.

He shook his head, dismayed that his stomach was trying to rule his life again. Well, enough was enough; he was going to forgo eating for a change and try to do something to help others, as Lively had done for him.

Rosenstein looked intently at the manuscript in his hand for several long seconds, then placed it on the desk near the TV with resolve. One area mentioned in the Big Book was giving him an itch that was proving too strong not to scratch. In the manuscript's margins, Lively had written of a place called the gold room, where the ceiling was made of pure gold. And if that wasn't amazing enough, it got even better because next to that room was a brand-new IBM 4321 Mainframe computer system. He wasn't sure which excited him more, the thought of the gold or the technology. He gave a small chuckle, thinking that if he had to choose between the two, he'd take the mainframe over the moola every time.

After a brief moment, Ricky once again found the switch in the mirror's ornate frame, and it slid open, revealing the dim, red passage behind. His heart pounding in his chest, he removed his shoes before stepping through. He was going to try to do his best impression of a ninja back there since the last thing he wanted was to show up on the radar of anyone, or anything, that happened to be shambling around the Sinclair's mysterious innards.

CHAPTER FOUR

December 29th, 2021 1615 hours

Almost ready to leave, Amanda Jansen gave a final glance about the living room of her small Port Moody home. At the same time, she tried to recall anything else she may have forgotten. Next to the front door, her overnight bag sat packed and ready to go. Outside, rain pounded into the ground, turning small depressions in her lawn into miniature lakes.

This evening, she would be visiting her sister. Her plan was to spend the night and then get an early start for Entwistle the next day when the break in the storm fronts was supposed to occur. Though she'd spent time at her sister's house on Christmas day, it had been more of a family visit with Cassandra, her husband Geoff, and their two daughters.

More and more, as the days slipped toward the end of the month, Amanda felt she might never return from the Sinclair if she stepped through its doors once again. So, tonight was going to be more of a chance to see Cass on her own, just two sisters, one last time. Her brother-in-law and nieces were catching a concert and spending the night at a hotel downtown. With Cass being her only remaining family, she figured she'd best pay her a visit, just to be safe.

Amanda smiled sadly as she looked around the room. Never marrying, she'd been proud of the little house that she'd renovated mostly by herself over the final decade of her career with the RCMP. After years of saving, she'd finally had enough to buy something outright back at the turn of the millennium, just before the market exploded and prices went through the roof. Though she loved the house, she was sad that it had only ever known her presence and nothing more.

Over the years, she had often fantasised of what their home may have been like if Danny had lived. What house would they have bought together? Would it have heard the laughter of children? They probably would have stayed in Entwistle to be near his folks, especially if they'd had kids. Was there a reality somewhere where that had actually happened, she wondered. She wiped at the corner of her eye with the sleeve of her cardigan as she briefly entertained the fantasy. There was no way she would ever know the answer to that. However, if she could somehow be a part of bringing back all the missing people, then perhaps it would finally allow Danny to be at peace, and then whatever happened to her would be incidental, even if it did cost her her life.

Willamina slunk herself around Amanda's legs, her throaty purr barely audible over the falling rain. Upon seeing Amanda packing her bag, the tortoiseshell-coloured cat had known something was up, and she had been even more omnipresent than usual. Of ancient Germanic origin, the cat's name meant 'determined protector', and that was something that her little puffball certainly was. Since adopting Willamina as a kitten from the BCSPCA almost a decade before, the little fluff of fur had been with her every minute she was at home, rarely leaving her side. After Amanda's retirement, they had grown even closer. Now, with the black, collapsible mesh cat carrier sitting in the hallway next to her bag near the door, the cat was even more agitated and wouldn't let Amanda out of her sight.

Reaching down to give the tortie a gentle scruff behind its

ears, Jansen said, "I'm sorry, honey, but you have to go. I can't leave you here alone." Still bent over, she patted the top of her left shoulder with her right hand, and the cat jumped up, draping itself across her shoulders as if its spine had suddenly dissolved. It nuzzled the side of her head, began purring in her ear and gave out a soft, questioning meow.

"We're going to go to Cassandra and Geoff's for the night, and then you're going to stay there for a little while, and Auntie Cass is going to look after you." The cat meowed at her again as she spoke as if protesting the need for a babysitter. Amanda continued, "I shouldn't be gone for more than a couple of days." She silently hoped that would be the case as the cat nuzzled the back of her head and continued to purr in her ear.

Fortunately, if something did happen to her, she knew Willamina would be going to a good home. When she'd prepared her last will and testament a couple of years back, Cassandra had agreed to take the cat, in the event of Amanda's premature demise. She was now glad she had that little peace of mind that her fur baby would be safe and sound, and that gave her one less thing to worry about.

In the overnight bag near her feet, the obsidian stone extracted from Will Weston's palm lay nestled in the rags in which it had been wrapped four decades before. Despite the layers of clothing and the wall of the hard-shell aluminum case between the stone and her legs, she thought she could still feel the cold emanating from it.

When she'd dropped Weston off at the hospital that afternoon so many years ago, that had been the last she'd ever talked with the man. After he'd been released from the hospital, he'd filed his story with his editor and then immediately requested a transfer to a different office of the Golden Press Group. His request had been granted, and to the best of her knowledge, he'd been living in Ferring's Point, a small town just south of Prince Rupert, ever since.

Amanda thought of her own experience at the Sinclair, which had ended there that same evening. After dropping Will at the hospital entrance, she'd parked the cruiser to seek attention for her own hands due to the serrations caused by the broken welds of the well cap. Just thinking of that incident once again made her hands itch slightly, and she looked briefly at the network of thin white scars still visible in the heel of one palm and across the fingers of the other hand.

***

A vast wash of stars cascaded across the night sky. Beneath their sparkling splendour, a crescent moon edged over the jagged, snow-capped mountains to the east. Now just a couple of minutes before nine o'clock in the evening, Amanda was finally done at the hospital and currently winding her Crown Victoria toward the top of Overseer Mountain. She hadn't been in touch with the inspector for several hours and hoped everything was well.

Her mind returned to dwell on Will Weston for a moment. Whatever had happened to the newsman up on the hill this afternoon before they found him was either something he couldn't remember, or something so traumatic he was having a hard time verbalising it, fearing they'd think him crazy. The chief inspector was of the belief it might be a kind of amnesia similar to shell shock, like soldiers he'd known in the war. Whatever it was, Weston was certainly acting odd, and she was glad to no longer have him in the cruiser.

After several miles of driving in silence, Amanda turned on the radio, meaning to catch the news update at the top of the hour from the local radio station, CJIF. Billy Joel had just finished telling how it was still rock and roll to him. The music was replaced by the clicking and clacking of teletypes in the background, over which a musical chorus announced the call letters of the station and the word 'news'. The announcer began with the Sinclair incident as the lead story. Will Weston must have worked quickly and posted it to the newswire as soon as he left the hospital. The silence up at the Sinclair would be ending very shortly, and they would be swamped with eager reporters and looky-loos wanting to snoop around the resort and Entwistle itself.

"Got some breaking news here, folks. The Sinclair Resort Hotel up on the hill has had something extraordinary happen that defies logical explanation. It has just been reported that an entire ballroom full of people taking part in the annual media awards gala on New Year's Eve have disappeared, apparently without a trace. The Entwistle RCMP are not releasing any further details at the moment but have said that a statement from Chief Inspector John Harder will be forthcoming shortly. A spokesman for the hotel could not be reached for comment at this time. Stay tuned to this station and we'll keep you updated as further details roll in. In other news..."

Amanda shut the radio off and continued the drive in silence. Rounding a final curve, the lane leading to the resort came into view. She drove through the imposing front gates, her headlights sweeping up the winding lane ahead, their piercing beams reflecting high, white walls of plowed-back snow on either side.

The Sinclair Hotel stood starkly outlined from the snow-covered forest behind, cold, grey, and brutal in the waning moon's pale light. With its spiralling turret and castle-like design, it didn't seem something that belonged here at the top of this remote mountain in the interior of British Columbia— almost like spotting a penguin at the North Pole. She pulled the Crown Victoria under the porte-cochere entrance and killed the engine. Harder's Suburban was still there, his wife's Malibu just behind with Weston's Chevette sitting next to it. Amanda had collected the hatchback's keys from the newsman and assured him that it would be driven back down to his house by tomorrow afternoon at the latest.

Jansen stepped across the threshold into the hotel once more, and she felt her simmering anxiety suddenly return tenfold. Grabbing her shoulder mic, she said, "Chief Inspector Harder, this is Corporal Jansen. Come in, please." After no response for several seconds, she tried again, saying, "Inspector, what's your twenty?" But once more, there was no answer.

The oppressive silence of the empty hotel was broken only by the whistle of the wind that had suddenly begun shrieking through small gaps in the thick oak doors at her back. Reluctant to explore the hotel's depths further, she only wanted to be done with this horrid place once and for all and then to never, ever, see it again. But before she did that, she needed to locate the inspector.

Though hoping that nothing else unforeseen had happened while she'd been absent, a part of her knew the lack of response from Harder was not a good thing. A sense of panic swept over her as she moved into the Sinclair, her breathing becoming more laboured the further she went. It was as if the ponderous weight of the colossal hotel itself was bearing down upon her and trying to smother her very soul.

CHAPTER FIVE

Minerva froze in her tracks with a gasp. It seemed that, like Esso gasoline, the Sinclair Hotel had put a tiger in its tank, or at least in its model. The Siberian tiger was posed sitting upright inside the model's halves, its green glass eyes drilling into hers. Keeping her gaze steady on the orange and black predator, Minerva held up the silver tray defensively and the white towels tumbled onto the floor in a small pile. Backing from the room, she said, "Nice kitty."

When the door entered her peripheral vision, she let her tray shield drop to her side. Her eyes never leaving the cat, she grabbed the handle and pulled the door slowly shut. Almost as soon as the door latched, a crash came from the other side as the tiger launched itself from where it had been seated. Minerva jolted back from the door in surprise. With wide eyes, she listened to the cat scratching furiously away on the other side. How was she supposed to get the ebony box from the model now?

Returning to the executive gaming lounge, Minerva discovered that she now had more problems on top of her problems. The polar bear was no longer next to the bottom of the steps. She looked around the gaming lounge but couldn't see it anywhere. Moving slowly, she made her way toward the lounge entrance where the gorilla still stood pounding its chest.

Her eyes on the big ape, she was almost to the door when she could resist no longer and stole a glance toward the video games. She figured the row of four machines looked like a perfect spot for a beast the bear's size to hide, and now, it seemed she'd been correct.

Crouched behind the tall arcade machines, the tip of the beast's white muzzle and black-tipped nose just peeked out from the edge of the Space Invaders unit next to Ms. Pac-man. If she'd gotten the urge to play a quick game of Ms. P, it would no doubt have been a very short one that ended with her being gobbled down instead of a white power pill.

Realising her gaze had lingered too long on the bear, Minerva turned back to the doorway just in time. With her focus elsewhere, she hadn't been paying attention to the ape, and it was dangerously close to her now. It had moved several feet out from the entrance, partially blocking the path to the doorway, its muscular arms outstretched as if ready to envelop her in a deadly hug. Her eyes now locked onto the creature, and she moved between the snooker and poker tables to give it a wide berth and avoid its dangerously long reach.

The carpet runner was still where she'd left it, rolled up against the bottom of the door. She would have to move it out of the way to exit, which meant she'd have to take her eyes off the ape for a moment. Trying to move as quickly as she could, she scooped the carpet aside with the edge of the serving tray then reached for the doorknob. As she stood and turned to open the door, something grazed the side of her head, and she jerked back in surprise.

The ape had turned around while she hadn't been looking and it now reached out toward her, its thick, black fingers almost close enough to grab her by the hair.

Backing rapidly across the threshold, Minerva slammed the door, then glanced about the small foyer for anything else that might be out to get her. Fortunately, the painted wolf wasn't anywhere in sight at the moment.

Beneath the vestibule's single narrow window was a small cafe table with a pair of low-backed wooden chairs to either side. Minerva dropped the serving tray with a clang and grabbed a chair, jamming its top edge underneath the door handle. Though the door opened inward, she hoped that the tension with which she wedged the chair's back underneath the knob would be enough to keep it closed, just in case the gorilla, with its opposing thumbs, tried to get the door open. The last thing she needed was a polar bear and silverback gorilla stalking the halls of the Sinclair as she tried to figure things out.

Collecting her tray-shield from the floor, Minerva moved carefully down the spiralling turret stairs to the hotel's third floor. Where was the painted wolf, she wondered. Was it still impaled by the steel sword? Since it hadn't been waiting for her outside the lounge, she considered that a good sign. Now, about to round the final curve in the staircase, she realised she would discover the wolf's status in just a couple more steps.

The sword still stuck upright from the floor where she had impaled the canvas predator, but that was all. The wolf must have only been playing possum when she stabbed it to the wood, and now it seemed to have torn itself free. A small scrap of canvas remained stuck into the floor by the sword's tip. She wondered if the injured beast was as dangerous as a real wounded wolf might be and said aloud, "I hope I never find out," but suspected otherwise.

With a grunt, she pulled the sword from the floor and the piece of canvas came free along with it. She tugged it off the blade's tip and grimaced as she looked at it. When the animal finally pulled itself free, it had left behind a little memento, but not one suitable for framing. She tossed the scrap of grey canvas away, saying, "Next time I'll use turpentine."

Ever so slowly, she opened the door and peered into the third-floor corridor. There was no sign of the wolf at the moment, but that didn't mean it wasn't there. It could be just around a corner, pressed against the wall near the entrance to one of the suites, ready to peel off as she passed and wrap its painted paws around her. She hoped that her little game of stabby-stabby with the sword earlier would slow the creature down somewhat or at least make it more audible to her as it moved about thanks to the big tear it must have in its canvas body now.

Keeping her eyes going in every direction at once, Minerva moved down the corridor, her sword draped over one shoulder like a sentry's rifle. Weighing well over five pounds, the large piece of steel was not something she was about to brandish out in front for any length of time. In her other hand, she still held the silver tray by one of its handles. Between the two, she felt almost like Robert E. Howard's character, Red Sonja. She'd always found those stories inspiring as a girl and admired any woman who could swing a sword and kick-ass the way Sonja did, fictional or not.

At the top of the grand staircase, she paused and tried to devise another plan since her previous idea to grab the ebony box had failed. There was no way she could go back up to the gaming lounge, not with the three stuffies so energetic, and especially not alone. Perhaps if she saw Doppelively somewhere in her travels, she could persuade him to help her with her mission? But then she thought, what if he disappeared in a puff of smoke on her, right when she needed him most?

Obviously, whatever force was animating the stuffed creatures was also using them to guard the miniature Sinclair and the ebony box inside, of that she was quite sure. Now, she had to figure out how to get the box out of the model, past the stuffies and then downstairs to the ballroom, all without touching it at any point. With a sigh, she began to descend the grand staircase to the second floor, keeping an eye out for duplicates of her brother, slithering paintings and giant spiders.

CHAPTER SIX

December 31st, 1981 2045 hours

Edward Sinclair moved into the bathroom and turned around. Beaming proudly, he stood next to the platform on which the clawfoot tub sat. The blonde bodyguard had followed him through the door and now stood off to one side of the entrance.

Lively entered the bathroom, followed closely by the bald bodyguard. Now with a bulging bad boy standing on both sides, he said, "Really, I'm okay. As much fun as it might have been to have a bath with my dad when I was a little guy, I think I'm kind of past that stage now, thanks."

Sinclair laughed heartily and said, "That's what I've always loved about your mother, her sense of humour, and I can see you've inherited it."

"Gee, thanks. I like to keep people entertained with the odd caper and jape. I find it helps to keep them off guard."

Edward nodded in agreement, "Oh, I'm sure it does."

With a glance about the room, Lively said, "Listen, since we're obviously not in here to make sure I wash behind my ears, would you kindly mind telling me why we're all standing around here in your little 'salle de bain'?

"Indeed, why not get to the point. I like your directness. Definitely a Sinclair trait."

"I've been meaning to ask you about that, Dad." Lively threw in another 'dad' as he spoke in order to lull Sinclair into believing he was more on-board with things than he actually was.

"What's that, Son?"

"How do you know I'm your son?"

"I don't understand."

"I mean, how do you know that you're my father. Mom is an attractive woman and all, and..."

Nodding with a look of comprehension, Edward said, "Ah, I see what you're saying. You're concerned that she had a dalliance with another suitor before I put her under my spell, so to speak."

Lively found that to be an interesting choice of words and said, "Something like that."

"Rest assured, there is no doubt of the blood in your veins or your lineage. Anyway, I can see it in your eyes. You have the exact same colour as your grandfather."

"If that's the only thing I share with my grandfather, I'll consider myself lucky," Lively said.

"Now, why would you say that? You've never met the man." Edward stepped onto the first of the three steps to the tub and said, "In any event, let me introduce you to the reason I brought you here tonight. Something that will, I believe, defy your expectations." He gestured grandly toward the clawfoot monstrosity at the top of the raised platform.

Lively watched Edward's performance, thinking it almost sounded like the man was unveiling a new model of car, rather than a bathtub, even if it could fit four people comfortably. He looked around at the twin bodyguards standing nearby. Both seemed unimpressed, no doubt having seen their boss's spiel many times before over the years, or decades, as it were. But he wondered at the location of the bathtub. It wasn't something he'd considered before, but as he plotted things out on his mental map of the hotel, he realised that this bathtub lay directly overtop the grand ballroom and the gold room below.

With a flourish, Sinclair turned the faucet around one hundred and eighty degrees so that it faced upward. He pressed the plunger button to close the drain, and Lively was surprised to see the tub smoothly and silently lower down inside the raised platform as a thick metal cover slid overtop the recessed tub. On its surface were four spots that, to Lively's eye, looked like the teleporter units from the original Star Trek series.

Frowning slightly, Lively said, "Well, that was unexpected."

Sinclair climbed onto the gleaming platform and gestured for Lively to do the same, saying, "Join me and experience your destiny."

Lively mounted the three low steps and stood next to his father on the platform. Looking over to Edward, he said, "So what now? Are you going to beam us up to the mothership?"

Shaking his head, Sinclair said with a chuckle, "Not quite. But don't worry, we use this all the time. It's perfectly safe."

"That's what they said about hydrogen on the

Hindenburg." Lively replied, looking questioningly around the platform.

With a smile, Edward said, "No doubt." He reached into his jacket pocket and added, "Before I forget, you need to put this on." He handed Lively a golden cameo-styled bracelet with a gilded letter S in the centre.

"Is this going to be a particularly painful experience?"

Edward shook his head and said, "No, not in the least. Perhaps a little disorienting at first."

Lively nodded, saying, "That's good to know."

Sinclair added, "Unless you try to use this machine without a bracelet".

"What would happen then?"

Edward shook his head and said, "You'd never be able to come back from whichever frequency you went to. We learned that lesson the hard way." He pressed down on the top of a tile in the low wall surrounding the tub on three sides, and a small control panel popped up. A row of seven-segment LED displays showed a series of numbers. Below them lay a numeric keypad with several black dials, and at the very top, a large red button glowed invitingly.

"What do you mean by frequency?" Lively asked.

"Don't worry, all will be explained shortly, Son." Sinclair looked around at the group and added, "All right, since we're dressed for success, let's have a little fun. We'll start with one we know." He spent a moment punching things into the keypad, then turned several knobs to varying positions. As he did this, the Beefy Boys moved onto the platform and stood in front of Lively and Edward.

"So, what do you call this little contraption?"

"The Harmoniser," Edward said, pausing his index finger over the luminous red button.

"Sounds like a jukebox brand, but okay." Lively nodded in acceptance.

"You're not too far off. We call it that since it harmonises our frequency with other continuums and allows us to travel between them." With no further explanation forthcoming, Sinclair said grandly, "Okay, hang on!" then pressed the red button with a flourish.

Hang onto what, Lively wondered. He was half-expecting some sort of humming, or maybe a vibration and a zapping noise. But his expectations were sorely disappointed when the only sound produced was a popping similar to a magnum of champagne being opened. After a tugging sensation in the centre of his chest, a brief wave of nausea washed over him. The world faded away like the end of a scene in a movie, just before the next one begins. Things lightened once again, and he looked about, blinking rapidly. It smelled of alcohol for some reason, and his eyes watered slightly from the fumes.

"And here we are!" Edward exclaimed. The room seemed the same, and it didn't appear they had gone anywhere.

The Beefy Boys stepped down from the platform. The blonde exited the bathroom into the suite. The bald one stayed near the door, keeping an eye on both his companion and employer at once.

"Where is here? It looks the same to me."

"That it does, but trust me, there are differences," Sinclair said as he moved down from the platform.

"Fair enough." Lively felt his eyes watering slightly and

asked, "Why does it smell like a Virginia moonshiner set up business in here all of a sudden?"

Edward sniffed the air and said, "Ah yes, the alcohol. It's amazing how you don't notice it after a while. Anyway, it helps with the cooling. Once the alignment is complete, the spent alcohol used in the process is drained off using the tub's plumbing."

"Really?"

"Indeed. It gives our system greater efficiency and almost twenty percent more cooling thanks to its lower boiling point of one hundred- and seventy-four-degrees Fahrenheit compared to water's two hundred-and-twelve."

Lively looked at Edward with a slight tilt to his head and asked, "Okay, that's interesting? But how does the Harmoniser work exactly?"

"Oh, don't worry about that right now. You'll find out in good time." Edward laughed at his words and exited the bathroom. Bald Beefy waited near the doorway for Lively to join Sinclair.

"After me, I'm sure," Lively said as he brushed past the taciturn bodyguard.

Lively gawked about the royal suite for a moment. It looked very royal indeed this evening, seemingly decked out to welcome guests from the furthest kingdoms of Europe and beyond. The furniture looked even more expensive than what had been in the suite before, although Lively recognised a couple of pieces, including the King Louis XIV chair. And yet, there was something else. The artwork on the walls had changed as well. Instead of hand-painted masterpieces dotting the walls, dozens of black velvet paintings hung in their place, everything from gruff dogs and adorable cats to playful unicorns and sad clowns. On the wall, just to the side of the snack rack, a life-sized painting of Elvis Presley posed in the mid-gyration.

"Fans of the King here, are they?" Lively said with a nod to the painting.

Edward waited for him at the entrance to the suite. "Amongst other things." He gestured into the hall, sweeping his arm out. "Come with me, Son, and see some of what your kingdom contains."

Lively followed Edward out the door and joined him. They walked side by side down the luxuriously carpeted hallway, one bodyguard taking point in front and the other at their backs. Wondering about the continued security, Lively asked, "Is the rest of this Sinclair as crazy as the decorations?"

Edward looked to Lively, slightly confused. "I'm sorry?"

"Our little entourage here. Are they here for our protection?" He nodded to the bodyguards.

"Ah, you mean Simon and Simon."

"Simon and Simon, really? Like the Pieman or the detectives?"

"Neither actually. They're with us in case things get out of hand. While it's not particularly dangerous around here, the residents do love their parties."

Nodding at the bodyguards walking ahead, Lively asked, "Do these men have a last name?"

"They do."

"Would it be Wright by any chance?"

"It would."

"And they are not identical twins, are they?"

"No, they're not."

Lively had almost expected that answer at this point. He'd realised both men bore an uncanny resemblance to professional wrestler Sonny Wright and now his suspicions were confirmed. Curious regarding other aspects, he said, "You mentioned earlier that if I don't keep this on," he waggled the bracelet on his wrist, "I could never get back?"

"That's correct."

If all of that were true, Lively posited to himself, then his other assumptions might also be correct. Some of the people here were obviously free to come and go to who knew where through the Harmoniser, but others were not. And without a bracelet, a person could be sent to whatever universe Edward decided and then be abandoned there with no way back. Lively could imagine that would be the perfect way to make somebody disappear. Who needs a shovel and a shallow grave like the Mob when you could just dump a body in a convenient parallel universe somewhere. Or better yet, if you wanted the person to suffer, leave them alive and let whatever anomalies existed in those universes have their way with them. Lively shuddered slightly at the thought.

Edward noticed his son's tremor and said, "Are you cold?"

"No," Lively lied, "just kind of excited."

"You should be! Momentous things are afoot now that you're here!"

They'd reached the elevator, and Bald Beefy stood holding the doors open for them to enter. At the same time, the blonde bodyguard began to descend the stairs, presumably to get to the lobby ahead of them.

Lively could hear music from a distant location in the hotel, possibly the same nine-piece band, the Glenn Millers, that played in the ballroom in the other Sinclair. As he stepped onto the elevator, he asked, "Might I ask where we're going?"

Edward pressed the 'L' button for the lobby, and the doors began to close. He turned to Lively and said with a broad smile, "Why, we're off to see the wizard, of course!"

Looking around at the garish decor as they descended, Lively said, "Well, I didn't think we were in Kansas anymore, that's for sure."

CHAPTER SEVEN

December 31st, 1981 2055 hours

All seemed quiet behind the walls as Ricky Rosenstein moved stealthily down the corridor. Though he realised he wasn't as athletic as Lively (okay, he wasn't athletic at all) and knew he couldn't battle the bad guys like DeMille, he hoped he could still somehow aid the man in his quest. Of course, overriding everything this time was his new number one priority, not to get caught again. And so, he tried to make like a church mouse and make as little noise as possible as he crept along in his stocking feet.

When he'd hid in Lively's shower earlier, he'd strained to hear the conversation when DeMille had answered the door. Unfortunately, he'd recognised the distinctive voice at the door as being the same man who'd introduced him to the concept of the in-room smorg, the Bowler Hat Man. With Lively now in the hands of the enemy, Ricky realised his cavalry might not come to the rescue this time if someone stumbled across him wandering around the dim red corridors.

Fortunately, the hidden hallways behind the walls had sufficient carpeting so that he could keep the noise to a minimum. As he moved with caution, he glanced inside some of the suites through the two-way mirrors. Not naturally a voyeur, he was still incredibly curious about what his fellow 'tenants' were up to in this prison hotel out of time.

Most of the suites were empty, but a few still had guests preparing for the ball. Though 'preparing' might not be the best word to describe what he saw. Ricky stopped to watch, fascinated.

A woman sat at a vanity applying her makeup. Seeming almost catatonic, her movements were robot-like, as if she were on autopilot. Wearing a rose-coloured satin robe to not get any makeup on her clothes, her face was expressionless as she applied some pressed powder. Judging by her ghostly whiteness, she had been making the same repetitive motion for some time now. She would tap the puff gently into the powder, then tap it onto her lovely face, then back into the powder and onto her face again, and again and again over the same spots she'd already covered. Despite her almost clownish makeup attempts, dark smudges still shone through under her eyes.

Ricky moved to the two-way mirror in the sitting area next to the bedroom. A man relaxed in an off-white leather lounge chair, presumably the powder puff girl's husband. His face reflected the same catatonia as hers. A highball glass in hand, he rested it on the edge of the chair's arm. He took a sip, mechanically raising the glass to his lips, then put it back down. A few seconds later, he would raise it and take another sip. Except he wasn't taking any sips at all. He was merely raising the glass to his lips and touching the alcohol to them but not imbibing in anything. It was like watching one of those sippy birds in the red hat that sat at the edge of a water glass, forever dipping their little beaks in the liquid but never, ever taking a drink.

So mesmerised was Ricky by this display that he almost didn't notice a person dressed in white moving silently down the corridor toward him until it was almost too late. He ducked into a partially open doorway as they passed. It was the same black-haired woman, Kandi, who'd been playing nursie in his suite earlier. After she passed, he popped his head out to see where she was headed. At the end of the corridor, she pressed the elevator's call button, and the doors slid silently open. She entered and descended to the lower levels.

Looking both ways to ensure the coast was clear, Ricky moved toward the stairs next to the elevator, the same ones that he'd climbed earlier with Lively after his initial rescue. Descending once more into the hotel's depths, his heart began to quicken in his chest, and his palms began to sweat as he slid them down the spiralling staircase's cold, cast-iron handrail. Near the first floor, he paused and listened before continuing. No sound could be heard, and he peeked around the corner, then almost screamed like a little girl in surprise.

Rapidly approaching along the corridor was none other than the Bowler Hat Man.

As silently as he could, Ricky backed up the staircase several steps until he was out of sight around a curve. The Bowler Man's footsteps grew louder as he approached, and Ricky tensed for a confrontation. However, after a moment, he exhaled a silent breath of relief when the thin man carried on down the passage and turned off into a different corridor.

With his curiosity about the mainframe now close to boiling over, Ricky continued down into the basement. At the bottom of the stairwell, he cautiously peered into the dim corridor and saw Nurse Kandi moving around the corner out of sight.

Curious to see what the woman was up to, Rosenstein followed silently from a considerable distance, just in case Kandi turned around and he had no place to hide. The tunnels beneath the resort were long with little opportunity for a person to hide, should the quarry they were tailing happen to look back. So, Ricky made sure to only move to the next safe observation point when there was sufficient time to do so.

Nurse Kandi entered a door just past the one where Ricky had his duct tape bindings removed. Taking a deep breath, he poked his head around the edge of the doorframe, but the woman was nowhere in sight. Staying low like he knew Lively would do, he moved into the room.

A glass observation window was inset along one wall. A dim room beyond the glass appeared to be empty. To Ricky's right, in one corner, stood a white cabinet filled with an assortment of drug vials. It must be where Lively had grabbed his stash of drugs earlier. The ones he'd used to subdue the blonde Adonis and his cohort, Mr. Clean. Thinking that it wouldn't be a half-bad idea to arm himself with the same, Ricky grabbed several handfuls of drug vials and a few syringes and loaded them into his tuxedo jacket's pocket.

In the middle of this room was what looked like a shallow bathtub, but the drain was in the wrong place. With a sudden flash of disgust, Ricky realised he was looking at an embalming table. Above it hung some strange contraption that made him think of another of his passions. A long-time fan of Universal's Monsters from the thirties to the fifties, he'd watched everything from Dracula and the Mummy to the Wolf Man and the Creature from the Black Lagoon. He almost expected to see Colin Clive wander through the door at any minute, ready to reanimate Boris Karloff on the embalming table, while somewhere in the distance, Lon Chaney Jr. bayed at the moon.

Still looking for Kandi, Ricky continued his exploration. He moved cautiously to the open doorway next to the observation window and entered what appeared to be a control room. His eyes lit up when he discovered he'd found one of the objects of his quest, the IBM mainframe system.

A crack of light was coming from a partially opened door at

the other end of the control room. Tearing himself away from ogling the massive computer for a moment, Ricky moved cautiously toward the doorway. It had to be where his least favourite nurse had gone.

With a deep breath, Ricky pulled the door open and took a tentative gander into the room beyond. He blinked rapidly and gasped as he took in the golden wonder stretching out before him. Down one wall along the far side of the room, he spied his nurse stepping through a doorway and seemingly vanish.

A sudden burst of chattering electronics came from the darkened room at Rosenstein's back as the mainframe came alive, and he turned. Whatever was going on with the system now, it had just started since Nurse Kandi stepped into the hidden room.

He looked to the spinning tape storage reels, listening to the machine click and whir for a moment. A wave of dizziness swept over him, and his knees felt weak. Being in the same room with such computing power was rather intoxicating for him. These days, he was used to the eight-bit operating systems of the Commodores, Apples and Ataris that he sold to retailers through his distribution company. He'd had some experience on mainframes in his college days, though it had been nothing as advanced as this machine. But knowing it was Cobol based, he didn't think he'd have a problem examining its programming, thanks to his previous experience with the computing language.

Text suddenly started crawling up the screen on a CRT on the other side of the room. Ricky moved to it and hunched over the display, watching as someone accessed a remote terminal on the mainframe, possibly Nurse Kandi. A list of options was presented to the remote user.

'Initiate Aggregation - 1'
'Dissipate Aggregation - 2'

'Initiate Translocation - 3'
'Reverse Translocation – 4'
'System Reset - 5'
'Enter choice?'

The user selected the first option and hit enter.

'Programme already executing. All systems are nominal. Please standby...'

After a brief pause, the screen flashed:

'Reset sequence initiated for 0000 hours.'

A hum of machinery from somewhere below gradually increased in volume. Next to where Ricky stood, a row of monochrome CRTs showed the views from several closed-circuit cameras located in the interior of the gold room. Overtop what looked like a gigantic silver satellite dish, a large piece of complex machinery slowly moved into place. It appeared something like the whatchamacallit over the embalming table, only much larger and with added bells and whistles.

Wondering what would happen next, Ricky was shocked to see the nurse suddenly exit the hidden room and begin rapidly approaching the control room where he now stood. Apparently, his remote learning tutorial course had ended, and he needed to make himself scarce.

Rosenstein ran through the doorway to the operating theatre, then paused for a discreet peek into the corridor beyond before he blundered out the door. He was glad he did—the Bowler Hat Man was rapidly approaching. In a panic, he ducked back inside the room, unsure what to do. Suddenly, his junior high school days of outwitting bullies came flooding back to him. And so, he decided to use the same strategy as back then, and he started looking for a place to hide.

After rapidly scanning the room, he was dismayed to see that the only place which could properly conceal his well-nourished form was the white enamelled housing that wrapped around the embalming table's base. He manoeuvred around behind the table and ducked down just as Nurse Kandi entered the room from one door, and Bowler Man entered from the other.

Ricky Rosenstein pressed his face against the cold white porcelain and realised his current position was not unlike the adage regarding being stuck somewhere, except that instead of a rock and a hard place, he'd scored himself a couple of sociopathic lunatics.

CHAPTER EIGHT

December 30th, 2021 1005 hours

Due to her experience with the painted wolf and everything else that had happened in the Executive Gaming Lounge and model room, Minerva had decided she'd had her fair share of fun and called it quits yesterday afternoon.

After grabbing another MRE from the dining room, she'd barricaded herself inside her suite for the evening. Once she'd placed a chair under the doorknob, she'd moved a dresser up against the sliding mirror along the far wall to stop anyone, or anything, from entering without her permission.

Overnight, there had been a couple of occasions when she'd awoken for some unknown reason and then lain in bed listening carefully, unsure what had disturbed her. There had been one incident in particular that stood out, however.

She'd jolted awake at 3:07 A.M., according to the digital flip clock next to the bed. Propping herself up on one elbow, she'd listened intently for several minutes as she'd looked about the darkened room but hadn't seen or heard anything threatening. Just ready to lie back down and snuggle into the bedcovers once again, she'd suddenly seen the slightest change in the quality of light coming from underneath the door leading to the corridor. Someone had been standing on the other side of the entrance, unmoving for a very long time, and had just moved away.

Climbing silently from the bed, she'd padded to the door and looked through the small, glass security portal. No one was in sight. She quietly moved the chair, unlocked the door and threw it open with a crash. She thrust her head out, but the corridor had appeared empty in both directions.

And then she'd felt it with her toes and looked down.

The carpeting outside her door was soaking wet as if someone had been standing there for several minutes without moving, right after they'd gone swimming. Who, or what had been outside her door, and for how long? If it had been something malevolent, why hadn't it tried to get inside, she wondered. Or had someone or something been out there guarding the door while she slept? And if so, from what? With those disconcerting thoughts swirling in her mind, she'd returned to bed and settled into an uneasy sleep.

About a half-hour ago, she'd finally awoken, surprised both at the time and that she'd fallen back into such a heavy sleep after her unsettling experience in the night. Feeling well-rested, she did a quick stretch and got downward with her dog a few times. Invigorated, she'd decided to head back down to the ballroom to gather another MRE for breakfast.

On her way, she made a discovery so startling that she now needed to do some more research with Lively's iPad Mini and the satellite hotspot. In fact, this revelation had been staring her plainly in the face the whole time she'd been at the hotel. She couldn't believe she hadn't seen it at first, especially after what had happened to her recently at the Slaughtered Sheep in Ireland.

Minerva had been indulging in her addiction, re-examining the large painting over the mezzanine for the umpteenth time when the epiphany had come to her. She'd been looking to see if the painted wolf or little boy had made it back to the landscape once again. It turned out that both had still been absent, and she realised she would need to stay on the lookout for them for the foreseeable future.

Minerva had just stepped back to the edge of the stairs to take the massive painting in all at once and get the lay of the land, so to speak, when it had come to her out of the blue. It seemed that as her eyes had taken in a bigger view of things, her mind had done so as well.

With a shake of her head, she realised she hadn't been thinking large enough. Til now, thanks to her fascination with the model and painting, she'd been micro-focused on everything. But now, pulling back to macro mode, she realised there was another connection for why this hotel was located where it was, and it was not from psychic energy caused by incidents that had happened on the land before or after the resort had been built.

It appeared that the Sinclair was not only rich because of the precious metals in Overseer Mountain below; it was also rich in power because of something else that ran directly beneath its foundations—ley lines. It was a concept whose existence was hotly debated amongst the scientific and paranormal communities across the world.

Plotted on a map, ley lines were a series of alignments between various geographical landmarks and historic structures around the world. In the early part of the 20th century, the idea had come to prominence, with true Ley line believers maintaining that these alignments were also recognised by ancient civilisations who had erected important structures along them all over the planet. This gridwork of lines was also known as the World Energy Grid. The structures that other societies had built along these lines of power were supposedly able to benefit from this positioning. Stonehenge, the Pyramids of Giza, religious sites and temples, the list went on and on, all connected through this gridwork of lines crisscrossing the globe. Some even thought the lines were used by ancient astronauts to navigate when they'd visited Earth in millennia past.

Staring at the painting, lost in thought, this revelation had flooded into Minerva's mind all at once. More than familiar with the concept of ley lines, she was surprised that she hadn't thought of them sooner. In fact, just north of Dublin, the Slaughtered Sheep ran directly over one. And from everything that she remembered of their positioning on the maps she'd studied at the time, she was almost one hundred percent certain that the Sinclair Hotel was located directly over top of one.

According to Doppelively, in his reality, there had been a massacre on this site at the end of the Yakima Indian War. And even in her reality, the area had supposedly held great spiritual significance to the Aboriginal people who had lived in this part of the world before Western influences had changed their lives forever. Was their sacrosanct cognizance regarding this mountain due to the ley lines, she wondered. And had the battles waged in and around this castle back in Scotland also been fought overtop similarly powerful ley lines? That was one of the things she would have to research, but she wouldn't be at all surprised to discover that Castle Sinclair had been located along a line of power in the old country as well.

Were these ley lines, or World Energy Grid, the source from which this hotel feasted and drew its immense power and ability to seemingly make things appear out of nowhere? Had the machine in the basement caused this directly or indirectly due to whatever they'd been experimenting on here? And was this power tapped from the ley lines now being left to run unchecked and separate from whatever else the machine had unleashed?

Minerva wondered again at her forgetfulness and the fact

that she hadn't put things together sooner. Part of it might have been caused by the sheer number of things that seemed to be going on inside, underneath and around this hotel. It was enough to baffle Sherlock Holmes himself. But still, she was not usually a forgetful person. She realised that some of her brain fog might have been caused by all of these elements coalescing into one big miasma of malevolence known to the world as the Sinclair Resort Hotel.

Lost in thought and hungry to boot, she decided she would check the kitchen before grabbing her MRE in case a meal was laid out for her. She wouldn't want to miss out on something delicious intended solely for her after all, and she moved to the basement via the stairs next to the front desk.

Disappointment was pretty much the only thing waiting for her in the kitchen. However, there was one thing that piqued her interest. The box of newspapers waited for her on the gleaming, stainless-steel countertop, right where she'd left them. With all the excitement of having lunch with Doppelively and everything else the other day, she'd forgotten them. She felt sad, since Charlie had been so insistent she read those papers. Well, it was something she could add to her growing list of things to check after she'd picked up her MRE for breakfast.

When she moved to pick up the box, she saw it now contained something that hadn't been there when she'd pulled it from the storage room a couple of days ago. Inside, lying on top of the newspapers, was a wide-mouth mason jar. Inside of it was an unexpected treat. Stacked one on top of the other like a jar of sugary Pringles were some of the most delicious-looking chocolate chip cookies she had ever seen, almost a dozen in all.

"Well, thank you, Mystery Chef!" she said aloud. She presumed that she had the same entity to thank for the cookies as well as the earlier mac and cheese. It was like this had been intended for her dessert. Perhaps something to snack on while she looked through the papers in the box she was supposed to examine? How did this entity know that her favourite cookies were chocolate chip? Of course, most people liked chocolate chip cookies, she realised, and many would list them as their favourite, so it wasn't too much of a stretch, but still.

With the box in hand, she moved back upstairs to the lobby. She left the cardboard carton at the foot of the grand staircase. There was no use carrying the rather weighty box all the way to the ballroom and back for no reason, just so she could grab an MRE. Though she didn't like to admit to ever growing old, she knew her number of years on this planet had given her insight when it came to unnecessary strain on her joints.

Her Grandma Nell had had osteoarthritis. It was something Minerva knew she may have inherited as well, and she tried everything she could to avoid things that would trigger it and make it flare up. Watching her diet and avoiding sugar had been a large part of her plan, combined with a liberal daily dose of yoga–something she'd had plenty of time for over the last couple of days.

As she moved toward the ballroom, she thought more of the mysterious cookies and knew she shouldn't have them, but just like dark chocolate, it was a good-food, bad-food kind of thing. Good because of the antioxidants in the dark chocolate chips, and bad because of the butter and refined white sugar in the cookie dough. But either way, she would no doubt eat them and enjoy them, but only after getting something more substantial in her stomach first.

The grand ballroom lay in darkness when she arrived at the doorway, the table containing the MREs only a dim outline in the middle of the room. Though she'd had several drapes pulled back the other day, they all appeared to be pulled tightly shut now. Outside the windows, she listened to the wind-whipped snow as it scratched and skittered against the glass.

Thinking of the ley lines as she looked about the darkened room, her eyes settled upon the bar, and she moved to where the ebony box had presumably sat on the far end. As she moved down the long piece of polished mahogany, she ran her fingers along its surface, slightly tented, so that only the tips were making contact. Images flooded her mind of people laughing and jostling each other as they ordered drinks at the bar during whatever event they had been part of over the years. Other images showed partygoers dancing and smiling, but she didn't think any of it was related to the people who disappeared. However, when she reached the end of the bar, where the ebony box was supposed to have been placed, things changed dramatically, and she stopped in her tracks.

Her breath started coming in short gasps, her hand now flat so that the palm made full contact with the bartop. Cold, so very cold. The surrounding room was warm enough, but this part of the bartop felt like it had been buried underneath an avalanche and then just brought inside right now.

Pulling out her lightsabre, Minerva turned it on and lay it on its side so its high-intensity beam could illuminate the bartop. She turned her head this way and that as she examined the wood. Was there something inlaid in the wood grain? Looking closer, she could see what appeared to be super fine wire filaments running through the wood. It was something that didn't show up under the regular lighting in the room. In fact, depending on how she angled her flashlight, it almost didn't appear at all and would be very easy for a person to miss. However, with a super bright light like hers held at the right angle, they almost seemed to glow as they ran through the wood, all appearing to converge on a spot near the end.

Moving behind the bar, Minerva scooched down and examined the underside. After shining her light about a little, she saw that, sure enough, the fine filaments converged from various directions into one wire underneath. She traced it back along the framework of the bar and down into the floor where it presumably connected to the machine in the gold room.

Minerva now knew that she and Lively had to be correct; the ebony box was key to, if not everything in this hotel, at least the mass disappearance in the grand ballroom. It had to be the concentrator which the Aggregator in the gold room required to operate. But with the three stuffies in the turret keeping it under guard, she had no way to get to it. Her elbows leaning on the bar, Minerva propped one hand under her chin, forgetting her empty stomach for a moment as she stared, lost in thought, at the spot where the ebony box had sat forty years before.

CHAPTER NINE

December 30th, 2021 1112 hours

The snow was thickening, and Amanda's wipers had already threatened to clog several times. Much to her dismay, the storm had already broken when she'd awoken at six o'clock this morning. After a home-cooked breakfast (Cassandra insisted), she got on the road just a little past eight.

Road conditions on Provincial Highway #99, also known as the Sea to Sky Highway, were moderately acceptable as far as Whistler and through to Pemberton. However, things deteriorated rapidly when she turned onto Highway #96, which led to Entwistle. It seemed the break in the storms had been shorter than the weather office had anticipated, and it was now storming full-tilt once more.

Despite the weather, Jansen was glad to be driving her pimped-out police cruiser. The vehicle stuck to the road like glue thanks to its weight of over two tons and the high-quality, studded snow tires she had installed on it for winter driving. The cruiser was one that the RCMP had decommissioned when it reached the end of its useful life cycle several years before. After Amanda's many years of driving a Ford Crown Victoria P71 as part of her job in the field, she had grown accustomed to its handling and responsiveness. And so, when she had the chance, she'd purchased one at a great price at an auction and had it fixed up.

After the car's 'sneeze-guard' between the cop and the 'cargo' section had been removed, she'd had the interior reupholstered and a shiny new paint job applied to the exterior in her favourite colour, forest green. Apart from installing a kick-ass stereo system with a six-disc changer, that was about all she'd altered. Though the kilometres on it were well over three-hundred thousand, its high-powered, high-performance engine from its days as a highway patrol car was still under its hood. Thanks to regular maintenance, it had only needed a minor tune-up when she bought it.

As she drove, she felt something she hadn't in quite a while, at least since she'd retired from the RCMP. Inside her chest, a feeling of fluttering tension grew and grew the closer she got to Entwistle. The roads weren't helping things, she realised. But still, the thought of returning to the horrible place after all these years was daunting. The closer she got to the place where she'd experienced some of the most electrifying and horrific things in her life, the tenser she became. She was soon threatening to strangle the steering wheel and had to consciously loosen her grip in order to drive safely in the deteriorating conditions.

Amanda had been to visit John many times over the years, but not any time in recent memory. A feeling of guilt temporarily flooded her mind. She'd been meaning to go, and meaning to go, but hadn't had the time. The irony was not lost on her that now that she finally had the time, she didn't want to go. Of course, she wanted to see John, but still, the thought of just turning around and going home had also entered her mind. Even though she agreed to come and take him up to the resort, she still didn't know if she could go inside.

Her wipers laboured to scrape the thickening snow from her windshield the further north she went. Now almost six hours since she'd departed Vancouver, she finally breathed a sigh of relief when the snow-encrusted blue highway sign marking the turnoff to Entwistle appeared out of the white nothingness before her.

Judging by the depth of the snow around John's condominium block, it had been snowing for quite a while here. The sidewalks looked to have been shovelled about six inches ago. Amanda realised that the rate at which the snow was currently falling meant only about an hour or two had elapsed since that had occurred. What must it be like up on the hill right now, she wondered.

Ringing the buzzer to John's condo a couple of times, she waited and waited, then waited some more. There was no response from the intercom security system on the wall, and the door remained locked. Pulling her cell phone from her pocket, she tried John's number, but there was no answer. She was now becoming rather concerned. No need to panic quite yet, she told herself; perhaps John was just in the washroom or out picking up some last-minute items for their trip up the hill? Unfortunately, she doubted that last supposition. She knew John had sold his car several years ago and knew that he would have a hard time going anywhere on foot in the deepening snow that currently fell all around.

Moving down the lane at the side of the building, Amanda looked for John's apartment. His unit, #104, must be located on the ground floor, and his enclosed balcony would have to be a couple of units down one side, she reasoned, but she didn't know which side, and she chose the right. Though she hadn't been to this particular condominium complex before, she knew where it was located from her years working in Entwistle before transferring to Vancouver. Her guilt returned with this thought when she realised how long it had truly been since she'd seen the chief inspector. If her guess was correct, John's condominium should be just up ahead.

With wide eyes, Amanda saw that she was correct.

However, John was not sitting inside sipping a coffee and watching TV as he waited. No, he was lying face down on the living room floor, surrounded by papers.

"Oh my God, John!" Amanda cried. She pushed through the snow at the edge of the lane and was, fortunately, able to access a small gate that allowed entry to the ground floor terrace. She hoped intensely that John had forgotten to lock his sliding balcony door as many people in apartments tended to do. With a massive sigh of relief, she found it to be the case and slid the door open and entered.

Placing a couple of fingers on John's neck, Amanda found his pulse strong and steady. "Thank goodness." She gently tried to rouse John, and after several seconds, he began to come around. His lips were cracked and dry, and it looked like he'd been on the floor for quite a few hours. "John, it's Amanda Jansen. Can you hear me?"

Harder's eyelids fluttered for a moment, and then he opened them and blinked several times. In a rough, dry voice, he said, "Amanda. So glad to see you. I—"

Amanda shook her head and touched John gently, saying, "Don't try to speak. Let's just work on getting you upright. Do you think you can move?"

John nodded, and she helped him sit up. He did so with a slight groan.

"Do you think you can stand so we can get you to a chair?" she asked.

Harder nodded again, and she helped him slowly to his feet and supported him as he shuffled over to a nearby La-Z-Boy recliner, where he sat with a grateful sigh. He felt so frail compared to the powerful man she remembered working with in Entwistle over the years. Even when she'd last seen him, which must have been five years ago, she recalled guiltily, he'd gone downhill.

"What happened, John?"

Shaking his head, Harder said, "I don't know. I took a dizzy spell."

"I'll be right back." Amanda moved to the kitchen to get some fluid to treat John's dehydration. Returning with a glass of room temperature water, she handed it to him and asked, "How long were you lying there?"

"I don't know." John accepted the water gratefully and took several small sips, undoubtedly having difficulty swallowing due to dehydration. After a breath, he sipped the water again and then asked in a rough voice, "What time is it?"

"A little after two in the afternoon."

"What day is it?" he rasped.

"December 30th."

"Oh my God."

"What is it?"

"I've been lying there since yesterday afternoon."

"Oh no! How are you feeling right now? Should I call the ambulance for you?"

Harder shook his head and sipped the water again. "No, apart from being thirsty and needing to use the washroom, I'm not doing too bad." After a brief pause, he added, "And now that I've gone and said it, I need to take care of business."

Amanda brought John's walker to him and helped him to

his feet from the recliner. "Are you sure you're going to be okay?"

"I'll manage, thanks." With that, John shuffled down a short hall to a half-bathroom near the kitchen.

Bending down to the spot where John had lain, Amanda began to pick up some of the mess of papers he'd dropped when his dizzy spell had overcome him. With a gasp of surprise, she discovered something that may have caused his fall. Underneath several sheets of paper, gleaming darkly in the centre of the floor, was an obsidian stone, just like the one in her suitcase. Close by were some rags, in which he must have wrapped it, and she used them to pick the gemstone off the floor. She took great care as she handled it, not wanting to touch it as if it were something she'd found in her cat Willamina's litter box. The cold gnawed at her hand through the rags, and she didn't know how John could have it near him. After placing it on the coffee table, she collected the remaining paperwork and put it in a manila folder lying nearby.

Straightening the papers, she noted they were printouts from various RCMP reports, including handwritten notes and several of Johns's ubiquitous little black books. While she worked, she couldn't help but look at what was on the papers. She wasn't surprised when she saw that they all had to do with the Sinclair Hotel, including a publicity still from the front of the resort.

When John returned from the washroom, Amanda was just placing the folder full of documents onto the coffee table. He moved to the recliner and sat down with a puff. Taking another sip of water, he nodded toward the folder, saying, "Thanks for doing that. I was looking through that folder when the dizziness overcame me."

Sitting on a small sofa near John's recliner, Amanda asked, "Was it caused by that, do you think?" She nodded toward the obsidian stone nestled in the plaid rags on the coffee table. Just being near it made her feel lightheaded, almost like the feeling she recalled from when she was a teenager painting her nails in her small bedroom without proper ventilation.

John looked to the stone and shook his head, saying, "I don't know. Maybe. I'd had it nearby. There was a photo I'd been looking at and..."

Amanda handed the folder to John, saying, "It's in here. Maybe it will help you remember."

Harder flipped the folder open and saw the picture of the resort resting on top. Without looking at the photo too closely, he handed it to Jansen. "It was this picture. I'd been going over everything for more hours than I care to remember and needed to take a break. When I returned, I noticed that the photograph had changed. That folder had been lying on top of the stack with this photo showing. Take a look."

Examining the photograph in her hands, Jansen saw that it was most likely from the publicity department at the resort. It was a gorgeous shot showing snowcapped mountain peaks and a marshmallow-covered forest in the background. The foreboding hotel stood in the foreground, one of its front doors open.

"Do you see her?" John asked.

Amanda shook her head, saying, "See who?"

"Helen!" John held out his hand, and Amanda passed the photo back to him.

Harder studied it and shook his head. "I swear to God that Helen was in that doorway! She was there for almost a full day. Then, yesterday afternoon, I was going to try scanning it into my computer so I could enlarge it, and that's when the dizzy spell came over me. But now she's gone! How is that possible?" Harder picked up an antique magnifying glass next to his chair and studied the photo for a moment longer, his eyes moist with unshed tears as he searched desperately for any sign of his missing wife.

"I believe you, John. I believe you." Amanda said with a small smile of reassurance. "I've seen things recently that I can't explain either, and it's only been getting worse the closer we get to December 31st."

John put the magnifying glass down, slipped the photo into the folder, and placed it on the small end table near his chair. "I agree. And I believe we must get back there before midnight tomorrow night."

As if in response to John's assertion, the Sinclair's publicity still slipped from its folder and fluttered to the ground. It landed on the carpeting near the coffee table, and they both stared at it, unwilling to touch it, eyes wide in shock.

In the main entrance of the Sinclair Hotel, a blonde-haired woman stood once more, one arm raised invitingly, appearing to beckon them both inside.

CHAPTER TEN

The elevator swept down to the lobby, its cast iron and brass cage gleaming as if freshly polished. Lively gawked around as he and Edward descended. Things looked the same architecturally, but the crazy decorating scheme continued, and tawdry multi-coloured furniture contrasted against carpeting with such a busy pattern it could make a person dizzy if they stared at it too long. Keeping pace with the elevator, Bald Beefy kept an eye on the descending car, his scowl fixed on the cage and more specifically, on Lively.

Many questions swirled rapidly inside Lively's mind, and he asked one at the top of the list, "So, how many versions of the Sinclair Hotel can you access through your Harmoniser?"

"Why, all of them, of course. Though there are some less desirable than others."

"So, was that how you provided food to us, through these alternate versions of the hotel?"

"Providing food to you? What do you mean?"

With a ding, the elevator arrived. They stepped out and

were greeted by Blonde Beefy, who'd gotten there just ahead of them. Continuing the conversation as they crossed the lobby, Lively said, "The beer and wine? The Christmas Eve buffet? Breakfast in the kitchen? None of that ring a bell?"

Edward shook his head, then said, "No, that wasn't us. We can access the stores of any and all Sinclair's that happen to be in the same frequency range that are similar to us, and thankfully, that is an almost limitless supply. However, nothing was ever sent to 2021."

"Why?"

"The Harmoniser is not a time machine, we can't travel forward or back in time, only to other realities in this same bubble as us."

"So, this looping you've created affects all of the other realities as well?"

"To different degrees, yes. Some are unaffected such as this one, and things are relatively normal, but in others, not so much."

Lively pondered this. If his father didn't provide the food and drink, then somehow, the hotel itself must have managed to harness some of the power that Edward and Schreck thought they were controlling. If anything, Lively now realised, things seemed relatively far from their control, and he asked, "What about the Sinclair hotels that aren't in the same frequency range?"

"I'll show you one of the subfrequencies when we're done here. They're not very pretty."

As they moved through the annex to the ballroom corridor, Lively recalled his earlier thought on the topic, and said, "Sounds like they'd be a pretty good place to 'lose' somebody for a while."

"Or forever. You're very astute, Son. I like the way you think."

Lively hadn't meant his comment to imply he could think of people he'd like to banish, per se, but it seemed Edward had taken it as such, and he had now managed to further ingratiate himself with his father and his plans for... whatever they were. "Always looking for an angle, that's me," he said, shrugging his shoulders slightly.

"I can believe it."

The snaky wallpaper which lined the passageway in the other frequency had been replaced with a chintzy-looking, foil paisley print.

Edward stopped in the doorway to the ballroom and glanced about. Turning back, he smiled with a slight nod, saying, "He's near the back at his favourite spot."

The group entered the ballroom, both bodyguards scoping the joint as they moved. Lively was surprised that Edward had seen anybody across the enormous space. The air was so thick with cigarette and cigar smoke it almost felt like a physical presence holding them back. Despite his initial shock of seeing people smoking when he first arrived in 1981, he was even more surprised now.

Back in the other '81, people were smoking here and there, and it seemed that maybe half of the partygoers were smokers. However, in this 1981, almost every person around them, without exception, was smoking a cigarette, cigar or in some cases, a pipe. But whatever their poison, it looked that everyone around them was actively engaged in destroying their lungs and their health. Coughing slightly, Lively said, "Looks like they could use to improve the ventilation system around here."

"Yes, that's one of the interesting things about the subfrequencies. There's always something different, sometimes in surprisingly subtle ways, and other times, a little more noticeable, like here, with their preoccupation with garish colours and tobacco products." He gestured at the smoke-filled air.

Always a sucker for an old movie on TV where a haze of smoke-filled some lounge or bar, Lively hadn't considered how hard it would be to breathe in such a situation in real life. By the time he was a teenager, smoking in most public buildings had been banned and he hadn't experienced too much of it until he'd joined the Canadian Armed Forces. He'd seen many fresh-faced cadets get hooked on the devil weed of Big Tobacco over his time in the military but had fortunately never succumbed to the temptation to try it himself. And now with another slight cough, he was glad he hadn't. His eyes were starting to water from the thickness of the smoke, and he wondered how people could enjoy any food, let alone breathe around here. Despite their two-dimensionality, movies had never left him gasping for air as this ballroom currently did.

This New Year's party seemed much more sprightly than the one occurring in the other 1981. The Glenn Millers were currently belting out a horn-heavy version of Boogie Wonderland to great effect.

Out on the dance floor, partygoers were laughing, shrieking, and having a grand old time as they gyrated and ground against one another. Their eyes were wide and wild, their parted lips wet and leering in flush-cheeked lust. At this ball, the reveller's faces were uncovered, as opposed to the masked ball of the other 1981, and boy, were they ever getting down, Lively noted with amusement. Some bopped and swayed to the bouncy boogie while others were engaged in what could only be described as vertical sex. At least their clothes were on, so far. He wondered what happened around here when it got closer to midnight. Was this frequency less sexually inhibited somehow, and not just due to alcohol or smoking their brains out? Judging from what he'd seen so far, it seemed a fair bet.

A group of people sat at some tables off to one side of the dance floor. Lively recognised several, supposedly killed in assorted plane crashes, drug overdoses and car accidents over the years. Were they all from his own reality and merely paying for the privilege of hiding here, one frequency down in this bacchanalian lustfest? Had the incidents that supposedly killed the people back home perhaps not been those actual people after all, but rather, in the cases where bodies needed to be found, duplicates of them pulled from other realities and sacrificed in their stead? His father had admitted that a select group of individuals were aware of what was happening at the Sinclair, undoubtedly paying vast sums of money for the privilege of living forever in these bubble realities. Were these famous people seated around the nearby tables some of this elite group, he wondered.

In one corner of the room, a table larger than the rest occupied a sizeable portion of floor space. Sitting in a rather plain-looking wooden chair, a small, grizzled man with a shock of bushy white hair glowered at their approach. Next to him sat another man that looked remarkably like...

"Edward Sinclair! How are you?" Standing from his chair, then moving toward them to shake hands was another, older version of Edward Sinclair. Lively noted that the man looked to be the age his father would have been in 1981, had he not undergone whatever rejuvenating process he'd received. The grizzled man remained seated at the table, his glower deepening at their arrival, but saying nothing.

Older Edward looked Lively over with keen interest and said, "Is this who I think it is?"

"Yes. I'm surprised you can't see the resemblance," Edward the Younger responded.

"Well, I thought there was something special about him! Sit down, please, and join us." Older Edward shook Lively's hand vigorously for a moment, then took a seat.

Eyeing Lively up and down as he claimed a seat at the table, the sour-looking senior said, "Who's the gommy lad?"

"Dad," Edward the Younger said, "I'd like you to meet your grandson, Lively."

"Lively? What kinda numpty name is that?" Thomas Sinclair asked, his Scottish brogue thick as mist on the moors despite his many years away from the Highlands.

"It's the name my mother gave me," Lively said. He reached forward to shake his grandfather's hand, but Thomas only looked at it.

"Yeah, well there's no accounting for taste, I suppose. Sit down, sit down."

Older Edward sat next to Thomas and Edward the Younger sat to the right of his alternate self. As Lively sat across from the three men, Older Edward leaned forward and said, "You'll have to excuse Dad, he's a bit of a crabbit today."

"I'm a bit of a crabbit every day, ya daft gowk," Thomas agreed with something on his wrinkled face that approached a smile but careened into a sneer.

Edward the Younger agreed, saying, "He's not lying. He can be a sour old bugger sometimes." He looked to Thomas briefly, then corrected himself and said, "Okay, all the time."

Thomas nodded approvingly at the correction.

Lively looked at the three Sinclair men. He could see the family resemblance, sort of. It was almost like looking at one of the evolutionary charts he'd seen in science class at school.

On the left, as if just out of the primordial ooze, Thomas Sinclair was an angry-looking, 'crabbit' of a man, his face settled into a permanent frown. To his right, Older Edward looked like a slight advancement on the evolutionary side of things, until arriving at the handsome and much more youthful-looking Edward the Younger, his supposed father.

Thomas Sinclair looked over at Lively and said, "Ya must be brimmin' over with questions, judgin' by your befuddled expression."

Lively felt fortunate for his multi-year exposure to James Doohan in the role of Scotty on the original series of Star Trek or TOS, to Trekkies like himself. Though he was aware of the controversy surrounding Trekkies and Trekkers, he had personally never felt maligned when someone would describe him as a Trekkie to friends and family. Other people had differing opinions, and to be called such were fightin' words to them, but not him. Regardless of fan classification taxonomy, listening to Doohan's Scottish accent over the years had helped Lively, and he was able to decipher most of what his grandfather was saying. The irony was not lost on Lively that Doohan was only imitating a Scot, and like the infamous captain of the good ship Enterprise, was also a fellow Canadian. Looking to his grandfather, Lively said, "I thought you were dead?"

"Nay, I was pulled into this frequency, durin' one of the first tests of that confounded machine!"

Edward the Younger shook his head, saying, "He was adamant to try it."

"When the prototype was run, he ended up swapping places with my father, the Thomas from this reality," Older Edward added.

"Aye, and it killed the poor bugger," Thomas said with a grave shake of his head.

"But, if you traded places, why didn't you just go back?" Lively asked.

Answering for his father, Edward the Younger said, "He can't. When he swapped with the other Thomas it altered his core frequency and now, he's stuck here." He held up his wrist to show the bracelet just peeking out from his shirt's cuff. "That's one of the reasons why we now wear these to travel. As I said earlier, you'll be stuck there if you try to translocate to another frequency without one."

"Like me," Thomas said with a nod, then added, "Edward can bring me back for a visit to the prime frequency, but I need to wear one of those damnable bracelets the whole time. But I don't go very often. I prefer this frequency." He looked to the gyrating partiers on the dance floor, adding, "It's much more liberated here."

Gesturing to the room around them, Lively looked to his father, saying, "You all keep using the same expression, 'frequencies' when describing things, why?"

Nodding, Edward the Younger said, "Because its the correct term. Each of the realities we access vibrates at its own unique frequency."

Older Edward nodded, saying, "Some are closer than others to the original frequency, of course, such as here."

Nodding, Edward the Younger said, "The closer to our core frequency," he pointed at himself and then Lively, "the more similar the universe. About the only thing we don't seem to share here is the postal code and taste in interior decorators."

Smiling broadly, Older Edward said, "Yes, we're practically next-door neighbours, isn't that right, Brother?"

His younger doppelgänger nodded, and they laughed.

Lively found the twin Edward's use of that word interesting. 'Brother' was exactly how his doppelgänger had addressed him when he'd stepped out of the movie screen and grabbed a handful of his popcorn. He wondered if that Lively had been pulled from a subfrequency like this one. Looking around the room, he asked Thomas, "Are the Sinclair's rich in all the frequencies?"

"Aye. The wealth that the Sinclair family has amassed spans universes, lad," Thomas said, a grave and greedy expression on his face.

"But how are you making money at this?"

"Think of it," Edward the Younger said, "If people are looking for you, for whatever reason, and if you want to disappear, what better place to hide than in another reality?"

"So, you're selling access to alternate universe hideaways?"

"Oh, it's much more than just that," Older Edward said.

"That was something we provided, at least until we had our wee problem," Thomas added with a nod.

A nubile young woman approached Lively with a dinner menu. He waved her away, saying, "No, thanks." Food was the last thing on his mind right now.

Older Edward suggested, "You really should try the steak—it's melt-in-your-mouth grass-fed Wagyu. Quite delicious and decadent, just like everything else here." He looked about the room with satisfaction and added, "Besides, you need to keep your energy up."

Lively shook his head, saying, "I'm not hungry, thanks." But he wondered at the comment. Keep his energy up? For what? Needing clarity from his grandfather, he asked,"What was the problem you had? An entire ballroom of people disappearing?" Lively asked.

Edward the Younger answered, "Oh, heaven's no! We planned that, of course. We just didn't plan on getting trapped inside our own bubble for forty years."

"Trapped?"

Edward the Younger nodded. "We miscalculated the power required for the initial alignment and it took more than we anticipated. However, now that you've come along, things are looking up!"

"But how did you bring me here?"

"Do you have your keychain?" Older Edward asked.

"My keychain?" Lively felt around in his suit jacket pocket, found his pocketknife, and pulled it out. His house keys jingled musically as they dangled down from a loop at one end.

"Your keys opened more than just doors around here," Older Edward said with a laugh. "That pocketknife is made of the same material as the bracelet you wore to travel here."

Surprised by this news, Lively looked more closely at the pocketknife, marvelling at the small Christmas gift from decades before. Though Edward had said there'd been an issue with the power required to further their little experiment after the ballroom disappearance, the fact that there had still been enough energy leftover to allow him to enter this alternate reality gave him some small hope. If he could be pulled through to here, it followed that he should be able to push himself, and hopefully everyone else trapped at this resort, out of the past and back to the future.

CHAPTER ELEVEN

December 31ˢᵗ, 1981 2111 hours

Ricky Rosenstein felt his legs cramping due to his current position. Fortunately, the table's skirting was just big enough to hide his girth, but he found it hard to stay bunched behind it. Parts of him kept threatening to protrude and expose his hiding place, and he was constantly readjusting his position as silently as possible to remain hidden.

A very short distance away, on the other side of the embalming table, stood his playmates in this deadly new game of hide-and-don't-be-seen in which he'd suddenly found himself.

Bowler Hat Man said, "Is everything prepared for tonight's alignment?"

In an excited and breathy voice, Kandi asked, "Yes, Maxi. The reset is scheduled to run as usual."

"I've asked you not to call me that when we're working."

"What? There's no one else around."

"Even so, there's a time and place for everything."

"You are *so* right," Kandi purred.

There came a sound that Ricky couldn't quite identify, and when he did, he was repulsed by what he was hearing. Nurse Kandi and the Bowler Man were kissing quite passionately. He shuddered, wondering how anyone could kiss that man's jumbled jawful of dental dementia.

With a wet smacking of lips pulling apart, Kandi asked, "Is Edward still in the dark?"

"Indeed. He's never been able to see too far beyond his own ego. But after tonight, that won't be a problem anymore."

In a breathy voice, Kandi said, "Oh, Maxi, you're so wicked."

More lip-smacking emanated from the other side of the table, and Ricky shivered again. After a moment, the couple broke lip-lock and moved away from where they'd been standing.

Rosenstein tensed, ready to feel a hand fall on his shoulder. But it never came, and he issued a cramped breath of relief as Maxi and Kandi moved into the corridor leading to the elevator and stairs, their voices gradually receding until he was once more left in silence. He remained hidden for a moment longer, thinking of what he'd just heard. Were Kandi and Maxi conspiring to stage a coup or something like it? Whatever sort of surprise they had planned at midnight, he figured it wasn't likely to be good for Edward Sinclair or anyone else.

Ever so slowly, Ricky peeked over the edge of the embalming table. He half-expected to see the Bowler Man grinning wickedly before him, Nurse Kandi at his side with a roll of duct tape in hand, their departure only a ruse to flush him out of hiding. However, he was pleasantly surprised to discover he was alone in the room. In the distance, through the open doorway, he could hear the lift being engaged and moving off to higher floors.

This seemed an excellent opportunity to check what else they had running on this mainframe. Moving silently, he made his way through the control room toward the partially open door leading to the gold room. He wanted to access the computer on the remote terminal from the confines of the hidden room where Kandi had disappeared. That seemed a much safer proposition than doing so in the main control room's more open spaces.

Pushing on the door ever so slightly, Ricky poked his head into the gold room like a red-headed gopher. The room was huge, seeming to take up much of this hidden level between floors. Thick, shining steel columns, spaced at regular intervals, supported the massive load of the castle/hotel hybrid above. The polished aluminum floors and walls reflected the golden ceiling's warm yellow colour, giving the entire room a relatively mellow vibe, considering its location.

This place was everything Lively had said in his manuscript and more. Blinking rapidly, he shielded his eyes from the glare after being in the dim control room. Due to the open layout of the ample space before him, there were very few places to hide, and he wanted to get out of sight again as quickly as possible.

With an exasperated sigh, Rosenstein saw he now had a problem. Kandi had closed the door to the hidden room when she exited. Now it was hard to say exactly where it lay along the gleaming wall. He moved slowly, his eyes scanning for the door.

Ricky was temporarily distracted by the immense depression in the floor where the dish he'd seen on the monitors resided. Overtop of it, the complicated piece of machinery looked even more intriguing in person than it had in black and white. He stood back for a moment, taking it all in, and leaned against the wall as he tried to imagine how the machine worked.

With a sudden yelp of surprise, Ricky realised he'd found the hidden control room.

Now presented with a supine view of things, Rosenstein looked briefly about. A row of black and white monitors up along one wall showed the large dish in the floor and the crazy machine above it from various angles. Beneath the monitors was the object of his search, the remote terminal. After verifying all of his assorted bits and pieces were still functional, he stood with a grunt and brushed himself off.

Closing the door, Ricky examined the small room. There wasn't much to see. Apart from the closed-circuit monitors, the only other thing of interest was a five-and-a-quarter-inch floppy disk drive squatting next to the CRT on a shelf just above the remote terminal keyboard. Nearby, a comfortable-looking office chair on casters awaited its next occupant. Oddly, a couple of pairs of sunglasses lay next to the floppy drive. Strange to have those in a windowless room, he thought. Shaking his head, Rosenstein sank into the leather chair with a sigh, then wheeled over to the terminal. Rolling up his sleeves, he cracked his knuckles, about to see what he could see.

With a few key clicks, he brought up the file directory listing and found what he presumed was the main programme's executable which controlled everything. He entered the editor and scanned through the code. Most of the programme seemed to be command calls made to various nodes and access points connected to assorted pieces of equipment located within the hotel. Interspersed in the code were calls to a couple of things he'd read about in Lively's big book—the gigantic silver satellite dish and the Harmonic Universal Alignment Aggregator. One of the nearby CRTs had a red plastic label underneath its display that verified his guess that the funky-looking machine over the dish outside was the Aggregator. All of this code was scheduled to execute tonight at midnight, all controlled by the programme he'd seen Kandi reinitialise a short while ago.

Ricky knew that he needed to find Lively, wherever he currently was, ASAP. But first, he wanted to make a slight alteration to things while he was here. In a flurry of keystrokes, he added a few personal touches to the mainframe's executable code, wanting to give it that Rosenstein touch. After a few minutes, he sat back in the chair and cracked his knuckles again, a smile on his face. At midnight tonight, the Sinclair would be running his new custom-modded version of their reality-alignment programme, or whatever it was.

Until he'd met Mr. DeMille, Ricky Rosenstein's life had been enjoyable enough but with little excitement. There were exceptions, of course, such as when a new computer system was released or perhaps when a new programming language was announced. And then there was always his first love, of course, smorging. But none of that had ever fulfilled him, and he'd felt strangely empty. But now, after the work he'd just done, he felt full to bursting with newfound courage, and it was a feeling that he wanted to last, hopefully forever.

But one thing he didn't want, for himself or anyone else, was to continue to live through this endless hell of parties, night after night for all eternity. Now that he'd been thrust into this topsy-turvy world where everyone seemed out to get him, he felt strangely excited and was enjoying this new feeling of living by the seat of his pants. Though he knew he had no skills in subterfuge, he still had certain aptitudes that he thought might prove useful in helping everyone out of their current predicament. He glanced at his watch and saw he would find out if that were true relatively soon.

Nodding in satisfaction, he stood from the leather chair and moved back into the gold room. His next stop was going to be his suite. In addition to his little mod, he'd had another idea and needed access to some of the goodies he'd packed in his bags upstairs. And so, with that helping spirit glowing in his chest, Ricky moved past the embalming table and crept silently into the dim red corridors once again.

CHAPTER TWELVE

Feeling guilty yet hungry, Minerva took the last chocolate chip cookie from the mason jar. She hadn't been down to grab a breakfast MRE yet and needed something to hold her over. Though she knew that a cookie was not a wise nutritional choice, her hunger overrode her better judgement. Taking a bite, she looked sadly at the empty jar and said, "And that's why I don't keep these around at home."

After leaving the ballroom yesterday, she'd spent some of the previous afternoon and evening reading some of the newspapers. After rising early this morning, she'd continued the process and had been surviving on the sugary, chocolate chip-infused delights in the jar. Except now, they were almost gone. She looked to be nearing the bottom of the cardboard carton and decided to forgo further sustenance for the moment. As soon as she was done, she could grab an MRE. With a small sigh, she picked up another newspaper from the box and said, "All the news that's fit to print."

When the Sinclair Resort Hotel opened in December 1946, it had advertised the addition of a young and upcoming blue-ribbon chef to its talented staff. Amelia Walden, a young woman originally from Winnipeg, Manitoba, had been appointed as head of the kitchen and would oversee everything from the Pinnacle Dining Room to the Snowdrop Lounge, along with room service and catering for the numerous balls and events held in the ballrooms.

Employing a woman in such a major position was unheard of at the time. However, she was backed up by her credentials as she had received training at numerous gourmet cooking schools across Europe before the war. When the Second World War broke out, she had been assisting Georgina Landemare, a fantastic chef and mentor who taught Amelia many things. And thanks to that good luck, Amelia had begun working with Landemare just as the woman had been appointed as the personal cook to then prime minister, Winston Churchill. It was a position Georgina would stay with for many years and one that opened many doors for Amelia as a result.

Churchill himself was quite the gourmand, enjoying fine food wherever he went. But when he was at home, he relied on Landemare and her staff to keep his ample belly full. It turned out that Thomas Sinclair was an acquaintance of Churchill, the two having met in Africa just before the Second Boer War. Churchill had been a young British newspaper correspondent trying to make a name for himself, and Sinclair, a wealthy industrialist, hoping to find business opportunities on the dark continent.

Well, find them he did. And thanks to several successful business ventures involving the South African diamond industry, his already sizeable fortune from gold in the Kootenays and Yukon had been enriched considerably. Many years later, when he'd begun pining for his ancestral home back on the Scottish moors, the idea of the resort incorporating the castle had been born, or so the story went. As one of Canada's first billionaires, he had the wherewithal to do most anything he desired, and so, he'd decided to bring his Old World heritage home to the New World.

Shipping containers filled with castle stone weighing hundreds of tons each had already taken the journey across the ocean to the port of Vancouver. Hauled by transport truck up the recently paved Highway #96 to the town of Entwistle, where it wound its way up Overseer Mountain to the site of the resort. After a little over one year of round-the-clock construction, the hotel was preparing to open near the end of 1946. When Sinclair had mentioned to his friend Churchill that he'd been looking for a head chef for his new hotel, the prime minister had recommended Amelia Walden for the job, and Sinclair had listened.

And that is how Amelia Walden ended up working for one of the wealthiest, most powerful and connected families in Canada and possibly the world. With the Sinclair resort almost complete, Amelia had had plenty to keep her busy with new menus to plan, larders to stock, and kitchen staff to hire.

When the hotel opened, Walden's food was an instant success, and as a result, she spent many happy years cooking at the resort. However, by the mid-seventies, there had been whispers of friction between her and the management at the hotel. Rumours had begun floating around that she was considering taking a position elsewhere.

These disagreements came to a head just as Amelia was preparing to celebrate thirty years in the Sinclair's kitchen. It was common knowledge that everyone who had eaten at the resort said that they would follow her wherever she went if she ever did leave the hotel. However, when Amelia finally departed the Sinclair Resort, she went to a place none of her customers could ever follow, at least not right away. On the afternoon of September 30th, 1976, Walden died after falling from one of the lookouts high in the hotel's singular turret.

Amelia Walden had been with the Sinclair for almost three decades before her accidental death. But Minerva doubted it was an accident and had a strong feeling that instead, someone, or something, had murdered her. After such a long and presumably enjoyable career at the hotel, she doubted that Amelia would have taken her own life, least of all by flinging herself from its highest parapet. But what if she'd been led up to the turret? Or something had drawn up there somehow? With a sudden shudder, Minerva wondered if someone had instead pushed her to her death once she got up there?

Suddenly, like watching a clip from a horror movie in her mind, she watched the silverback gorilla silently juddering its way up to Amelia's back, lifting her high overhead in its mighty arms, then hurtling her to the ground far below. Minerva shuddered at the thought.

The kitchen in the hotel had always felt welcoming, much like how she'd felt in her own Grandma Nell's kitchen. And now, Minerva thought she knew the reason why—Amelia Walden was obviously still here. And if that were true, could her spirit somehow be accessing the interdimensional rifts she and Lively suspected were dotted around the hotel? Was Walden somehow reaching through those portals and bringing food for them? Was she, in fact, the Mystery Chef? If that were the case, then it seemed her passion for the kitchen, cooking and caring for people far outweighed other minor considerations, such as her own death.

CHAPTER THIRTEEN

December 31st, 1981 2141 hours

After the meeting with Thomas and Older Edward, Lively had been toured around the hotel for a short time, his father citing the variations between the two realities as they went. There weren't too many significant differences, as he'd seen earlier, just the change in decor and the slightly less inhibited people that seemed to inhabit the frequency. As they were moving back through the lobby, a naked woman chasing after a naked man streaked past them and flew up the grand staircase, presumably to either get some clothes on or just plain get-it-on.

"Does that often happen around here?" Lively asked, a bemused smile on his face.

"Surprisingly, yes. The inhabitants of this frequency seem to have few inhibitions when it comes to exposing to the world what nature has bestowed upon them."

Thinking of his father's words, Lively asked, "Speaking of exposed to the world, who do you have on the outside in 2021 overseeing that holding company for you?"

"A trusted associate," Edward replied vaguely, then added,

"We realised that there would be numerous liability claims against the Sinclair Corporation once our procedure was initiated and everyone in the ballroom had shifted frequency. So, well before that happened, a majority of the corporation's assets were moved to an offshore holding company. Much of the family fortune was placed into technology stocks with companies such as IBM, Apple and the like. All of it shielded from any prying government eyes, of course."

They had arrived back at the elevator, and the bald bodyguard held the door open for them once more. As they stepped aboard, Lively asked, "Then who sent me the invitation to investigate this hotel?"

"We also hired a well-established private investigative company and paid them handsomely all these years to continue surveillance of you and your sister until the time was right." Edward pressed the button for the third floor.

This was shocking news, and Lively asked in surprise, "So you had people spying on us our entire lives?"

"Spying is such a harsh word; let's just say 'under observation' instead, shall we?"

"Semantics," Lively said with a shake of his head.

"There's so much about you and your sister that you don't understand right now, and I can't explain it all at the moment. Suffice it to say, when the time was right, the agency had been told to send out the contract proposals and remuneration packages that you both received." The elevator arrived with a ding, and the doors opened to reveal the unsmiling face of the blonde bodyguard waiting for them.

Stepping from the lift, Lively said, "So you had this all prepared in advance with our information packages gathering dust at that agency that whole time until we were deemed ready?"

"Yes. We had everything ready to go in early 1981 before you were even born." Gesturing to the air around them as they approached the entrance to the royal suite, Edward said, "Can you feel it?"

"Feel what?"

"The power that surrounds us."

"I've felt something, I think. Is that all from the people in the ballroom?"

"Hardly."

"Then what powers this whole process."

"More than just the electricity from the hydroelectric dam your grandfather built, that's for sure.

"Such as what?"

Almost to the entrance of the royal suite, Edward turned and said, "You've heard of the World Energy Grid?"

"You mean ley lines? Yes."

"Good. Then you must be aware that two of them converge directly underneath this hotel. They provide us the extra boost we need for our process."

Lively's eyes widened at this news. "Well, that's something I never considered." He'd pondered the connection between the gold in the gold room and the Sinclair family's gold rush connection to Lawless. With a jolt of newfound cognisance, Lively realised that that small mountain town of Lawless might also be situated over one of the same lines that converged beneath this hotel and most likely Entwistle itself. His mind began to race, and he asked, "Did Thomas know of these ley lines when he found this mountaintop to build the resort on?" Lively still couldn't bring himself to call the elder Sinclair 'Grandpa', not quite yet.

"Your grandfather knew there was something special about Lawless, but not why. However, when he was guided to this mountain, he learned of the power they truly contained."

"You mentioned that earlier. Guided by my grandmother, Margarethe, correct?"

"Yes, she led your grandfather to this spot just after the turn of the 20th century. Much like you and your sister, your grandmother had a feeling for things unseen, both in this world and outside of it."

Lively thought about that for a moment; he knew from his previous conversation with Edward that his grandmother got 'feelings' for things. Now, he realised it may have been more than just feelings. Perhaps she had been not unlike Minerva and himself? If Edward were to be believed, he now knew where part of their talents came from.

Stepping into the royal suite once again, Edward said, "Come, let me show you something else while we still have time."

"Time till what?"

"The frequency realignment, of course."

"Frequency realignment?"

"At midnight when we reset everything." Furrowing his brow, Edward asked, "Are you going to repeat everything I say?"

Looking somewhat embarrassed, Lively shook his head. "Sorry, just trying to process everything you're saying is a challenge sometimes. There's a lot to learn here."

"No doubt." Edward nodded and added, "Well, don't worry, you'll know everything you need to know soon."

Lively could see his father seemed to be buying his interest in the family business, so to speak. He wanted to keep up the charade as long as possible to hopefully facilitate the rescue of the people who had gone missing. Thinking of them, he asked, "How do the people in the ballroom fit into all of this?"

"Are you familiar with how an atomic bomb operates?"

Thinking for a brief moment, Lively recalled some information from high school science class and said, "An atomic blast occurs when two subcritical masses are brought together to form a supercritical mass. Generally speaking, a smaller explosion, usually chemically induced, ignites and frees neutrons from fissionable material and initiates a bigger explosion; in this case, a nuclear reaction."

"Quite so!" Edward said, appearing impressed. He entered the ensuite bathroom, the bald Simon preceding him through the door. Lively entered next, followed by the blonde Simon.

"So what're you saying, that this place is nuclear as well?" Lively wondered aloud.

"Hardly, but the principle is similar." Edward stepped onto the platform over the clawfoot tub again and gestured for Lively to do the same. He continued, saying, "The energy provided by the partygoers is one of the subcritical masses, the chemically induced explosion as it were. This is directed at another subcritical mass, the power from the ley lines, and each night at midnight, we reintroduce the two to each other and reach supercritical mass once again, thus reinitialising the harmonic alignment for another twenty-four hours."

"And what if that didn't happen each night?"

"If the alignment were improperly terminated, the consequences could be dire."

"But if it was done correctly, it could be ended?"

"In theory, but we've never tried, of course. One of the major side effects of all this is temporal stasis."

"You mean you don't age like you mentioned earlier?"

"Correct. And if the realignment were ended in our frequency, so would this stasis."

"It would introduce discordance then."

"Yes! And we need harmony for all of this to work." Edward tilted his head and asked, "Are you aware the Earth resonates in the key of C-sharp?"

Lively nodded, saying, "I've heard something like that."

"Good. However, you might not be aware that all of the planets in our solar system have their own unique vibrational frequency and are in harmony with each other. As such, our entire universe operates in a similar harmonious fashion." Edward held up his hand and exposed the bracelet on his wrist, adding, "And much like that harmony in planetary frequency, these bracelets are attuned to our reality's unique prime frequency."

"Prime frequency? Your 'brother' used that same phrase."

"That's because that's what it is."

"How do you mean?"

"The universe that propagated the aggregation is the prime frequency, and the others are all subfrequencies, or daughter universes, if you will, and they align with that. I'll show you another right now, in fact." Edward began punching numbers into the keypad, adding, "Fortunately, there's still power here in this frequency to do so. Otherwise, we'd have to travel back to the prime frequency before initiating another trip." As he spoke, the bodyguards joined them on the Harmoniser's platform, standing protectively in front of them once again.

"We don't always need to come back to this location to initiate travel between the frequencies?"

Edward nodded. "No, only for the initial departure from the prime frequency. After that point, recall is automatic, no matter where we are, thanks to a preset count-down timer, and once that time is up, it pulls us back.

"So, your twin and Grandpa Tom can't just pay you a visit?"

"Due to differences in the vibrational frequencies, the Harmonisers that exist in these daughter universes can't initiate travel to our prime frequency. If they want to visit prime, we have to bring them there."

"They can't use the Harmoniser at all then?"

"They can, but only to travel to other subfrequencies of their own respective daughter universes." Edward finished his input on the control pad and said, "Bearing all that in mind, if you need to return home early, there is always the panic button as a last resort. In fact, you've already got one with you."

"I do?" Lively asked. He raised his wrist so that his shirt cuff fell away, revealing the cameo-styled bracelet with the gilded S. "In here, I presume?"

"Twist the Sinclair S on the front clockwise."

Lively did so and was surprised to see the gilded letter pop open to reveal a small red button beneath.

"Whoever is wearing the harmonic bracelet is the person that returns with it, along with whoever they happen to be holding, or anyone else wearing a bracelet that originally shifted frequencies from prime with them. The activation of the panic button on one bracelet triggers them all."

"What if it gets broken, lost, or somebody steals it and uses it instead of you?"

"That wouldn't be a good thing."

"How so?"

"Well, you'd be taking up permanent residence there since you'd have no way back and you'd be permanently synced to that reality." He shook his head sadly, then perked up at once and said, "And on that note, I'll show you one of the wastelands."

"The wastelands?"

"Yes, not all sub-frequencies were as unaffected as this one here. A few had some rather unforeseen outcomes." He looked to the control pad, then at Lively and asked, "Are you ready?"

Unsure if he'd ever be ready to be ripped from one universe to another, Lively simply nodded and said, "Make it so."

With a grin on his face, Edward hit the red flashing launch button and initiated the sequence. After another popping noise, the room around Lively blinked away to darkness as it had before. The tugging sensation in his chest came again, and then the world resolved around him again, the feeling of brief nausea paying him a return visit as well.

It was very dim here, almost dark, actually. Minimal light entered the room, what little there was coming through a window high on the exterior wall of the bathroom. However, it was enough for Lively to see that things were not good here.

Both bodyguards pulled small flashlights from their jacket pockets and turned them on, then stepped down from the raised platform and shone them around the room. Bald Beefy moved off to the suite's other rooms, the blonde standing nearby and waiting patiently with his flashlight to illuminate their way.

Dirt, decay, and destruction were everywhere, and it looked as if this version of the Sinclair had been abandoned since the ballroom incident forty years before.

"This frequency was impacted rather hard," Edward said, stating the obvious.

"What do you mean? Impacted by your moving between realities or the initial ballroom disappearance?"

"The ballroom most definitely. Here, let me show you," Edward said, stepping off the platform again. He nodded toward the powerless keypad as he did, saying, "As you can see, this Sinclair hasn't had power for some time now. It's one of several frequencies that had what we would call a rather untoward outcome."

Lively shook his head and said, "All caused by you and your experiment. So where did everyone go that was in this reality?"

"We're not quite sure, but sacrifices must be made in the name of science."

"You're not quite sure?" Lively was shocked at his father's cavalier attitude toward human life and added, "It looks to me that all the sacrifices you've made in the name of your science project so far have been human sacrifices."

"Well, we didn't know this would happen," Edward said defensively. He gestured to the blight that surrounded them as they moved into the royal suite's bedroom, and he said sadly, "It's all very regrettable."

It seemed that was as close as Edward would ever get to an apology, and Lively asked, "Did you ever stop to think of the consequences before you started?"

Turning, Edward entered the sitting area and said over his shoulder, "They were of minimal consideration in light of a discovery with such far-reaching potential."

Following his father into the sitting area, Lively was stunned at the condition of things. Through the jagged and torn curtains, a crescent moon illuminated the suite with its faintly luminous light. Mildew covered most of the carpeting, chairs, and sofa, with large patches of black mould growing in several corners near the ceiling.

"Well, your potential certainly seems to have reached this far," Lively said, shaking his head in disgust.

Lively took in the view through the window. "Why is the moon visible here when back home there's nothing but that killer fog surrounding the hotel?"

"Yes, for whatever reason, our access to the rest of the prime frequency is limited outside the hotel, but more leeway is available in many of the subfrequencies. The size of the bubble varies from place to place. Some frequencies are quite limited, like back at home, while others stretch for miles in every direction, at least from what we've experienced in our exploration of them so far. This one, for example, despite the devastation, has a great amount of freedom outside its doors."

"How many frequencies have you visited since you initiated the loop?"

"Thousands and thousands. We've been cataloguing them as well. Some of the more 'exotic' frequencies have very interesting foodstuffs and wildlife. It can make for a rather interesting experience at times."

They moved through the suite and into the hotel corridors. Dust, mould, and broken furniture lay everywhere as they moved along. Many of the doors to the suites had been seemingly vandalised with their doors broken open, some hanging from only one hinge. Curious, Lively asked, "What happened here? Vandals?"

Edward shook his head and said in a hushed voice, "No, crawlers," but would say no more.

With Bald Beefy taking point and Blonde Beefy walking close behind, the bodyguards guided them silently through the ruined hotel toward the Executive Gaming Lounge. They seemed to be on high alert for anything else in the immediate vicinity, presumably the crawlers that Edward had mentioned. Several minutes later, they stood in the model room near one of the narrow windows that looked out onto the valley below. The miniature of the hotel in this frequency lay shattered into thousands of pieces, the delicate and detailed minutiae from inside scattered across the floor in all directions.

"You wouldn't have seen anything back home with that fog, but you can see a bit here with the moonlight helping outside." Edward stood back and let Lively peer out the window.

The moon bathed the landscape beyond in its pale, silver light. The snow was a smooth, unbroken white blanket overtop of everything. It appeared so deep, the lane leading up to the hotel was barely visible beneath the thick mantle.

Lively could see his breath as he peered through the window. Fortunately, he was fairly sure this cold was not from anything supernatural but instead from Mother Nature herself. With no electric heat inside this building, things were decidedly chilly. After a moment, he stepped back from the window, saying, "There's a lot of snow out there, but that's about all I can see."

"From this window, you should be able to see the lights of Entwistle twinkling away down below," Edward observed, glancing back out the window.

"I didn't see anything like that."

"No, you wouldn't. Because there's nothing to see."

"Why?"

"There's no one in the town below."

"What?"

"When our prime frequency initiated the sequence in the ballroom, as I mentioned earlier, it had unforeseen circumstances in other realms, such as this one, and it was impacted more than others."

"So, everyone disappeared from the hotel here and town below at the same time everyone was kidnapped from the ballroom in our reality?"

"As far as we know. But I wish you wouldn't call it that. Technically, since we never issued a ransom note, it wasn't a kidnapping," Edward said in a petulant tone.

"Call it what you will, but where did all the people go?" He gestured toward the window.

"We're not sure."

"Not sure? Several thousand people go missing, and you're not sure where?"

"We believe that initiating the sequence in the prime frequency had repercussive and cascading effects in some of the other subfrequencies. Not a lot of them, but enough to be of concern."

"What would happen if you shut off the machine running the sequence in the prime frequency now? Would they come back?"

"Couldn't tell you. We can't shut it down."

"What? You've got to be kidding me."

"Absolutely not," Edward said gravely. "For whatever reason, we can only reset the alignment from within the loop and have no control over stopping it. We believe it can only be shut down from the outside. And even then, we don't know if it would be successful, or instead end up killing us all."

This gave Lively some small hope, with a slight addendum to the part regarding everyone dying as a possible outcome. Perhaps if they could reverse things, and everything unfolded as he hoped, then everyone missing from here would return along with everyone else from the ballroom in 2021. But it begged a question, and he asked, "You mentioned other frequencies were affected as well. Are there realities that are worse off than this one?"

"Several. In fact, there's one where we believe that most of the Province of BC and part of Washington State were affected.

"That would be..."

"Almost ten million people."

"Oh my god!" Lively couldn't believe what he was hearing. Here was his father, if he was to be believed, now telling him that the incident in the ballroom had unforeseen side effects which had impacted millions of lives. And that was just in one of the affected realities. Lively wondered how many more were devastated, just like this one, that they hadn't yet discovered.

Seeming bored with the conversation, Edward looked at his watch and said, "It'll be just another few seconds now."

"Until what?"

"Translocation. When the auto-recall function kicks in." Glancing down at his watch, Edward said, "And three... two... one..."

The room darkened around them, and then they were suddenly standing back on the platform over the clawfoot tub in the prime frequency. Lively blinked several times as his eyes adjusted to the bright lights.

"Well, I can see that it's getting close to time. We should get back to the festivities."

Lively began to remove his bracelet and return it to his father, when Edward said, "You might as well hang on to that for now."

With a nod, Lively placed it back on his wrist. He'd noticed earlier that both bodyguards had been wearing bracelets before they underwent the initial translocation to see his grandfather. And now, both retained their bracelets afterwards and did not give them back to Edward. Noting this, Lively asked, "You mentioned that when you're in other frequencies, you need to wear one of these bracelets, but is there any other reason for wearing them?"

"Being out of sync with the frequency you're visiting is disadvantageous to one's health, let's say."

"Is this from what you've personally witnessed?"

"Science demands sacrifice and experimentation. And yes, I have witnessed it happen. Unfortunately, people have laid down their lives so that we may enrich our own."

"And you're okay with that? Along with all the other people who've likely disappeared from realities you're not even aware of yet."

"As I said, without sacrifice, science, and the very progress of mankind itself would stagnate. I don't view what has happened to a few unfortunate souls as something that should stop us from achieving our ultimate goal."

"A few unfortunate souls? Try millions! And all for what, money?" Lively was aghast. Here was his father, telling him that he'd seen people die before his eyes, all in the name of his own family's enrichment and their quest for fame and power. And it seemed that Edward was okay with many more dying or disappearing as well. A feeling of nausea suddenly overcame Lively, but it was different from translocation. This sick feeling in the pit of his stomach was from realising he was part of a family that seemed responsible for the disappearance and possible deaths of millions of people across multiple realities.

Crushing guilt overcame Lively as he and his father's entourage moved back toward the grand ballroom. His mind was chattering away, overloaded by everything he'd just learned. At the top of his mind was how he would ever come to terms with this new knowledge, let alone tell Minerva the fact that their father and grandfather before them were basically mass murderers on a scale not seen since the Second World War.

CHAPTER FOURTEEN

December 31ˢᵗ, 2021 1049 hours

Minerva folded the last yellowed newspaper closed and looked to the others scattered across the duvet. From the disarray, it appeared as if she were expecting a puppy with a leaky bladder to climb onto the bed next to her at any moment.

Lost in thought, she sat on the edge of the bed, her chin resting on the back of one hand. Charlie had indicated she didn't need to read all the papers, but most of them had contained a least one article that dealt with the Sinclairs, Amelia Walden or the hotel itself. It was as if someone were keeping them all together to put into a scrapbook someday. Taking a moment, she mulled over everything she'd read, trying to unpack all of the information into neat little compartments in her mind.

Despite the revelations in the newspapers, Minerva felt no closer to figuring out how to get the ebony box out of the model room and into the ballroom than she was yesterday. At the thought of the ballroom and the MREs contained therein, her stomach rumbled loudly. She looked at the empty cookie jar and felt tempted to pour the remaining crumbs into her mouth. Instead, she checked the time and her eyes widened in disbelief. It was almost eleven o'clock in the morning! She'd completely lost track of time. Her grumbling stomach had long ago finished digesting the chocolate chip cookies from this morning, and she wasn't surprised it was complaining.

Now, in light of her current hunger situation, and especially after reading about a blue-ribbon chef, amongst other things, she was curious about the kitchen once more. Was something else waiting for her to dine on downstairs, pulled through from some alternate Sinclair's kitchen? If there was a chance for her to not have another MRE, then she was open to alternative possibilities, even otherworldly ones.

With her stomach giving a particularly aggressive growl, Minerva removed the chair resting against the door. Its rear legs had kept a rolled-up bath towel firmly in place—her defensive strategy from any slithering canvas predators out in the halls. Kicking the towel aside, she creaked the door open and peered into the passageway, sword in one hand, silver tray in the other. The coast seemed clear in both directions, and she stepped into the corridor.

As Minerva rested the sword on her shoulder, she glanced up, and her heart did a somersault.

Perhaps just thinking of her favourite creepy-crawly tour guide as she'd sat on the bed had been enough to summon him forth because there it was, clinging to the wall just above her suite's doorframe. Though Charlie, as of yet, hadn't seemed in any way malevolent, she nonetheless stepped back a pace into the corridor so she would not be too close to the substantial spider.

Adjusting the sword on her shoulder, Minerva said, "Well, well. If it isn't my little eight-legged librarian friend."

The spider waggled a leg at her in response.

"You'll be happy to know I've finished all the course

material you gave me and was just on my way to get some late breakfast."

The wolf spider scuttled down the edge of the door frame until it was eye-level with Minerva, then waggled two of its legs in the air, perhaps to wave off her current desire for food as being unimportant.

"Okay, fine, I'll hold off on breakfast. So, where to now, short, dark and hairy?"

The spider gave another waggle as if to say, "Tally-ho, follow me!" Scrambling down the doorframe, it raced down the passageway toward the grand staircase.

Minerva had expected the arachnid to move toward the hotel's lower levels since that's where she'd mostly encountered it. Instead, Charlie scampered quickly up the staircase toward the third floor. With a little less alacrity, Minerva mounted the stairs in pursuit.

Though curious to see where the spider was leading her now, she was also keeping an eye out for other things and didn't want to let her determination to keep up with Charlie blind her to any other hazards that might be in the vicinity.

As she'd expected, the spider was waiting for her at the top of the stairs, tapping one leg as if to say, "What took you so long?"

"Sorry, Charlie, I only have two legs, not eight. It takes me a little longer than you to get up here."

Seemingly uninterested in excuses, the spider turned and rushed down the corridor toward the royal suite. However, it stopped when it was a couple of suites short of the royal's door.

"What's in there?" Minerva asked.

The spider didn't respond but merely moved off to the side for her to open the door. "I don't have a key with me, and Lively has his snap gun with him, so let's hope this is unlocked." To Minerva's surprise, it was. The spider scampered around the doorframe and disappeared into the darkened room beyond.

Smaller than the royal, this suite still appeared well decorated, though the antiques seemed minimal. Located on the outer wall of the east wing, the room's two windows faced out onto several clay roque courts, currently buried under eight feet of snow. With the drapes pulled tight, it was quite dark in the room, and minimal daylight leaked through their velveteen fabric.

Off to one side of the windows, a couple of small amber lights glowed intriguingly on a desk. Minerva flipped on the overhead lights as she entered the suite, surprised to see one of the amber lights belonged to an Atari 800, a beige-coloured personal computer from the early '80s. The second glowing light was coming from the front of a shoebox-sized device next to it, an Atari 810, five-and-a-quarter-inch floppy disk drive. Beside them, the handset of the house phone was pressed into the rubberised acoustic coupler of an Atari 830 modem.

"Oh, my stars! Where've you been for the last forty years?" Minerva wondered aloud. The equipment appeared new, with the CPU unit and disk drive the same light tan colour as a Tim Horton's double-double. Connected to all of this, a thirty-two-inch Sony Trinitron TV sat at a slight angle so the computer's user could see its screen.

Looking about the room, there appeared no sign of the spider, and she presumed it had scuttled into, onto, or under something or other. She'd just have to keep her eyes open.

Having not been in all of the hotel's innumerable rooms,

Minerva wasn't surprised to see the odd thing left behind. Previous tenants had left the odd thing behind in some of the rooms she'd investigated, despite the RCMP supposedly clearing out their personal effects. However, it wasn't unexpected as some things were bound to get missed; it was just human nature. And over her time here, she'd discovered a few items, including Esmeralda Cruz's diary and the odd toiletry, like the Mr. Bubble found next to her bathtub. But she hadn't found anything too exciting, until now, with this intriguing computer setup.

So that begged a question: if all the personal items found in the suite, along with the food and alcohol, had been catalogued as evidence and long since removed, where did this 8-Bit computer from the 1980s come from? It seemed a strange thing for the hotel to materialise if that's what had happened. Or was it here for another reason, and that was why Charlie had introduced her to it? Had something changed where Lively now resided to cause its appearance here? This seemed very encouraging. And although she hadn't been steered wrong by her sizeable spider-friend yet, she was still skeptical of the arthropod's assistance.

With tiny embers of hope beginning to glow in her chest, Minerva powered on the television. It was turned to channel three, and static currently danced across its screen. Looking to the side of the computer, she saw a small black power rocker. Flipping it on, she was rewarded with the sound of the disk drive groaning to life with a click and a clack. The Sony's screen flashed a brilliant blue, and a white cursor appeared at the top. A series of electronic beeps and boops began emanating from the TV's speaker as the computer happily booted up whatever was on the floppy disk already in the drive.

After a moment, the Trinitron displayed 'Rosenstein Computer OS'. Below was a series of prompts for various options the user could load from this personalised operating system. Minerva selected the most helpful option, 'Remote

Chat', and began to type.

CHAPTER FIFTEEN

December 31st, 1981 2158 hours

Apart from his computer and mathematical studies, one of Ricky Rosenstein's minors at McGill University was the study of psychology. He recalled that Carl Jung had said that events that seem to smack of synchronicity were nothing more than chance occurrences, statistically speaking. Astrologers, psychics, palm, and tarot readers all provided the curious and those who wanted to believe with the same thing— information that they wanted to hear and nothing more. However, Ricky realised many people chose to assign these occurrences meaning because they appeared to validate paranormal and supernatural concepts they held. He was never quite sure if he believed himself to be one of those people, but it now begged the question: was his meeting with Lively DeMille serendipity, or was it fate?

Ricky had always felt that he'd lived his life for a reason. And he also believed that his mother had survived Auschwitz for a reason. Perhaps, he thought now, her reason was to give birth to him so that he could fulfil his reason for being— meeting and assisting Lively DeMille. Was it his destiny to help unravel this dastardly plot and rescue not only himself, but everyone else inside this building as well? With this sense of newfound purpose filling his soul, he knew there was no way he was going to let his beloved mother down, peace be upon her, or Lively DeMille either, wherever he was now.

When he travelled about the country and the world, Ricky always carried samples of his wares to show prospective clients. Since he'd just been coming off the heels of yet another successful sales trip, he had several examples of his personal PC line accompanying him on his stopover at the Sinclair. The computers and peripherals travelled in their own large, padded suitcase, so large it was almost the size of a steamer trunk in reality. And due to its size and weight, transporting it around on his business trips on a regular basis cost him dearly.

Rosenstein realised he could probably bring an assistant along instead and have them lug all of his gear around. However, he enjoyed the freedom and travelling about and meeting new people and potential clients on his own, without anyone to distract his spiel. Surprisingly, he was quite effective as a salesman, presumably since he was so unassuming and low-pressure in his dealings with people.

Safely back in his room, he dialled in the combinations on the suitcase's locks, popped the latches and opened the lid to reveal his 'babies'. Nestled inside several layers of custom-cut foam rubber were a Commodore Vic-20, TI-99/4A, and an Atari 800, along with all their assorted cables and peripherals. Now, he just had to figure out which one he wanted to use.

Though he loved the Vic-20, he was more partial toward the Texas Instruments and the Atari since they both packed a huge sixteen kilobytes of RAM compared to the Vic-20's meagre five. With a smile, he decided and unpacked the Atari CPU, disk drive and modem. Setting them on the desk next to the Sony Trinitron TV, he connected them and then turned everything on.

When he'd been down in the gold room on the remote

console, he'd crafted himself a little back door into the mainframe's code because everything needed a back door, in his opinion. Soon, he would not only be able to monitor what was going on down in the gold room, but he would also be able to modify any of the IBM's settings if he so desired.

One of Ricky's other hobbies, apart from 'smorging', was coding. Compiled in 6502 assembly language, he'd built his own front-end system for the Atari, and its interface glowed colourfully on the screen before him now. He removed his suit jacket and rolled up his sleeves, a gleam of excitement in his eyes. Wheeling over the desk's leather executive-style chair in front of the computer, he sat with a puff and began to type.

After a few minutes, Ricky picked up the telephone receiver handset and plugged it into the modem's acoustic coupling interface. Though the hotel's internal copper-wire-based telephone system was part of the mainframe's lifeline to the outside world, it also worked in reverse, and he'd been able to burrow his way in locally.

After logging into his new back door, he was at the top level of the homebrew mainframe interface when something unexpected happened that made him sit back in his chair in surprise.

On the TV screen before him, one word was typed out before his disbelieving eyes.

'Hello?'

Had he been hacked? It didn't seem possible since he'd just logged on. As far as he knew, there was no one down at the computer terminal in the gold room. But if that were the case, then who was accessing his Atari? He supposed there was a chance it was Nurse Kandi at the other end, toying with him, but how had she realised Ricky had gained access to the mainframe's system so quickly?

Ricky frowned fiercely. If this was a hack, they were pretty open about it. He returned the salutation, typing, *'Hello. Who is this?'*

Several moments later, the response came back: *'A friend.'*

He wondered at this for a moment. A friend? What friend? He didn't have any, at least none nearby, unless he counted Mr. DeMille. Since the little hack he'd pulled off with the mainframe wasn't one that involved connecting with the outside world, that meant the person that he was communicating with must be someone within this hotel.

After another brief pause, the person on the other end reciprocated and asked, *'Who are you?'*

Ricky typed in, *'Someone who is wondering what's going on around here.'*

A few seconds later, a response flashed upon his screen, and he laughed as he read it.

'That makes two of us!'

Typing again for several seconds, Ricky entered, *'How did you gain access to this computer?'* Wondering what the response would be, he hit the return key and then waited.

Shortly, a reply came back, and it was not one he'd expected.

'I didn't 'gain access' to the computer. I found it.'

Found it? Found it where he wondered. His fingers flying over the keyboard, he posed the exact same question to the person at the other end.

'In suite #304 of the Sinclair Hotel.'

What? How was this possible? He was in suite #304 of the Sinclair hotel, two doors down from the royal suite! He typed, *'But that's where I am!'*

There was no response for a long time, then the other user replied.

'We're both in the same place, but somehow not.'

Ricky looked about the room at his back to verify there wasn't someone else in the suite with him. He shook his head, not comprehending how such a thing was possible. But then a possibility popped into his head, was he communicating with someone else from the future? With nervous fingers, he typed, *'What year is it there?'*

'2021'

Ricky sat back in his chair, shocked. If the person at the other end was telling the truth, then everything Lively had told him was also true. Previously, he'd held some small part of his belief in check when Lively told him where he was from, just in case the man had recently escaped from Sunnybrae Mental Institution on the coast. But now, it seemed his last little bit of doubt had been erased, and he felt renewed hope that he was on the right path; his actions in the past, the act of putting this system together just now, were having repercussions into the future. He patted the top of the sturdy beige computer, pleased to know the unit was still working dependably after all those years.

He recalled Lively's Big Book of Busting and the notes he'd made in the margins of it. Pulling it from his suit jacket, he leafed through it, and then typed, *'Are you Minerva?'*

'Yes, I've been staying here with my brother, Lively, trying to figure this place out, but he's disappeared.'

With a smile, Ricky replied, *'Well, you don't have to worry anymore. He's here in 1981 with me. By the way, I'm Ricky Rosenstein.'*

'Pleased to meet you, Ricky. Do you know where Lively is right now? I need to speak with him.'

The smile on his face faded, and he shook his head as he realised he had no answer for that at the moment. He didn't know what had happened to Lively since he'd disappeared with the Bowler Man. Clacking away on the brown plastic computer keys, he replied, *'He is with the Bowler Hat Man, and I don't know his location. Will keep you posted and try to have him respond ASAP.'*

Minerva replied, typing in a passphrase for him to share with her brother so that he'd know it was her, if and when they were able to communicate.

As Ricky watched her type it in, he sat back with a sigh, wondering if the person he was talking to in the ether really was Lively DeMille's sister, or was it only a ruse by this hotel or whatever was ultimately in control of things around here? Well, he figured, there was only one way to find out, and that would involve finding the man in question.

CHAPTER SIXTEEN

December 31st, 1981 2205 hours

As they approached the elevator on the third floor, Lively marvelled at the intricate iron latticework that comprised the exterior cage surrounding the shaft. It reminded him of something, and he said to Edward, "Before we head back to the soiree downstairs, could you tell me what happened here on Christmas Eve, 1963?"

Edward studied Lively a moment as if assessing his intent with the question, then said, "Why do you ask?"

Lively seated himself in one of the nearby borne settees situated about the second-floor common area to await an answer. As he sat, dozens of reflected Livelys did the same. "I've been curious about what happened up there that night since the police report proved inconclusive."

Edward didn't sit, but looked at his watch briefly, then said, "Time is short, and there's still much to do."

"Short? I thought time was something you had plenty of around here?"

"We do, or rather we did."

"What do you mean?"

"I'm sorry to say we only have time for one question at the moment."

Though realising he had so many more questions he wanted to ask than just the one, Lively stuck with the original and asked, "So tell me about 1963."

Edward looked at his watch again and was about to speak when Max Schreck appeared as if from nowhere. "Excuse me a moment, please." Edward walked a short distance away with Schreck and began conversing animatedly about something.

Lively was left with a Beefy Boy standing to either side of him. He looked from one to the other, then said, "Just so you know, our little tete-a-tete in the basement was purely business, guys. Nothing personal."

At Lively's admission, both of the massive men squinted at him a little harder but said nothing. He wondered at that. Did they speak? Could they speak? As he pondered the possibility that they'd been rendered mute by some procedure, Schreck and Sinclair returned from their conference.

Nodding to Schreck, Edward said, "My associate, Mr. Schreck, will answer some questions for you. But unfortunately, I have other matters that need tending to."

With a nod, Lively said, "I'm sure this hotel must take up much of your time."

"Yes, in fact, it takes up all the time," Edward said with a chuckle, then departed, his bodyguards following close behind.

Lively watched Edward walk away, thinking his choice of words rather odd. What did he mean by that exactly?

Schreck folded his gangly body into a chair opposite Lively, smiled his Grinchy smile, and then said, "Ah, here we are again. And alone at last. You must have so many questions right about now?"

"You must be psychic."

"Oh, I have my ways."

I'll bet you do, Lively thought, but instead said, "How long have you been with the resort?"

"Oh, I'm not exactly 'with' the resort. I'm here as more of a consultant. But to answer your question, I have been here since just after it opened. However, I rarely interact with any of the local staff or customers. I travel a lot, you see."

"I bet you're a real jet-setter."

With a dismissive shake of his head, Schreck said, "I never use them."

"So, you're a consultant. To what?"

"Scientific pursuits, mostly." Schreck shifted in his seat to look at Lively directly, then asked, "Are you aware of my history, Mr. DeMille?"

Lively shook his head and said, "Not at all. But since we're now on the topic, I was wondering if you could explain something you said to me earlier."

"And what was that?"

"You said you were related to the actor Max Schreck 'in more ways than one'. How many more ways are there, apart from by blood?"

"Is that what keeps you up at night, Mr. DeMille?" Schreck laughed lightly.

"Amongst other things like giant spiders and the Ghost of Christmas."

"Really?" Schreck seemed caught off guard by this.

"Wasn't that part of your little welcome package here at the Sinclair?"

"Oh, heaven's no." Schreck looked genuinely interested, however, and said, "But do tell."

This was something that struck Lively as surprising. If Schreck was to be believed, the phenomena they had witnessed before he'd arrived in 1981 hadn't had anything to do with the disappearance, at least not directly. And if that were the case, it certainly furthered the supposition that the hotel had gained sentience and was now somehow able to access the multiple realities co-existing here.

But what of the supernatural aspects? Were they due to the arcane items that Thomas and Edward collected over the years? Had they been affected by the experiment in the ballroom, and were they now responsible for the assorted nightmares which now roamed the Sinclair's halls? It could be a combination of all of these factors, but there was no way to tell which was which.

With a shake of his head to dispel the myriad of thoughts, Lively said, "You were supposed to be answering my questions, remember?"

Smiling gruesomely again, Schreck seemed to be enjoying his little interview and said, 'Quite so. Now, where were we? Ah yes, my relationship with actor Max Schreck is quite simple, really. He was my uncle. I was born Klaus Zoller in Munich. Schreck was my mother's maiden name, and

Maximilian was my uncle. I took to using my uncle's famous name when I came to Canada after the war."

"Which war? The First or Second?"

"Oh, you are a scamp," Schreck said, then added, "Why the Second, of course. However, unlike my uncle and his silver screen fame, I pursued more academic goals. After college, I attended university at Oxford where I majored in physics and psychology."

"And that's where you met Edward."

"Quite so!" Schreck said. "Due to our shared passion for physics, Edward and I had many of the same classes. When I found out that Edward had interests in the occult as I, well, naturally, we became friendly."

"Naturally."

"Georges Lemaître first hypothesised his Big Bang Theory in 1927, just after I started at Oxford. I recall it was making the rounds and causing intense debate whenever anyone brought up the topic." Schreck looked wistful for a moment as he recollected his colourful, and no doubt sordid, past. He continued, "From then on, the advancements that took place in the field of physics, especially over the next half-dozen years, were phenomenal. Edward and I began collaborating on a ground-breaking project, but that was interrupted when the war broke out, and I was recalled to the fatherland. However, we kept in touch through some mutual connections. Then, after the war, I came to Canada under my assumed name of Schreck, and we continued to work on it together."

"So, my father aided and abetted the Nazi party?" Lively asked, aghast at the thought.

Schreck chuckled, then said, "No, not directly. But as you must know, the Sinclair Corporation, like many multinationals during the war, sold munitions, supplies and equipment to both sides of the conflict. Oftentimes that was through subsidiary companies, especially when it came to the Axis Powers. However, our collaborative project was for neither the Nazis nor the Allies; it was solely for our own benefit."

"And where is your little project now?"

"Why, you're inside of it, of course."

Lively was taken aback. He'd thought that only the gold room, ballroom, and royal suite above were part of their elaborate machine, but now, he was shocked to hear otherwise and said, "The entire hotel is your machine?"

He nodded. "Quite right. All thanks to the concentrator."

That name rang a bell, and Lively asked, "And what is that, exactly?"

"Oh, I'm sure you've figured that out already. Though it looks like it's made of wood, it didn't test as such through any of the processes we used."

"You're talking about the ebony box."

"Is that what you're calling it? Yes, quite so. It was discovered in North Africa, a couple hundred kilometres south of Cairo. Thomas had been there on several curio-hunting expeditions over the years, his first at the turn of the century and his last in the mid-1930s. We initially thought it was a sort of small prayer cabinet, but we know that definitely isn't the case now."

"Why is that?"

"No prayers were ever said over that box because it predates organised religion."

"How old is it?"

"We don't know for sure since its origins are obscured by time. But according to the carbon dating we had done in the late 1940s, it's well over fifty-thousand years old."

"So that box is key to everything?"

Schreck nodded. "Undoubtedly. Without it, we'd never have achieved what we did."

"Can you access it from this reality as well?"

"No, there is but one box. And where it is right now, inside the model, is the only place it is, or ever can be, if we want things to continue the way as they are each night, that is."

"But what if it was placed back in the ballroom?"

"In theory, things might be reversed, but that can't happen as long as the nightly harmonic realignment is enabled, so the point is moot."

"You can't disable it?"

"We've never tried."

"What, really?"

"Why would we want to? Everything is in balance right now. And as far as we know, the consequences of shutting it down could be catastrophic."

Catastrophic for whom, Lively wondered. Perhaps for those relying on the accumulated energy within the box to continue their loop of time, but not for the captive partygoers—to them, it would most certainly be liberation. He had to ask, "But I heard Edward say you were all trapped here."

With a dismissive shake of his head, Schreck said, "Edward is so dramatic. I wouldn't call it trapped, but rather 'constrained' in the where and when." An odd smile crossed his face, and he concluded, saying, "But hopefully, that will be remedied soon." He looked at his watch and stood, adding, "Speaking of getting around, we'd better make our way back to the ballroom."

Apparently, Schreck's little 'Biography' moment was at an end, Lively saw. Though he had more questions, he put them on the back burner for now and joined Schreck, following him down the grand staircase toward the lobby. As they descended, he processed all of the information recently divulged to him. With what he'd learned from Edward about their goals and achievements, and now with the information from Schreck, he firmly believed the ebony box was key to everything that had happened here. He and Minerva had been on the correct course, and now, he just needed to communicate this to her.

In addition to his skills in lie detection and chemical interrogation, another area of training that Lively had received over the years involved disappearing when he needed to. As he followed Schreck down the corridor toward the ballroom, he looked for an opportunity to give the man the slip. In addition to contacting his sister, he wanted to see what Ricky Rosenstein had been up to for the last little while. Hopefully, between the three of them, they could figure out a plan. For whatever reason, Lively didn't think his experiencing a reset would be a good thing, and unless he did something pretty quick, he would be looping here with the rest of the gang indefinitely.

His chance came near the main doors to the ballroom. There seemed to be a bit of confusion at the entrance as some latecomers arrived at the ball. Several men in tuxedos, accompanied by their wives or girlfriends, were arguing about something with one of the doormen and the girl in the blue silk gown. One of the men seemed very inebriated. He turned unsteadily toward Schreck, grabbed his arm, and with a very pronounced slur, proceeded to explain the 'sitcheeashun' to him.

Lively took this moment to begin moving slowly and quietly backwards from the group as he attempted to fade into the background. Thankfully, his training served him well, and he was just about to step into the service corridor when a familiar voice at his back said, "Leaving the party so soon?"

CHAPTER SEVENTEEN

After picking the resort's photo from the floor, Amanda had inserted it back into the manila folder once again and then placed it on a side table. She sat a box of facial tissue on top to ensure it didn't eject any more of its contents. After that, she'd brewed a good hot mug of tea for them both.

Since the storm outside had still been raging, and at John's insistence, for safety's sake, she'd decided to spend the night on the sofabed in his living room. Part of her had actually been relieved at postponing her visit up the hill for just a little while longer, however.

That evening, they'd had a lovely pasta dinner together, along with a couple of bottles of wine. John had remarked at one point that it felt a little like a last supper, and that had dampened the mood a bit. But for the most part, their time together had been mostly positive, and they'd reconnected, rekindling their relationship. She had viewed John as a father figure for a while now, especially since her own had passed away two decades before at the relatively young age of sixty-four.

When they'd been getting dangerously close to the bottom

of the second bottle of wine, John had remarked that Amanda was truly like the daughter he'd never had. She had told him of her own father then and of how she felt toward him. His eyes reflected his contentment at her company, and she could see that he genuinely appreciated their time together.

She'd wished she'd had more time to visit last evening and had not wanted it to end. But that had been the way of her life, always looking for more time, not only now but in the past as well. Especially her past with Danny, who she'd been thinking of more and more with each passing hour. Though their time together as a couple had been brief, it had been one of the most electric and intoxicating experiences of her young life. Every day since Danny's passing, she missed him just as much, the years doing little to diminish her love or the pain of her broken heart.

Later that evening, she'd been washing her hands in the hall's small half-bathroom, and just as she finished, she'd looked up and seen Danny behind her in the mirror.

But it had been handsome Danny, the man she loved. He'd just been standing there, smiling his crooked smile. She hadn't turned around because she'd known he wouldn't be there if she did, so she had kept her gaze locked on his for the longest time until he'd eventually faded away like an old photograph. She'd looked at herself then, her eyes shining like pearls and her heart beating like a hummingbird's.

In that brief moment, her resolve to go back up to the resort had solidified, her earlier trepidation now gone. Amanda knew she must go to the Sinclair and do whatever she could, up to and including laying down her own life in the process. If it meant that the missing people were found, she felt that, perhaps then, Danny, as well as herself, might finally be at peace.

The snow had finally tapered off just after ten o'clock this morning, and she'd spent almost a quarter of an hour digging the Crown Vic out of the drifting snow which had built against its sides, along with the additional snow pushed up against it by the snowplow.

By the time she'd been done, it had been approaching eleven o'clock, and she'd been more than a little hungry. When she'd gone back inside to warm up and get ready to leave, she'd been grateful that John had prepared her something to eat until she discovered what it was.

With reluctance, she'd managed to choke down half of the peanut butter and mayonnaise sandwich on the white Wonderbread he'd made for her. With a smile, she'd told John the rest was 'for later' and wrapped the other half in a piece of paper towel, placing it into her parka pocket. She didn't have the heart to tell him that 'later' would never come for that other half.

Though eating the sandwich had been pretty hard going, it wasn't as hard as the going currently was on the winding winter roads through which she now manoeuvred the Crown Victoria. And to add icing to her snow-topped cake, just as they'd pulled away from John's condo complex, the snow had started falling again.

***

Another gust of wind rocked the cruiser. It was like being sand-blasted in a gale. Sitting in the passenger seat, John had watched as some of the stronger gusts threatened to rip the steering wheel from Amanda's hands. Though the road had been recently plowed, there was already another half-foot of snow covering it, and it just kept falling.

Before they'd left, John had helped Amanda place the cable chains onto the cruiser's already aggressively studded snow tires. They had both figured it would be safer to chain up before leaving the condo rather than attempting to connect them in the deep snow at the side of a road in the middle of nowhere.

Trying to keep the cruiser on the road seemed to be taking all of Amanda's concentration as they slowly made their way to the top of the mountain. John didn't try to make any small talk, not wanting to distract her. And besides, they'd done most of their talking last night over dinner. He looked through the passenger-side window into the snow-filled afternoon. Everything around them was a shifting, blowing mass of white nothingness. No matter how bad the weather was in Entwistle, it was always worse on Overseer Mountain.

As they climbed toward the resort, John could feel something coming over him and wondered if Amanda was experiencing a similar feeling. It had started as a tightness in his chest and then spread to the rest of his body. It had to be anxiety. He hadn't been back up to the Sinclair since the investigation had stagnated in the early months of 1982. And he still wasn't sure how he felt about returning there after all this time. But he knew that he had to since he needed closure.

After four decades of the Sinclair incident preying on him and the trauma of what he experienced up there lurking in the back of his mind, he felt he was about done with it and done with life as well, for that matter. He had now spent more time alone than he had with his wife, Helen. Marrying in 1956, this year would have been their sixty-fifth wedding anniversary. When Helen had initially gone missing, John hadn't known how he would survive, but survive he did. He had stayed at his position of chief inspector with the Entwistle RCMP until 1991 and then retired. The work had helped provide some distraction from his loss, but once retirement had afforded him more free time, it had become so very much harder.

John looked over to Jansen and saw with alarm that she was nodding off at the wheel. Despite his not wanting to distract her, it seemed something needed to be done to keep her awake, or they would go off the road and end up somewhere at the bottom of a ravine. "Amanda!" he said in a loud voice, but not sharply since he didn't want to startle her.

"Are you all right?"

Looking suddenly wide awake, Jansen stared out the snow-filled windshield with large eyes, saying, "I'm okay, John, thank you. I just haven't been sleeping well at night because of the dreams and all. Last night on the sofa was a little hard on my back, and I didn't get much sleep then, either. But I've been wondering if maybe some of the things I've been seeing are a result of this lack of sleep?"

"Seeing things? Like what."

"Danny. Last night at your place, and also at my house."

Sighing, John said, "Me too." He wasn't surprised, somehow.

"Really?"

"Yes." John shuddered slightly as he thought of waking up and staring into his son's rotting face the other night.

"It's strange, though."

"You've got that right."

"No," Amanda clarified, "I mean, I saw Danny at first all blackened, burnt and dripping as he must have been from the accident. But now..."

"Now... What?"

"I saw him the other day at home, in the mirror as well, and he was the Danny I knew and loved, whole, handsome and smiling, and it gave me such a feeling of hope. Hope that maybe, whatever happens to us up at the resort, we can make a difference after all these years and help him to be at peace, along with all the other souls who've gone missing at that horrible place."

Nodding his head, John said, "I think you're right. With everything we've learned, we might finally stand a chance of doing some good up there once and for all."

The wind kicked up another scouring gust of snow, shaking the car, and John watched Amanda's hands squeeze the wheel into a stranglehold. She slowed their progress to a crawl, perhaps fearful they'd get blown off the high mountain road into a ravine thousands of feet below. It was as if the weather were conspiring against their ever arriving at the top of the mountain alive. Giving his head a slight shake, John wondered if, in addition to everything else that had and was occurring at that cursed resort, was it also able to control the weather now?

CHAPTER EIGHTEEN

December 31st, 2021 1201 hours

The leather chair creaked slightly as Minerva sat back. She felt stunned as she reread everything on the screen she'd just shared with Ricky Rosenstein. She was happy, scared and potentially hopeful, all at the same time. Lively was alive! She hadn't known that for sure before since what he'd carved into the tub's linoleum, and the bed's headboard, had been done almost forty years in the past, and she hadn't had any updates since. But now, to have what amounted to instantaneous verification of Lively's whereabouts was a wonderful thing.

But before she did anything further, she needed a bit more corroboration. Reaching into Lively's courier bag draped across her shoulders, she rummaged for a moment. She'd taken to carrying it with her as she went about her business at the hotel since it gave her some comfort and felt like a little piece of Lively was still there with her.

After a quick consultation of the Big Book of Busting's list of missing persons, she saw that Rosenstein was indeed among them. But still, it might only be the hotel toying with her once more, and she might not have been chatting with the actual Ricky Rosenstein after all. She wouldn't know for sure until she could talk to Lively directly, if such a thing were possible.

Minerva sat staring at the TV screen for a few more minutes, hoping Lively might suddenly come online and begin typing to her. But it didn't happen, and she sighed in frustration and loneliness. She missed chatting with her brother. Even when they were apart and doing their own thing in the world, they usually contacted each other almost daily, unless one of them was in a position where they couldn't due to a job or other complications of life getting in the way. In addition to a quick hello text, they would often have a Facetime chat at least once a week. She made a mental note to come back and check this computer every few hours in case he left her a message.

A rumbling in her stomach reminded Minerva that she was still hungry and hadn't had anything to eat—and she was dismayed to see it was now past two, according to her wristwatch. She stood from the computer and removed the towel and chair leg defence from the bottom of the door. Any opening that something could slither under was one she now blocked, especially one to which her back was turned.

Verifying the coast was clear through the viewing portal, Minerva grabbed her sword and silver shield-tray and stepped cautiously into the corridor. Everything appeared calm and peaceful at the moment, though that seemed to mean little around here, she thought sadly—this hotel liked springing its surprises on people when they had their guard down.

Taking a deep breath, she stepped out into the passageway and moved toward the grand staircase. She arrived without incident on the mezzanine and then cursed her weakness once again. Unable to resist the siren song of the massive painting, she had stopped to marvel at the detailed artwork, now standing in front as if mesmerised.

The painted boy was still missing from the hotel's portrait, but the wolf was back. On the right side of the colossal canvas, the painted predator peered out from some brush, just as it had when she'd first seen the large landscape.

Nodding her head in satisfaction, Minerva said, "Went home to lick your wounds, huh?"

There seemed no response forthcoming from the wolf, and she turned away. But just as she did, she thought she caught motion from the corner of her eye. Had something moved in the portrait just now? She turned back and studied the massive artwork for a moment longer. With nothing further occurring that she could see, she began to look away when what had changed suddenly caught her eye.

The painted wolf was missing once again.

Minerva backed toward the edge of the lobby stairs and was almost to the top of the flight when her eyes went wide with disbelief.

Seeming suddenly fluid, the painting's surface rippled almost imperceptibly. Then, in the lower right corner next to the gilded wooden frame, the picture bulged, just a bit, as if maggots wriggled beneath its corrupt canvas skin.

Backing slowly down the stairs, Minerva watched in horror, her eyes never leaving the painting.

A claw-tipped paw poked out from behind the edge of the frame where the artwork met the wall. Razor claws scraped the rich rosewood panelling as the painted wolf dragged itself out of the portrait a bit at a time; another paw, then the snout, and finally the rest of its head popped out.

The only thing to which Minerva could liken what she was witnessing was childbirth. A scratching sound, like dead skin scraping across cold gravestones, accompanied the creature's efforts to pull itself free. After a bit more squirming, the rest of the animal's body wriggled out from behind the painting. It rippled down the wall and then crumpled to the floor. For a moment, it looked like nothing more than a thin pile of folded canvas. But then it stretched itself to its full length and rippled upright. It appeared whole once more, and any sign of her sword's wound now seemed fully healed.

Though horrified at what she was seeing, Minerva marvelled at the incredible detail of the painted wolf, each hair on its fur-covered body exquisitely defined, thanks to the artist's photo-realistic representation. Careful of her step, she held her sword at the ready as she backed down the final flight of stairs to ground level. The last thing she needed was a broken neck, left lying on the cold marble lobby as the wolf slithered across her paralysed body to finish its job.

Fully born once more, the painted predator turned its attention toward Minerva, and its head seemed to vanish. When the rest of its body twisted in the same direction, she almost lost sight of it. With a dry hiss, it rustled to the edge of the stairs and paused before descending as if wondering what to do. All at once, it collapsed to the floor at the top of the mezzanine and then rippled down the steps toward her like a deadly waterfall.

Finally at the foyer floor, Minerva backed across the lobby as the canvas creature reached ground level. The beast squiggled upright and began rustling rapidly across the floor toward her.

As it drew near, Minerva brought the sword down on the creature, but it was quick, almost cobra-like in its movements. The wolf nimbly rippled out of the way before the sword struck, easily avoiding the blow. The blade clanged off the marble, sparks flying as the steel's edge chipped a chunk from the floor.

The beast came at her again with lightning speed. Minerva dodged out of the way just as it swiped one of its painted paws toward her legs. Its claws were just as sharp as ever, and two of them grazed the side of her boot, scoring the leather. Fortunately, it didn't cut through to her leg beneath.

Minerva followed through on her dodge and spun around, winging her silver tray into the side of the wolf's head, and it was slapped back across the lobby. The weight of the canvas beast was surprising. She'd expected it to weigh next to nothing, but when the tray connected with the wolf's head, it had felt surprisingly solid.

Perhaps it was the silver in the tray having some effect on the animal, but for whatever reason, it seemed making contact with the platter had temporarily disabled it. Minerva reasoned that whatever had just happened wouldn't last for long. Not wasting any of those precious few seconds, she hustled toward the Snow Drop Lounge—she had an idea. At her back came the familiar sound of rustling as the painted predator stood once again and resumed its pursuit.

Racing into the lounge, Minerva slammed into the bar, dropped the sword and tray on top with a clatter, and then began loosening her floral-patterned silk scarf from around her neck. With the scarf in hand, she climbed onto the end of the mahogany bar where the bartender's trap door was situated. Assorted glassware was still spread across the bartop, and it crashed to the floor as she scampered up.

Minerva clearly remembered the force with which the weighty bartender's door had slammed closed behind their backs. Fortunately, it was now open and tilted back against the wall, just like she'd left it on Christmas Day after checking in the small bar fridge and discovering another bottle of Moosehead missing from the case inside.

With panicked fingers, Minerva knotted one end of her scarf to the pull handle on the underside of the trap door where the barkeep would grab to close it. Ravelling the other end of the scarf around her hand, she squatted a few feet back from the lip of the bartop where it met the trap door's hardwood edge. With a glance toward the entrance, she watched the painted wolf squiggle toward her like a canvas anaconda.

Giving a hissing howl, the animal lunged toward the end of the bar, its knife-edged claws shredding the mahogany as it tried to drag itself onto the bartop.

Minerva leaned backwards and pulled with all her might, yanking the heavy trap door back into position. It smashed down onto the painted wolf's back, pinning it between the bar's edge and the trap door.

The beast let out a squealing, shrieking bleat of what Minerva could only imagine to be pain. And then it tried to wriggle out of the predicament in which it had found itself. But the trap was heavy, the wood's sharp edges straight and true, and the mahogany door held it securely in place.

Moving tentatively toward the hissing, shrieking creature, Minerva stopped when she was within inches of its snapping, painted fangs. With a smile, she said, "Hi-ho Silver, away!" then dropped the weighty tray onto the wolf's head, flattening it to the bartop with a clang. Though it had sounded pained before due to the trap door, now, the creature sounded like it was in true agony. With one of her booted feet, Minerva stepped down onto the tray, hard. She could feel the wolf wriggling under the silver platter as it squealed and writhed, and then she pressed down even harder.

As the creature shuddered and spasmed, the smell of burnt hair filled the air. The silver was doing its job and immobilising the creature. But it seemed that it was doing more than that, the silver having a reaction, not unlike a silver bullet would have had on a werewolf. Minerva smiled grimly as smoke began to curl out from under the tray's edges.

After a while, the squirming under her boot diminished and then finally stopped. With no further movement for several seconds, Minerva tentatively lifted her foot from the tray. She crouched down, slowly raised the platter, and then peered beneath. With a grimace, she said, "Fade to black."

The painted wolf had been seemingly burned from the canvas, and now only a smouldering, sooty blackness was in its place.

Minerva climbed down from the bar, breathing more easily now that the nightmare stalking her was disabled and hopefully laid to rest. She placed her hands on her hips and let out a puff of breath, blowing a stray strand of hair from her eyes while wondering what other surprises the Sinclair had in store.

A noise at her back caused her to turn in surprise. Standing behind her with a look of concern on his face was the painted boy.

CHAPTER NINETEEN

December 31st, 2021 1301 hours

The cruiser turned into the entrance of the hotel. One gate was open, hanging back against the stone wall off to one side. The snow seemed deeper here, and John was sure they would get stuck, but they wound their way up the lane without incident, thanks to Amanda's expert handling of the Crown Vic.

Neither of them spoke as the Sinclair Hotel appeared through the snow-streaked windshield. Still monolithic, its appearance seemed unchanged after almost forty years in the elements at the top of this windswept mountain, which hardly seemed possible. In fact, to both their eyes, the resort appeared as if open and ready to welcome guests for the evening's ball. Amanda pulled the cruiser up under the hotel's covered entrance near the front doors. Two vehicles were already parked there, a Toyota 4Runner and a very expensive-looking BMW.

With a nod, Amanda said, "Well, that's a good sign."

John looked to Amanda as she shut off the engine and said, "I think you know as well as I do that seeing vehicles parked in front of this hotel doesn't mean that something hasn't happened to the people inside."

A couple of minutes later, Amanda stood next to John at the top of the stone steps, the ornately carved wooden doors to the Sinclair Resort Hotel standing firmly closed before them. She wondered once again if things would be resolved before they left here, if they ever left here, that was.

In their possession were the two things which they thought might prove vital to their success, the obsidian stones. Before they'd left, she'd transferred hers from her travel case to her shoulder bag. Despite the freezing temperatures that surrounded them as they stood in the sub-zero weather, she was certain she could feel the intense cold emanating from the gemstone inside her bag. John had stuffed his down into his parka pocket, wrapped up once again in its plaid rags. She was surprised he hadn't complained of the cold coming from it. Perhaps after his prolonged exposure, he was inured somewhat from its influence.

Jansen shuddered slightly, initially from the cold and then from a sudden recollection of events on her final evening here. The memories had just now come flooding back, and her anxiety had returned with them. Now she felt frozen to the spot, unsure if she would be able to enter the building.

John noticed her shudder and said, "A lot of memories, eh?"

Nodding her head slowly, Amanda said, "Too many, and very few of them good."

***

After arriving back from dropping Will Weston at the hospital, Amanda had found Inspector Harder nowhere in sight, and she'd reluctantly entered the Sinclair Hotel once more. Receiving no response on her radio, she had also called out to him as she'd entered, her voice echoing off the lobby's hard surfaces as if a dozen Amanda Jansens were already there and on the case.

She'd moved through the annex and was nearing the grand ballroom when she heard what sounded like a heavy door slamming shut somewhere within the hotel. She felt relief, thinking that Inspector Harder was on his way to her location from elsewhere within the huge building. However, her sense of relief didn't last for long.

As she grew closer to the grand ballroom, there came more pounding from within the depths of the hotel as if something substantial rushed in her direction, getting louder and louder the closer it got.

Whatever was approaching had now made its way into the annex leading to the ballrooms. She looked back to the far end of the passageway to see who, or what, would appear. The crook of her palm rested on the butt of her revolver, still in the holster, the leather catch which held it in place now undone.

Unfortunately, the unknown entity remained unknown as it thumped toward her down the corridor. Her heart slammed in her chest, seeming to match the rhythm of the heavy footfalls. The sconce lights on both sides of the hall dimmed and then brightened again as the thing hurried down the corridor toward her. She moved quickly into the ballroom and pulled the heavy doors closed just as whatever was approaching slammed into the other side with a crash.

Backing into the room, Amanda held her hands over her ears as the thing on the other side began to pound relentlessly on the door, the noise booming through the empty space like a series of shotgun blasts. Her breath came in panting gasps, and suddenly, vapour began to pour from her mouth and nose as the temperature in the room plummeted.

The doors, though firmly closed, now seemed to bow

inward from the force of each blow from the other side.

Then, just as suddenly as it started, the pounding stopped, and silence reigned once more. Amanda breathed a huge sigh of relief and then became concerned about the temperature change. From her time watching old horror movies on late-night TV over the years, she knew that was never a good sign.

Amanda's eyes searched the now silent room. It was dim, with only a few of its numerous chandeliers currently illuminated. After the forensic team had finally arrived on New Year's Day, they'd tested everything on the tables for toxins and drugs. Once they'd finished, the food had been left where it was, drying out and going rotten since the kitchen staff had all been dismissed after questioning. Though she realised some supervised personnel would need to be brought in to clean up at some point in the future, as far as she knew, that time hadn't yet arrived. But now, amazingly, only the centrepieces, wine bottles, glasses and ashtrays remained, and all the food had been removed. Where had it gone, she wondered.

The light from the chandelier overhead cast Amanda in sharp relief as she turned in a small circle exploring the room with wide eyes. She suddenly halted as she spied something that made her heart skip a beat. In one darkened corner of the room, barely visible, a man stood motionless.

"Who's there?" she called out. "This is Corporal Jansen of the Entwistle RCMP! Identify yourself!"

As if that were the cue that the man had been waiting for, still shrouded in both darkness and silence, he began approaching where she stood.

With her own flashlight still MIA and having forgotten to grab the spare from the patrol car on the way back up the hill, she did the only thing she could think of and once again rested the edge of her palm on the grip of her service revolver.

The man slowly drew closer and closer. He finally spoke, saying, "A-m-a-n-d-a."

Recalling the last time she'd seen the abomination that had once been her beau, Amanda began to pull her revolver from its holster when she suddenly stopped.

Danny Harder stepped into the light, and she saw he wasn't burnt, rotting, or dripping wet. No, he was whole, smiling and as handsome as ever. He spoke to her again, saying, "R-e-m-e-m-b-e-r."

He reached out, and she took his hand, tears flooding her eyes. She did remember—the laughter, the love, the joy, the happiness. She recalled it all and missed it so much that her heart felt like it would tear itself from her chest. Since Danny's death, he had never been far from her thoughts, and now, seeing him here again like she remembered gave her renewed hope.

Releasing her hand, Danny turned and moved toward the ballroom doors. Though he was out of the light, he seemed energised somehow from Amanda's touch, and he continued to look like the man she remembered, his form outlined with a faintly luminescent glow.

As he approached the ballroom's entrance, the doors flew open of their own volition. Whatever had been on the other side pounded away back down the corridor, fleeing into the depths of the hotel once more. Danny took one last look over his shoulder and smiled that crooked smile she loved so much, then faded away to nothing as he stepped out into the corridor and moved in the direction of the loud and invisible entity.

**

John looked at the woman standing next to him as she

stared at the closed doors of the resort, lost in her own internal world of thought.

His own experiences that final night had been nothing short of traumatic. It had been an event, like the well room, that he'd blocked out until now. But this hadn't taken place in the bowels of the hotel; no, it had occurred at one of its highest points. John's hip throbbed anew as the memory washed over him.

When Amanda had taken Will Weston down the hill to have his hand, and her own, tended to, he'd been alone in the hotel for a handful of hours. He'd been standing in the lobby when he'd heard a voice, Helen's, faintly echoing down from the upper floors. He'd flown up the stairs calling her name. Fortunately, this time he hadn't had any problems arriving at the top of the stairs and no tricks were played on him by the hotel.

Expecting the royal suite to have been his ultimate destination, he was surprised when proven wrong. After standing motionless at the top of the third-floor stairs for several long moments, he strained to hear Helen's voice again. Silence for the longest time, and then it came once more, faintly, from the west wing and the location of the Executive Gaming Lounge.

John sprinted down the corridor. Up ahead, the door to the turret lay open. Had Helen's voice come from the games room like he suspected? He knew Jansen had checked it earlier today during their initial sweep upon discovering Helen's car outside. He'd been up to the turret only once before during the initial phase of the investigation and had largely dismissed the area as one of interest, until now.

He'd stopped in front of the lounge's entrance. To his left, the door to one of the suites stood open, and he glanced inside, wondering if that was from where Helen's voice had emanated, but it seemed empty, and he turned his attention back toward the spiralling stairs in front of him.

"Helen! Are you up there?" What she would be doing in the turret, he didn't know and didn't care; he just wanted her back more desperately than anything he'd ever wanted in his entire life.

After a momentary silence, John had his answer when he heard what he thought was a shriek somewhere up above, and it had sounded like Helen. Taking the steps two at a time, he raced up the spiralling staircase. The door at the top was open partway, but something seemed to be blocking it. He pushed hard, and whatever was in the way was pushed aside enough for him to enter.

Strangely, the gorilla that stood guard near the doorway had somehow been moved into the door's path. But how was that possible, he wondered. These things didn't move of their own volition, or at least he hoped that wasn't the case. He called out, "Helen? Helen Harder, are you up here?"

No further response seemed forthcoming, and he glanced about the room, unsure what to do. Then he saw the other stairwell leading upward. Was Helen up there right now? Could it be, all along, that she'd been held against her will in the castle's turret, like a fairy tale princess? There was only one way to find out. Stomping rapidly up the final flight of stairs, John was presented with another door. Turning the knob, he found it unlocked.

Pushing through into the room, he thought it seemed familiar somehow, although he couldn't recall ever being up here. He felt almost unsurprised when he saw the massive model of the hotel sitting in the middle of the round room. Had he actually been up here before and just didn't recall it for some reason?

Flashes of remembrance came to him—glimpses of his hands picking up the ebony box from the ballroom bar and then carrying it up to this room high in the turret. But what had happened once he had the box up here and what he'd done with it, he didn't know. Was it inside the model right now? If so, he had no idea how to get the thing open. Stooping down, he peered through the tiny windows in wonder, noting the detail of all the little figurines inside.

He moved around the model, his eyes searching for a catch or release somewhere on its exterior. There had to be a way to open it up, he reasoned. Something as elaborate as this duplicate of the hotel must surely have a way inside in order to view its internal wonders.

Wrapped up in concentration as he was, John barely heard what moved into the room behind him.

CHAPTER TWENTY

December 31st, 1981 2214 hours

Rubbing at his eyes, Ricky Rosenstein was overcome by a massive yawn, the extremes of the day finally catching up to him. In the middle of another yawn, he froze when a sudden knock came at his suite's door. His breath held, he moved quietly toward the entrance. He peeked through the peephole in the heavy door and was pleased to see Lively Deadmarsh standing on the other side. He unlocked the door and opened it, surprised to see a beautiful woman standing beside him.

"May we come in?" Lively asked.

"Of course, Mr. DeMille!" Ricky stepped back and allowed them to enter.

"Hope you don't mind; I brought my mom," Lively said as Selene stepped across the threshold.

With wide eyes, Ricky took in Selene, saying, "You're his mother?"

"So he tells me," Selene replied as she stepped into the suite. She glanced about as if wondering how the other half lived. Fortunately, most of the mess Ricky had left during his in-room smorg had been cleaned up when the smorg itself had been cleared away.

Following Selene into the room, Lively said, "I was just at my suite to check on you. When I saw you gone, I figured you were back here again." He noted the blanket that Ricky had draped across the two-way mirror, still unsure if doing so was effective, but he hoped that would be the case. Turning to his mother, Lively added, "Just as I was about to head upstairs, I bumped into Selene here. Mom, I'd like you to meet a friend of mine, Ricky Rosenstein."

Blushing slightly, Ricky said, "Pleased to meet you."

Taking Ricky's sweaty hand in her own, Selene flashed a quick smile, then said, "Just Selene is fine." Looking to Lively, she added, "For both of you." Seeing her son's crestfallen expression, she clarified, adding, "Nothing personal, Lively. It's just that learning everything I have recently is a bit of a shock all at once. You're going to have to give me a little time before calling me Mom on a regular basis."

"No problem, M—" Catching himself at the last moment, Lively corrected course and said, "I mean, Selene. That's quite understandable."

Looking from Lively to Selene, Ricky said, "Well, whatever you want to call each other is fine with me." A look of excitement skittered across Ricky's face, and he said, "And by the way, it's getting to be a real family reunion around here!"

"How's that?" Lively asked.

"I was just talking to your sister."

"What?" Lively said, shocked. He looked to Selene and then back to Ricky, adding, "Don't tell me she's been captured by this place as well?"

Realising the confusion his comment had caused, Ricky clarified, saying, "No, no, sorry about that. I talked to her on here." He gestured toward the Sony TV with the Atari 800 connected. A white prompt flashed patiently at the top of a blank blue background, awaiting input.

"She sent you an email?" Lively asked, surprised.

Ricky looked confused for a moment and said, "A what? Like on CompuServe?" He shook his head, saying, "No, nothing like that. But she was just chatting with me a few minutes ago, honest."

Now it was Lively's turn to look confused, and he said, "How did she start communicating?"

Gesturing to the computer once again, Rosenstein smiled and said, "Well, I set up this emulated telnet terminal to monitor the modification I made in the mainframe's code downstairs. I was just going to log in when she started a remote chat and—"

Interrupting, Lively said, shocked, "You've been in the basement?"

Ricky nodded, looking sheepish, and said, "You'd mentioned the mainframe in your Big Book of Busting, and I just had to see it." He picked up Lively's manuscript from the table and handed it to Selene for a look-see.

"Just a little bit risky, don't you think? Considering what's already happened?" Lively asked.

"Well, yeah," Ricky admitted. "But I figured if you were in trouble, maybe I could do something that might run interference on the mainframe. You're very inspiring, Mr. DeMille."

Selene looked over to her son upon hearing this, a small

smile on her lips, and she said, "You seem to leave quite an impression, Mr. DeMille."

With a modest shrug, Lively agreed, saying, "I guess so." Looking toward the computer on the desk, he asked Ricky, "You know about mainframes and stuff, too?"

Ricky gave a proud smile and moved next to the Atari, where he began listing off his college and university degrees, along with the programming languages he had studied over the years. After about thirty seconds of this, Lively cut him off, saying, "I believe you, I believe you," then sat down in the wheeled office chair.

With a slight grimace of distaste, Selene sat down on one end of the white leather couch, three cushions down from its other current occupant, the remnants of a turkey leg someone had devoured. Ricky noticed it at just about the same time as Selene. He swooped in to cover it with a hand towel he'd grabbed from a side table, then whisked it away. Selene gave a small nod of thanks.

Lively nodded toward the computer, saying, "So you were texting through this, and you think it was Minerva that responded."

"I didn't type anything. She typed to me first."

"And she said she was Minerva?"

"Well, no. At first, she said she was only a friend, but after we'd been typing back and forth for a while, I asked if she was your sister, Minerva, and she said it was."

"I hate to break it to you, my friend, but I don't believe this hotel has anyone's best interests at heart. In fact, there's a pretty good chance that whomever you talked to was probably not my sister."

"That's what she said you were going to say, and she left me a passphrase to give to you just in case you didn't believe me."

"Oh, trust me, Ricky, I want to believe."

"Well then, let me help you do it."

With a confident nod, Lively said, "All right then, if I'm not mistaken, I believe the passphrase Minerva gave you was, 'Mrs. Tolbert's Cat'."

Ricky's jaw dropped open. "Wow, you're right!"

Lively smiled. "I figured it would be the same one she'd used with me here at the resort in our own time."

Selene looked over to Lively questioningly and asked, "Why was she using a passphrase if you were the only one there with her?"

"Because the me she'd seen around the hotel on a couple of occasions wasn't necessarily the me she grew up with." Both Ricky and Selene stared at Lively strangely for a moment, then he added cryptically, "Sometimes I'm not even sure if I'm me around this place." Giving his head a shake, he turned to his mother, saying, "Your head must be spinning right about now, Selene."

"Oh, trust me, it's been spinning for a while now, especially regarding you being my son. But I'm a little more in the loop with things around here than you might think."

"How do you mean, 'in the loop'?

"Well, I've noticed some things just today, too. One of the most annoying being the déjà vu I keep having. It's happened several times so far."

Ricky nodded and added, "I've had it a lot, too."

"But it didn't start happening until I met you," Selene looked to Lively.

Ricky said gravely, "Same for me. I believe Mr. DeMille is a catalyst for change around here. And that what we're experiencing, this déjà vu, is a sign that we can alter things here and end all of this."

Selene looked to her hands, lost in thought for a moment, then said, "I hope you're right. It all feels so hazy sometimes."

"What's the last thing you did before coming here for this party," Lively asked.

"Well, I'd spent almost all my time recuperating here since your supposed stillbirth. Edward had been generous enough to let me stay in the royal suite to recuperate as long as I needed. But just the day before yesterday, Edward had Simon drive me to my condo in Vancouver to pick up a few things, and then we headed right back here. He'd been so insistent I be here for his New Year's party."

Lively said, "That's why you said you'd only been here for a day when I met you this afternoon."

"That's right, though you're now telling me it's been four decades." She looked at Lively and locked eyes, adding, "Just so you know, we never married. Edward can be a generous and funny man, but he has a dark streak, and I wasn't sure how I felt about that. But despite everything, I honestly never suspected he was capable of spiriting my children away at birth, then hiding them from me their entire lives, and keeping me captive here to boot."

You don't know the half of it, Lively thought. When Selene learned what Edward's greed and avarice had done to the other realities, she would know it was more than just a 'dark streak'. Instead, he said, "He seems to be full of dirty little secrets."

"Well, I don't know how it is now, but having children out of wedlock wasn't something you'd broadcast to the public back then, unless you wanted to damage your career. When I came full term, Edward had some of the best doctors flown in from around the world to help with the delivery. But then, when they told me you'd both died in childbirth, I was heartbroken."

Lively looked to his mother and said, "But Grandma Nell and Grandpa Robert raised us, saying you'd passed away giving birth. At least, that's what we were told as we grew up." He reached into his pocket and pulled out his keychain with the small, bone-handled pocketknife attached. He showed it to Selene.

Selene shook her head back and forth, saying, "What's that?"

"This was Grandpa Robert's. He gave it to me for Christmas when I was six, and at the same time, Grandma Nell gave Minerva your old locket."

"Grandma Nell and Grandpa Robert? Who are you talking about?"

"Your mom and dad?"

"Those weren't my parents. My mother and father's names were George and Estelle Deadmarsh."

"What?" Shaking his head in confusion, Lively asked, "If they weren't your mom and dad, then who were they?"

"I don't know. You'd have to ask Edward about that."

"Here, let me show you; maybe that would help." Lively

reached into the inner pocket of his tuxedo jacket, pulled out his iPhone and unlocked the screen. He pulled up a photo of Robert and Nell he'd downloaded a while back and handed the phone to Selene, saying, "This is them."

Selene held the phone delicately and looked at the picture closely, then shook her head, saying, "I've never seen these people before in my life."

This is crazy, Lively thought. In the last day, he discovered that not only was his deceased mother actually still alive but that his previously unknown father was a mass murderer of people in other realities. And now, on top of all that, he had just discovered that the two people he loved most in life, apart from his mother, were actually imposters.

"What is that?" Ricky asked, his eyes like saucers as he marvelled at what Selene held in her hands.

Selene handed the phone back to Lively. He brought up the home screen and passed the cell phone to Ricky for a quick gander.

"That is a pocket computer containing, in no particular order, a cellular telephone, telephoto camera, video player, jukebox, level, compass, measuring tape, and portable library, and is probably a heck of a lot more powerful than the mainframe downstairs."

Rosenstein looked at the colourful icons that represented the apps on the phone's screen, asking, "And what are all these?"

"Those icons represent the various programs currently stored in the computer's solid-state memory."

"Solid state memory? How many kilobytes?"

"Five hundred and twelve gigabytes of storage and six gigs

of RAM."

"Gigabytes!?" Ricky looked almost ready to have a case of the vapours like a southern belle at her debutante ball.

With amusement, Lively watched Rosenstein for a moment as he flicked through the apps on the phone. If it were possible for the man to make love to the piece of technology in his hand, Lively was pretty sure Ricky would be hard at it right now if they weren't in the room. Fortunately, Lively had an iPhone 13 Pro Max, and the battery life was significant, so it could withstand some of Ricky's stress tests, which seemed to consist of trying every app at once. However, his charger was in his courier bag back in 2021, along with everything else he had, and he wasn't sure how long it would last, despite the phone's bigger battery.

A shout of surprise came from Ricky's lips, and he said, "Hey! You even have an emulator that can pretend this phone is that computer." He pointed to the Atari 800 next to the TV. He looked through the folder to see what other systems the phone could emulate and asked, "What's a Commodore Amiga and an Atari ST?"

"You'll find out in about four years." Being a retro '80s kind of guy, Lively loved all of the emulators that were able to pretend to be old game systems from previous decades, and he loved to still play those games on his phone when he travelled. On his iPhone were emulators for almost everything, from Nintendo Gameboy to Sega Game Gear, SNES to Wii, all the way up to and including Xbox and Playstation 2 games.

"You really need to let me look this over for a few days, Mr. DeMille."

Lively extended his hand, palm upward, saying, "Tell you what. If we get out of this alive, I'll give it to you. How's that sound?"

Rosenstein handed the iPhone back, sounding both reluctant and excited at the same time, and he said, "You've got a deal!"

A sudden electronic 'boop' came from the speaker on the TV at Lively's back as the Atari 800 received a message from beyond.

CHAPTER TWENTY-ONE

December 31ˢᵗ, 2021 1305 hours

The painted boy had led Minerva up the grand staircase and guided her back toward suite #304. He hadn't rustled as loudly as the wolf when he walked but instead made a gentle susurration, like the rush of water in a small stream.

Now, having just followed him into the suite, she partially closed the door behind her out of habit—she'd begun feeling uncomfortable leaving doors wide open at her back around here, and with good reason.

The boy pointed toward the Atari 800 computer.

"Do I have a message?" Minerva asked.

Still saying nothing, the painted boy turned and moved toward the door. He turned sideways, slipped through the small half-inch gap between the door's edge and frame, and then disappeared.

There hadn't been any new messages from Ricky showing on the screen. But Minerva figured she'd been brought here for a reason. After blocking the gap under the door, she sat in front of the computer. Though not expecting an answer right away, she typed a quick message. However, this time she was delighted to receive a response almost immediately, and it had been from Lively.

The whole experience seemed surreal. In some ways, it was like any other text chat she may have had with her brother, yet in other ways, it seemed completely crazy. Not only was he not sending her a text message by phone, but instead from a four-decade-old 8-Bit computer that was somehow communicating through time and realities to allow them to converse.

Unfortunately, something happened before they could finish their conversation, and they were disconnected. She hoped that whatever Lively planned to do, it worked in conjunction with what she was already planning with the box.

But this brought her back to her main problem: how to deal with the stuffies that called the gaming lounge home and seemed guardians of the ebony box. She'd been going over possible scenarios that would allow her to remove it from the model and none of them seemed too promising. She'd considered the suit of armour located in the entrance to the turret at one point but couldn't envision trying to easily move around in what amounted to the medieval version of a tank.

Deciding she needed some inspiration, Minerva departed suite #304 and headed once more for the lobby. Despite all of her ideas, she still seemed to come back to the thought that she would need more than just herself to access the box. With Lively unavailable, she needed to think of something in this hotel that could help her do the work of two people.

The lobby was silent as a morgue as she tapped her bootheels across the marble floor. There was something different about the place now, almost like when she'd first arrived here several days before. Fortunately, she wasn't experiencing another Limey this time, and she was glad. One was enough for her in a lifetime. With that thought, she recalled another thing she only ever wanted to experience once in her lifetime.

Since she was in the neighbourhood, she decided to check on the Snowdrop Lounge. After her recent experience, she wanted to verify that her nemesis was still a blackened mess wedged between two pieces of heavy wood. When she arrived at the bar, a satisfied smile played across her lips.

The wolf, or what was left of it, was still wedged between the bartender's trap door and the bar, the silver tray shining brilliantly on top.

Knowing she'd need the tray's assistance in the future to move the box, she peeled it off the wolf's blackened head. Not knowing if she might encounter other entities in need of a good chop or stab somewhere else in this hotel, Minerva grabbed her sword as well and rested it across her shoulder like a sentry with a rifle, then marched from the lounge.

***

Amanda stood next to John, feeling the oppressive weight of silence all around them. When she'd followed the inspector through the door into the resort, she'd been expecting something strange to happen rather quickly. And now that they were inside, she was saddened to see that she had been correct in her expectations.

Across the lobby, an attractive, auburn-haired woman with a sword over her shoulder and a shining silver tray at her side exited the Snowdrop lounge. She stopped a moment when she saw them, perhaps wondering if they were real or not, then began moving in their direction.

"Minerva Deadmarsh, I presume," John called out to the approaching woman.

"Well, it certainly isn't Dr. Livingstone." With a smile, she added, "And you must be Chief Inspector John Harder."

With a nod, John said, "Retired." He looked to his left and introduced Amanda, saying, "This is RCMP Inspector Amanda Jansen."

"Amanda is fine. And I'm just as retired as he is." She looked questioningly at Minerva's sword and tray and added, "Going into battle, are you?

Glancing to the sword on her shoulder, Minerva said, "No, thanks, just had one," as if that were the only explanation required for why she was armed like a medieval knight. She shifted the weapon into her left hand, where she held the shield and briefly shook hands with them, saying, "It's nice to meet you both. But I wasn't expecting you to come up here after I contacted you, Inspector Harder."

"John, please."

Minerva nodded, saying, "John. But since you have, and now that you're both here, I'm actually quite glad. There's something that I believe needs to be done that I can't do alone, though I have tried. But if we can accomplish this task, we may be well on our way to bringing everyone back."

A grim smile on his face, Harder said, "That's why we're here, to do something that none of us could have done alone." He paused for a moment, sniffed the air, and then said, "What is that smell?"

That was something Amanda had noticed when she'd first walked in the doors, even before spotting Minerva, and one of the last things she had expected to smell upon entering this hotel—the scent of freshly cooked food.

"I noticed it too. It's coming from the basement." Minerva began moving toward the stairs next to the front desk, saying, "I'm taking the stairs, but the elevator is working as far as I know."

"Stairs should be fine, going down at least," John replied and began tapping his cane across the lobby after Minerva.

Amanda joined him at his side, offering her elbow for assistance.

John smiled at her and shook his head, saying, "I'm okay for now, thanks."

They descended to the basement with Minerva in the lead. Amanda stayed next to John should his footing prove unsteady. The inspector took his time, one hand on the railing, the other grasping the handle of his cane tightly for support.

As soon as they stepped onto the dogleg to the basement, Amanda wondered, could it be? When she arrived in the kitchen moments later, she saw that indeed it could.

Waiting for them under several silver cloches was a dish she'd cooked on several occasions and one of Danny's favourites: roast beef, yorkshire pudding, mashed potatoes and all the trimmings. Laid out around the food on the stainless-steel countertop were place settings for three.

With a slight frown, John said, "Looks like we're expected."

CHAPTER TWENTY-TWO

December 31st, 1981 2221 hours

Lively watched as the white cursor began to move across the computer screen as someone started typing at the other end.

'Ricky, have you had any luck reaching Lively yet? It's imperative I speak with him.'

With a small smile playing at the corners of his lips, Lively sat in the leather chair in front of the computer and began to type.

'Hi, Sis!'

'Lively, is that you?'

'Yes, Mrs. Tolbert's Cat told me you wanted to talk.'

'Thank goodness! After a brief pause, Minerva added, *'You're all right, aren't you?'*

'Right as rain and fit as a fiddle, at the moment.'

After that statement, Lively noted a pause in the communication, and then Minerva began typing again.

'Sorry, but when you typed that just now, you gave me a flashback to your doppelgänger. He said the exact same thing just a little while ago.'

'Well, he is me, as far as we know, and I suppose he would say similar things. So, what's happened since I got zapped here this afternoon?'

'Plenty. And what do you mean, since this afternoon?'

'Why, what's the date there?'

'I don't believe we are experiencing time at the same rate. You've been missing since Christmas Day—and it's now New Year's Eve! Except for these messages, things aren't elapsing at the same rate for some reason.'

'Six days? It feels like not even half a day has passed here.' Lively sat back and dropped his hands from the keyboard and thought about everything he'd just learned. It was true; to him, it seemed that he'd only been gone half a day, but in the 'real world' (as he thought of it now), it appeared that six entire days had passed. Unsure how long their communication portal would last, Lively began to type again, *'You need to get the ebony box back to the ballroom.'*

'I realised that as well, and I'm working on it.'

Lively wondered how she would move the box down to the ballroom and then remembered the gloves he'd left there. But even with those, he didn't know if she could handle touching it for any length of time. About to type another quick thought to his sister, the connection ended abruptly, and the white cursor dropped down a couple of lines on the screen, saying, *'Connection Lost.'*

"Well, isn't that just peachy." Lively swivelled around in the chair and added, "Sorry, Selene, I was just going to introduce you to your daughter, but we lost our connection to the Twilight Zone."

With a small shake of her head and a sad smile, Selene said, "Perhaps it's for the best." She brightened a little and added, "That way, when this is all over and I meet her in person, it'll be that much more of a happy surprise."

Lively nodded, grateful for her understanding, and said, "Let's hope that day is today." Tilting his head from Ricky to the computer, he said, "Tell me more about the 'interference' you ran on the computer downstairs. What did you do exactly when you hacked into it?"

Ricky nodded to the Atari, saying proudly, "Not just hack into it—I also patched the programme they're running."

"Patched the programme? And what, exactly, is running on that system?" Lively asked.

"Well, it's fairly hi-tech what they've got going on down there." After reconsidering what he said for a moment, Ricky added, "At least it's hi-tech to me in 1981."

"I'm sure that whatever they've got going down there is quite hi-tech, despite the age of the equipment they're running it on." He gestured about the room and finished saying, "That is, if what they've achieved around here is anything to go by."

Selene said to Ricky, "And what did you do to their computer?"

"Well, fortunately, they'd coded everything in Cobol, and I was able to tweak a couple of things."

"A couple of things? Care to share?" Lively asked.

"I reworked a few things in the program and altered the temporal sync to their realignment subroutine."

"Which means?" Selene inquired.

"Things shouldn't repeat anymore after tonight."

"And what'll happen then?" Lively asked, concerned.

"I don't know." Ricky shrugged his shoulders. "But it should stop things from looping and hopefully end this for us."

With a slight nod, Lively said, "Well, some plan is better than no plan at this point, I suppose." However, he wondered about the ramifications of Ricky's dabbling in the computer's code downstairs. Would it help or hinder things? Looking at his wristwatch, he said, "At least we won't have long to wait." He patted the computer again and added, "Let's hope 8-bits is going to be enough."

Nodding gravely, Ricky said, "It was enough to get mankind to the moon, so I hope it's enough to get us out of the Sinclair."

Selene asked, "So what now?" She'd moved next to Lively at the computer and was staring at the words written by her daughter.

"So now we try to make it look like we have a plan."

"How can I help?" Selene asked. From what Lively could determine, she seemed enlivened and excited by the prospect of having her children in her life.

"I think you can help by keeping Edward distracted."

"How do you I do that?"

Lively looked at his mom in her red satin gown and said, "Do whatever comes naturally. I don't think you'll have too hard a time distracting him in that dress."

Selene looked down at her frock and the 'V' of her breasts on display thanks to the dress's strapless design and said, "That's a good point."

"What about me?" Ricky asked.

"I think you need to stay here and monitor what's happening with that computer downstairs."

"I can do that."

"And you said that your patch will kick in at midnight when this tries to loop again?"

"It should..." Ricky trailed off, distracted, his eyes going wide as a noise in the corner of the room drew his attention.

All watched in a mixture of surprise and alarm as the large, blanket-covered mirror slid aside. Stepping through into the room from behind was none other than the blonde Simon. The massively muscled man surveyed the group, an intense frown upon his face.

Lively regarded the slab of beef on legs standing before them, doing an internal threat assessment to determine his upcoming course of action.

Ricky and Selene stepped back behind Lively as they watched the monstrous male moving toward them.

"Easy now, big fella," Lively said, stepping up to the man as he approached.

Simon stopped halfway into the room, put both hands up in the air, palms outward, and said in a deep baritone voice, "Just wanna talk."

Lively was tense, suspecting a trap or some other ruse, but he stepped back and let the man speak his piece. "Your name is Wright, right?"

"Yeah, and I'm done."

Peering timidly from behind Lively, Ricky questioned, "Done?"

The large man nodded. "I'm tired of the same old shit every night. I've had enough, and I want out." He held his hand out and said, "Name's Simon."

Lively reached out and shook the man's hand, feeling tendons and muscle like steel cables engulfing his own. He fully realised that Simon could crush all the bones in his hand to powder with one squeeze if he so desired, and he said, "Edward mentioned that, but I thought your first name was Sonny?"

"It is, in professional circles, but my real name is Simon."

"Professional circles? So you are, in fact, Sonny Wright, the wrestler from my reality who disappeared, correct?"

With a slight nod, Simon said, "That was me."

"So, how did you end up here?" Selene asked.

"Through Schreck. He's the one that does most of the recruiting."

"Recruiting?" Lively asked.

"That's what Schreck calls it when he travels to a new subfrequency, looking for people to tempt and bring into the fold."

Schreck's earlier comment about travelling but never using

jet airplanes came back to Lively. Of course he wouldn't, not if he spent most of his time jumping from one universe to the next utilising the Harmoniser as he sought help for their little operation. Wanting to ensure they were on the same page, he asked, "You said you wanted out?"

"Yeah, out of this repeating hell."

"So, you're aware of it what's occurring?"

"Oh yeah, big time. Been helping them out for years now, since before the loop. And it depends on what you mean by occurring. Nothing much occurs around here. It's the same damn thing every single day and night—like an old folks home playing a broken record."

"But how is it that some people are aware of what's happening, and others are oblivious?" Lively looked to Selene and Ricky as he finished his sentence.

"These." Simon held up his left arm, and his shirt cuff fell away, revealing a bracelet like the one Lively had worn earlier during his wild ride on the Harmoniser.

"But I thought those were for counteracting the side-effects of travel between the frequencies," Lively said.

"They are, but they also stop the realignment from affecting your mind. It keeps you tuned to the core frequency. Without it, you'd drift slightly out of sync as the day progresses, making you forgetful. Without a bracelet, for most people around here, every day is a new day, not just another one like the day before and the thousands before it." With a sad shake of his head, he added, "It gets so monotonous, man."

"But I'm aware of what's going on now," Selene said.

"Yup, and at midnight tonight, when the frequency resets,

you'll forget it all again."

Lively wondered at this. He'd been forgetful but had the key fob, yet it had only partially protected him. Perhaps the metal's more medicinal properties, such as counteracting the amnesiac effects of the realignment, were only effective when in contact with a person's skin to complete the circuit.

Obviously still dealing with the after-effects of his kidnapping, Ricky didn't seem to be buying everything Simon said and still stood slightly behind Lively. He said, "So you've re-evaluated your life and turned a new leaf? Just like that? And we're supposed to believe it after everything you've been part of, including my kidnapping?"

"Yeah, sorry about that little guy. But I was still following orders at the time."

Looking to Lively, Simon added, "By the way, thanks for hitting me up with that ketamine, twice." The man rubbed the back of his head lightly as if still feeling the drug's effects.

Lively shrugged slightly, saying, "Sorry, but you have to work with what you've got. At the time, I didn't think you'd be willing to just stand down if I asked."

"You never gave me a chance; you just snuck up and stabbed me with a needle without warning. But I gotta say, that second dose really got me wondering about things, at least when I finally woke up in that laundry cart and started thinking for myself once again. I think it was those drugs that brought me all the way back."

"Brought you back? From where?"

"Back from wherever Schreck had me, or Zoller, or whatever you want to call him. Somehow, he can influence people to do his bidding. If fact, I don't even recall the first couple of decades over here."

Lively believed he knew that some of what Simon was saying was true from his own experiences with Max Schreck. And he thought he knew how he accomplished it—his dazzling diamond stickpin. When he'd first met the man in black, he remembered he'd had difficulty looking away from it.

Selene asked, "So you and the other bald Simon aren't twins?"

"No. Schreck and Sinclair wanted enforcers around that could make people do what was required of them, even if they didn't want to do it. Once they had me, they began looking for more."

"How many of you are there altogether?"

"Here? There're four of me, but Schreck has other versions working for him in some of the other frequencies."

"Are they very different, these other realities?" Selene asked, looking concerned.

Nodding his head, Simon said, "Some are very different and very dangerous. He looked at the oversized wristwatch on his massive forearm and said, "Look, I've got to go now. They're probably wondering where I am." He stepped into the frame once more and looked at each of the group as he spoke, saying, "But just so you know, I'm ready and willing to help end this, if it can be ended, whenever you guys are." With that, he pressed the button, and the mirror slid closed again.

"What now?" Selene asked.

Lively held out his arm for Selene to take and said, "Like I was saying just before we met our new co-conspirator, we need to get down to the ballroom and keep up appearances." He opened the door to the hall and looked at Ricky, saying, "Keep an eye on that computer."

Ricky gave a small salute, saying, "Even better, I'll use both."

CHAPTER TWENTY-THREE

December 31st, 2021 1315 hours

John Harder held a forkful of roast beef and mashed potatoes covered in glistening brown gravy. He sniffed it again. It smelled as delicious as it looked, and he took a tentative bite. His tastebuds came alive, reminding him of better times and the homecooked meals Helen would make for him and Danny. Looking to the food in the middle of the stainless-steel island, he said, "So you think this was made by the longtime chef here at the hotel, Amelia Walden?"

"Well, that's what I'm going with right now. Perhaps she's still alive in some other reality."

"I've read a bit about her in my research on the hotel," Amanda said.

"Yes, she'd been with the Sinclair since it opened. From everything I've read, she seemed to have loved her job at the hotel. Apparently, she won numerous prestigious awards for the resort over the years. Right up to the time of her 'accidental death', in fact." Minerva took a small mouthful of roast beef and yorkshire pudding.

"You say that like you don't believe it was such?" John

noted. He shrugged out of his heavy winter jacket as he spoke, then draped it over his stool. Whenever he ate out somewhere in winter, he always took it off to dine because he found it ungainly, not to mention how overheated he got as his body began metabolising whatever food he was eating at the time.

"No, I don't. It was either suicide or murder," Minerva said.

Amanda agreed, saying, "I'd go with the latter."

"Why do you say that?" Minerva asked.

"Because of my connection to this hotel—Danny Harder, John's son." Amanda looked to the inspector, smiled softly and patted the top of his hand. "Danny and I were going to be engaged when he died in an accident. He'd been working security here on his days off from the RCMP and said once he'd earned enough money for a nice engagement ring, he would quit the moonlighting..." Amanda's breath hitched slightly in her chest at the thought, and she trailed off.

John looked kindly at Amanda and finished for her, saying, "But before that could happen, he was killed in that accident."

Amanda said, "I think he may have seen or heard something here that he shouldn't have and was silenced as a result, just like Amelia."

Harder nodded toward the food in the middle of the steel tabletop and added, "I actually met her a couple of times."

"Really?" Minerva prompted.

"Yes, Helen and I had eaten up here several times over the years before..." John trailed off for a moment. "Anyway, Walden was a great chef, and we really enjoyed the food. She would even come into the dining room to greet the guests when time permitted. And we actually met her on a couple of our visits. We usually came up here for anniversaries and birthdays and such, so it would have been one of those times." He scooped another large spoonful of the buttery mashed potatoes onto his plate and topped it with a liberal dollop of gravy.

"What was she like?" Minerva asked.

A faraway look of better times suddenly recalled entered John's eyes, and he said, "Very friendly and professional. She seemed dedicated to making sure every dish that came out of her kitchen was the best it could be, just like my Helen." He smiled wanly and fell silent as he took another forkful of tender gravy-covered beef.

"She seems to be carrying on that tradition," Minerva said.

"That is, if it is her," Amanda added.

"I found a box of old newspapers in a storage room that I believe may have belonged to Amelia," Minerva said. "They covered a lot of things that had happened at the hotel, the restaurant and various events hosted up here over the years."

"Maybe she was going to put it all in a scrapbook but never got around to it. Too busy cooking up a storm," Amanda said.

With a nod, Minerva added, "Or maybe she was going to use information in them along with whatever she'd discovered up here to expose the Sinclair family somehow."

"And you think she was silenced, just like Danny?" Amanda asked.

Minerva nodded.

John looked to Minerva, saying, "Speaking of what was going on here. What about your brother? Have you heard anything more from him?"

"Yes! It appears he's alive and well and living in 1981."

As one, John and Amanda said, "What?"

"It's a long story." Minerva went on to briefly detail her experiences at the hotel so far, up to and including her recent text chat with Lively on Ricky's Atari 800. When she was done, she looked to the inspectors as if expecting them to be somewhat disbelieving of some of the things that had occurred, but they were silent.

"I'm sure every room in this hotel has a different story," Amanda said finally.

"And a different horror," John added, then asked, "Tell me of Lively. What do you know of his situation?"

"It seems he found the missing people."

"That is amazing news!" Amanda interjected.

Minerva nodded, saying, "It is, except that he's now trapped there with them."

This truly was wonderful news, apart from Lively's disappearance, of course. Secretly wondering if Deadmarsh had seen his missing wife as well, John asked, "There? Where exactly is there?"

"This hotel."

"They're all still here in this hotel?" Amanda said, surprised.

"In a version of it, from what I understand. Listen, to get your mind around that, I'll need to show you something before we go back upstairs. I believe it's partly responsible for everything that's happened here. And after that, I'll show you our little problem in the model room since it will take the three of us to solve it."

A series of images suddenly flashed through John's mind as Minerva mentioned the model room in the turret, and his hip flared in pain. For many years, he'd struggled with arthritis and the after-effects of an old injury sustained on his final evening here at the Sinclair Resort. Most days, it only growled at him, but in colder weather like today, it barked like a junkyard dog. The injury was one he thought he'd sustained due to his own carelessness. However, now that he was back here, it must have triggered something buried deep inside, and he recalled what had truly happened in the model room that night.

***

Whirling around, Harder's hand automatically dropped onto the butt of his sidearm as he sensed a threat.

The silverback gorilla was just inside the doorway, leaning forward onto its knuckles, seeming to regard him with barely contained hostility. Its mouth was partly open, perhaps in mid-roar, its fangs sparkling in the model's spotlights. John edged toward it, his mind overloading at the prospect that what he was witnessing could actually be possible.

With wide eyes, he edged past the creature, then quickly glanced out into the stairwell. There was no one in sight and no sound of anyone trying to flee silently down the spiral staircase.

Turning back, Harder stared at the beast from behind, wondering how it had gotten up the stairs. Considering the armature underneath and the furry pelt overtop, it couldn't be too light. And judging by its girth alone, he figured it would probably require two good-sized men, at least, to bring this beast up the stairs.

John re-entered the room and continued around the model of the hotel once again, looking for a culprit. There was nothing out of place, and no one hid behind it. He returned to the grotesque gorilla but stopped short and looked questioningly at it. Was it standing slightly taller now? He was almost certain it had been on its knuckles earlier, yet now, it was almost fully erect.

Though he realised he'd been missing out on some sleep recently due to this investigation, was what he was witnessing due to this deprivation, he wondered. Was the creature even actually standing there in front of him right now? There was only one way to find out.

He reached cautiously forward and ran his fingers over the short, wiry fur of the great ape's head. Probing further, he was surprised to touch the beast's skull beneath. Unlike most modern taxidermied animals, this creature had been stuffed many years before styrofoam forms, and its actual skull had been used as a form underneath. Presumably, the rest of this beast and those down in the games room were stuffed with excelsior around a lightweight wood and wire frame. However, with the inclusion of the creature's skull, it was hard to say how many other parts of the animal's skeleton lay beneath without cutting it open.

But all of that begged the question: how did this animal get up here? He realised he still had Jansen's Maglite, and he shone it into the creatures glittering glass eyes. There was no reaction, of course. There couldn't be; it was dead after all. He turned back to the model for a moment, wondering once again how to get it open. This hotel was a regular house of horrors, but unlike at the carnival, this one could kill you if you weren't careful. With that thought capering about in his head, a heavy hand dropped onto his shoulder.

Harder jerked away and spun around to find himself face to face with the gorilla. It had moved to within inches of his location and now held its arms out as if to pull him into its powerful grasp. He backed up in reflex and bumped into the model, cracking his elbow against one of its sharp corners.

A flash of tingling pain from his funny bone distracted him momentarily, but that had been enough, and then the beast was upon him.

John gagged from the reek of tanned leather and dusty fur that suddenly filled his nostrils. Unable to see, wiry hair ground against his face as he was dragged by his neck and shoulders across the rough stone floor toward the top of the turret stairs.

CHAPTER TWENTY-FOUR

December 31st, 1981 2232 hours

Selene exited the suite with one arm draped over Lively's. They took the elevator down and made their way through the lobby toward the ballroom once more. All around them, people laughed and shrieked, having a grand old time.

Lively took it all in, wondering if every evening here was as raucous as this? What must it be like to have a celebration like this every night for the last forty years? Though he enjoyed a good party as much as the next guy, he didn't think he could handle that much of a good time. Then again, maybe these people didn't know how good their times were each night?

Thanks to Simon, they now knew the realignment process affected the memory of the people inside of it unless they wore a bracelet. His own forgetfulness was a prime example of that. If he spent too long here without one, he wondered, would he ever have any desire to leave? Or would he become like the rest of the people, forever unaware of their situation due to a side effect of the very thing that kept them prisoner?

The Glenn Millers were just ending a set when Lively and Selene re-entered the party. Across the room, Edward had been entertaining a couple of guests at their table, and he excused himself when he saw them approaching. Patting Lively on the shoulder, he ushered them over to his table, saying, "There you are! We thought we'd lost you!"

"Sorry, just seeing some of the sights around the old place. It's not every day I get to see such a party as this," Lively said. He still wanted to play along with Edward and stay in his good graces as long as he could until the time came to try and effect a rescue of some sort.

"Better get used to this if you're going to be staying around here," Selene said under her breath. Lively pulled out a chair for her. She gave him a small smile in thanks and sat down.

With a pleased expression on his face, Edward said, "I'm so glad you're enjoying it! This is a moment in time of which I've long dreamt; my son becoming part of the Sinclair empire."

Lively was pleased to see his job of buttering up his dad was doing the trick, and he said, "It's just been such a shock over the last few hours here. Learning that mom is still alive, as well as yourself, and how I'm somehow a part of all of this as well. I'm sure you can imagine..."

"Of course, it must be quite overwhelming to have all of this thrust upon you," Edward agreed.

Wanting to corroborate some of the information he'd been trying to assimilate, Lively said, "So is there any way these people could ever be brought back to the present?"

"Sadly, it seems to be a one-way ticket for them."

"Really? It can't be reversed?" Selene asked.

"There is a chance it might be possible, but it might also kill everyone in the process."

"Maybe that would be a good thing," Selene said, shaking her head sadly.

Edward frowned slightly, about to speak, when the band started up another number, and dozens of couples began jittering and jiving across the dance floor. Moving through the throng of bodies, Schreck approached the table, freshly back from an errand in another part of the hotel.

"Does that help?" Lively asked over the band's bass-heavy boogie, his eyes on the dancers. "The music and everything, I mean?"

Schreck answered the question as he sat down, saying with a tangle-toothed grin, "Oh, absolutely. The endorphins released by the music help with their mental state, along with liberal amounts of alcohol as well, of course."

Edward nodded in agreement, saying, "It most definitely helps with the reset. Speaking of which, I'd recommend you have a couple of good stiff ones before midnight, Son. It helps lessen the headache afterwards." Sinclair signalled O'Malley at the bar.

Simon had made it back down to the ballroom and now stood to one side of the table once more, with Bald Simon on the side closest to the bar. He saw Sinclair's gesture and moved to retrieve a bottle that had been placed on a silver platter by the barman. Returning with the bottle, the bodyguard placed it on the table along with several shot glasses. It looked like the Glenfiddich that Lively had shared with his sister or another bottle of the same. Either way, he knew it wouldn't be too hard to knock back the multi-thousand-dollar liquor, despite his preference for milder, brewed beverages.

Schreck poured an ounce into each shot glass and distributed them to Selene and Lively, then Edward and lastly himself.

"What does it feel like?" Lively asked, sniffing the shot. It smelled the same as what he'd shared with Minerva. Not that it wasn't easy to mask the smell and taste of other substances in alcohol. For all he knew, it could be drugged. However, like Toucan Sam, he trusted his nose and figured he should be okay.

"The reset? It feels like you've had the insides sucked out of you and then blown back in, all at once."

"Well then, it sounds like a little something to deaden the nervous system couldn't hurt."

"Absolutely!" Edward held his glass up to the rest of the table and said, "To new life and old money!"

A rather odd toast, but Lively went along with it, and he and Selene downed their shots. Delicious, just as he'd remembered, but not something he would regularly seek out in the world—Moosehead was still more than enough for him. But just as he downed his shot, he noticed that Schreck and Sinclair had only brought their glasses to their lips but not downed any of the alcohol themselves.

Selene drooped against Lively as he placed his glass back on the table. He turned to her and began to say, "I think you'd better slow it down a bit, Mom, because..."

That was as far as Lively got. He slumped suddenly forward, his head thudding onto the hardwood table as the world around him faded to black, and he knew no more.

CHAPTER TWENTY-FIVE

December 31st, 2021 1410 hours

Are you all right, John?" Amanda queried. Harder had been seemingly enjoying his meal when he stopped eating suddenly, and a look had come across his face.

Coming out of his trance, John said, "Sorry, just recalling my final time upstairs in the model room. Somehow, I believe those stuffed animals are guardians of that ebony box."

"I agree," Minerva said.

Amanda stiffened slightly and said, "Was that what had happened when I found you, John? Was it one of them?"

Nodding in remembrance, John admitted, "Yes."

Leaning forward in anticipation, Amanda asked, "Was it the tiger?"

"No, the ape."

"Well, I think those stuffies are just as active now as they were forty years ago," Minerva said. "Judging by the damage to the door to the model room at least. Lively had a run-in with one of them just before he disappeared." A look of concern crossed Minerva's face, and she added, "When we get back upstairs, I want to show you something in the Snowdrop Lounge."

"What happened in the lounge?"

After gathering up her sword and serving tray shield again, Minerva said, "It's not just the stuffed animals we need to worry about now."

***

With their meal done, Minerva led her companions back to the bottom of the basement stairs. Turning back to speak to them, she said, "Before you head up in the elevator to the lobby, there's something else I need to show you." She took the lead up the short flight of steps to the dogleg landing and waited for the inspectors to arrive.

Once they were all together again, Minerva said, "Since we're going right by it..." She turned, toed the unseen switch in the corner and pushed on the side of the wall to reveal the hidden revolving door.

John shook his head in amazement as he looked at the secret passage that now lay before them. "I always suspected there was something hidden away within the walls of this hotel. And now I see how right I was."

"This is only one of many, as you can imagine," Minerva said, shining her lightsabre down the dim passageway.

"Was it through a hidden door that everyone was taken from the ballroom?" Amanda wondered aloud.

"Perhaps, but probably not a doorway like any we've ever seen before. Follow me." With that, she revolved out of sight.

John went through the door next, followed by Amanda. Once they were all on the other side, Minerva shone her light down the long, red-hued corridor and said, "Just down here a way."

A few minutes later, they stood before the polished aluminum door leading into the gold room. Minerva opened the door and stepped inside, hearing her two companions gasp appropriately as they entered behind her.

"My Lord!" John said, shaking his head.

"I can't believe this was just beneath our feet the whole time," Amanda noted, her eyes wide as she tried to take everything in all at once.

Minerva agreed, saying, "Amazing, isn't it?" Looking upward, she added, "And yes, that's real gold lining the ceiling."

They walked further into the vast room, and John moved to where the collector dish lay, marvelling at its size. "Is this the machine that did it?"

"We believe so." Minerva moved along one wall for a short way and then popped open the door to the hidden control room. She stepped inside, saying, "Cozy, huh? We believe this is the computer that operates it. Or at least, this is a remote terminal that accesses the mainframe in the other room which controls it." Minerva propped her sword and tray against the wall and wheeled the executive leather chair toward John, saying, "Would you like to sit down?"

"Yes, thanks." John sank into the office chair with a grateful sigh, saying, "Ever since I stepped through the front door of this place, my hip's been acting up again." He looked up at the monochrome security monitor displays and then down at the typewriter-styled terminal underneath the green CRT, asking, "So there's a program you can run on this?"

"Actually, as far as we know, it's already running." Minerva leaned over John and pointed at the screen showing the menu with the list of numbered options. She was about to say something about how they still needed the concentrator when she noticed the screen had changed. Beneath the fifth option was a new one which said:

'Enter password to disable override - 6'

"Well, this is new," Minerva said.

"What do you mean," Amanda asked. "I didn't think anything was new around here."

"Neither did I, but this menu option wasn't there the last time I looked."

"What? How is that possible?" John wondered aloud.

"I think it's possible because of my brother. His very presence in 1981 is disrupting the timeline, or whatever you want to call it. Apparently, that computer I told you about in suite #304 that I used to communicate with Lively was owned by some sort of early proto-hacker, one Ricky Rosenstein. So, he may have had something to do with it."

Nodding her head, Amanda said, "I remember that name from the list of the missing."

John said with a slight smile, "Despite everything else that's been happening, this might be some genuinely good news."

Minerva nodded, saying, "Let's hope so because that's something in relatively short supply around here."

***

With the basement level of her grand tour complete, Minerva brought the inspectors back out through the hidden sliding door behind the storage room's shelves.

"This is where we found Will Weston," Amanda said quietly. She grasped John's arm firmly for a moment, perhaps more out of a need for her own comfort than actually giving John support.

A few moments later, as they moved down the corridor past the kitchen, Amanda said, "I was thinking John and I should take the elevator back up."

"That might be an idea," John said, "My hip is barking at me right now."

Minerva said, "I've been reluctant to take it myself being all alone. But you guys go ahead. I'll still take the stairs just so all of our eggs aren't all in one basket, so to speak."

Amanda pressed the button, and the doors opened immediately with a musical ping. They entered the car, and as the doors slid shut, John said to Minerva, "See you in the lobby, I hope."

Climbing the stairs, Minerva wondered at her new companions and what it must be like for them to be back here after forty years, along with all of the thoughts and memories that no doubt came with the visit. Arriving at the top of the stairs, the elevator gave a ding in the lobby and John Harder click-clopped out the door with his cane, followed closely by Amanda.

Minerva smiled slightly as they approached and said, "Nice to see things work as they should around here sometimes."

"Yes," John agreed. "Sometimes. However, Amanda and I had issues on a different service elevator, not this one."

The group began to move toward the lounge, continuing their conversation.

"Is it the one that comes up in the ballroom service corridor?" Minerva asked.

"That's the one," Amanda said, nodding in agreement. "It never went where we wanted. Is that what happened to you?"

"No," Minerva shook her head. "I had a different adventure." A slight shudder ran through her as she recalled the corrupt, bloody fingers that had grasped at her hair from the black gap. Now almost to the bar, she began, "Like I was saying downstairs, it's not just the stuffed..." She trailed off, suddenly staring at the bartop up ahead.

Noting her concern, John asked, "What's wrong?"

The polished wood of the mahogany bar shone dully in the muted overhead lights of the Snowdrop Lounge. The trap door lay open once again. The wood looked dark and scorched where the painted wolf's head had been, but the canvas carnivore was nowhere in sight.

Looking about the room for any sign of the animal, Minerva said, "It's what I was going to show you and my reason for this sword and tray, the painted wolf."

"This creature is proving harder to put out of commission than I would have thought. Just before you arrived, I'd had it pinned here by the bartender's trap door."

"How did it get loose then?" John asked.

"I think something else aided and abetted its escape," Minerva said as she pictured the silverback gorilla swinging down from the gaming lounge above and lifting the trap door to rescue an ally in need. It now seemed obvious the silver of the tray had been effective in at least keeping the beast in abeyance. She held it up, saying, "I figured I needed this, but I guess I shouldn't have removed it in hindsight."

"It's always twenty-twenty," John said in commiseration.

"So true." Giving the tray a flourish, Minerva said, "Okay then, I need to stop by my suite to pick something up." Resting her sword on her shoulder, she added, "On the way, we can admire some art."

CHAPTER TWENTY-SIX

December 31st, 1981 2249 hours

Ricky Rosenstein was getting antsy again. He'd promised Mr. DeMille he'd stay put this time and wouldn't leave his suite. But he wondered what was happening elsewhere in the hotel as he sat there. And the more he wondered, the antsier he got. One thing that had always been Ricky's biggest fault was his curiosity. In another life, he figured he must have been a cat.

Though he was monitoring the computer for any further messages like he'd agreed to do, it didn't seem that Minerva was willing or able to communicate at the present time, despite his attempts to call her attention. Hoping that all was well down in the ballroom, he looked at the clock on the wall; it was approaching eleven o'clock. What was happening with Lively and Selene, he wondered. It had been almost a half-hour since he'd last seen them, and he was becoming concerned.

Deciding action seemed the best course rather than inaction, Rosenstein moved to the mirror on the wall. Engaging the switch, he marvelled as the massive piece of glass slid aside seemingly of its own volition. "Yeah, that just never gets old."

Rosenstein looked through the mirror's frame, torn. Lively arriving had been a good thing. It had interrupted his routine of gluttony and being kidnapped every night for forty years, and he was eternally grateful for that. And though he'd agreed to stay where he was, he figured there was a reason for his freedom, and that reason was Lively's doing. Breaking his promise, he gave a small sigh, then whispered, "Sorry, Mr. DeMille, but sometimes a mensch has gotta do what a mensch has gotta do." And then he stepped through into the dim red corridor.

Standing in the semi-darkness, still in his stocking feet from before, Ricky was indecisive as to what he should do next. The ballroom was off-limits; he knew that. If he showed his cute little button nose anywhere in the vicinity of the party, he was sure he would be captured again. And the way things were going, he didn't think Lively would be able to help him out anymore since the man probably had his hands rather full at the moment.

He crept through the dim corridor toward the spiral staircase, moving with surprising stealth for a small man of such large size. In the two-way mirrors looking into the suites he passed, all were now dark and empty, the occupants taking part in their nightly revelry, no doubt.

Drawn to the basement and the mainframe computer once more, he crept slowly down the stairs from the third floor. When he arrived on the second floor, he discovered he had a problem.

His back to Ricky, a man was standing in the middle of the corridor near the staircase, his shoulders slumped forward, and head tilted to one side. He stood almost completely still, as if in a trance. Who was this, Rosenstein wondered. At first, he'd thought it was Lively but then saw he was mistaken. Though the man was about the right size, he didn't have the same muscular build that Lively had and appeared slightly less fit.

Ricky felt around in his tuxedo jacket pockets and discovered a half sleeve of Rolo chocolate-covered caramels. He unwrapped the foil from one end, removed a candy, and placed the remaining roll back in his pocket. That done, he took a quick peek back into the corridor and saw the man hadn't moved. Who was he? Was he one of the guests who'd accidentally found their way through one of the sliding mirrors? If so, why was he stopped in the middle of the corridor?

Targeting just over the unknown man's shoulder, Ricky let the Rolo fly. His years of balling up scrap papers and tossing them in the trash can on the other side of his office had prepared him well. The caramel shot past the man's head, then bumped and rolled along the floor for several yards down the passageway. It wasn't a loud noise, but it was loud enough. The man took notice and moved jerkily in the direction of the small chocolate. He seemed rather unsteady on his feet, and Ricky wondered if he'd been drugged.

From the alcove, Ricky watched as the man approached the candy. He appeared oblivious to it and stepped on the chocolate, squishing it into the thick carpeting that lined the hallway. Continuing along, the man arrived at the junction near the stairs and elevator, and Ricky thought for sure he was going to stop again. But fortunately, the mystery man turned and shambled down another dim corridor that stretched out into the hotel's west wing.

Utilising his stealthiest of movements, Ricky slowly descended the spiral staircase again. The first floor seemed clear, and he continued toward the basement without incident.

Now back in the hidden bowels of the hotel, Rosenstein snuck down the gloomy passageway, approaching the room with the embalming table. He was almost to the door when the lift at his back began to descend to his level. Slipping inside the room, he peered around the doorframe to see who the newest visitor to this basement underworld might be. Was it the unidentified man from the second floor?

Fortunately, he didn't have to wonder for long. The doors opened, and Mr. Clean exited the car first, followed by a gurney just like the one he had been strapped to less than six hours before. At the other end of the gurney was blonde Simon, who'd recently admitted to having had enough of partying every night. Last in this little conga line of crazies was his least favourite nurse, Kandi, still in her uniform. She peeled off from formation and entered the prep room to get something while the terror twins continued to push the gurney toward his location.

Ricky's eyes widened in horror when he saw who was going for a ride on the wheeled stretcher this time—Mr. Lively DeMille. As the group grew closer, he looked around in a panic, needing a place to hide again, and he didn't think the embalming table was the best of spots after almost getting caught last time, not to mention that it was most likely the destination of the gurney.

Scurrying silently on stocking feet, Rosenstein retreated to the control room. He was just about to flee into the gold room beyond when he discovered he could squeeze his bulk behind the mainframe and the rear wall. Fortunately, the gap was rather sizeable thanks to the hulking computer's cooling requirements and its need for plenty of airflow to keep from overheating. Just milliseconds after Ricky hunkered down behind it, the ceiling brightened slightly as the high-intensity lights over the embalming table were turned on.

Through a speaker in the ceiling of the control room, the audio from the other side of the glass was relayed. A deep male voice said, "Are you sure this is what they want?"

"As far as I know," came the reply. It was the same deep voice again as if the person was talking to themselves, but

Ricky knew better. Simon and Mr. Clean were having a little tete-a-tete.

"I thought they wanted to make him part of things," the first voice said.

"They do, but not how we figured, I guess. But this came down directly from the big guy. And you know we're always the last to know about things around here."

"Yeah, you're right about that. Okay, let's get him into position." A moment of grunting came next, presumably as unconscious Lively was lifted onto the table.

Another voice joined the conversation, a woman. Kandi had returned from the prep room with whatever she needed to get. "What's wrong, boys? Is there a problem?"

"No, ma'am, no problem. We're getting him secured now, and we'll get the electrodes attached next."

"Good. When I'm done with this, I'll get things loaded up on the mainframe and then we'll be ready for the transfer."

Ricky risked a peek over the hulking mainframe and watched the trio working away. Kandi was wearing thick, insulated work gloves as she inserted what looked like some kind of dark stone into the crazy-looking machine overtop the embalming table. Lively's jacket and shirt had been removed, and he'd had electrodes placed on various points around his muscular torso and head.

Ready for the transfer? He wondered at that. Transfer DeMille into something? Or transfer something into DeMille? The question was, which one? There was a chance they might be foiled by his little alteration of the mainframe's code, but he didn't know for sure. Either way, he couldn't let anything happen to Lively and wondered what he could do about it.

Kandi turned from the table and approached the control room door.

Ricky ducked back down and felt around in his tuxedo coat's pockets for some more inspiration. In the pocket opposite the one containing the Rolos, he suddenly found something that just might help.

***

His head throbbing, Lively gradually came around. Voices seemed to surround him from all sides, and he kept his eyes closed as he swam upward toward consciousness, resisting the urge to open them and give away the only advantage he had on his captors right now. If they were unaware of his current state of consciousness, so much the better.

Just as he felt the straps tightened, he'd woken up and was still trying to focus. Someone, a woman, said something about a transfer. What kind of transfer, he wondered. Physical? Mental? Either way, It couldn't be a good thing, and he felt his alarm rising. He needed to see what was happening and risked a squint through one eye. The hazy outline of a very large person was visible through his narrow slit of vision, and he presumed it to be one of the Beefy Boys. Squinting a little harder, Lively saw that it was Blonde Simon, and he risked a brief look at the man. The other Simon was grabbing something from the white medicine cabinet in the corner, his back to the table. Seeing that Lively was awake now, Blonde Simon nodded imperceptibly and gave a slight wink.

Bald Simon approached from the other side of the room and said, "All right, I'll just inject this into him, and he'll be ready for the transfer."

***

Sweat beaded on Ricky's brow as he hunched behind the mainframe. Part of it was from nervousness, and part of it was from the heat that the computer's exhaust fans put out. The air coming from them had to be over one hundred degrees Fahrenheit, and he was currently right next to two of them.

Nurse Kandi had been working away at the computer keyboard for a few moments. With a sigh, she stopped typing and activated a microphone saying, "Are you guys all set in there?"

"Yes, ma'am," came the reply.

There was a clicking of computer keys as Kandi tried to bring up whatever program was needed for the transfer. Suddenly, she said, "Okay, who's been screwing around with the mainframe? Has one of you guys been playing Zork on here again?"

Ricky listened to the sound of heavy footsteps approaching. Mr Clean and Simon entered the room and stopped just inside the doorway. One of them said, "Wasn't me."

"Nope, me either."

"Well, something's been done to the programme. I've been trying to enter the secondary menu for the transfer, but all the menu options are unresponsive, and it's asking me for a password now!"

Ricky smiled and covered his hand with his mouth as he almost brayed laughter. It seemed his little modification job to the code was working as he'd hoped.

"Well, don't look at us." Said one twin.

"So, what's going to happen then," the other asked. "You still want us to get him ready?"

"Yes, go ahead. Have you administered the sedative yet?"

"No, I was just gonna do it when you accused us of breaking your computer."

"I didn't accuse you of breaking it; I accused you of playing games on it again. Go finish prepping him and standby. I'll see if I can figure out what's going on here."

"Yes, ma'am." There was a sound of heavy feet shuffling away.

Nurse Kandi muttered to herself, apparently reading the screen, "Enter password to disable override? What override? What password?" After a moment, Kandi resumed her clickity-clacking on the keyboard as she no doubt attempted to crack Ricky's code.

In his jacket pocket across from the Rolos, Ricky had found the vials and syringes he'd previously liberated from the medicine cabinet in the operating theatre. He now drew what he hoped to be an adequate amount of fluid into one syringe, then carefully moved from his hiding place. He didn't want to risk jabbing the woman in the neck with the needle and accidentally sever an artery or something, even though he was sure, after everything she'd done to him over the years, she most certainly had it coming. Instead, he crept cautiously behind Kandi and jabbed the syringe into her thigh, partially visible through an opening in the side of the chair.

"Hey! What gives!" Kandi exclaimed, swatting her hand to her leg as she felt the needle's sting. But by then, it was too late, and Ricky had unloaded the entire syringe into her curvaceous, creamy thigh. She started to turn and saw Ricky crouched down and grinning innocently behind her. "You! You little bast..." Her words trailed off, and a look of discombobulation spread across her face as she slumped back into the chair unconscious.

From the other room came the sound of heavy footfalls as

one of the twins came to investigate, but by then, Ricky had crept back behind the mainframe once again.

"Hey, what in the hell happened to you?"

Ricky peeked around the mainframe and saw it was Mr. Clean and not Blonde Simon. The muscular man was currently giving Kandi a shake, trying to rouse her with little success.

Suddenly, the bulging brute caught sight of movement as Ricky ducked back behind the mainframe, and he hollered, "Hey! What are you doing back there?!"

Reluctantly popping up from his hiding place, Rosenstein said, "Computer maintenance?" He held up one of his business cards to support his claim, but it didn't seem to sway the man, and he stepped menacingly toward Ricky.

"Why you little—" Mr. Clean's words were cut off along with his breath as Simon came from behind and put his twin in a chokehold, saying, "Sorry, brother."

CHAPTER TWENTY-SEVEN

December 31st, 2021 1555 hours

The gargantuan painting loomed over the group as they studied its detail. It was not lost on Minerva that, as they stood there, if the landscape came loose from the wall, it would crush all three of them to a bloody pulp, and that would be game over. She stepped back slightly as the thought came to her. Since this hotel now seemed much more aggressive in its actions, she wouldn't have been surprised by such an eventuality.

"I always wondered about this painting," John said as he studied the forest behind the resort. He peered closely at the blackened smear amongst the lush green foliage, which Minerva said was the wounded wolf.

"Yes, me too," Minerva replied. "I've always been fascinated with odd paintings ever since watching reruns of a show called Night Gallery when I was a little girl."

"I know the show you mean," Amanda said. "The one with a painting of a cemetery next to a house, and how it changes each time it's viewed."

Minerva smiled and nodded, "That's the one."

John asked, "Has anything else changed that you know of?"

Minerva scanned the painting, trying to take it all in at once. "Not that I can see. There was a little painted boy in the picture, but he's been missing for a while now. Like the wolf, I've seen him out and about in the hotel since."

"Really?" Amanda asked. "Has he been menacing toward you?"

"No, he's been helpful so far. When I first arrived here and saw this painting, I talked to him, just in jest, of course. I don't make it a habit of talking to paintings. Little did I know, I'd eventually be following him around the hotel. Back then, he had a little painted dog, too." She pointed to where the collar had been on the painting's green lawn, which she'd eventually found in the royal suite upstairs.

"I don't see one now."

"No, I think the wolf ate it."

"Sounds like you're lucky it didn't eat you, too," Amanda said.

"I agree. But remember to keep your eyes open around here because..." Minerva trailed off, suddenly staring hard at the painting.

"What's wrong?" John asked, seeing her expression.

"There is something different."

"Really? What's that?"

"There was something else in the forest that's no longer there." Minerva pointed at the flora on the opposite side of the painting, saying, "A large brown bear used to be hiding amongst the leaves and branches here."

"Well, that's just what we need," Amanda said. "Something else to worry about."

Minerva nodded, concerned. How were they going to deal with something like that? The wolf was dangerous enough, however manageable, but this bear could be more of a challenge. And the thought of something its size sneaking up on someone unsuspecting and then wrapping itself around them like a python made her shiver.

"Did you just feel a cold spot?" Amanda asked? "They seem to be all over this place from what I remember."

"Yes, they are, but no, that's not what made me shiver. Just thinking about my encounter with this wolf here." She pointed to the dark smudge on the portrait and added, "If that bear is anything comparable, then we could have big trouble right here in River City."

John smiled slightly at Minerva's reference, saying, "And it's definitely not a pool hall."

"Everyone just needs to be on extra high alert," Amanda said.

"That's my natural state around here already," Minerva added.

They continued to the second floor, Amanda at John's side, aiding him with the climb. As they neared the top, Minerva excused herself and jogged to her room to retrieve something she believed might assist them in their mission. She kept her eyes open for anything large, brown, and thin as she moved, the missing bear still at the top of her mind.

A few moments later, she returned to find John and

Amanda resting on one of the borne settees in the mirrored common area. Harder had beads of perspiration dotting his forehead and looked somewhat winded.

Noting John's condition, Amanda said, "I think we should take the elevator up to the third."

With a nod, Minerva said, "I think that would be best since we have the climb to the Executive Gaming Lounge after that."

With a tired look, John said, "I agree."

Minerva pressed the call button while Jansen helped Harder stand.

The elevator arrived, and John shuffled into the car ahead of Amanda. Once they were both in the car, the petite inspector turned and tried to give Minerva a faintly encouraging smile as the doors closed. The car began to rise toward the third floor, and Minerva sprinted up the stairs, taking them two at a time. She arrived at the top of the stairs just as the bell rang and the doors slid apart.

The lift was empty.

"Oh, no, not again," Minerva said, shaking her head in disbelief. She stepped slowly forward and peeked inside the elevator car, reluctant to enter. However, she could see no one was inside and recalled when she'd first met Doppelively and how he'd disappeared under similar circumstances. Had John and Amanda not been real, either, and had they now vanished like her brother's double?

The doors slid shut.

Minerva stepped forward and pressed the call button. The doors slid apart again, and there stood John and Amanda, looking startled that she was already there ahead of them.

"Where did you go?" Minerva asked, confusion knitting her brows.

"What do you mean? We were right here in the elevator since you saw us last," Amanda said, surprised. "How did you get up here so quickly?"

"I got here a few seconds ago, just as the elevator arrived—and it was empty."

John said, "That's not possible."

Shaking her head, Minerva said, "Even the impossible seems possible around this place." She wondered about what had just happened. To John and Amanda, it seemed as if they'd had one continuous journey in the elevator car, and to them, hardly any time had elapsed, making it seem as if Minerva were the Flash or something. Were there areas inside this hotel that somehow operated in different pockets of time, with some progressing slower, like where Lively was? And an even more terrifying possibility, were people now being teleported to other realms at the whim of this hotel? If one were to get on this elevator again and ride it to the lobby or the basement, would their trip actually end there, or would they instead descend into the molten core of the very earth itself?

Jansen stepped out of the elevator behind Harder, a frown on her face. "Despite your lack of enthusiasm for stairs, John, I think it might be better if we used them instead of this elevator from now on."

Nodding, Harder said, "I agree. But even stairs can have issues around here." He glanced over at Jansen as he said that, and they shared a look.

Minerva asked, "Did you have something happen using the stairs?"

"Let's just say they sometimes don't go where you'd expect," Amanda said.

"That pretty much describes everything in this hotel," Minerva agreed.

As they began to move along the lengthy west wing corridor, Minerva paused to grab a serving cart parked down a narrow service passage. She wheeled it out, saying, "I saw this earlier and figured we could use it for our little procedure." She rolled it over to John and added, "As a bonus, until we get to the turret stairs up ahead, I thought you might like to use it. When I used to take my Grandma Nell for groceries, she liked to hold the grocery cart like a walker. I figured this would work the same for you."

With a grateful smile, John said, "Thank you, that's very thoughtful."

A couple of minutes later, Harder left the cart at the bottom of the turret stairs as the trio began their climb. By the time they'd all arrived at the top, it appeared that John was ready for another break.

Taking the lead, Minerva entered the room first, followed by John and then Amanda. She looked about the room, noting where the stuffed animals were located and felt slightly relieved to see they all seemed back in their original positions. Beside her, the two inspectors did the same. Minerva was pleased to see they all seemed to be on the same page and said, "We can't take our eyes off of the stuffies, or bad things might happen."

Nodding gravely, John and Amanda both said, almost at once, "I know," then looked at each other in surprise.

John moved to a high-backed chair at a round table with a green felt covering. It looked freshly cleaned and dusted as if in anticipation of an upcoming evening of five-card stud. He sat facing the door, looking at what stood next to Amanda and Minerva. The silverback gorilla pounded its chest, its glass eyes appearing filled with barely contained rage as it seemed to stare directly at him.

Minerva moved behind the bar and disappeared for a moment, then came back with a couple of small green bottles of Canada Dry ginger ale, saying, "I found these earlier when I was getting some towels. Would either of you care for one?"

Nodding slightly, Harder said, "Please."

Amanda shook her head, saying, "No, thanks," as she moved to get a better view of the striped predator on the other side of the room. It crouched next to the Ms. Pac-Man machine as if lying in wait for an unwitting arcade player to drop a quarter in. Off near the stairs to the model room, the polar bear towered over all.

Still at the bar, Minerva watched Harder and Jansen for a moment. Both looked to be dealing with their own internal demons regarding the taxidermied animals; Amanda stared at the tiger and John at the great ape. She popped the top from both bottles and brought them over to John, handing one to the seated senior and holding onto the other for herself. She raised hers slightly and said, "To everyone missing, may they come home safely to the ones they love and the lives they'd left."

John smiled and said, "Well put," then sipped from the small bottle and let out a slight, satisfied, "Ah."

Now keeping her eyes on the polar bear, Minerva said, "The reason I couldn't get to the ebony box sooner was because of these animals. That cat over there was sitting next to the model upstairs when I last saw it. Somehow, it's gotten back down here again. They seem to move when you're not looking at them or when no one is around."

Both retired officers spoke almost in unison once again, with John saying, "Yes," and Amanda finishing with, "We know," a grim smile on her face.

"So, what now?" Harder asked.

"The only way I can see this working is with Amanda at the bottom of the stairs trying to keep all the animals within sight."

"Why, where will we be?" John asked.

"Upstairs, getting the ebony box out of the model. I am so sensitive to the power that emanates from it that I can't handle touching it without overloading myself."

"Okay, so I take the box and do what with it?" John asked.

"It needs to go back to the ballroom in the exact spot where it was on December 31st, 1981." She glanced quickly to her companions, then back to the bear once again and asked, "Okay, so we're all on the same page?"

"I think so," Amanda said, nodding slowly. "But how will I keep an eye on all three of these creatures at once?"

"I have something that might help us out here." Minerva rummaged around in Lively's courier bag. Though she'd been carrying the bag with her for a while now, she'd left one crucial item behind in her room that she needed to retrieve before their climb to the turret—the iPad tablet. As a break between reading newspapers and just before bed last night, she'd indulged in a guilty pleasure and played several rounds of Bejeweled that Lively had installed on the tablet. The only reason the game was on the iPad was for her, she realised, since he didn't play it, and it made her love and miss him all the more.

With a small smile, she pulled the tablet from the bag along with three of the GoPros that her brother had been using in the model room. Placing everything temporarily on the poker table, she began setting up the cameras in various spots about the round room. The first was pointed at the gorilla, the second sat on a chair directed at the tiger, and the third perched on the edge of the billiard table aimed at the polar bear.

"You're going to record them?" Amanda asked, glancing at what Minerva was doing and also around the room at the stuffed animals at the same time.

"Yes, and no. You're going to watch them while this records them." Minerva picked up the iPad Mini from the table and turned it on. She loaded up the GoPro app she'd found on it while figuring out the satellite router's internet connection. After several taps and a couple of colourful metaphors, Minerva had everything set up the way she wanted. She handed the tablet to Amanda, saying, "Here you go. I would have you come upstairs with us, but unfortunately, these cameras have a limited range when connected to the tablet, and I'm sure all that stone would get in the way."

"Yes, that would have been nice to stick together, but okay," Jansen said, accepting the tablet. She saw that she now had live feeds of the trio of GoPro's streaming on the iPad's screen. All three stuffies were framed within each shot, and she could easily keep an eye on them all at once while John and Minerva retrieved the ebony box.

They moved slowly toward the model room stairs, Minerva helping John. Amanda trailed behind them with her eyes glued to the tablet.

At the bottom of the stairs, "Here, you can use this if you need it." Minerva handed her sword to Amanda but held onto the tray, adding, "I need this to place the box on once we get it out."

Jansen took the sword gratefully, saying, "I hope I don't need it."

With the silver tray tucked under one arm and John holding tight to the other as she began to ascend the stairs, Minerva said, "That makes two of us."

From over his shoulder, as he climbed, John said, "Three."

CHAPTER TWENTY-EIGHT

December 31st, 1981 2304 hours

Edward Sinclair surveyed his kingdom, sipping from a champagne flute, Max Schreck at his side. They stood near the doorway leading to the service corridor. Sinclair said, "So, after all these years, tonight's finally the night."

"Yes, it is," Schreck agreed, eyeing Edward from the corners of his eyes.

Draining the last of the champagne, Sinclair placed his flute on a nearby serving cart, saying, "Well, I guess there's no time like the present."

"Or the past," Schreck added, and Sinclair laughed.

The party in the ballroom appeared to have kicked into high gear now. The music from the Glenn Millers pulsed through the room, and the revellers seemed even more agitated than they had before as if they somehow sensed what was about to happen. With brays of laughter and shrieks of delight at their backs, the men departed through the service door and made their way to the basement.

Sinclair stepped through the doorway into the operating

theatre first, followed closely by Schreck. From one side of the door, Lively grabbed hold of Edward and held his arms behind his back, while Simon nabbed Schreck from the other side, immobilising the man in a big bear hug.

"Unhand me!" Edward said, struggling briefly.

"This is outrageous!" Schreck complained.

Still feeling the effects of the drug he'd been slipped, Lively was able to function well enough to handle his father at the moment but felt glad Simon had a hold of Schreck since the thin man appeared to be a slippery and devious individual.

He'd expected his father to be stronger due to his youthful appearance, and though Edward struggled briefly, he ultimately gave up due to his son's superior physique. Though looking only slightly less fit than himself, Edward seemed only to have the strength of an elderly man. This apparent physical weakness would explain the need for beefy bodyguards constantly nearby for protection. Nodding toward Schreck, he said to Simon, "Check our friend there for accessories, will you, big guy?"

"What are you doing? Let me go, Simon!" Schreck struggled briefly, but resistance was futile since the man holding him was impossibly strong.

"Sorry, Boss, I've had about enough of you." With his boulder-like bicep able to crush the thin man to death with a single flex, Simon kept one massive arm around Schreck as he began the shakedown. He removed several items of interest from Max's person, seeming to know just where to look. Brass knuckles bulged in one pants pocket, a stiletto hid in the other, a fully loaded syringe lay stashed in his suit jacket, and a spring-loaded derringer was strapped to one wrist.

"My, but you do come prepared, don't you?" Lively said to Schreck as Simon removed the handgun. "Were you ever a

Boy Scout?

A vicious gleam in his eyes, Schreck said, "I like to be prepared for all contingencies."

"Oh, I'm sure you do," Ricky Rosenstein said, emerging from the control room. He pushed the wheeled office chair in front of himself. Kandi, her head lolling back and forth, sat unconscious in its seat. With a slight shove, Ricky pushed the chair into the room, and Kandi spun around several times before coming to a rest next to the embalming table.

A flash of anger streaked across Schreck's face, and he said, "What have you done to her?"

Rosenstein said calmly, "Nurse Kandi is on a short sabbatical from consciousness right now and won't be able to verbalise anything for a little while."

"You'll rue this day if you've hurt her in any way," Schreck said coldly.

"Oh, trust me, I rue this day already. She's fine don't worry. But while she's gone, maybe you could tell us a little more about the plans you two had for Edward, which I overheard you discussing just a little while ago." Rosenstein gave Kandi another spin for emphasis. "What do you say, Maxi?"

His eyes wide with surprise at this revelation, Sinclair looked from Rosenstein to the thin man and said, "Maxi? Plans? What's going on, Schreck?"

Lively watched this play out with some bemusement. It seemed a double-cross was occurring between his father and his henchman, and Ricky had stumbled upon it during his explorations. He was impressed at Rosenstein's newfound bravado and let things play out for the moment, taking it all in.

"He doesn't know what he's talking about, Edward," Schreck said in a placating voice.

Ricky shook his head while looking at Lively and Edward, then said to Schreck, "Oh, I overheard you both quite clearly. After you'd finished checking each other's tonsils, you said, and I'm paraphrasing slightly, 'After tonight, Edward's ego isn't going to be a problem anymore'."

"What?" Sinclair's eyes drilled into Schreck with shock and indignation.

"Don't listen to him, Edward. You know I'd never betray your trust," Schreck said defensively.

"It's true, Mr. DeMille," Rosenstein said, looking at Lively with sincere, puppy dog eyes.

Lively didn't doubt the little computer man, but he wanted to set a few other things straight before he got into that can of worms. He nodded toward Schreck, saying, "We'll get to that shortly. In the meantime, could you press his mute button, please, Simon?" He nodded to Max, still firmly clasped in the strongman's arms.

Schreck struggled ineffectually for a moment, then the blonde giant changed up his grip and slapped one of his oversized hands across the thin man's mouth.

Edward's eyes burned in anger at this disclosure of Schreck's treachery, and he said, "Really, Max? After all these years?" He shook his head sadly, then tried to look over his shoulder to Lively, who still held him from behind. His demeanour changed in a flash from anger to open-eyed innocence, and he said, "Son, what's going on? Why are you doing this?"

Lively laughed, saying, "Why am I doing this? Self-defence, mostly. I don't really enjoy being strapped to embalming tables against my will." He pointed Sinclair toward the table, still holding him tightly from behind. It was not that he expected the man to be any danger, physically, but he didn't want to allow him too much freedom until he could establish Edward's part in things.

"What do you mean?" Sinclair asked, acting surprised.

"I mean, why did you drug Selene and me?"

"It's not how it looks," Edward equivocated.

"Really? Well, I think it looks pretty suspicious. But why don't you go ahead and tell me how it's supposed to look."

"I only wanted you to become part of this, Son. You and your sister."

"What do you mean? I thought you said I was going to be part of the Sinclair empire already."

"Well, you were, but just not in the way you'd anticipated."

Ricky stood on his tip-toes, reached up to the machine over the embalming table and opened the panel in the side. He pointed, saying, "I don't know what this thing is, Mr. DeMille, but it's part of what's going on down here. I saw Kandi put it inside." He reached in to take the black gemstone out of the machine.

"Don't touch it!" Lively said with alarm.

Jerking his hand away, Ricky asked, "Why? What's wrong?"

"That's good advice; you might want to listen to him," Edward said.

Giving his dad a small shake, Lively said, "What was that stone for?"

"Something to facilitate your becoming part of things like I promised. You and your sister are far more special than you can ever imagine. Just the very fact that you're here is amazing!"

"You still haven't told me what you were going to do with your contraption there?"

With a small sigh, Edward said, "As you know, the human brain is similar to a computer, with electrical impulses travelling throughout the body to regulate everything from our thoughts to our breathing and even our very heartbeat." He squirmed in Lively's grasp a moment and then continued. "However, we've found that some individuals shine brighter than others, metaphysically speaking, that is. And you and your sister are two such individuals. Utilising that gemstone your little friend pointed out, you were going to be brought completely into this frequency at midnight tonight."

"But I'm already here."

"No, you wouldn't exist in your physical body in the same way as you do now. Instead, your life force would be there, inside of that." He looked to the obsidian gemstone in the machine over the embalming table.

"What?" Lively felt stunned. He had just come within a heartbeat or two of ceasing to exist. "How could you do that to me?"

"I wasn't doing it 'to you'," Edward said, his voice dripping with condescension, "I was doing it 'for you' and for the benefit of the Sinclair empire."

"And what about Minerva?"

"As I said, you're both very special. Once you'd been processed, your sister was going to join us here and become part of things too. With the power inside both of you, we would have the ability to bring our little experiment to the next level, not only in this frequency but in the infinite frequencies beyond. Then the universe would see what we could accomplish with almost unlimited power!"

With his father going off on an egomaniacal tangent at the moment, Lively said, "Regular masters of the universe, aren't you?" He shook his head, then asked, "What about all the other people in the ballroom? Is that what happened to them, too?"

"Yes, but on a much larger scale. Apart from an elite few, the essence of almost everyone in this frequency has been stored inside those obsidian stones. Though their corporeal being still exists, most of them are now more like automatons than people. However, their energy pales compared to what we could accomplish with you and your sister."

Lively shook his head in disgust and said, "Okay, that's enough for now." He wondered if his father had run any of this 'ruling the multiverse' concept by Selene, and he doubted it. Most megalomaniacs figured everybody was always on board with whatever their little scheme might be, so self-assured as they were of their own superiority.

Releasing his hold on Edward ever so slightly, Lively gave him a quick frisk, looking for items he might use as a weapon. It wasn't that he expected his father to be carrying a switchblade or pistol like Schreck but knowing the history of drug use around the resort, he'd decided he could never be too careful. Reaching into Edward's jacket pockets, Lively felt something familiar and pulled out a pair of syringes and two glass vials. He held them up in front of Edward's face, saying, "Well, well. Like father like son. Going to use this on me if the drugged drink failed?"

Sinclair only shrugged, saying nothing more.

Before Edward and Schreck appeared, Lively found enough time to get his shirt and jacket back on. However, he'd now dispensed entirely with his bow tie at this point. Thanks to his time in the armed forces and then in CSIS, Lively had learned quickly that in hand-to-hand combat, anything grabbable, like a tie already strung around your neck, could give your opponent a surprising advantage, which was not a good thing. And when he'd been required to wear a tie during his time at CSIS, it had always been a clip-on for that reason. Taking Edward's vials, Lively placed them into his suit jacket pocket where his bow tie now resided.

Her head drooping to one side of the chair, Kandi began to come back to consciousness with a snort. She shook her head groggily, then sucked back a string of saliva dripping down the side of her face. Trying to stand, she discovered she couldn't and said dreamily, "Wha... What's going on?"

Simon had provided Ricky with a roll of duct tape. As he'd buttoned his shirt, Lively had watched Rosenstein take quiet pleasure in making sure that the woman was firmly taped into the wheeled chair with no chance of escape.

Giving her head another shake, Kandi blinked her eyes a few times, then looked over to see Simon holding Schreck and said, "Maxi! What's going on? Did you..." She trailed off, finally seeming to realise the gravity of her situation. With a swivel of the chair, she turned to see Ricky standing nearby and said, "You! You little piece of—"

Rosenstein had moved near Kandi as she'd regained her wits. He had a strip already torn off the roll of duct tape, and he plastered it across Kandi's shiny red lips with obvious delight, saying, "Sticks and stones."

With Kandi muted, Lively said, "Thanks, Ricky." He turned to Edward and asked, "Is there anything else you haven't told me?"

Edward appeared reluctant to speak at first, and Lively gave one of his arms a twist of encouragement. "Ah! Stop it! Yes, I'll talk."

Nodding slightly, Lively said, "Go ahead then, spill it."

"As I told you, you don't know how powerful you truly are." His voice swelled with pride as he added, "But thanks to the work Max and I did, both of you were destined for greatness at a very young age."

"What work?"

"I mean, Max and I helped you along, unbeknownst to Selene."

"And speaking of which, where is Selene right now?"

"Your mother is safe, for the moment," Edward replied, his voice low and threatening.

Lively gave another small twist of Edward's arms and said, "Safe? Safe where?"

"Let's just say, if you ever want to see her alive again, you'll let me go."

Lively was torn. He didn't want to let Edward do something that would further jeopardise either himself, anyone close to him, or any of the partygoers. Reluctantly, he released his grip on Sinclair and stepped back, but only a pace. Turning to Simon, who was still holding Schreck, he said, "Hold onto that slippery little snake for a little while longer, would you?"

Simon nodded in understanding, his face grim. Giving Schreck an uncomfortable-looking squeeze, he said, "My pleasure."

Lively turned back to his father, his brow furrowed in anger, saying, "How did you 'help us along'?"

A frown on his face, Edward attempted to brush the wrinkles out of his suit jacket's sleeves caused by Lively's manhandling of his person. Tearing himself away from his self-grooming, he said, "Some of my other studies in university, apart from physics and architecture, were human physiology and genetics. Thanks to Max's assistance and our experimentation on various subjects over the years, we developed several different gene therapies."

Lively wondered if the 'various subjects' had been volunteers or shanghaied into doing so. "Okay, good for you. And did you win a Nobel Prize?"

"Hardly. But one of the more successful gene therapy procedures we developed was implemented on you and your sister while you were still in your mother's womb."

CHAPTER TWENTY-NINE

December 31st, 2021 1646 hours

Thanks to the wide-angled view of the camera lenses on the GoPros, each of the taxidermied animals were posed, filling their respective frames in full, high-definition glory. Amanda Jansen's eyes ticked from one to the next to the first and back around as she tried to keep all of the animals in view simultaneously within the app.

Despite this electronic view, Amanda couldn't resist the odd glance up to the real deal every now and again to ensure that these creatures' electronic representations weren't lying to her. She adjusted the sword resting on her shoulder and stole another glance up from the tablet to the gorilla across the room. It was then that her first problem reared its ugly head.

A scratching sound, like claws on stone near the Ms. Pac-Man machine. Out of reflex, Jansen's head whipped over to the cat, and her heart jumped into her throat. Though still crouched, now, its head was up, like it was peering over the tall grass of the Serengeti, and it only had eyes for her. She whipped her eyes back to the iPad and saw that the tiger's pose on the screen matched what she'd just seen with her own wide-open eyes.

"No, no, no," Amanda said, shaking her head slowly back and forth, not wanting to believe what she was seeing was real. Keeping her gaze locked to the tablet, she scanned from camera to camera to camera. To her dismay, she saw that things had changed with the other animals as well, and suddenly all she could hear was her own elevated heartbeat.

In its window on the tablet, the gorilla no longer pounded its chest and instead stood on its knuckles, glaring in her direction. Next to the towering polar predator, she saw herself looking concerned as she studied the tablet at the bottom of the stairs. The bear's head was now angled slightly down and toward her, its razor teeth gleaming as it snarled in frozen rage. She brought the sword down from her shoulder, backed up a couple of steps into the stairwell, and then rested the sword's tip on the stone steps. She felt more than just a little uncomfortable at being so close to the menacing creature.

The GoPros were relaying everything exactly as they should to her eyes; she knew that now without a doubt. And yet, once more, Amanda felt an overwhelming urge to look at the Siberian tiger, unable to stop the reflexive nature of her inbred human survival instinct that wanted to see the actual predator in the room with her and not its image on a small screen. And so, without even thinking of it, she glanced at the cat again.

The tiger was low on its haunches, its muscles taut as steel cables. They seemed to ripple ever-so-slightly through its Halloween-coloured fur as if the beast were straining to contain its powerful pounce.

Jansen backed up the stairs another pace. As she stepped onto the next riser, the sword Minerva had given her tangled in one of her bootlaces. Amanda stumbled slightly, almost losing her balance and dropping the iPad. Fortunately, she stayed upright and avoided damaging the expensive tablet. However, the distraction had given the trio of taxidermied terror the brief moment they needed to further their advance, and she shrieked aloud when she looked to the tablet once more.

The gorilla seemed ready to push off its knuckles in a full-tilt charge across the room. And her orange and black nemesis was poised at the beginning of a mighty launch into the air.

A sudden noise above Amanda's head caused her to look up with a start from the tablet, and her lungs suddenly seemed incapable of drawing another breath. The polar bear had turned its body toward the stairs. One massive paw was clawed into the stone wall as the creature began to drag itself around the corner to get to her. Small fragments of stone trickled down from furrows gouged into the wall by its claws. The razor talons seemed to quiver ever so slightly as if readying to lash out and slash into her soft body and rend her flesh from her bones.

Amanda put the tablet into her shoulder bag and then held the sword up in both hands in front of her face, ready to swing at anything that got too close. Slowly retreating up the stairs, her eyes were laser-focused on the entrance to the staircase below. She continued to back up around the curving corner, and eventually, the bottom of the stairs and the predators wound out of sight.

Drawing a quick breath, she turned and fled, her snow-booted feet slapping on the stone steps as she sprinted up the hard, stone stairs. Up and up and up, she ran. How far was this model room anyway? She didn't recall there ever being so many steps when she'd been up here four decades before. They seemed to go on forever and ever, and after a few moments, her lungs burned for air, and it felt like her heart was going to explode in her chest, yet still she ran. Even without the tablet, she could tell that the animals were still coming for her—she could hear their paws and claws quite clearly as they scrambled up the stairs behind her.

***

John had felt his heart begin to beat faster and faster in his chest as he'd ascended the stairs to the model room. He knew that part of it was the exercise, but part of it was also anxiety. He hadn't been up here since the day Jansen had found him at the bottom of the staircase with a broken hip and multiple contusions.

It seemed doubtful that Minerva's plan with Amanda monitoring the cameras would work, but they had to try something. John knew all too well that despite seeing something relayed by camera, the human urge to see things with their own eyes was powerful, and he wondered how Amanda was faring below.

Arriving at the top of the stairs just now, flashes of his younger self shot through his mind. Memories of the day after the disappearance in the ballroom. Suddenly, he saw himself standing near the ballroom's mahogany bar. Then he was on the winding stairs, his hands numb from the cold as he carried the ebony box up to the top of the turret. And then a final image came to him of his arms, illuminated by the sickly yellow light from inside the model as he inserted the ebony box into its last resting place. He'd been unable to recall any of that until this very moment when he finally arrived at the top of the spiral stone staircase with Minerva. And now, he wished he hadn't.

"Are you okay, John?" Minerva asked.

With a deep breath, Harder said, "Sort of. I just recalled something. It was me who carried the ebony box up to this room forty years ago. Something compelled me to do it. I suffered some sort of fugue state, and I never recalled doing so until now, and I have no idea why I did it."

Minerva replied, "Because of the same reason anybody does anything around here. Something in this place just seems to get inside your head, and it messes with you big time. But with that said, this is good news in a way. It means we know for sure that you're the person best qualified to remove the ebony box."

"Hooray for me," John said.

The model room door was standing wide-open, and Minerva ushered John inside. The spotlights were still turned on and illuminated the miniature Sinclair in a harsh light, accentuating its rough surfaces and sharp angles.

"There's a catch somewhere near the eaves, according to Lively," Minerva said, placing the silver serving tray on the edge of the rooftop parapets.

"Does anything about this seem familiar, John?"

A flash of black fur and excruciating pain jolted through John's mind as he took in the room and the sizeable model in its centre. "Yeah, all of a sudden, it's all too familiar."

Minerva put on the gloves that Lively had left behind, then felt along the edge of the roofline, looking for the hidden release. After a moment, she said, "Ah, there you are." There was a soft click, and she began to push the model's halves apart. "I'd left this wide open when I was last here after I found the tiger sitting between the halves. I presumed by closing the door that I'd secured the cat inside this room, and I don't know how it got out or how the model got closed."

John thought he could imagine exactly how it got closed and the cat out of the room. In his mind's eye, he saw the gorilla climbing the stairs to the model room to let its companion out and then close the model up again. "It certainly seems that this hotel doesn't want us to remove its heart," John said.

"Interesting you should call it that." Minerva pushed the

model halves apart to reveal the topic of their conversation. The metal shield was still hanging open, exposing the ebony box like a cancerous tumour in the centre of the miniature Sinclair. She didn't approach the box but stood near the periphery of its influence outside the model. Picking up the fallen hand towels from before, she placed them on the model's roof, saying, "Whatever happened here forty years ago, this ebony box has been influencing everything around this hotel ever since."

"Exactly. Like that event somehow gave life to the thing." John said gravely. "And like any living thing, it will utilise anything it can for its own protection and survival."

Through the partially open doorway at their back came the clamour of booted feet rapidly climbing the stairs. John stepped away from the door, and Minerva spun around just as Amanda Jansen came flying into the room. Still holding the sword in one hand, she grabbed the door's edge with the other and slammed it shut just as something heavy crashed against the other side. The door had a lock, and she engaged the mechanism with trembling fingers.

Almost immediately, the sound of claws gouging into the wood came from the other side of the door as the bear, or the tiger, or perhaps both tried to shred their way through the thick oak.

Shaking her head back and forth in denial of what was happening, Jansen backed away from the door, her eyes like saucers.

If someone had told John three months ago that he would be back in this hotel experiencing its horrors anew, he would never have believed them. And yet here he now was, not only in the hotel but the very model room where his experiences with the Sinclair had ended four decades before. In a strained voice, he said, "My God. This is madness."

"You won't get any argument from me," Minerva said, looking urgently about the room at the same time.

The scratching stopped suddenly, and all three were ready to breathe a sigh of relief. But after just a moment, they watched in renewed horror as the doorknob began to wiggle back and forth just slightly, as something on the other side, presumably the ape, tried to turn the door handle.

"Thank goodness I locked it," Amanda said in a shaky voice. As the words came out of her mouth, deafening pounding came from the other side of the door as the great ape began to batter relentlessly against the thick wood. Jansen backed further into the room and dropped the sword with a clatter, then pulled out her Smith and Wesson and aimed it at the door.

With each resounding blow, small puffs of dust came from the edges of the doorframe near the hinges as the aged steel screws began loosening their grip from the ancient stone walls.

CHAPTER THIRTY

December 31st, 1981 2316 hours

"So let me get this straight." Lively grabbed Edward by his jacket's lapels and pulled him close. Despite his father's threat concerning Selene, he felt his emotions getting the better of him once again. "You used some sort of genetic manipulation on both of us before we were even born? How could you do that!"

Edward looked at his son in surprise and said, "It wasn't what we did to you; it's what we enhanced within you! We made you the best you can be." There was a wide and wild look, and he finished saying breathlessly, "And look how well you turned out! Haven't you ever wondered how it was that you and your sister were so gifted?"

"Luck of the draw, I guess." Shaking his head in disgust, he released his grasp on Edward.

Flattening down his lapels, Sinclair said, "Hardly. It was through years of research and sacrifice that your abilities and those of your sister were imbued within you." He nodded toward Schreck, adding, "As you know, I hired Max to work for me after the war."

Unable to corroborate anything, the man in black merely glowered at Edward. Having received a piece of duct tape from the roll Ricky was holding, Simon had stuck it across Schreck's distorted dental work in lieu of his hand. The bodyguard now held his captive with both enormous arms wrapped tightly about him as if they were now inseparable BFFs.

Edward continued, "His work went a long way in assisting our little endeavour, bringing along a great quantity of information that he'd gleaned from his experiments in some of the treatment groups he assembled during the war."

"Treatment groups during the war? It sounds like you mean prison camps." Lively nodded to Simon to uncover Schreck's mouth, saying, "Want to clarify things, Max?"

A small smile playing at the corners of Simon's lips, he ripped the duct tape from Schreck's mouth but kept one hand on the thin man's shoulder, ready to reel him back into his vice-like grasp if need be.

Schreck didn't say anything for a moment and merely scowled as he rubbed his face where the tape had been. Lively nodded, and Simon gave the man's shoulder a good, hard squeeze.

"Ah! Stop! I'll talk, I'll talk. Yes, prison camps. We did studies on various genetic modification techniques through several groups that I'd put together. We'd just arrived at a promising in vitro method, but unfortunately, we had to stop our testing at that point when the war ended."

Ricky's eyes narrowed at this news, and he began advancing on Schreck. "It was you, wasn't it!"

"Me?" Schreck asked, surprised by Rosenstein's vehemence.

"You! At her prison camp—at Auschwitz! She said a 'doctor' came by every few weeks. He toured the camp, looking for subjects for his tests. Both of her sisters and her only brother were taken away and never seen again after he did his 'tests' on them! I remember she said he was very tall and thin, dressed in black, and always very polite, and everyone he chose seemed to go willingly with him when he took them away."

With a wicked smile, Schreck confirmed the charges against him, saying, "That was me, yes."

"You piece of filth! Garbage! Animal!" Ricky began moving threateningly toward Schreck, the empty hypodermic he'd used on Kandi held high in the air as if ready to plunge it repeatedly into Schreck's black heart.

Lively saw where this was going and called out, "Ricky! Stand down!"

Ricky continued forward for a brief moment, then halted, breathing heavily as he held himself in check. He brought the syringe back to his side and asked in a low and threatening voice, "What did you do to my aunt and uncle?"

"Suffice it to say, everything they endured was for the greater good."

"The greater good?" Rosenstein almost shrieked the phrase and began to advance once more.

"Ricky," Lively said again. He spoke calmly, but there was something in the way he said it that seemed to get past the anger clouding Rosenstein's mind, and the small man stopped once more and looked to Lively, who said, "Just relax for a minute, my friend. We'll deal with all that in good time. But let me finish things here first, okay?"

Rosenstein nodded and said, "Yeah, sorry, Mr. DeMille.

It's just that my mom told me tales of her life during that time. And though I never witnessed some of the horrors she described, I feel like I lived them through her stories. Now, to see someone in front of me that caused my mother so much anguish and so many nightmares throughout her life, I just got a little swept up."

"Completely understandable. Just give me a moment here, and we'll figure out something appropriate for Mr. Schreck." Lively nodded to Simon, and the bodyguard reapplied Schreck's dental tape once again.

Turning his attention back to his father, Lively reached out and grabbed the man's lapels and pulled him close. Although he'd talked Ricky down just now, he felt his own pent-up emotions still threatening to boil over. "Everything you and Schreck learned came at the expense of untold suffering and loss of human life, and then you went ahead and applied this knowledge to the unborn fetuses of your very own children?" He punctuated the word children by shaking Sinclair so hard his teeth chattered like castanets.

"But it wasn't just you! I experimented on myself as well. There were other gene therapies we discovered, including some that affected the ageing process through AMPK gene manipulation."

Not only had the man before him altered the very fabric of his children's being for his own research and gain, but he'd experimented on himself as well, and also shown absolute disregard toward their mother in the process. Lively was emotionally untethered, unsure how to feel, except for the anger; that was something he could latch onto big time right now. His eyes burned into the man who'd kept them under the constant gaze of two imposters as they'd grown up, and then continued this surveillance long after they'd left home and made their way into the world—two guinea pigs in a madman's science experiment. And the icing on top of this layer cake of duplicity and deception was the fact that the madman was their very own father.

With a deep breath, Lively lowered Sinclair down from the tiptoes the man had been standing on while he'd held him close. Losing control right now wouldn't help the current situation in any way, Lively knew. He needed to figure out where to go from here. Throwing his father up against the wall and beating him senseless for his aiding and abetting crimes against humanity was a very strong urge but one he knew he must ultimately fight, for now. He had Minerva to think of, and Selene as well, of course. Edward was holding his mother captive somewhere in this hotel, and he couldn't incapacitate the man in any way until he was able to locate her.

Lively patted down the lapels on Edward's tuxedo jacket and said in a slightly ragged voice, "Okay, what do you propose? Bear in mind, you and I still need to work things out when we're done." As he finished, he glanced to the elaborate machine over the embalming table containing the obsidian stone.

Edward's eyes ticked from Lively to the machine and back, and he said, "Quite." Craning his neck slightly to look up at Simon, a slight pucker to his lips, he asked, "Since we might need the assistance, I need to ask what you've done with the other Simon?"

"Oh, he's stretched out on a cart in the other room, though he won't be much good to anyone for the rest of the night after that rhino-sized dose of ketamine Mr. DeMille pumped into him."

Edward turned back to Lively and said, "Really, I do wish you'd stop drugging my staff, Son."

"I'll see what I can do." Lively nodded his head toward the duct-taped dominatrix and asked, "What about nursie there?"

Sinclair tsk-tsked and shook his head slightly. In a troubled voice, he said, "Kandi, Kandi, Kandi, what happened? You've been a trusted associate in this little venture over the years, just as much as Max—even longer, in fact." He gave a small sigh, then added, "But sadly, because of your complicity in things, now I need to decide what to do with you." He propped one elbow on his forearm and rested his chin on his closed fist as if considering his options. "You do have some medical training and those computer skills are a bonus. I'd hate to lose those abilities if I were to banish you with Max."

Kandi wriggled in the chair at the mention of banishment, and Lively said, "Could you take the tape off her mouth for a moment, Ricky?"

Rosenstein said, "With pleasure," and ripped the tape from her lips, glossy red lipstick and all.

Wincing from the pain, Kandi said, "It wasn't my idea!"

"Oh, I'm sure it wasn't," Edward said. "However, it does bring one question to the forefront of the conversation, and that is: what sort of subterfuge did you two have planned?"

Nodding her head toward Lively, her eyes glistening with the slightest hint of crazy, Kandi said, "What do you think? We wanted all their power for ourselves! Your focus is so narrow, you would have wasted it!"

His eyebrows raised in surprise, Edward said, "Well now, that certainly helps make my decision easier." He moved to the chair to which Kandi was taped and removed the golden bracelet from her wrist, saying, "Let's just have you forget this treachery and still retain your services. I'll banish Max instead; how's that sound for a deal?"

Schreck said nothing, the duct tape over his mouth doing its job, but his eyes spoke volumes and burned into Edward.

In a voice on the verge of tears, Kandi said, "Please, Edward, don't make me one of the forgotten. Remember, it's like you said, I can help you with the mainframe." Her eyes widened suddenly, and she added, "And I didn't tell you, something's happened to the program for tonight! I think the code's been altered, and it needs a password to proceed with the realignment. I think it was the little computer man who screwed with it!"

Edward's eyes flashed to Ricky, and he said, "You did what?"

Ricky crossed his arms and nodded, saying, "Yes, I've set your little realignment programme at midnight tonight on pause, and I also locked you out of it."

"What? You can't do that! No one knows what will happen!" Edward said.

"Give Mr. DeMille his mom back, and then we'll talk, but not until then."

Shaking his head, Edward said, "I don't know where she is."

Now it was Lively's turn to be surprised. "What, did you lose her or something?" He stepped toward Edward, his hands feeling the need to rattle some more teeth if his father didn't talk.

Backing up a step, Edward said, "Hardly. I had Max take care of her new temporary accommodations, and only he knows where she is." He shook his head sadly and added, "You're going to have to talk to him directly."

Lively turned to Schreck and said, "All right, what's your angle?" With a nod to Simon, the big man ripped the tape from Schreck's lips.

A smug little smile formed on the thin man's lips as he gave them a rub with one gloved hand, saying, "My angle? Why, I still want to have your power for myself, Mr. DeMille, but that doesn't seem to be a viable option at this point in time." He seemed to mull things over for a moment, then said, "Tell you what, once Selene is back, you can give me Kandi, then she and I will banish ourselves to a subfrequency of our choosing."

"I'll tell you what; when I get my mom back, then we'll talk. In the meantime, you just tell Simon where you stashed her in the hotel, and he'll go and get her."

Schreck shook his head, saying, "It's a little more complicated than that."

"How so?"

"Because she's no longer here in this hotel, or this reality."

CHAPTER THIRTY-ONE

December 31st, 2021 1655 hours

The pounding on the door continued unabated, the screws now so loose, the hinge plates rattled in the doorframe. Amanda Jansen stood to one side of the entrance, her .38 trained on the door. She called out, "I kept this after we'd upgraded—just for nostalgia's sake, and now I'm glad I did."

"Maybe you won't need to use it. I think I have an idea," Minerva said, then moved back to the model and peered intently inside for a moment.

With a grunt, John bent down and picked up the fallen sword. He held it up with some effort, his eighty-eight-year-old muscles struggling with the weight of a weapon ten times their age. Glancing at Minerva, he said, "Whatever you do, you'd better make it quick."

Minerva looked frantically about the interior of the miniature hotel. Three tiny animals stood in the turret, just outside the model room door. On one side was the tiger, the polar bear on the other. In the middle stood the ape, its tiny fists resting against the door in mid-pound. Minerva frowned and said, "Let's try something." Using the tips of her crimson-coloured fingernails, she tweezed the minuscule figure of the ape between her fingers and picked it up.

The pounding outside the door ceased almost immediately. A small smile played across Minerva's lips as she said, "Let's see if you can swim." She placed the small ape onto the surface of the model's swimming pool and then turned her attention back to the other tiny animals at the turret door.

The mini polar bear was now in front of the model's door, and from the other side of the real door, great rending scratches sounded as the arctic beast tried to tear its way through the thick wood.

Tweezing the bear by its head, Minerva picked it up and placed it on top of the pool's surface next to the ape, and the scratching stopped immediately. She turned her attention back to the miniature model room door, ready to grab the tiger, but it had disappeared, perhaps sensing it might be next.

Silence now filled the room. All three stood looking to the other, their eyes wide and disbelieving as to what had just happened.

"That was inspired," Amanda said shakily. "I would never have thought of that."

"Thanks," Minerva replied, smiling weakly, then added, "From what I'd observed, the little figurines inside the model sometimes represented what's happening in the actual hotel, so I thought it might be worth a try."

With an appreciative nod, John said, "Your intuition may have just saved all our lives."

"I'm just glad it worked out," Minerva said as she moved to the door. She was curious if the large, stuffed cat was actually gone from the other side. She reached into Lively's courier bag and removed the endoscopic camera. Turning it on, she fed the fibre optic lens cable under the door. The coast seemed clear, and she coiled the camera cable up as she stood again.

Taking her sword from John, just in case, Minerva popped the lock and slowly turned the handle, creaking the door open. The cat really was gone. At least, there was no sight of it anywhere on the landing or down the portion of the spiralling staircase that she could see. But despite this apparent good news, she knew they'd have to be on their guard once they got the ebony box out of the model.

"But where did the tiger go," John wondered.

"Somewhere to lay in wait for us when we're least expecting it, no doubt," Amanda said, shaking her head at the thought. She opened her revolver and checked the ammunition inside the cylinder, then snapped it shut with a click and gave the cylinder a spin. Placing it back in her shoulder bag, she said, "Well, at least we're somewhat prepared for other eventualities."

With a slight shake of his head, John said, "I don't know how much good that might do against things that aren't alive."

"Well, I loaded it with hollow-point cartridges."

John nodded approvingly. "That's good. Maybe it can at least put a good-sized hole in something if need be and help slow it down," He held up his cane, adding, "I use this for traction when I'm out in the snow and ice at this time of year, but it might also come in handy right about now." With the press of a button beneath the handle's grip, a two-inch spike sprang from the cane's non-slip tip.

Minerva said with a slight smile, "I like that. You get right to the point." She closed the door to the stairs and moved back to the model, saying, "Okay, Amanda, here's the deal. Through previous experience, I know I can't touch this box even with gloves on without getting overloaded with sensations."

"Okay..." Amanda looked at Minerva doubtfully. "And?"

"And as you know, I was going to have John remove it, but he's a little unsteady on his feet already, and I don't know how heavy the box might be. But either way, I really don't think John will be able to walk and hold it at the same time, especially down those two flights of spiral stairs."

"I agree," John said with a slight nod. He moved next to Minerva to get a better look at the ebony box.

Minerva continued, saying to Amanda, "So, I think since you're here, you might be the better candidate to carry the box, and hopefully be unaffected by it. Once we get it down the stairs to the bottom of the turret, we can put it on that serving cart. Then, we can wheel it to the elevator and roll it right into the ballroom." She picked up the gloves and handed them to Amanda with an encouraging smile.

Sighing reluctantly, Amanda took the gloves and pulled them on, wriggling her fingers as she did, trying to adjust the oversized glove to better fit her smaller hand.

Minerva gently patted Amanda on the arm and said, "Just take it slow and easy. Tell me if you feel anything as you get closer, okay?"

Amanda said nothing and merely nodded. Minerva figured she was probably mentally steeling herself to touch the box.

John said to Minerva, "I'll let you monitor Amanda. I'll take the lead down the stairs and keep an eye out for that tiger. I have this if I need it." He held up the cane, its steel spike shining brilliantly in the room's high-intensity spotlights.

"Okay, thanks, John. Are you sure you'll be okay?" Minerva asked, concerned.

"I have no choice," he replied with finality and moved toward the door to stand guard.

***

Amanda tensed herself as she approached the ebony box. She only had a vague remembrance of seeing it on the first day of the investigation, and it had disappeared after that. Minerva grabbed the hand towels from the model's roof and handed them to Amanda to give her extra insulation against the cold of the box.

The gloves on her hands were cumbersome. Despite the thickness of the leather and its shearling lining, her hands felt cold as she approached the box, and she wondered what would happen upon touching it. Hopefully, it would feel like nothing more than pulling a Christmas turkey from her freezer at home to thaw, and then she'd have it on the cart downstairs in no time. Taking a breath, she reached into the model and placed a towel on both sides of the box. As soon as she made contact, her hopes were proved incorrect.

Minerva kept an eye on John near the door as well as what was happening with Amanda, her attention torn. However, as soon as Jansen touched the box, it became undivided.

Amanda stiffened as if electrified, her breath coming in short gasps. Slight wisps of vapour flowed from between her parted lips, the air around the box suddenly freezing. Though not having any visions from touching it, she felt overwhelmed, nonetheless. She was happy, sad, scared, angry, and almost every other emotion she could think of, all at the same time, and she felt smothered by the intensity of the experience.

Minerva asked, "Are you okay?"

Jansen didn't respond for the longest moment, then finally said in a soft inflectionless voice, "I think so. I'm being bombarded by emotions, and my hands are tingling from the cold already."

"Do you still think you can carry it down the stairs?"

"Like John said, I have no choice. So here goes nothing."

Amanda was just about to pull the box free, and Minerva said, "One other thing!"

Jansen paused and withdrew her hands, jolting slightly from the shock of Minerva's excited voice and asked, "What is it?"

"I think it would be best if you try not to tip it or jar it in any way."

"I'll do what I can." Now feeling as if she were handling a potentially unexploded bomb, Amanda took a deep breath, reached inside the model once again and began to pull the ebony box from its decades-long perch.

CHAPTER THIRTY-TWO

December 31ˢᵗ, 2021 2325 hours

Ricky Rosenstein's mission of the moment was to check for any further messages from Minerva on his Atari 800 and also try to communicate to her what had happened. He trailed a short distance behind Simon and Schreck, currently on their way to retrieve Selene from wherever the Bowler Man had secreted her. Max was in the lead as they moved down the third-floor corridor, Simon following close at his heels and watching his every move. The thin man in black couldn't be trusted to bring Selene back unsupervised, so Simon had volunteered to go with the man and keep an eye on him.

DeMille was currently in the control room overseeing Edward and Kandi to ensure the pair didn't try to override the patch he'd installed, not until Selene was brought back at least.

Ricky had departed the basement at the same time as Simon and had asked the bodyguard if he could tag along since he was going that way anyway. He'd also mentioned he'd like to see the Harmoniser in action, if possible. The big man had agreed and now they were almost to the royal suite and Ricky couldn't be more excited—he felt like a kid at Hanukkah. Though only given a brief description of the

Harmoniser and its capabilities so far, his brain had been set alight with curiosity, and he hoped to get a chance to check the machine out a little bit while Simon was preparing for departure.

All of this excitement to see new and exciting technology first-hand came with a caveat, of course; he'd have to be on his toes and paying attention at all times. He was fairly sure if given the opportunity, Schreck would try to slip out of this situation faster than a slice of his beloved mother's chocolate babka slipped into his own stomach. In fact, thinking now of his mother, Ricky knew she would be getting one heck of a mother's day gift if he ever got out of this, and if she were still alive, that was.

Entering the royal suite, Schreck stayed in the lead, with Simon and Ricky following the thin man into the bedroom and ensuite washroom beyond. He marvelled at the size of the bathroom when he entered. It was so much larger than his own! Despite that, he thought it seemed strange to have something as ground-breaking as the Harmoniser located within any bathroom, no matter how luxurious it was. But then again, despite his brilliance, one of the people attributed to the machine's creation, now standing near the room's royal throne, was himself an incredible turd. And so, the Harmoniser's location, he realised, seemed quite appropriate after all.

"Okay, you," Simon pointed to Schreck and then over to the toilet. "Sit. There."

"What? You want me to sit there?" Schreck asked, looking at the porcelain throne with distaste.

Tilting his head, Simon asked, "Wasn't I clear enough just now?"

"If you ever want to be able to sit again, you might want to do what the man says," Ricky interjected.

Nodding, Simon said, "I'd listen to the little guy. He's pretty smart." The big man folded his arms and looked from Schreck to the commode.

With a sigh, Max sat and said, "Oh, very well. But I still need to punch the coordinates for Selene's frequency into the Harmoniser."

Shaking his head, Simon said, "No, you don't. You can relay them to me, and I'll punch them in when we're ready to leave." Turning to Ricky, Simon added, "And you can keep an eye on him in the meantime, little guy."

And with that, Ricky was left guarding Max Schreck. He found himself torn between trying to keep an eye on the Bowler Man and trying to watch what Simon was doing at the same time.

Acting as if what he was doing were nothing out of the ordinary, the muscular man twisted the faucet around one hundred and eighty degrees and pressed the plunger down. The tub lowered smoothly into the platform, and the metal cover slid out over the top.

Ricky couldn't help himself and gawked in awe, saying, "Okay, that is seriously cool."

"Thank you," Schreck said from his place on the throne.

Jolting back to the task at hand, Ricky looked back to the thin man and said, "Don't go trying any of your Jedi mind tricks on me."

"Whatever are you talking about?"

"I've seen how people around the hotel here seem to cooperate with you no matter what. Just like when you proposed that in-room smorg to me."

"Ah, yes, the smorg has proven to be a popular programme." Smiling thinly as he regarded Ricky, he added, "And some people are easier to entice than others."

Schreck adjusted himself on the toilet seat as if trying to get comfortable. The diamond stickpin in the centre of his red silk tie glimmered in the recessed lights that dotted the bathroom's ceiling. The way it sparkled was quite fascinating to watch. Its numerous facets flashed and sparkled, drawing Ricky's eyes into the centre of the amazing-looking diamond's surface, seeming to spiral down and down and down...

"Hey! Little guy!" Simon's voice called at his back, breaking Ricky from his trance. "You doing okay over there?"

Ricky snapped his head briefly over his shoulder toward the blonde giant, saying, "I'm okay, I think." What had happened just now, he wondered. He felt like he'd been drugged but was pretty sure that hadn't been the case. It had to have been Schreck and his diamond stickpin. It must be how he got people to do his bidding and acquiesce to his wishes. His mother had said the man led people willingly into the black trucks that came to Auschwitz to collect 'volunteers'—the same trucks that had taken away his aunts and uncle. And now he had almost succumbed to the man's mind control himself! He shook his head in dismay at the thought.

Simon said, "Good, just keep things together for another few seconds." He pressed down on a tile, and a control panel popped up.

Ricky took a deep breath and said, "Yeah, okay." He took this moment to further grill the man in black, asking, "How do you live with yourself, the way you treat other people?"

"As a scientist, I must be progressive in my pursuit of answers."

"To what end?"

"The meaning of our existence. Not only our own, but those in other, parallel universes to this one."

"But at what cost? How many people have died in those other universes due to what you've done?"

"Those realities are an unfortunate recipient of our successes sometimes. High-level things such as what occurred at this hotel's ballroom usually have an equal and amplified negative effect in one of the subfrequencies."

Ricky shook his head in disbelief of Schreck's callous attitude toward other people, even if they lived in a mere subfrequency. He was about to probe further when Simon said, "Okay, ready for transport. Just need the coordinates now."

Schreck remained seated on the royal throne, unwilling to move.

"C'mon, get up," Simon said, an edge of frustration entering his voice, but still, the man in black didn't move. Stepping down from the platform, the now angry-looking giant stalked toward Schreck, who sat there seemingly unafraid. The bodyguard reached out with one massive arm to grab the thin man and drag him kicking and screaming onto the platform if need be.

But that didn't happen, and Schreck did something completely unexpected. He feinted backwards on the toilet seat, barely avoiding Simon's grasp. At the same time, he removed the stickpin from his tie in one fluid, practised motion, and jabbed it into Simon's beefy forearm.

"You sneaky son of a..." The words faded on Simon's lips as he collapsed to the floor unconscious.

At least, Ricky hoped he was only unconscious. He stepped backwards several paces as Schreck stood and moved threateningly toward him, the long silver shaft of the stickpin still gleaming wickedly in his hands, a twisted smile on his lips.

Rosenstein looked rapidly about the washroom for something to use as a weapon, but the only thing he could find was a bath towel. He grabbed it from the rack and spun it rapidly into something more streamlined.

Schreck lunged with the shining stickpin, and Ricky dodged out of the way, jumping backwards out of the thin man's long reach, but only just.

Cocking his arm, Rosenstein snapped the towel out, and Schreck's hat flew off as the white cotton connected like a whip with the side of his head. Thanks to his time as a water boy on the high school football team, Ricky had learned how to snap a towel with the best of them. He'd needed to learn the technique as a way to defend himself from the prank-playing jocks who delighted in snapping their own towels at the lowly water boy as he passed.

"Why, you little beast!" With his hat temporarily gone, thin wisps of hair shot up in all directions from the top of Schreck's mostly bald head. Cursing in German, he bent down to grab for his bowler.

Ricky lashed out at the hat, and it rebounded off Schreck's legs and skittered across the floor several feet, landing in front of the steps leading to the Harmoniser's platform. As the man in black reached down for his bowler a second time, Ricky snapped the towel again, and this time, he connected with Schreck's face.

The thin man screamed as the crisp and clean cotton loops of the towel flicked across his eyeballs. Though temporarily blinded, he still held the stickpin in one hand and wicked it back and forth in the air, trying to jab Ricky. Just as Schreck's fingers traced across the brim of his hat near the edge of the platform, Ricky bundled up the large towel in both hands, held it out in front of himself and ran head-first at the man in black.

Schreck flew backwards onto the platform and howled in pain as the back of his head collided with the cold hard metal, his hat flying from his hand.

Rosenstein scuttled around the platform like a fiddler crab and slapped his hand down onto the large red button on top of the control panel. He hoped it might send Schreck anywhere but here right now.

A popping sound suddenly occurred, and Max Schreck was no longer in the room. One moment he was there, and the next, he was gone. Ricky had expected something dramatic to happen and see the man dematerialise like on Star Trek, but the reality was much less exciting than what TV and movies portrayed, not that he was particularly surprised at that being the case.

A groan came from the other side of the room, and Ricky moved to Simon. He crouched down to assist the man, saying, "Oh good. I hoped you weren't dead."

"Gee, thanks," Simon said as he sat up. "I suspected Schreck's little stickpin was used for some sort of hypnosis, but I never expected it to be drugged at the tip. With a deep breath, Ricky helped the mountainous man to his feet. Simon said, "Where's Schreck?"

"I was able to get him onto the platform and then hit the big red button."

Simon stepped shakily onto the platform, looked at the display, and then said, "Ooh, that's not good."

"Why? What happened?" Ricky wondered.

"You sent Schreck to the machine's last destination."

"Oh, really? Which was where?"

"One of the wastelands."

"Wastelands?"

"Yeah, they're not the best place to be."

"Why is that?"

"There's nothing there. Plus, they can be kind of nasty."

"Sort of appropriate, considering who Schreck is."

"Yeah, well, we should still be able to bring him back since he's still got his harmonic bracelet on." Simon held up his wrist to show the golden band about his meaty forearm. "I'll just do an auto-recall on his bracelet."

Looking slightly sheepish, Ricky said, "Well, maybe not. I took this from him when I tackled him." Ricky held up the golden bracelet that Schreck had been wearing, now on his own wrist. While Schreck lay incapacitated with pain on the platform, Ricky had seen the device and snatched it off before hitting the Harmoniser's launch button.

"Well, he's going to have fun then."

"How's that?"

Shaking his head, Simon said, "Where Max Schreck is right now, at the top of that other Overseer Mountain, there's nothing alive for hundreds of miles in any direction. And since we have no way to pull him back without his bracelet, he could be anywhere."

His eyes wide, Ricky added, "Which means we have no way to bring Selene back from wherever he hid her."

CHAPTER THIRTY-THREE

December 31st, 2021 1710 hours

The intense cold of the ebony box leached through to Amanda's hands, despite the layers of towelling and the thick leather gloves. Now finally down to the gaming lounge, she paused and placed it onto a nearby billiard table to take a break. Removing the gloves, she crossed her arms and put one hand under each armpit in an attempt to warm them up.

"Are you okay, Amanda?" John asked, concerned. He took this moment to sit down and rest his undoubtedly aching hip.

Amanda frowned and said, "I don't know. This thing is so cold, it feels like I'm getting frostbite, even with these gloves and towels." But there was more, of course. The constant onslaught of images was almost overwhelming. Some were of things she'd never seen before, and others she never could have imagined in a hundred lifetimes, so she knew they weren't pulled from her memory. But almost all of them, without exception, were things she never wanted to see again.

"Thanks for doing this," Minerva said, nodding toward the box. "I don't think I would have survived if I'd tried to carry it, especially with the psychic energy that box emits. How are you doing with that aspect, by the way?"

"Well, let me just say, I'm sure glad we have that cart waiting down at the bottom of the stairs." Amanda blew into her cupped hands a couple of times in an attempt to garner some extra warmth, and then she pulled the gloves back on. With a deep breath, she picked up the ebony box once more with the towels and moved to the lounge's exit.

There had been no sign of the stuffed cat, yet. However, they were all on high alert, unsure if the striped beast would be bold enough to try and attack all three at once. Moving toward the turret's final flight of stairs, John took point with his cane, followed closely by Amanda. At their backs, Minerva held the sword aloft once more, keeping it at the ready as they descended.

When they were finally at the turret's base, Amanda said, "I can't feel my hands anymore." It was as if someone had shot both of them full of novocaine at the dentist's office. Fortunately, the serving cart John had been using as a walker was still there, and she gratefully placed the ebony box onto it. As soon as she released her grip on the box, the feeling began to return to her numbed digits.

Minerva reached in to pull the turret door closed when motion on the back wall of the small foyer caught her attention—a slight rippling movement from behind the large tapestry hanging behind the suit of armour. "There must be a draft somewhere," she said, beginning to pull the heavy door closed. Suddenly her eyes widened in alarm, and she finished closing the door with a slam, saying, "We've got problems."

John asked, "What is it? What's wrong?"

Just as the words came out of Harder's mouth, a rustling came from the bottom of the door. The trio watched in horror as two painted brown forepaws popped out, followed by an ursine head. With a deep, rattling hiss, the canvas bear began to pull itself out from beneath the door's edge.

Raising her sword high in the air, Minerva slammed it down, piercing the canvas head of the painted bear and pinning it to the carpet. The creature let out a high-pitched squeal like a stuck pig and tried without success to pull the sword free from its head, but the steel was buried deep, and its painted paws couldn't gain purchase on the slippery shaft.

John stood next to Minerva, his face a mask of disgusted rage as he stabbed at the bear repeatedly with his cane's spiked end. The painted predator gave up on the sword and turned its attention to John's cane tip, trying to knock it from his hand with quick, snake-like jabs of its paws.

"I think I have an idea," Amanda said. "Minerva, could you give me a hand?"

While Harder continued to stab away at the beast, Minerva and Amanda carried a heavy leather wingback chair, which they both struggled to lift, from a conversation alcove nearby. They placed the chair's back against the turret door, dropping its rear legs onto the bear's body and the front legs onto its forepaws. With the beast now pinned to the floor, Minerva pulled the sword free, saying, "Just in case I need this for later."

Amanda returned from the conversation alcove with one more item, a black metal trash-can/ashtray combination, the top filled with white sand, making the whole thing quite heavy. With a thud, she dropped it on the bear's hissing head, and it stopped moving. "That should hold it, but I doubt that it's out of commission for good."

"I agree. These things are very hard to kill," Minerva said, shaking her head. "Hopefully, it's not going to go anywhere else."

"For now at least," John said. He retracted the spike at his cane's tip and placed the cane next to the ebony box, then took hold of the cart's handles. With a nod to his companions, he began pushing the serving cart down the corridor toward the elevator.

Each time they approached another alcove or service passage, Amanda tensed as if expecting some new horror to leap out at them as they moved past. Unfortunately, they couldn't move very fast due to John's limited mobility, and it seemed to be taking forever to get to the other end. Feeling exposed with the long, empty passageway at her back, Amanda would glance over her shoulder every once in a while to ensure the painted bear was still where they'd left it. At the same time, her mind flashed back to her experience with the tiger in the second-floor corridor many years before.

They found the lift waiting for them as they rounded the corner at the end of the corridor, and John wheeled the cart into the elevator car.

Amanda asked, "Are you going to ride down with the box, John?"

"I believe I'm going to have to. I don't think I could handle any more stairs."

Minerva said, "Okay, but let's take it one floor at a time, all right?" She reached into the car, pressed the second-floor button, and said, "See you there."

The doors closed with their usual musical ding, and the car began to descend. Minerva and Amanda trotted down the stairs, trying to keep up with the descending elevator. On the second floor, the doors pinged open to reveal John standing next to the cart. He gave them a slight wave and a thumb's up, then pressed the button inside the door to select the ground floor, and the doors closed once more.

Moving quickly, the two women made it down to the lobby just as the elevator doors were opening.

Minerva said, "Okay, John, let's get that..." She trailed off, her mouth still partially open with unspoken words as she looked inside the lift.

John Harder and the ebony box had disappeared.

***

Pushing the cart out of the elevator, John looked about. Where were the ladies? He'd expected that they would have been down here by now. He called out, "Hello? Amanda? Minerva? Where did you ladies go?" His voice echoed throughout the lobby, sounding old and frail, not how he remembered it the last time he was here. Shaking his head at not receiving a response, he presumed that the women had gone on ahead, and he pushed the cart toward the grand ballroom annex.

Rolling the cart along, John reflected on the previous forty years since he'd last been up here. His loneliness during that time had been overwhelming. What should have been a happy retirement with Helen had been four decades of unrelenting solitude. He'd never remarried or really even looked at another woman in that time. In his heart, he felt that he would be betraying Helen somehow. And for all those years, despite everything he knew, he'd held out some small hope that she would miraculously walk through the door one day and all would be well again. But that had never happened, of course.

The grand ballroom lay just ahead, its two oaken doors firmly closed. As he grew closer, John slowed more and more and eventually rolled to a stop, feeling unable to go any further. He remembered when he'd first been called to this hotel and stood in front of these very same doors, early in the morning of a brand-new year, just before this insanity had started.

He was fairly certain he recalled almost everything now, except for whatever else he may have been up to whilst in his fugue state when he'd moved the ebony box. What had possessed him to do that, he wondered, and had he done anything else at the same time? He had no answer and doubted he ever would.

But he suspected it wasn't just him and that many more individuals at this hotel over the years had ended up doing something they would never, ever normally think of doing. His mind suddenly flew to Helen once again. Had she been overwhelmed by this evil place as soon as she'd walked through the doors? Wherever she'd gone, had she done so of her own volition, or had her beautiful mind become ensnared within this hotel's tangled web of deceit and horror? And though he'd had no revelatory flashbacks regarding his wife, he was still not entirely convinced that he hadn't had something to do with her disappearance.

He thought of Amelia Walden from the kitchen. Maybe it hadn't been someone or something that had pushed or thrown her from the parapets like Minerva suspected. Perhaps she had jumped instead, but not from depression or anything like that. No, due to his own experiences here, he wondered if something from deep within the lightless heart of this hotel had burrowed its way into her mind and compelled her to do what she did; controlling her, much like he had been when he'd moved the ebony box all those years ago.

It was frustrating not knowing anything for certain and believing whatever horrible thing his tortured mind could dream up. Sometimes, he reflected, the things a person doesn't know can be even scarier than the things they do.

Taking a deep breath, John reached for one of the door handles, turned it and slowly pulled the door open. The knob was cold to the touch but not freezing as he'd encountered in other places around the hotel.

"Hello? Ladies?" Silence lay beyond the door. He tried again, "Minerva? Amanda?" Still nothing. Where could they have gone? Why would they disappear like that when they knew they were in the middle of moving the ebony box?

The room was quite dim—just bright enough to see no one in the immediate vicinity. The snow-filled afternoon beyond the tall windows had now been replaced by a snow-filled evening, and it did little to brighten the large ballroom. Only a few sparkling chandeliers were currently working; their limited circles of light dotted the floor beneath with small pools of radiance, a sea of darkness all around.

John stood in the doorway, unwilling to enter the room for the moment, his breath hitching in his chest as he took it all in. He blinked rapidly several times, unsure if he was seeing what he thought he was seeing. Though he knew that the food had been cleared away long ago, he was stunned to see the tables now looking as they had on that very first morning.

Uneaten meals covered the plates. Wine and champagne glasses were filled to the brim, and the ashtrays overflowed, several containing cigarettes that still burned. It looked as if the party had just ended. What was going on here? There was no way any cigarette or cigar could burn for forty years. If they did, tobacco companies worldwide would have been out of business long ago.

Streamers and balloons were piled high in the centre of the dance floor like he remembered. However, they were not deflated after four decades as he would have expected, but rather, all seemed freshly inflated.

Shaking his head in dismay and wonder, John pushed the cart further into the ballroom and wheeled it toward the mahogany bar. The shelves running along the mirrored wall behind were once more lined with alcohol of every description, ready to make a drink for any partygoer that wandered by.

The end of the bar was empty, awaiting the box's positioning once more. John took another breath to steel himself and lifted the ebony box from the cart, placing it in the spot he'd found it four decades before. As he did, a feeling of electricity passed through his arms like he was completing a circuit that had lain open for all those years.

All around, the world dimmed away, and soon John was in complete blackness, losing his sense of orientation. If he hadn't had the bar directly in front of him to lean on, he might have fallen to the floor—it was as if he were suddenly in outer space. He couldn't see his breath but felt it must be steaming from his open mouth in great clouds. That was if the full-body shivers he was currently experiencing were anything to go by. He'd taken his parka off when he'd eaten his lunch and neglected to put it back on afterwards, leaving it draped over the stool on which he'd sat. Now, he wrapped his arms about himself as he tried to keep warm. Wherever he was, John realised he was freezing to death, and there didn't seem to be anything he could do about it.

CHAPTER THIRTY-FOUR

December 31st, 1981 2351 hours

After Ricky Rosenstein and Simon had departed with Max Schreck, Lively had allowed Kandi to check the mainframe to get an idea of what the little computer man had been up to. Sitting in the wheeled leather chair, the faux-nurse had been clicking and clacking on the mechanical keyboard for several minutes now.

Shaking her head, Kandi said, "Everything looks the same to me, but I can't tell for sure what that little butterball has changed in the code."

Lively stood nearby, watching her work. It wasn't that he trusted Kandi in the least at the computer. But he figured if he monitored what the woman was doing while she poked around, maybe she'd find a way to unpause what Ricky had altered in the realignment code, which might be a good thing. He still wasn't convinced that what Rosenstein had done was the best course of action. This was especially so in light of the fact that Ricky and Simon still weren't back from collecting Selene from wherever Schreck had sequestered her. And though he wanted to end things here tonight, Lively also wanted to do so with minimal risk to everyone involved, and he wasn't sure how risky what Ricky had done to the code might actually be.

Edward stood just behind Kandi, peering at the monitor as she worked. He placed a hand on her shoulder and said, "Can't you at least scan through the programme and make sure it's okay?"

"With that password he's placed at the top level, I can't seem to do much more than bring up the directory." Kandi looked up at the clock on the wall over the monitors and added, "And even if I could get in, there's over three million lines of code and a little under five minutes to check them all. But, yeah, sure, no problem."

"There's no need for sarcasm," Edward replied tersely.

Kandi said, "Okay, let's try this again." She updated the menu, and the screen refreshed, listing her options:

'Initiate Aggregation - 1'
'Dissipate Aggregation - 2'
'Initiate Translocation - 3'
'Reverse Translocation – 4'
'System Reset - 5'
'Execute Subroutine Break - 6'
'Enter choice?'

"What did that little Oompa Loompa do?" Kandi wondered aloud, then selected '5' and pressed enter. A prompt appeared on-screen:

'Enter Password:'

"Password? What password?" With a shake of her head, Kandi sat back in the chair and said, "Well, this is out of my league. I don't know the password or how to get past it, and I've tried everything I could think of."

It was now just a couple of minutes before midnight.

Somewhere below, the thrumming bass vibration that was already running ramped up and became louder and louder. On the computer monitor in front of Kandi, lines of code began to scroll past as the machine executed operation after operation as it prepared to realign the frequencies.

Lively watched the clock on the wall, counting down as the reset approached. He looked to Edward and then to Kandi. His father seemed to have the slightest sheen of sweat on his forehead as he watched the witching hour approach, while in front of him, Kandi continued to try and break the password that Ricky had created, but to no avail.

With less than ten seconds on the clock, Ricky and Simon appeared in the doorway of the operating theatre and then made their way into the control room. With alarm, Lively noted that Schreck was no longer accompanying them, and there was no sign of Selene either.

"Finally!" Kandi exclaimed. "I can't get into the mainframe because of your password protection!"

"Didn't think you would," Ricky said with a slight smirk.

"Don't you understand what might happen?" Edward asked.

"Well, it looks like we're going to find out," Lively said, then looked to the clock and counted down, "Three, two, one…"

Suddenly, it seemed as if every molecule of Lively's being was being agitated at once as if in a giant microwave. Unlike the slight tugging sensation in the centre of his chest and brief wave of nausea with the Harmoniser, this felt more like ants crawling over every single nerve cell inside his body. The thrumming vibration from below wound higher and higher, building to what he thought would most likely be a crescendo of noise and vibration. But instead, the machinery gave a final thrumming surge, and the vibration ceased, the machinery below winding down until there was nothing but deafening silence.

On the computer screen, the prompt now read:

'Programme paused. Enter password to continue:'

"Oh no!" Kandi said. She looked to Ricky and said, "You did this, little man! Fix it!"

Rosenstein looked to Lively, who nodded affirmatively. "Move aside," Ricky said, and Kandi evacuated the chair so he could sit down. His fingers flew over the keys, and after a few seconds, the thrumming started up once more beneath their feet. "There you go, all better."

Kandi moved next to Ricky to see what he'd done. She examined the readout from various sensors and said, "No, not all better. You've restarted things, but we're not aligned to where we were."

"So?"

Edward answered for Kandi, saying, "So, if we don't get things realigned again, the further we drift from the stasis we've achieved after all these years, the greater the chance of our frequency's evanescence."

"Evanescence?" Lively inquired. "I thought they broke up."

"No, as in, vanish, dissipate, cease to exist," Edward clarified.

"Okay, that's definitely not a good thing. Is there anything you can think of that could assist us in getting realigned somehow?" Lively peered at the computer screen as he spoke. "What about the fifth option? System Reset?"

"It could stop us from phasing out of existence, but..." Kandi trailed off without finishing.

"But what?" Ricky asked.

"I don't know what will happen—it might help, or it might accelerate things and further shorten however much time we have left."

Lively shook his head and said, "All right, then let's hope that whatever Minerva's doing at her end might help."

Ricky offered, "With everything that happened, I didn't get a chance to check my computer yet for any messages from your sister. But I can do that right away, Mr. DeMille."

"Thanks, you read my mind, Ricky," Lively responded.

"Well then, let's hope she has some success," Edward said.

That crisis dealt with, Lively moved to the next and looked to Simon, saying, "Speaking of success, where's Selene?"

"And Maxi?" Kandi asked.

Giving an apologetic look, Ricky said, "We had a little problem."

"Yeah," Simon agreed, "We lost Schreck."

"No!" Kandi said in disbelief.

"You lost him? How do you lose someone around here, unless it's intentional, of course?" Edward asked.

With a sigh of embarrassment, Simon said, "Well, he jabbed me with that stickpin of his and knocked me out."

Jumping in to tell his part of the tale, Ricky said somewhat excitedly, "With Simon down, I slapped Max around with a towel and was able to headbutt him onto the platform. Then I hit the red launch button on the console to try and put him somewhere temporarily before he recovered and came at me again."

Lively's eyes had widened somewhat as he listened to Ricky's description. It seemed the little computer man was stepping up, and he felt some small amount of pride in helping him to do so, though it was tinged with concern for his mother's wellbeing. But now, Lively was left with a question, and he asked, "And where is Schreck now?"

"Well, the Harmoniser was still set to its last destination, the wastelands," Simon said.

Ricky held up his wrist and showed off the golden bracelet saying, "And I grabbed this off his arm just before he disappeared."

"Well, that's it then," Edward said. "The wastelands without a bracelet..." He trailed off and shook his head somewhat sadly.

Sounding angry yet tearful at the same time, Kandi said, "He's now synced with that frequency, thanks to you!" She looked daggers at Ricky.

"And you must realise that this means we can't bring Selene back from wherever he's put her since only Max knows where she is," Edward said to Lively.

From his previous conversation with Edward, Lively knew that someone who translocates without one of the harmonic bracelets would then become a long-term resident of that subfrequency, much like his grandfather in the party land Sinclair reality. "Well, this calls for an alternative plan," he said, moving to the doorway.

"What's that?" Ricky asked.

"Looks like Simon and I need to go on a little trip."

The blonde giant nodded, saying, "Sure, where to?"

"The wastelands to find Schreck and get him to tell us where Selene is."

Ricky asked, "What if he won't talk?"

With a pop of his knuckles, Simon said, "That won't be a problem. I've never met anyone who wouldn't talk to me, eventually."

CHAPTER THIRTY-FIVE

December 31ˢᵗ, 2021 1755 hours

"But where did John go?" Amanda asked with an incredulous expression.

"I think there're spots around this hotel that go to other places," Minerva said, a frown on her face.

"Other places? Where?"

"Here."

"I don't understand."

"Let's walk and talk," Minerva said as she started toward the ballroom corridor. "So, I believe there are entrances to other realities around this hotel, somehow created by whatever it was that made all those people disappear forty years ago."

"And you think that's where John has gone?"

"Maybe."

"Will he come back?"

"Maybe." Minerva hated to give the same response twice, but she knew that was probably the safest answer she could give. She honestly had no idea what had happened to John Harder. "When you and John vanished from the elevator, you reappeared almost immediately, so let's hope John does the same this time."

Now approaching the doors to the grand ballroom, they saw one of them ajar, muted light shining through the gap.

"Thank goodness, maybe John is already here," Amanda said, relief heavy in her voice.

Minerva pushed the door open, and the two women peered inside but saw no sign of John. All about the room, the few chandeliers that were illuminated looked exceedingly dim.

Together they moved through the murk toward the mahogany bar. At first, the room dimmed more and more until they could barely see their hands in front of their faces. But as they drew closer, the single chandelier overtop the bar grew gradually brighter, and they finally saw that there was, in fact, someone there.

John Harder leaned heavily on the polished mahogany, arms wrapped about himself and shivering as if he'd just been outside for a sub-zero stroll. Next to him, the wheeled serving cart was abutted against the bar's end. As the women arrived, the chandelier returned to full brightness, spotlighting the ebony box that sat just below, exactly where it had been the night of the disappearance four decades before.

Amanda exclaimed, "John, where were you?" She removed her parka and draped it across the elderly man's shoulders, and he gratefully pulled it around himself.

"I was about to ask y-you the s-s-same," John answered through chattering teeth. "I c-came out of the elevator, and both of you were g-gone!"

"From our perspective, we stayed right where we were, and it was you that vanished," Minerva said. "How did you get here without us seeing you?"

"I-I don't know. I pushed the cart out of the elevator and made my way here, thinking you m-might have gone on ahead. When I arrived, all the tables around the room had f-food on them again, just like the night of the disappearance."

"What? How is that possible?" Amanda looked about at the tables and saw them bare, except for a few empty wine bottles and drink glasses here and there, with faux-flower centrepieces still in place on each. John didn't answer and only shook his head, perhaps not knowing what to say.

Jansen guided Harder to a nearby table and had him sit with the jacket wrapped about himself for several minutes. Once his teeth had stopped chattering, John said, "When I placed the box on the bar, everything grew dark, and I felt like I was in outer space. And the cold! So, so cold." He shivered again at the thought.

"There are many ways this hotel plays around with your mind," Minerva said.

Amanda said, "Perhaps it showed you what you remembered from 1981."

"Maybe," John said but looked unconvinced. He began to remove Amanda's jacket, his shivers almost entirely gone. "I'm just glad I've found you both again." He handed the parka back to Amanda, giving a nod of thanks, a grateful smile on his face.

"The feeling is mutual," Minerva said, nodding slightly.

As Amanda shrugged back into her parka, she looked to

Minerva for a moment and asked, "Since we're all together again, I was wondering if you could do us a small favour before we try running the machine downstairs."

"What's that?" Minerva asked, concerned.

"We were wondering if we could speak to Danny. Would you be able to do a quick seance?"

John nodded in agreement, saying, "Both of us have read of your psychic abilities, thanks to the internet, and it was something we discussed on the way up the hill. If you think it would be possible, do you think we might speak with him?"

Minerva saw the look in Jansen's eyes was shared by Harder, and she acquiesced, saying, "I suppose a quick one couldn't hurt." Though their time was growing short, she knew that some sort of closure for these two was in order, especially considering that the light of their life, Danny, had most likely been snuffed out at the behest of someone connected with the Sinclair Resort Hotel.

With faint hope in his voice, John added, "Perhaps we could talk to my wife, Helen, too, if she's out there somewhere, that is."

A compassionate smile on her lips, Minerva said, "We can try."

***

The ballroom lay in darkness, the chandeliers extinguished, and candlelight was the only illumination. Their flickering flames danced across the hopeful faces of John and Amanda. There had been no need to pull the drapes since the snow-filled evening beyond added only minimal light to the room.

Amanda Jansen looked across the round dining table at

Minerva Deadmarsh. The woman's eyes were closed, and she hadn't said anything for several minutes.

Within her heart of hearts, Amanda hoped that Minerva could contact Danny. After seeing him smiling handsomely in her home's bathroom mirror as well as in John's condo, looking so young and healthy as he had, it had been a powerful experience for her. She knew there must be something that Danny wanted to communicate to her but hadn't the strength or power to do so for more than a few moments outside of the resort's sphere of influence. Now, through Minerva's abilities, she hoped to finally hear from him again after all these years and perhaps even learn what had happened to him and gain some closure. John Harder was to her right, and he looked both saddened and hopeful at the same time. She was sure that he also wanted to see Danny due to his own visitations over the last few weeks.

After retrieving the crystal orb from her suite, Minerva had performed the requisite cleansing rituals, and she now appeared ready to raise what currently walked within the Sinclair's unhallowed halls. The trio clasped hands around the table, and then Minerva began to speak.

"Spirits of light, I call upon you today with compassion and understanding and ask that you join us here in our circle of love and light. Beings of darkness begone! You are not wanted or welcome here. I call upon those of light and positivity; please aid us as we seek one beloved soul, that of Danny Harder. Hear me, Danny. Those who love and remember you are here with me today and wish to see you once again."

Amanda looked about the room but saw nothing. With a slight shiver, she noted that she could see John's breath in addition to her own now, the temperature dropping rapidly around them.

Minerva began to speak once again. "We mean you no harm, Danny Harder. Please join us and have peace and love within our circle. You are welcome and safe here." As those words left her mouth, she began to breathe in short gasps, vapour puffing from her mouth in a series of small clouds.

Just behind Minerva, the darkened room appeared even darker than only moments before. Amanda held her breath as she waited and watched, wondering if Minerva's plea would be heard. The amorphous darkness moved slowly around the table until it was between Amanda and John but slightly back from them by several feet.

Minerva looked to the darkness, her eyes unfocussed now, and she said, "Come forth, Danny Harder. Come forth to those that love you and miss you."

The candles flickered wildly as if a breeze had blown through the room from an open window somewhere. Suddenly, the darkness seemed to roil within itself like a turbulent storm cloud, but after a moment, it began to thin, and a man stepped forth. He was transparent but almost solid at the same time. Tall and handsome, he was dressed in the work uniform of an RCMP officer from the previous century. As he looked from John to Amanda, a crooked but winning smile crept across his face.

John's eyes were heavy with unshed tears as he looked upon his son, appearing glad to have this moment once again after so many years apart.

Amanda blinked back her own tears as she saw her Danny again, exactly as he'd been on that final day so many years before, and her heart swelled as she recalled it briefly. She'd just been coming off a day shift, and he was preparing to go to work for an evening shift on that New Year's Eve in 1979. They'd made arrangements to be together for a little while the next day on New Year's when they would inform Danny's parents of their new life together.

The plan had been to have New Year's dinner with his

parents and bring a surprise along—her. Danny had wanted to introduce Amanda to his mother and father and then spring their decision of marriage on them all at once. But that day had never come to pass when Danny had been killed that evening. Amanda had been alone ever since, unable to find anyone that made her feel the way Danny had; someone who elevated her day, brightened her world and filled her with love.

That day before the accident had been a good one. She'd been busy getting things ready for her upcoming visit that had never happened with John and Helen. Once she'd gotten off shift, she'd spent the afternoon baking shortbread, mince meat pies, and Nanaimo Bars, some of his parent's favourite holiday treats. When Danny's shift on 'Christmas Light Patrol' ended at midnight, he was supposed to come directly to Amanda's place. But by one o'clock in the morning, he still hadn't shown. After giving him another hour, she'd called into dispatch to check on his status and had been informed at that time that Danny had been struck and killed by a suspected drunk driver. She had been absolutely shattered by the news. Her brief time of light and joy with Danny had been replaced by a life of sadness, loneliness and depression.

Looking at the apparition before her, Amanda knew that John was most likely having similar thoughts going through his mind right now. It was a double whammy of despair for the inspector, she realised. For the man to have lost his son to a grisly accident and then, less than two years later, to also lose his wife to this hotel must have been almost unbearable. Amanda was sure that whatever had happened to Danny, like whatever happened to Helen, both were somehow linked to this abominable resort.

"Danny, what is it you need," John said, emotion weighing heavily in his voice.

Minerva said, "Tell us, Danny, if you can, what is it that keeps you here in this mortal realm?"

The apparition looked to Minerva as she spoke, then turned back to John and Amanda. Danny's smile faded as he said in a faint but discernable voice, "Two into darkness; one into light." He suddenly looked over his shoulder into the darkness at his back as if something else were in the room causing him concern.

Amanda wondered, what could possibly cause a spirit concern? Whatever it was seemed only a temporary distraction, and Danny turned back to them, his winning smile on display once again. He looked to both John and Amanda, his gaze lingering on each for a moment, then began to slowly fade away.

"No, Danny, don't go!" Amanda called, her voice filled with sadness and loss. Seeing him again as he was, as she'd loved him, made her realise that no matter what happened here today, she still wanted to be with him more than anything she'd ever wanted in her entire life. And she now knew she'd do whatever she could to make that a reality.

The temperature began to return to normal, and the candles stopped their flickering like the open window somewhere had now been closed. Amanda looked to John and then Minerva. No one spoke for several long seconds.

John broke the silence, his voice wavering as he said, "I still wanted to ask him about Helen. I miss them both so, so much." A shudder seemed to pass through him, and Amanda suspected it wasn't from the cold this time but rather anguish, longing and loss. She patted the back of his hand, saying, "I know, John. I'm so sorry."

Looking from John to Amanda, Minerva said kindly, "There was something else you should know."

The two inspectors looked to Minerva as one, and John asked, "What is it?"

"It was a sensation I got from Danny when he was here."

"Which was what?"

With a small smile playing at the corners of her lips, Minerva said, "A feeling of hope."

CHAPTER THIRTY-SIX

December 31st, 1981 0000 hours

A sensation of anxiety ran through Lively as he noticed the first of what presumably would be the cascading effects of Ricky's pausing of the realignment. Moving through the bedroom to the royal suite's bathroom, things appeared dull and drab, as if the renewal he'd been experiencing in 2021 was now working in reverse. Everything around him seemed faded, like it had been bleached by sunlight over many years. With a shake of his head, Lively said, "I think it's happening like they said."

The platform for the Harmoniser was still activated and ready for transport. Simon nodded as he stepped to the top in two long strides, saying, "Yeah, I noticed things were looking a little dull on the way up here."

As he stood marvelling at the Harmoniser once more, Lively asked, "So, to the best of your knowledge, Schreck got himself harmonised with one of the wastelands. And that last destination was the wasteland we visited, correct?"

"Yes."

"I wonder..."

"Wonder what?" Simon asked as he prepped things on the control pad.

"If Selene is no longer in this hotel, and Max has placed her in some other subfrequency, why didn't he get zapped back to wherever that was?"

"Instead of the wastelands, you mean?"

"Yes."

Simon nodded at the control panel, saying, "Well, he might have erased the frequency he travelled to in order to cover his tracks. If he did, it would have defaulted to the last one in memory, which we travelled to with Edward a little while ago."

"I guess so," Lively said, still unsure if that were the case. "Can we bring him back here to interrogate him if he doesn't want to give us the information we need when, and if, we find him?"

"Well, he was sent through without a bracelet."

"So that means we can't bring him back?"

"Not necessarily." Simon punched in numbers on the keypad next to the platform for several seconds, then said, "We could, but he wouldn't survive here for very long since he's been synced to the frequency of the wasteland now. He'd have to wear a harmonic bracelet constantly to avoid separation."

"Separation? What's that?"

"It's what happens when someone is away from their core frequency without a bracelet. Without the stabilising effects of a harmonic bracelet, they're eventually torn apart by the difference in frequencies."

"Sounds kind of unpleasant. So that's why your twin wears one constantly—because he's not from around these parts?"

"Yup. Without it, he'd be a big pile of goo pretty quick."

"And you wear one around here all the time to help with the forgetfulness the realignment causes, correct?"

"Now you're getting it," Simon said, nodding in agreement. He handed a harmonic bracelet to Lively from a small storage compartment located in the low tile wall surrounding the tub. "Here, don't forget to wear one yourself unless you want to join Max in the wastelands for the rest of your life."

Stepping to the top of the platform, Lively held his wrist up, saying, "I still have mine from my earlier travels with Edward, so I'm all ready." He gave his hands a clap, then rubbed the palms together, adding, "Let's do this thing."

The blonde giant gave another nod, saying, "Okay, here we go."

Lively mentally braced himself for the upcoming sensation. Just like last time, he felt the tugging in his chest and a brief flash of nausea, but now it wasn't as bad as the first time he'd travelled, and he wondered if perhaps he was getting used to it. Blinking rapidly, he saw that he was indeed back in the wastelands. Everything looked just as derelict and cold as it had last time. However, it wasn't dark here now. Weak daylight filtered through from storm-swollen skies beyond the windows. This was a change from the nighttime world he saw when he was last here. Was this another example of the realities becoming unsynced?

Stepping down from the platform, Simon said, "Okay, since there's no power here, before we left, I set the Harmoniser to auto-recall our bracelets in one hour."

"Let's hope that's enough time," Lively said. He looked at his wristwatch, adding, "To expedite things, we should split up."

"Yeah, I guess so. But before I forget again, I should mention the crawlers."

"Edward said something about them when we first came to this frequency."

"He did. They first encountered them back when they'd dug the foundation for the hotel and began the mining down below. I think that stirred them up."

"Mining? Under the hotel?"

"Yup. That's where they discovered more of those black gemstones and a hell of a lot more gold."

"You said, 'more' of the black gemstones? Where were the others discovered?"

"Some right here in Canada. Back when Thomas first came to the country, I believe, in the interior of the province, near a little town called Lawless."

Lively's eyes widened slightly as he digested that last little bit of information. The gold rush was what everyone believed had been Thomas Sinclair's attraction to Lawless and the reason behind his subsequent success. But now he wondered, was the gold only secondary, and was Thomas's attraction to that area and this one due to an obsession with these powerful obsidian stones? If they had been found near both Lawless and Entwistle, two towns located along the same ley lines, how many other similar sites across the globe had his grandfather scoured over the years in his quest to amass more of the gems? Giving his head a slight tilt, Lively asked, "Did Thomas find other stones elsewhere?"

"Yes, but I don't know where."

Lively wondered if it had been in Africa somewhere near where Schreck said Sinclair had found the ebony box. And were these crawlers located at every site where the obsidian stones were? Thinking aloud, he said, "But what are they?"

"The crawlers or the stones?"

"The crawlers."

"Turns out there are native legends from around this area going back a couple of millennia at least."

"Legends of what?"

"The People of the Ground, or the Ancient People, depending on who you talk to. When I became involved in things here, the Sinclairs were well into the extraction process of the gold down below. As far as I know, there hadn't been any problems until they came across those gemstones. But after that, they lost several miners over the years down there, usually someone alone, even for only a few seconds. Vanished without a trace. Never found them or their bodies."

"Maybe they fell down an open shaft somewhere?"

"There weren't any nearby where some of the guys disappeared. And then there were the voices as well."

"Voices?"

"Searchers looking for the missing men reported what had sounded like voices whispering to each other. Sometimes it was off in the distance, down passageways that had been closed for decades because they were unsafe. Other times, it sounded like they were right there near them, just around the corner in the dark, or so I've been told."

"Have you ever seen them?" Lively asked as they moved into the suite's sitting area.

"Just a glimpse once when we were checking one of the wastelands during some early testing of the Harmoniser. They're bolder here than they ever were back in the prime frequency."

"That sounds rather disturbing."

"Yeah, they are. So, keep an eye peeled for them."

With a grim smile, Lively thought of Ricky and said, "Even better, I'll use both."

They moved through into the bedroom and then the sitting area beyond. Simon stopped at the suite's entrance and peered cautiously into the corridor. He looked over his shoulder to Lively before moving into the passageway and said, "Oh, and by the way, try not to let them see you if you can avoid it, especially when you're by yourself."

"Duly noted," Lively said, and they moved into the corridor. Once there, he added in a hushed voice, "Okay, why don't you take this wing, and I'll take the west wing and turret. We'll check each floor and then meet down in the lobby and take it from there."

Simon nodded and moved to check inside one of the nearby suites.

Making his way along the dim and dusty corridor toward the Executive Gaming Lounge, Lively was able to glance into the suites as he passed. Almost without exception, their doors were either busted inward or missing entirely. He could see more dark grey sky through the room's windows, those that still had windows at least. He didn't bother checking thoroughly inside each suite, as it seemed highly unlikely that he'd find Max Schreck cowering underneath a moldy bedspread or hiding in a shower stall in any of them. It appeared as if much of the damage to the rooms had been done in the past. With that being the case, he figured the dust on the carpet would be disturbed near the entrance of any suite Schreck may have entered, and he'd seen no sign of that yet.

The door to the turret was closed. Lively cringed slightly as he pulled it open, the hinges squealing like a litter of newborn rats. He'd been trying to make as little noise as possible as he searched, and that certainly didn't help things. At first, he'd considered calling out Schreck's name as he searched but then thought better of it. He recalled Simon's advice regarding the crawlers and also figured it would be best to catch the man in black by surprise if he could, instead of the other way around.

As before in the gaming lounge, things were in disarray, the gaming tables broken into numerous splintered pieces. Across the room, the Ms. Pac-Man and Space Invaders arcade machines lay on their sides, gaping holes in the middle of their shattered CRT screens, like someone had put their raging fists through the glass.

Lively crossed to the model room stairs. He was on the first couple of steps when he hesitated, fairly certain there had been a noise at his back in the lounge just now. He turned and surveyed the room, but nothing had moved or was currently moving that he could see. Whatever made the sound, it definitely wasn't made by one of the taxidermied animals, he knew that for a fact.

When he'd been through here earlier with his father, he'd noticed the stuffed guardians had been missing from their spots. Flaps of fur and skin covered the floor, their wooden taxidermy skeletons now twisted and dismembered. From the looks of things, they'd been toppled from their positions and ripped to pieces many years before.

At the top of the stairs, Lively stood outside the model room door and looked cautiously inside. The miniature hotel lay in numerous fragments, some large, some small, just like before. He moved into the room and looked more closely at the devastation wrought upon the miniature. It would have taken immense strength to damage such a solid-looking structure, yet there were no sledgehammers or other blunt objects anywhere in sight that anyone could have used to demolish it. He thought once more of the crawlers. If it had been them, they must have immense strength to do such a good demolition job.

Unable to resist a quick glance, Lively moved to the window and looked onto the ruination outside. Heavy snow covered most everything, but a few of the trees lay exposed, seeming diseased and dying, if not already dead. According to Edward, this desolation went for hundreds of miles in every direction. Had Schreck ventured out into this bleak wilderness in an attempt to reach some sort of civilisation?

With a sigh of frustration, Lively began to descend the stairs to the gaming lounge. Approaching the bottom, another slight noise came from below. As he stepped into the room, he noted it seemed a little darker now, the sun behind the cloud cover getting dangerously close to setting, and the circular room lay shrouded in deep shadows. Trying to keep his eyes going in all directions at once, Lively moved cautiously through the lounge. Though nothing was in sight to make it do so, the skin began to crawl along the back of his neck.

"Hello? Is anyone there?" There was no response, not that he'd expected one. When he reached the doorway, he stopped and looked back into the room. Had there been the briefest flash of movement near the small bar just now? He moved toward it to investigate, taking care to be as noiseless as possible. Perhaps it was a crawler.

Lively's eyes widened as he cautiously peered around the corner of the small bar. A person with long, oily hair cowered in a small ball, their arms wrapped protectively overtop their head. They looked impossibly thin beneath their ragged clothing, as if starved for many months, perhaps even years.

"It's okay. I'm a friend. I'm not going to hurt you."

The person unfurled their body and scuttled up against the cabinetry attached to the wall behind the bar. Through long, stringy hair, a man's bloodshot eyes stared unblinkingly back at Lively. A lengthy black beard sprouted from his gaunt face, appearing just as unkempt and greasy as the hair on his head. In a hoarse and halting voice, he asked, "W-who are you?"

Feeling some small relief that he was at least dealing with a human being and not a crawler, Lively held his hands up to show he had nothing in them and no intention of harming the man. "It's okay, my friend. I'm here to help. My name's Lively Deadmarsh."

"W-what kind of name is that?"

With a slight smile, Lively said, "It's the one I was given at birth." He reached out to the wasted man to offer him a hand up, saying, "Come on, my friend, let's get you back to some sort of civilisation."

The thin man pulled back against the cabinetry once more, and Lively said, "Okay, okay, not a problem. I'll let you do it yourself."

The man nodded slightly and then began to stand. From one ragged shirt pocket, he pulled a pair of thick-lensed, horn-rimmed glasses that were taped together at the bridge. He placed them onto his thin nose and blinked owlishly at Lively for a moment as if finally able to see what he looked like.

Lively nodded and asked, "What's your name, friend?"

The man looked lost in thought for a moment as if wondering that same question himself. Had he been here so long that he'd forgotten his own name, Lively wondered. But then, the man finally seemed to access the information inside his foggy brain and said, "Vincent." After another small pause, he pulled his last name from the past, speaking haltingly as if saying it was now unfamiliar, "Vincent... DaCosta."

Lively was dumbfounded. Vincent DaCosta, the front desk clerk who had disappeared almost six decades before. "I know you," Lively said.

Now it was the man's turn to be surprised, and he rasped, "How do you know me? Nobody knows me anymore. I hardly know myself anymore."

After a quick explanation of who he was and why he was at the resort, Vincent seemed a bit more at ease, and with a slight tremor of hope in his voice, he asked, "Are you going to bring me back to the world?"

Wanting to reassure the man, and possibly himself, Lively said, "I'll do my best to see that it happens."

A faint smile may have played at the corners of the man's mouth, but Lively was unsure due to his thick beard. But then it faded, and he said, "What about the crawlers?"

Lively moved to the door leading to the turret stairs and the third floor below. "I've been told of them, but haven't seen one, yet."

With eyes even wider than before, Vincent DaCosta looked about the damaged gaming lounge and said, "Well, don't worry, you'll know one when you see it."

CHAPTER THIRTY-SEVEN

December 31st, 2021 1959 hours

Minerva shone her lightsabre along the end of the bar in the ballroom. Thanks to the ultra-intense light, just visible were the numerous wire filaments that ran throughout the surface of the mahogany, all converging on the spot where the ebony box now sat.

"So, this is where the box was on New Year's Eve 1981, is that right, John?" Minerva asked.

"Yes." He shook his head in wonder as he peered closely at the fine wires and added, "I can't believe I never saw those before."

Minerva offered, "Perhaps it's because you weren't looking for them, and if you don't hold your light the right way, they're quite hard to see."

John nodded slightly and said, "I suppose."

Amanda asked, "I've been thinking about what Danny meant when he said, 'Two into darkness'? Do you think he meant the two of us, coming into the darkness that exists within this hotel?" She gestured toward John and then herself.

"I'm not sure," Minerva replied. "But don't forget he also said, 'One into light'. Hopefully, we'll figure things out as we go."

"So, what now?" John asked.

"Well, with this box where it's supposed to be, we've completed a major step. In fact, I think we should be about ready to give this a whirl and see what happens when we run the program downstairs in the gold room."

Amanda asked, "Do you think it needs to be done at a certain time?"

"Maybe," Minerva replied. "But the question is, which time is the right time?"

***

Standing in front of the computer in the gold room's remote terminal access, Minerva studied the screen. To her right, John Harder sat in the executive leather chair with Amanda behind, her hand resting on the chair's back.

On-screen, the choices were still the same, and nothing had been added since the sixth option, which she'd noted earlier:

'Initiate Aggregation - 1'
'Dissipate Aggregation - 2'
'Initiate Translocation - 3'
'Reverse Translocation – 4'
'System Reset - 5'
'Execute Subroutine Break - 6'
'Enter choice?'

Amanda said, "Which one is the right choice?"

Minerva furrowed her brow. "I pressed number two the other time, and it said that the concentrator wasn't in place. So, if the ebony box is supposedly the concentrator, I think we need to dissipate whatever had been concentrated or aggregated in this case."

John said, "So option two looks like the right choice then."

Minerva said, "I think so." She looked to John and Amanda and added, "Shall we give it a go?"

With both of her companions nodding in agreement, Minerva selected the second option and pressed enter with a small flourish. The prompt changed, and it now read:

'Dissipate Aggregation? Are you sure?'

Minerva typed the letter Y and the low-level hum ramped up beneath their feet.

"What is causing that noise?" Amanda asked.

Shaking her head, Minerva said, "I'm not sure, but there must be another room we haven't found that contains that machinery."

In a hopeful tone, John said, "It must be sizeable judging by its sound. But at least it's doing something at the moment."

They fell silent as they listened to the sound continuing to ramp higher and higher. When it reached a crescendo where it seemed something dramatic was about to happen, the hum suddenly dropped back down to its previous levels once more.

Shaking her head, Minerva said, "Well, that's not good."

On the terminal screen, the prompt now read, 'Operation cancelled. Insufficient power.'

"What?" John said, dismayed. "What else do we need to power this thing?"

Pursing her lips in thought, Minerva said, "There's something that we're missing; that much is obvious."

"But what?" Amanda asked, shaking her head in dismay.

"That's what we need to determine." Standing, Minerva said, "Perhaps another visit to the oracle would be a good idea."

"The oracle?" John queried.

"It's what I'm calling the computer in room #304 that I told you about. I'm hoping Ricky Rosenstein might be able to give us a few more answers."

**

A short while later, as he stepped onto the lobby floor again, John's heart was pounding far too rapidly for his liking, and his hip was killing him. He'd insisted on taking the stairs up from the basement, anything to avoid one of the malfunctioning elevators in this place. However, any further stair climbing was out of the question at the moment. With a pained sigh, he sat on one of the velveteen borne settees in the centre of the lobby.

Minerva hefted her sword and rested it on her shoulder once more. Looking toward the grand staircase and then back to John, she said, "I'm not sure if you want to take the elevator again after what recently happened."

Amanda added, "And I don't think any more stair climbing is in your future, at the moment, is there, John?"

Harder shook his head and said, "Not with how my hip is

feeling right now. I'm going to have to take a pass on this round." He'd decided not to mention how his heart felt, not wanting to worry them further. Thankfully, it was beginning to slow its hummingbird-like rhythm to something approaching normal. Over the years, he'd tried to be diligent in the taking of his blood pressure medication, especially since that's what Helen had brought up to him here at this hotel all those years ago. She had disappeared due to his own forgetfulness, and his guilt had made him faithful in his taking the medication for many years. But now, as he aged, he sometimes just forgot.

Amanda said, "I'll stay with you."

"No, I should be fine out in the open. I can see anyone or anything approaching from here. So, don't you worry about me." As if to emphasise his point, he held up his cane, pressed the handle's trigger, and the steel spike shot from its tip once more. He placed the cane across his knees and patted the seat cushions on either side, adding, "And besides, this is quite comfortable."

Reluctantly, Amanda said, "We shouldn't be too long," then followed Minerva toward the grand staircase.

John looked to the grandfather clock across the lobby from the front desk; it was approaching nine o'clock. He turned his attention to the women and watched as they ascended the stairs past the mezzanine.

Minerva seemed quite bright and competent, very much like her fraternal twin brother, Lively. He thought momentarily of the lost man and where he could possibly be inside the hotel. Was he perhaps in the very same lobby with him right now, but just on some other plane of existence, their awareness of each other only separated by a thin veil of reality? John shook his head at the thought.

Amanda had once again surprised John with her resilience

and strength in returning to the Sinclair. If they made it out of here alive, he was forever indebted to her for her kindness and care over the years since Helen had disappeared. She truly was the daughter he'd never had.

Thinking of children, Danny sprung to mind once again. And as that thought tripped other dormant connections in his brain, John recalled something else about that final evening here at the hotel, something which occurred just before his final encounter with the ape. Had he forgotten it earlier because of the other trauma he'd received that same evening? Whatever the reason, forgotten or not, all of it suddenly came rushing back to him.

It had been just before he'd mounted the stairs to the turret that fateful night, when he paused to listen again for the voice he thought he'd heard from up above, Helen's voice.

The quick glance he'd taken inside the open door to the suite beside him turned out to have been much more than that. His recollections of what had happened that evening seemed to skip over this part for whatever reason. Previously, he'd presumed he only listened intently for Helen's voice for a brief moment, then climbed the stairs. But now, he remembered it had been much more than that.

***

Harder stared into the room in astonishment. It was large, almost as big as the royal suite, and decorated in a similarly extravagant style. A group of men were in the centre of the room engaged in a soundless conversation. Only, they weren't actually there, and as he drew closer, he saw they weren't all men.

Thanks to a table lamp glowing on a desk near the window, he could see the closed drapes on the far side of the suite through their semi-transparent bodies. Though it looked like they were speaking quite animatedly, John couldn't hear anything, and they seemed to have no conscious awareness of him as he slowly approached them for a better look. Were they so intent in their conversation that they didn't actually see him, or were they merely echoes of things long past and, like a recording, oblivious to his presence? He didn't know.

There were five shades altogether, and John recognised two of them. Still unable to discern what they were saying, he kept moving closer until he could finally hear them talking, but he had to listen closely—it was as if they were speaking through a child's tin-can and string telephone.

A heavyset, balding man clutching a brown fedora said, "You've no right to do this."

Across from him, sitting casually on an off-white leather sofa, Edward Sinclair replied, "I have every right."

Next to Sinclair stood a tall man in black wearing a bowler hat. Smiling grotesquely, the thin man added, "You waived all your rights when you signed the contract."

"I didn't know it would be this way!" The heavyset man released one hand from his hat and clutched protectively at what John had presumed to be a small man at first. He now saw it was, in fact, a boy, perhaps eleven or twelve, and possibly the man's son judging by the resemblance.

The last of the shades was huge and looked to be the same extremely large man he'd seen in his vision down in the ballroom with the ebony box, the missing wrestler, Sonny, aka Simon Wright. Except, this Simon Wright appeared to be as bald as a newborn baby and, if anything, looked even meaner than the blonde giant he recalled. The bald behemoth stood near the heavyset man, hovering just over his shoulder in a threatening manner.

Pulling the boy close, Fedora Man said, "I won't let you take him."

"It said in plain but small print at the bottom of the form, 'rights to primary progeny waived upon signature'. Didn't you read the whole thing?"

The heavyset man shook his head, clutching his son even closer. Behind him, the bald giant reached around and grabbed the boy by the back of his jacket, wrenching him away from his father's grasp in one twirling move. Now, the bald man held the boy close to his massive chest, the child's feet dangling high in the air.

As John watched this unfold, off to one side, another shade had appeared briefly in the doorway, then ducked back out of sight just as he'd turned his head. It had looked like Danny; he was sure of it! This must have all occurred when his son had been working up here doing the security job of which Amanda had told him.

Thanks to the intensity of the conversation, it had initially appeared none of the others in the room noticed Danny. However, John saw with dismay that the angry giant had noticed Danny's brief appearance in the doorway, and when he did, he scowled even harder.

Was this what had gotten Danny killed, or at least precipitated the event, John wondered. Could Danny's unexpected appearance here, witnessing something he shouldn't have, be the reason for his 'accident' on that New Year's Eve in 1979? After this accidental introduction to some of what was really going on up here, had Sinclair and his minions tried to coerce Danny into going along with their foul deeds? John presumed that his son didn't agree, and as a result, the accident had then occurred, ending Danny's life.

Amanda had relayed to him what newspaperman Will Weston had said on their drive down to the hospital all those years ago. He'd admitted to having worked with Danny, using him as his 'insider' at the resort. Supposedly, Danny had uncovered some information that was quite damning to Sinclair, but his accident had occurred before he could divulge anything to Will. John figured that whatever it was, it must have been something relating to this incident and possibly whatever had ultimately occurred in the ballroom on New Year's Eve 1981.

But what of that boy he'd witnessed being wrenched from his father's grasp? What had happened to the young man? Had they used him for some sort of inhuman experiment up here? Did he ever see his father again? John's heart broke, thinking of the man's loss as well as his own with Danny.

The shadows of traumatic events past faded away, and he had been left standing alone in the room, a mixture of fear, anger and loss coursing through the core of his being.

But everything he'd just seen was pushed to the back of his mind as he heard another shriek from high up in the turret. He had renewed his frantic search for his wife, ultimately leading him to his encounter with the silverbacked guardian of the ebony box in the model room.

***

With ghostly recollections still reverberating through his mind, John came back to the present. The grandfather clock was just chiming its final notification that nine o'clock had arrived. He glanced about the empty lobby, noting how clean and sparkling things seemed despite the hotel's closure of forty years, looking almost ready to open its doors and accept guests into its numerous rooms once again. Thinking of the ladies in room #304, he hoped they'd have some good news regarding Minerva's interdimensional computer connection when they returned from their expedition.

A final revelation came to John as his eyes settled on the chair in which he'd awoken from his well room fugue state that final day. He felt around in the pockets of his parka for a moment. He was glad to have it back once more and thankful to Minerva for retrieving it from the kitchen. Before the seance she'd fetched it at the same time she'd gone to get her crystal orb from her room.

Harder withdrew the small bundle of plaid cloth from his parka pocket and unwrapped it. The golden key fob he'd taken from Constable Eggelson so long ago now shone brilliantly, seeming freshly forged. Its companion in the plaid nest appeared to do the opposite, the obsidian stone's sparkling darkness consuming any light that hit its surface. He recalled when he'd first seen it on the floor near the end of the bar. At the time, he'd wondered if it had come from the ebony box.

From the shadows of his past, his vision of the dancers in the ballroom suddenly sprung to the forefront of his mind. He recalled using the golden key fob to open the ebony box, but unfortunately, the vision had ended too soon, and he hadn't been able to see inside to verify that was where the stones went. But now, he felt a growing certainty that the 'two into darkness' to which Danny referred was the stone in his lap along with the one that Amanda currently possessed. They needed to go back inside the ebony box, and once that was done, the program on the mainframe would run; he was almost certain of it now. His excitement building, he wrapped the gemstone and key fob back up and placed them into his pocket once again.

With this new sense of surety, John decided to do a little investigating of his own, despite saying he'd stay where he was. He was too old and life too short to waste any more time sitting around. He thought of calling Amanda on his cell phone to inform her of his plan. However, when he pulled it out and looked at its screen, he gave a small sigh of disappointment. No bars were showing due to an apparent lack of cell phone repeater towers near the top of Overseer Mountain.

Having brought the serving trolly back from the ballroom,

Harder pulled on its handles as he stood with a grunt, appreciating the sturdy metal cart's use as a walker. Wheeling himself toward the ballroom once again, John hoped against hope that what he'd deduced might actually become a reality.

CHAPTER THIRTY-EIGHT

December 31st, 1981 0000 hours

Finding no sign of Schreck anywhere on the third floor of the west wing, Lively descended the grand staircase toward the second floor with Vincent DaCosta at his side. Things seemed even dirtier than the last time he'd been here with Edward, and he wondered if things in this frequency were drifting out of alignment as well. Curious to know more of DaCosta's plight and what he knew about things, Lively asked quietly, "How long have you been here?"

Seeming lost in thought for a moment, his hoarse voice hushed, Vincent said, "Well, it's hard to keep track. They'd been experimenting for years before I came on the scene. They sent me here just after the ballroom realignment at the end of '81. According to Schreck, they wanted to find out how long somebody could survive in an alternate frequency, if they were protected." He held up his wrist to show that he, too, wore a harmonic bracelet, except this one was plain and devoid of the gilded S cameo on the front like Lively's. Giving his head a sorry shake, DaCosta said, "Turns out, it was a long time, and I was that somebody." With a sigh, he concluded, "It must be at least a dozen years now."

"Hate to break it to you, my friend, but it's been a little

longer than that."

"Really? How much longer?"

"We'll talk," Lively said reassuringly.

As they'd ventured along the dim, dusty second-floor corridor, Lively noted that most of the doors were either broken inward, standing open, or missing altogether. However, the entrance to suite #217 was undamaged in any way and looked firmly closed. Trying the door handle, he found it locked and said in a hushed voice, "That's strange."

"What is?" Vincent whispered.

"Why is this door locked?"

"I don't know. I've been through all the suites looking for supplies. I leave the doors unlocked and open after I've grabbed whatever is in the bar fridges."

"What about the suites with the broken doors?"

"That was the crawlers.

"And the food stores down in the kitchen pantries, have you utilised those?"

"I've been there a few times but try to stay mostly in the turret since the crawlers don't usually come up that far. They seem to prefer the main floor and the basement levels. It's just so dangerous down there that it's not worth it."

"So, you've been surviving on peanuts, beef sticks and beer from the complimentary bar fridges all this time?"

"Amongst other things." A slight noise further down the hallway caught Vincent's attention, and his head snapped around in the direction of the sound. A large rat scurried down the hall and disappeared into a suite where the door hung askew. Vincent licked his lips hungrily, then looked back to Lively, his eyes cast downward as if ashamed.

Lively had watched this and felt compassion for the wasted man. What must it have been like trying to survive here in this decaying house of horrors for so many years? He turned his attention back to the locked door. After feeling around in his tuxedo jacket's pockets for a moment, he was unable to find the key to his suite and realised he may have left it with Ricky Rosenstein. Fortunately, Lively found something almost as useful and pulled the zip gun from his pocket, commenting, "I don't leave home without it." He fit the gun's steel rod into the lock along with the tension wrench, and after a couple of clicks of the trigger, the door unlocked.

Vincent reached into the numerous layers of dirty rags he currently called clothes, pulled out a chain from around his neck, and held it up; a key dangled at its end. "It's a master," he said proudly, then added, "Guess I should have mentioned that I had that a little sooner."

"What, and spoil all my fun?" Lively asked with a small grin and turned back to the door. He twisted the handle as he extracted the steel rod, then toed the door open slightly with the tip of his patent leather dress shoe and peeked inside.

Limited light from the tumultuous skies outside shone through the semi-closed drapes, and at first, Lively thought the room was empty. But just as he began to close the door, he caught movement out of the corner of his eye. He looked more closely and saw there was someone on the bed underneath the duvet cover. He moved into the dimness to investigate.

"Careful," Vincent advised in a hushed voice from the doorway.

Lively nodded as he approached the bed. Bracing himself, he whisked back the duvet and said, "Selene!" Her arms and legs had been bound to the bed frame, a rancid-looking rag stuffed into her mouth as a gag.

Sitting next to his mother on the bed, Lively noted her chest's regular rise and fall as she breathed. She was alive and seemingly unharmed, and he felt as if a weight had been lifted from his own chest. Her eyelids fluttered slightly but remained closed as if she were in the middle of some late-stage REM sleep.

With a grimace, he pulled the rag from Selene's mouth and began to untie the torn bedsheets used to bind her. Beneath the ragged sheet on her right wrist, a harmonic bracelet gleamed in the dwindling daylight. It was a basic model without the S cameo, like the one he'd seen on Vincent's wrist.

A gentle smile on his face, Lively gave Selene a couple of soft pats on each cheek, hoping she regained consciousness sooner rather than later. He loathed the thought of slapping her or anything as extreme as that. If it came down to it, he figured she wouldn't prove too difficult to cart around for a little while, at least until she woke up.

He tried one more time, saying, "Mom? It's your son, Lively."

Selene's eyelids fluttered open in the middle of this second round of cheek patting, and she said, "Lively! Thank goodness! I'm so glad to see you, Son." She sat up, wrapped her arms around him and hugged him hard.

Something swelled inside Lively's chest as his mother called him son. He sensed that she'd meant it truly and deeply, and it gave him a similar sensation to what he had with Minerva, yet different at the same time. A look of contentment crossed his face as he suddenly realised he'd received his wish: a hug from his mother. It was one of gratitude, to be sure, but it was also one of love—something he'd longed for over so many years. His voice cracking slightly, Lively said, "Anything for you, Mom, always."

Selene let go of Lively, but only slightly. Her eyes widened in surprise when she suddenly spied Vincent DaCosta standing just inside the doorway.

In a rusty voice, DaCosta said, "It's okay, ma'am. I'm with your son."

Lively agreed, saying, "He's all right, Mom. Just another one of Edward's volunteers."

Looking more closely at the man, Selene's eyes went from wide to startled, and she said, "Vincent? Vincent DaCosta? Is that you?"

Vincent nodded and said, "Yes, ma'am."

"You know each other?" Lively asked.

Selene said with a small smile, "Yes, Vincent was always one of the more decent people in an indecent place."

DaCosta moved further into the room and nodded again, saying, "Thank you for that, Miss Hammond."

"Selene, please." With a frown, she added, "They said you'd died."

"No, just abandoned here and long forgotten."

"I'm glad to see that another of Edward's lies has been exposed."

"If I can, I want to help your son end this madness."

"Let's hope that happens," Selene agreed.

Helping his mother to the edge of the bed, Lively asked,

"Are you going to be okay to walk? I can carry you if you need; no problem."

"I think the drugs have worn off, and I should be okay to get around under my own power. Nothing is broken or hurting that I can feel."

Still concerned, Lively asked, "You're sure?"

Selene nodded, then ran her fingers through her mane of auburn hair that looked so much like Minerva's. Looking from Lively to Vincent, then back again, she asked, "How did you know to find me here?"

"I had no idea you'd been stashed away here. I was looking for Schreck so he could tell me where he'd hid you." Lively nodded toward the entrance to the suite and added, "But when I saw the door closed, it seemed kind of out of place amongst all the others, and something struck me as funny about it. I just get these gut feelings sometimes."

"Your grandfather used to get those, too."

"Thomas Sinclair?"

"No, my father, Herbert."

Edward had told Lively that his paternal grandmother, Margarethe had her own abilities, which had helped Thomas locate this site of dark power and untold riches here in the interior of BC. But to now learn that his talent for finding people, places, and things was something that ran on both sides of the family was quite interesting, to be sure. And he had to wonder, had his father's dabbling in his own genetic code amplified those abilities in addition to this inherited talent?

A questioning look in her eyes, Selene asked, "Whatever happened to you, anyway? Were you also held captive here?"

Lively shook his head and said, "Actually, no. I wound up in the hotel's basement strapped to an embalming table."

One of Selene's hands flew to her chest, and she said, "Oh, no! That's horrible!"

"Not the most pleasant experience, that's for sure. But it could have been worse, I suppose."

"How so," Selene asked.

"Edward could have succeeded in what he had planned for me."

"What was that?"

"I'll fill you in later," Lively said as he stood.

"Well, I'm so glad you're here either way." Selene took a deep breath and stood from the bed, shivering slightly, her only clothing against the hotel's bitter cold, her red satin gown.

"Here, Mom, wear this." Lively gave his suit jacket to his mother.

Selene accepted it with a grateful smile and bundled up inside. Departing room #217, she leaned lightly on Lively for support as they made their way along the corridor.

The damage to the multi-mirrored common area seemed complete. Every mirror looked to be shattered into millions of glistening shards. The settees and wingback chairs had been torn apart and smashed into unrecognisable kindling.

Her voice low and filled with surprise, Selene asked, "What happened around here?"

"Just another example of the after-effects of Edward's grand plan," Lively said quietly, then began to lead the group toward the lobby.

The sprawling landscape of the hotel hanging over the mezzanine had been shredded, and only small scraps of fabric still hung from the top and bottom edges of the heavy, gilded frame.

Selene asked quietly, "His plan did that to the painting?"

Vincent shook his head and said, "No, it was—" Commotion in the lobby below interrupted his reply, and he moved stealthily to the railing and peered down. Turning back to Selene and Lively, he finished in a whisper, saying, "Crawlers."

But it wasn't just crawlers; it was Schreck and Simon as well. It seemed the bodyguard had found the object of their quest and had been bringing the man in black back when they'd encountered some trouble. The brawny bodyguard was currently backing toward the stairs leading to the mezzanine, one massive arm around the thin man, the other holding out a highbacked wooden chair in self-defence.

Schreck called out to the crawlers, uttering words of encouragement, perhaps hoping to break free of the strongman's grasp and escape if they were to suddenly attack. Did he somehow understand these creatures, Lively wondered. Would they do his bidding?

Impossibly thin and pale-skinned, the long-limbed crawlers seemed like an El Greco painting come to life. Though Lively had thought Vincent DaCosta had looked thin and wasted when they met, the grotesque things in the lobby below took the concept to a whole new level. A half dozen of the skeletally thin creatures scuttled and capered about in the shadows as they moved closer and closer to the two men. They made no noise save for a barely audible susurration, sounding as if they whispered amongst themselves.

Simon dragged Schreck into one of the few remaining pools of cloudy, late-afternoon daylight slanting down from windows high overtop the lobby's entrance. The creatures whispered and hissed, advancing slightly but staying just out of the light and remaining mostly hidden in the deepening shadows.

Lively felt Selene give a slight shudder next to him as she tried to wrap his suit jacket more tightly about her slender frame, no doubt feeling a combination of the chill of the lobby and a shiver of fear, both at once. He drew her closer, placing his arm around her shoulders as he watched the breath puff from her parted lips and his own, the cold seeming deeper here than it had been upstairs. Was it because of the crawlers, he wondered. Whatever the reason, Lively knew he needed to do something, and though reluctant to put Selene at risk, he moved to the edge of the railing and called out, "Simon!"

The burly bodyguard looked up to the mezzanine, and unfortunately, so did the crawlers. Calling out in a booming baritone, he said, "I found him! But he went and got these guys all pissed off!" Simon looked back to the creatures and saw they were drawing closer. The remaining daylight from the windows continued to fade as late afternoon approached early evening.

From the shadows of the basement stairs near the front desk, a new group of crawlers emerged and began approaching the shadows at the edge of the grand staircase as they moved to cut off Simon's escape route to the safety of the mezzanine. With a dismayed shake of his head, Lively called down, "We're okay! I found my mom!"

Schreck had begun to wriggle free and had slipped slightly from Simon's grasp. Now holding the man only by his neck, Simon called over his shoulder, "So what should I do with him?"

As if to answer his question, one of the more daring crawlers lashed out at Simon and batted aside his defensive chair, sending it crashing across the lobby's dusty, faded marble. Simon renewed his grasp on the thin man's shoulders just as a second crawler reached out with one long limb and snatched at one of Schreck's legs. Another joined in, and soon Simon was playing a game of tug of war with the crawlers, the thin man's body playing the rope.

Through the high windows, the last of the light disappeared, and darkness descended on the day. From all sides, whispering creatures closed on Simon and Schreck while another group scuttled their way up the mezzanine stairs toward Lively, Selene and Vincent.

CHAPTER THIRTY-NINE

December 31st, 2021 2101 hours

Though Minerva was fairly certain she'd closed the door to suite #304 when she'd left the room after her text chat with Lively, it was now standing ajar when she and Amanda arrived. Just two doors down, the door to the royal suite, which she'd knew she'd left open, now looked to be firmly closed. She shook her head, thinking that no door around this hotel ever seemed to remain in one state for very long. It was as if unseen guests came and went on a regular basis, doing what people do, and leaving the doors opened or closed behind them as they went about their business. Whatever the case, she didn't think a closed door would have affected what had happened here.

Inside suite #304, Ricky's Atari 800 and its peripherals had been smashed to pieces. Dozens of jagged shards poked up from the white shag carpet like beige plastic weeds. Next to where the computer equipment had sat, the glass screen of the Sony Trinitron TV now had a huge concave impression in its centre as if a massive fist had punched into it.

Minerva moved into the room, surveying the damage. "Well, this isn't going to help things much."

"What happened in here?" Amanda asked, seeming shocked by the havoc in the room.

Shaking her head, Minerva said, "I don't know. But it seems that someone or something doesn't want us communicating anymore."

In one corner of the room, Minerva spied a large suitcase almost the size of a steamer trunk. Though unsure what it contained, even if it were another computer to replace the broken one, it wouldn't matter. Antiquated computer systems were never something to which she'd paid much attention. As a result, she had no idea how to get it up and running again, let alone back to the state in which she'd first discovered it.

"So, what now?" Amanda asked. She stood just inside the entrance with her arms folded, next to the partially open door of the coat closet.

Minerva turned and looked at the destruction once more. "Well, I was going to see if Ricky had any more insights for us, but it seems that's out of the question now. So, I guess we'll just go back downstairs to see what we can—"

A rustling at her back caused Minerva to stop in mid-sentence. She whirled around and looked in horror as a length of painted brown canvas wrapped itself around Amanda Jansen's head and shoulders, then pulled her into the closet.

"Amanda!" Minerva ran to the closet door and wrenched it open.

The painted bear coiled the rest of itself around Jansen, pulling its canvas body tighter and tighter as it enveloped her from head to toe in its deadly embrace. Propped in the corner of the closet like a freshly bandaged mummy, Amanda jerked and spasmed as the painted predator smothered and squeezed the life from her quivering body.

"Oh, God, no!" Not wanting to risk cutting Amanda, Minerva propped the sword against the wall outside the closet, then reached in and tried to pull the thick canvas from Jansen's convulsing body, but it wasn't working. Changing her tactics, Minerva grabbed Amanda's feet and began to pull her from the closet instead. The woman slid down the wall and hit the floor with a muted thump as Minerva dragged her into the room.

Grasping one corner of the canvas near the top of Jansen's head, Minerva leaned back with all her weight, tearing it partially away as she did. A small gap had appeared near Amanda's mouth, and the woman wheezed thinly as she tried to catch her breath.

The canvas predator continued to constrict its painted body, and every time Jansen exhaled to bring more air into her lungs, the creature tightened itself further and further until she could only gasp like a fish out of water.

Minerva wracked her brain, unable to think of a way to get the painted bear to unravel and release Amanda. Whatever she did, she needed to do it quickly, or Amanda Jansen would die before her eyes.

The answer came to her in a musical jingle as she tugged futilely at the canvas once more. Recalling what had been effective on the painted wolf, she figured that the same rules must also apply to the painted bear, and she suddenly realised she had something almost as effective with her right now—her charm bracelet. Along with the bracelet itself, her mother's locket and several other charms were all triple-nine silver.

Minerva wrenched off the bracelet and pressed as many charms as she could into the side of the bear's painted face, currently wrapped around Amanda's head.

With a rattling hiss, the beast loosened its grip slightly. It was just enough to expose part of Jansen's face, and she took a gasping breath, trying to get more oxygen into her starved lungs, but the snake-like constriction about her body made it almost impossible.

Continuing to hold the silver charms against the canvas beast, its rattling hiss now mixed with squeals of what Minerva hoped was pain. Small wisps of smoke began to curl up from where the charms made contact with the painted horror, and it began to loosen its grip further on Amanda.

Without warning, a tendril of canvas shot out and tried to coil itself around Minerva's arm, the one inflicting the pain on it. She pulled away just in time, then leaned back in, pinning the tendril to the carpet with one knee and then she reapplied the shining silver with renewed fervour.

The beast unwrapped itself from Jansen all at once, and Minerva felt brief elation. Her plan had worked, but she now needed to stop this creature from getting away so it wouldn't ambush them again in the future. She stretched out her arm and grasped the sword propped near the closet door. Both knees pinning the beast to the floor, Minerva gave a small shriek of rage and revulsion as she drove the shining steel down into the creature and the thick shag carpet beneath.

Squalling and hissing like a stuck pig in a steam valve, the animal tried to buck Minerva off and wriggle under the partially open door into the corridor to safety.

***

Amanda sat up, gasping for air. Nearby, Minerva repeatedly drove her sword into the beast, but it appeared she'd still require some additional assistance. There had to be something with which to stop this monster somewhere nearby. And then her eyes widened when she saw it sitting on a side table, apparently never collected by the staff after the hotel shut down—a sterling silver cloche.

Still wheezing for air, Amanda scuttled on her hands and knees to retrieve the lid while trying to avoid cutting herself on the broken plastic shards sticking up from the carpeting. Dragging herself upright, she grabbed the cloche and then staggered back toward Minerva on unsteady feet.

Near the door, the ursine artwork renewed its efforts to wriggle free, the sword seeming to have minimal effect on it now. It continued to jerk and spasm violently as it tried to throw Minerva off its back.

A musical clang rang out as Amanda dropped to her knees on top of the bear's shoulders, slamming the silver cloche with all her might onto the creature's convulsing head. It hissed with renewed energy and redoubled its efforts as it tried to pull away, but it was pinned beneath both women now. Smoke poured from beneath the cloche, and Amanda and Minerva began to cough from the acrid fumes.

Minerva's face was a mixture of anger and revulsion as she repositioned herself over one of the animal's hind legs and began to slice the ancient blade through the aged canvas. The painted bear's rattling hiss changed to a shrieking wail of agony as she worked her way around its body, dismembering the beast one painted limb at a time.

***

The wheels squeaked slightly as the serving cart rolled along the corridor as if it were propelled by little white mice running around and around inside each wheel. Or at least that's what John thought it sounded like. However, why he would think that he didn't know. Perhaps because of everything happening to them at this hotel and everything that had happened in the past. It seemed as if they were all on their own little wheels, running themselves ragged as they tried to solve the mystery of the disappearance. Well, he thought with some consolation, at least there wasn't a giant cat after them at the moment.

Approaching the ballroom, John paused. What was that up ahead on the carpeted floor of the passageway? He drew closer and saw a series of footprints on the carpeting. It appeared someone soaking wet had exited the nearby service corridor and entered the grand ballroom just before he'd arrived.

John squeaked his way slowly into the grand ballroom, his apprehension growing in equal measure with his rapidly accelerating heart rate. The room seemed empty, and he couldn't see any sign of who or what had left the prints. They disappeared halfway into the room as if whatever had made them had just up and vanished in a puff of smoke. But that wasn't surprising around here, he thought with a sad smile.

He moved to the bar, trying to keep his eyes going in all directions at once. There was minimal light since most of the chandeliers were still off from after the seance, and he'd neglected to turn on any more of them when he'd entered. The room was quite large and open, but he didn't see anything nearby. Of course, that didn't mean something wasn't lurking in a darkened corner somewhere or perhaps behind one of the many dining tables.

Wheeling toward the mahogany bar, John angled his trajectory to partially see behind it as he approached. Fortunately, it seemed unoccupied. One of the few active lights was situated overtop the end of the bar. The ebony box basked in its glow, the white of its pearl trim muted in the soft light.

John bellied up to the bar and pulled the plaid bundle from his pocket. He unwrapped it and placed it on the bartop, staring at its contents for a long moment. Just as he was about to pick up the key fob and see if it could open the ebony box as it had in his vision, he paused, tilting his head slightly.

Wrapped in thought as he was, Harder hadn't noticed the

sounds and the smell at first. A slightly musical tinkling sound was followed by a plopping noise of liquid spattering onto the floor at his back, all accompanied by the faint but unmistakable smell of chlorine. And then he identified it all at once—water, dripping and dropping, along with more musical tinkling, that of dangling crystals.

Something dropped from the darkened chandeliers at his back, hitting the floor with a wet slap, and John whirled around.

It seemed that the creature that had made the footprints hadn't disappeared after all. It had taken to the air, so to speak, and managed to clamber up into the chandeliers overhead, where it had waited patiently for someone to approach the box as he had just done. And now, the silverback gorilla hulked before him, its water-soaked arms raised menacingly in the air, ready to finish what it had started with John forty years before.

CHAPTER FORTY

December 31st, 1981 0000 hours

Barely visible in the rapidly fading light, the Crawlers ascended the stairs toward their position. Thinking of only one thing to do, Lively called down to the lobby, "Hang on, Simon, I'm hitting the panic button!"

The bodyguard nodded, keeping his attention on the crawlers, at the same time trying to renew his failing grasp around Schreck's neck and shoulders. The crawlers were powerful creatures, and it seemed they wanted the man in black quite badly. Another had joined the game, and now three pulled on his legs, trying to drag him into the darkness. He shrieked in agony as the bony hands of the crawlers dug into his legs with their taloned fingertips.

As Schreck began to slip from his grasp, Simon hollered, "If you're going to do something, you'd better do it quick!"

With one arm already linked through one of his mother's, Lively said to Vincent, "I think the three of us need to be in physical contact for this to work. Can you hang onto Mom's arm on your side?"

DaCosta nodded and held his arm out. Selene took it

reluctantly, a slight grimace on her face as she noted the amount of grime covering it.

From what Lively understood, because he and Simon had shifted frequencies together, their bracelets would be in sync, and when he hit the panic button, it should pull the bodyguard and anyone he was holding back through with him. Selene and Vincent were a different story, however. He figured they should be in contact with the person wearing the panic button since they had travelled to this frequency separately. Lively twisted the gilded S in the centre of his harmonic bracelet, and the cameo popped open.

Crawlers had reached the top of the mezzanine and were now scuttling toward where the trio stood beneath the massive painting's empty frame. In the lobby below, Simon finally lost his grip on Schreck, and with a shriek, the man in black was yanked away into the surrounding murk.

Whispering excitedly, the creatures now approached from all sides, ready to drag everyone else back with them into their eternal darkness.

Lively said, "Okay, here we go!" He took a quick breath, mentally hoping that the panic function actually worked, and pressed the small red button.

The world went black.

Just as before, Lively felt the tugging sensation from within his chest, but this time there was no nausea, and he felt somewhat relieved. It seemed repeated use of the Harmoniser dulled some of the more unpleasant sensations of the frequency shifting.

In a blink of an eye, they were back on the platform in the prime frequency's royal suite bathroom. Simon stood in front, and Lively, Selene and Vincent were bunched together behind.

Lively released DaCosta's arm, grateful to not have the man too close any longer—his body odour was tremendous. Then again, after numerous decades without a shower, Lively supposed he'd be a little ripe as well. Looking to his mother, he watched her nose wrinkling in distaste as she released her grip on Vincent's arm, no doubt having similar thoughts of her own.

Simon moved down from the platform to allow the others to exit. Lively followed, stepping down just one step, then turned and offered his hand up to Selene to help her down.

DaCosta followed but kept a small distance between himself and the others. In the fresher air of the prime frequency, it seemed the man was now more aware of his own potent musk as well.

Lively said to Vincent, "We'll drop by my suite first thing so you can get yourself cleaned up a little."

Looking down at his filthy, dishevelled clothing, he nodded in agreement and said, "Or a lot."

***

With DaCosta showering and hopefully washing away a few decades of filth covering his body, Lively took the opportunity to get out of his monkey suit and change into his comfortable sweater, jeans, and bomber jacket combo. He'd left the tuxedo in the bathroom for DaCosta to wear when he was done since there was no way the man was going to go anywhere near the rags he'd been wearing in the wasteland. In the meantime, Simon had departed to track down Edward Sinclair.

Selene sat on the suite's off-white leather sofa, looking rather tired and bewildered. Lively didn't blame her, all things considered. He turned to the small bar fridge and opened the door, surprised to find it almost empty. Fortunately, one single-serving bottle of white wine had survived Ricky's healthy appetites. After removing the paper cover from the top of a glass tumbler, Lively poured some for his mother, saying, "Here, this should help calm your nerves."

She accepted it with a grateful smile and took a long sip.

After several minutes, Vincent emerged from the bathroom, looking somewhat more civilised with Lively's tuxedo hanging from his wasted frame. Though freshly scrubbed and washed, thanks to his straggly beard, hair and oversized clothes, he looked like he would be more at home somewhere on the prairies, propped on a post and surrounded by corn as he scared away crows.

Just as they were ready to depart, a rapid staccato of knocks came at the door. Selene and Vincent both looked to Lively, eyes wide. Moving to the door, Lively peered through the fisheye security lens. He stepped back and whisked the door open, catching Ricky Rosenstein with his hand poised to unleash another flurry of knocks.

Panting like he'd run the whole way there, Ricky said, "Mr. DeMille! Mr. DeMille! Am I ever glad to see you!"

"Come inside and tell us what's happening, Ricky."

Rosenstein stepped into the room, and Lively closed the door at his back. The small, spherical man huffed and puffed for a moment but smiled and nodded a little when he saw Selene. However, when he saw Vincent DaCosta standing off to one side, he did a double-take and gaped at the thin man with the stringy hair and beard wearing Lively's tuxedo. Shaking his head, he said, "You remind me of someone. Howard Hughes springs to mind, but I know he died back in '76."

"I feel like I've been dead for a while, that's for sure,"

Vincent rasped, his voice still hoarse from disuse. He held out his hand to Rosenstein. "I'm Vincent DaCosta."

Ricky shook the proffered hand, saying, "Ricky Rosenstein. You still seem familiar for some reason."

"Not surprised. You're probably having some déjà vu. I've seen you around here several dozen times before they sent me off for experimentation, but you probably don't remember me—the forgotten never do."

Rosenstein looked questioningly to Lively, who shook his head and said, "We'll fill you in shortly, Ricky. So, what's happening? You seemed rather excited at the door."

"I was! I mean, I am!" Appearing to suddenly recall his reason for the visit, the small man said, "I was in my suite, monitoring the Atari for any more messages from Minerva when it happened." He paused and nodded expectantly as if what he'd said explained everything.

Shaking his head, Lively said, "When what happened?"

Still vibrating from excitement, Rosenstein said, "Oh yeah! I was just about to leave the suite and check what was happening with you guys when I heard the mirror to the secret passage being opened on the other side of the room. I slipped out of sight into the closet near the door, and just in time, it turns out."

Concerned as well now, Selene said, "Why? What happened?"

"It was Mr. Clean! He destroyed everything!"

Lively realised that Ricky was talking about the bald Simon from another frequency and said, "What do you mean, he destroyed everything?"

"He smashed the computer, the modem, the disk drive and even the TV. I can't monitor anything from the mainframe now. I'll need to be down in the gold room."

"Okay, that shouldn't be a problem," Lively said. "We need to get downstairs now anyway." He opened the door to the hallway, and Selene rose from the couch, preparing to leave.

"But there was something else, too!" Ricky said, still agitated.

"What is it?"

"It's the frequency drift that Edward was talking about." He pointed out into the corridor and said, "Look around! It's getting worse!" The group stepped out into the hall.

It seemed that Ricky was correct. The drift in the currently paused prime frequency was having its effects known, even more so than he'd previously noted. Now outside the room, everywhere Lively looked, the degeneration of the hotel seemed to be progressing. Apart from being slightly faded, it hadn't been that bad when they'd made their way back to room #217 just a little while ago. But now, it seemed that things were degrading further. Looking more closely at his mother and Ricky, Lively wondered if they looked any different. Was the red of Selene's satin gown no longer as vibrant as it had been? Was Ricky's carrot-coloured hair just a little less orange?

They'd made it as far as the mezzanine when they encountered Simon coming up the stairs from the lobby toward them. Face scrunched up in concern, he glanced briefly about and said, "I guess you've noticed the drift?"

Lively gave a slight nod and said, "That we have."

The group descended to the lobby and now stood near the front desk. Lively said, "All right. Vincent, why don't you go with Ricky since you know the building so well. Maybe the two of you together can figure something out."

Vincent said grimly, "Anything I can do to get back at the bastards that stole my life, I'm all for it."

Ricky nodded vigorously in agreement, saying, "I'm with you one hundred percent, friend. Let's go see what we can do." Now with a newfound sense of purpose, the two men moved toward the basement service stairs next to the front desk.

The desk was currently untended, and the office behind lay in darkness. Lively noted that it was so much different from how it looked back when he'd first arrived. Then, it had just looked dusty and run-down from years of not being cleaned inside. Now, everything around the ornately decorated lobby was faded, even more so than they'd seen in the upstairs corridors. It made Lively think of the Roger's Video store that had been located near the house where he grew up. The rental shop had kept several displays of old VHS tapes in the same sun-drenched location for so many years that their box art had faded almost to monochrome.

"We may have another problem or two," Simon said as Rosenstein and DaCosta disappeared from view down the stairs.

"Don't we have enough already?" Selene asked.

Simon shook his head, saying, "Seems not."

"What is it?" Lively asked.

"Number one, I don't know where my bald counterpart is."

"Well, we know where he was," Lively said. "Ricky said he smashed up his computer inside his suite."

"Okay, well, I don't know where he is now. But our second problem is the two Simons that were guarding the grand ballroom's entrance."

"What happened," Selene asked?

"Well, only one is at the main entrance now, and the other is in the secondary corridor at the ballroom's service door. Looks like Sinclair is in there, and those boys have been told to keep us out."

"Do you think they can be swayed to join our cause?" Lively asked.

"Nah, I doubt it." Simon gestured at the hotel around them, saying, "This frequency is a step up for those guys. Trust me when I say they wouldn't want to go back to where they came from."

Lively nodded toward the ballroom annex, saying, "We'll need to deal with them before we can finish up with Edward, and I don't think it's going to be easy."

"I agree. They're just as strong as I am, maybe more so."

"Lovely," Lively said.

Moving along the ballroom corridor once again, Lively noted the colour seemed to grow more vibrant the closer they drew to the grand ballroom. It was as if the people inside were somehow keeping the frequency drift at bay outside the room, at least for the time being.

Up ahead, one of Simon's masked doppelgängers guarded the ballroom doors as he'd mentioned. Lively paused, saying, "I think I have a plan."

"What's that?" Selene asked, sounding hopeful.

"We go in through the main doors of the ballroom and see what happens."

"That doesn't sound like much of a plan," Simon said.

Lively nodded and said, "That's because I don't think we have much of a choice."

CHAPTER FORTY-ONE

December 31st, 2021 2120 hours

John stared unblinkingly at the great ape. If he turned his eyes away, even for a moment, he knew the creature would not throw him down any stairs this time. No, this time, it would crush him to death in its powerful arms and squeeze his insides out.

Taking great care, he reached toward his serving cart-cum-walker. Resting on top was the only thing he could think of to use as a weapon. He lifted his cane from the cart, brought it about to face the gorilla and pressed the release button in the handle. The two-inch spike shot from the tip with a metallic clack, and he said, "Keep your paws to yourself, you damn dirty ape."

The gorilla didn't respond to John's threat directly since that just wasn't its style. Silent, its movement unseen was the creature's preferred method of executing its business, with a heavy emphasis on the word executing.

With his weapon in hand and eyes locked on the beast, Harder grasped the bar's edge and carefully edged himself around the end as he moved to the other side. He wanted to try and put some distance between himself and the monstrous monkey, and he figured the nice, thick mahogany was better than nothing.

At his back, the doors to the ballroom slammed shut, but John didn't turn. He knew what would happen if he did. "Hello?" he called out. "Is there anybody there?" There was no response, and he continued to stare at the gorilla as he hoped that whatever had closed the doors at his back wasn't another member of the stuffed animal club sneaking up from behind.

***

Their booted feet echoing mutedly off the carpeted stairs, Minerva and Amanda rushed down to the lobby. After what had happened in suite #304, they both realised that John may be in need of assistance as well. Surely, if the hotel was as bold to attack Amanda as it just had, then it seemed all bets were now off.

They made it to the lobby without incident, only to discover that John was again missing.

"Where could he have gone?" Amanda wondered aloud.

Minerva said, "I think there's only one possibility," and then she rushed toward the ballrooms with Amanda hot on her heels.

As they neared the final bend at the end of the long corridor, Minerva suddenly stopped, and Amanda almost ran into her back.

"What's the mat—" Amanda didn't finish her sentence once she looked past Minerva and saw what had brought her to such an abrupt halt.

Outside the ballroom doors sat the polar bear, its fur damp, a small puddle of water around it on the parquet flooring near the entrance.

"I don't think we'll be going that way," Minerva said, bringing the sword off her shoulder and holding it in a protective manner again.

Amanda nodded and reached into her shoulder bag, withdrawing her Smith and Wesson .38.

Their eyes laser focussed on the polar predator, the women moved warily into the service corridor. Minerva closed the door behind them with a sigh of relief. As far as she knew, the bear couldn't open doors due to its cumbersome paws and their incompatibility with doorknobs. She was hoping it wouldn't receive any help from its opposing-thumbed, simian crony, wherever it was.

The grand ballroom's service door lay just up ahead, currently closed. Minerva held her hand up in a caution sign as she moved to the door. She pushed it slowly open and stepped cautiously inside, Amanda at her back. Minerva scanned the dim ballroom and wished her eyes would adjust more quickly. When her gaze settled on the bar, she exclaimed, "Oh, my stars! John!"

***

As if tending to business, Harder stood behind the mahogany bar. His eyes felt dry and raw from trying not to blink as he'd kept his gaze trained on the silverback gorilla. His arms were getting tired from holding the cane defensively out in front. Though not a heavy cane by any means, after years of retirement and lack of exercise, his muscles weren't used to holding anything at arm's length for any period of time.

Like an intoxicated customer demanding their drink, the gigantic gorilla loomed over John, its back to the room. It hadn't advanced any further in the last few minutes as far as he could see, but that was because he'd tried to use every ounce of willpower not to blink, sure that the creature would take advantage of every millisecond of inattention it could get.

Despite knowing better, Harder had been unable to resist a glance toward the women as they entered the room. Realising his error almost immediately, he looked back to the great ape with a jolt of fear, horrified to see it now reached across the bar toward him, its grasping fingers inches from his face.

Minerva approached the ape slowly from behind, saying, "I'm going to see if I can chop him down to size, John."

"Whatever you need to do, do it quickly."

"I'll cover you," Amanda said, holding up her service revolver.

As John watched Minerva draw closer out of the corner of his eye, he became convinced that the monster before him had now become almost fully sentient.

Minerva raised her sword as she prepared to attack. When she was within a yard of the ape, a cringe-inducing snap echoed through the cavernous room, and their worst fears were realised.

The silverback gorilla began turning its head toward Minerva as she prepared to swing the sword. One of the beast's massive arms creaked and cracked as it raised it defensively in the air to deflect the upcoming blow.

Amanda stepped suddenly forward from the bar's end and brought her .38 to bear on the ape. Holding the weapon only a couple of feet from the animal's head, she said, "Deflect this," then pulled the trigger three times in rapid succession.

The gorilla tried to move out of the way, but its real-time reflexes weren't fast enough, not yet at least, and the bullets punched through the side of the animal's head. Chunks of fur, skin and skull blew out the other side and scattered across the gleaming bartop.

John watched in wide-eyed horror as the ape jerked and jittered its head toward Amanda. From the other side of the softball-sized hole in the creature's head, Minerva stared back at him, her eyes equally wide.

Amanda stepped back, and Minerva released the cocked swing she had prepared with her sword. The blade whistled through the air and connected with the taxidermied gorilla, biting deeply into its neck. The sweeping blow severed the creature's head almost completely, and it now hung down one side of its body, a thin flap of leathery-looking skin the only thing keeping it attached.

The lack of a head didn't slow the stuffed ape down at all, and it turned toward Amanda and Minerva, a gurgling grumble of rage coming from the ragged hole where its head used to be. Minerva changed up her tactics and gave a low, sweeping strike with her sword. Her aim was clean and true, hacking into the animal just at the thigh, its sodden fur and tanned hide separating with ease as they met the sting of Minerva's cold steel. The amputated leg flew from its body, and with another rumble of rage, the beast tumbled to the ground with a crash, its head coming loose and rolling several feet across the floor.

The creature now scrabbled about blindly on the hardwood floor, trying to grab at the women's legs and pull them down into its powerful arms, but both danced back out of the way just in time.

Seeing another chance, Minerva lashed out and sliced into one of the creature's arms as it reached toward Amanda, severing that appendage as well. After a further bit of hacking and slashing, a slightly winded and dishevelled Minerva stopped to rest and survey the results of her handiwork.

Now missing both arms and legs, the gorilla lay in numerous pieces scattered across the floor. And yet, each individual fragment still jiggled and jived as if alive, seeming to only need a sturdy needle and thread to be good as new again.

Minerva moved to the netting which had held the balloons and streamers, currently hanging down from the ceiling in the middle of the ballroom's dance floor. Standing on a chair, she snagged the webbing with the tip of her sword, pulled it down, and then dragged it toward the dismembered ape. Spreading it out near the animal, she walked around the carcass, using the blade to flick the juddering limbs, legs and torso into the centre of the net while feeling like Captain High Liner hauling in his catch of the day. With that done, Minerva and Amanda dragged the quivering mass of body parts to a storage closet in a far corner of the room and closed them up inside.

***

The trio stood at the bar for a moment, looking at the ebony box. John said, "I came back in here because I think I figured out where that stone goes." He pointed toward the obsidian gem on the bartop. "I recently recalled something that had happened to me many years before here, and I'm convinced it needs to go back inside that box before we can run that machine in the basement again."

Minerva stared intently at the stone and golden key fob nestled next to it, keeping well away as if sensing the dark energy they contained. "I never knew those even existed."

"Neither did I, until my first day here. I found it near this box, just down there." John looked to the floor near the edge of the bar.

Amanda pulled her own bundle from her shoulder bag, opened it up and placed it on the bartop next to John's. The two gemstones weren't identical, appearing roughly hewn and slightly irregular in shape, but both still fairly uniform, each about the size of a walnut.

"Okay, this is progress. But how do we get the lock and chain off?" Minerva asked. Her breath came in small puffs, the temperature dropping around them as the two stones were placed next to each other.

Nodding, John said, "I think I know." He picked up the golden key fob using his winter gloves. Though not as cold as the obsidian stones, he could feel it nonetheless. Recalling his dream, he moved the fob toward the lock and felt it gradually growing warmer and warmer. As he placed it against the lock, the black wax covering its surface began to liquefy and run down its sides, dripping onto the mahogany bartop.

"That seems to be working," Minerva said encouragingly.

Soon, the lock beneath lay exposed, revealing a strange pattern on its face. Amanda said, "It almost looks the same shape as the key fob."

John nodded, saying, "I agree." He aligned the irregularly shaped fob with the lock face and pressed it into it.

The lock's shackle suddenly dropped open with a clunk, and each member of the group looked to the other, all seeing the same apprehension being reflected back.

CHAPTER FORTY-TWO

December 31st, 1981 0000 hours

Ricky Rosenstein followed Vincent DaCosta down the corridor. The pair moved cautiously, unsure what they might encounter in the dim passageway. Arriving at the intersection that led to the operating theatre and gold room beyond, Vincent held his hand up, and they paused. After a momentary peek around the corner, the coast seemed clear, and they made their way into the operating theatre.

Images of being strapped down, tied-up, taped, untaped, bruised and battered flashed through Ricky's mind. He suspected they were from his repeated experiences down here and elsewhere in the hotel over the years. But there was one thing that kept reappearing—a face. And not just any face, that of his shaven-headed nemesis, Mr. Clean. After his recent close encounter with the man breaking into his suite and destroying his Atari computer, the man was definitely at the top of Ricky's mind. He hated to think what would have happened if Clean had discovered him unawares at the computer and he hadn't had time to hide in the coat closet.

"How did you end up here? I mean, how did you end up working for these people?"

"I was greedy and lazy." DaCosta shook his head in disgust.

"What do you mean?"

"Back in the day, before I first came over. I felt I wasn't living up to my full potential, working the night shift at a hotel front desk in the middle of nowhere and all. Anyway, Schreck came along, promising me all sorts of things, including being part of, as he said, 'something that the world has never seen before'."

Ricky shook his head sadly and said, "Well, I guess he was right about that much."

They moved into the dimly lit control room, and Rosenstein checked the computer terminal to see what was happening. The program was still paused, as was the realignment. He tried to break into the executable but was thwarted when he discovered the computer had stopped accepting any input. It wasn't frozen exactly, and appeared to be running, but it just wouldn't allow him to do anything more to it either. Ricky wondered if he might need to reboot the entire system. But if he did so, what would happen?

A noise in the other room drew their attention, and they watched through the viewing window with large eyes as Mr. Clean strode into the operating theatre, his face clouded with barely restrained anger, as usual.

Vincent moved quickly to the exit leading to the gold room and gestured for Ricky to follow. Moments later, they were slipping inside the hidden terminal access. Just as they'd closed the door, Clean moved into the gold room.

With eyes glued to the CCTV monitors and their breath held, they watched to see what the man would do. At first, they were afraid he might come directly to where they hid, but fortunately, it seemed he had other plans and strode toward the concave impression in the floor where the huge dish was located.

Looking to be at least forty feet across and dipping down into the floor by almost twenty, the dish looked for all the world like a very large, very expensive sink basin. An intricate metal framework hung from the ceiling overtop the dish's expanse. 'Collectors' projected from all four sides, tapering to a point over the centre, connected to an elaborate machine, which, according to the monitor's label, was the 'Aggregator'.

The bare-headed bodyguard opened an access panel in the floor near the edge of the dish and began to adjust something. Whatever he was doing was most likely at the behest of Edward Sinclair. Ricky looked to Vincent with concern. It was a look which DaCosta seemed to share, as both realised that Clean was potentially sabotaging things as they watched, just as the monstrous man had with the Atari computer in suite #304.

Ricky's eyes widened as he saw the opportunity that had just presented itself, and he silently moved to open the control room door. Vincent saw this and put his hand out and held Ricky's arm momentarily, hissing, "What are you doing? Do you want him to know that we're in here?"

Ricky pulled away from Vincent, whispering, "I need to do something, and I need your help." After a quick explanation of his plan, he looked to the monitor and saw that Clean was still busy doing something next to the dish, his back to the room. This was their chance. Years of repressed anger mingled with fear toward this man coursed through Ricky's veins, and he knew he needed to do what he'd planned.

Creeping out into the gold room first, Rosenstein was followed by DaCosta, who moved silently off toward the periphery of the dish, just out of Clean's field of view, waiting for his cue.

Moving a little past where the bulky bodyguard worked on the aggregator, he watched the man cursing away under his breath as he tried to adjust something on the art-deco electrical oddity. Ricky's eyes widened as he noted how muscular the man actually was and knew if he screwed up or things didn't go according to plan, he and Vincent would be in a whole world of hurt, dead, or both.

"Hey, Yule Brenner!" Ricky called.

The bulging bald man turned, his eyes narrowing to slits, and he said, "You! You little rodent. This is all your fault!"

"My fault? You're the one aiding and abetting all this insanity!"

"The only thing I'm betting on is that I'm gonna break you in half. You've been a pain in my ass all these years." With his back now to the dish, Clean didn't see Vincent moving behind him at a tangent.

Making a show of bravado, adrenaline flooded through Ricky's veins as he approached the immense man. In each hand, he held a syringe that he'd pulled from his jacket pockets. They weren't actually loaded with anything, but he held them up at an angle as he brandished them toward the man, hoping he wouldn't notice. "I have enough drugs in these to put you into a permanent coma."

"All right. Let's dance then, little man."

Rosenstein came at the massive man as if he was going to jab him with the syringes and then, at the last minute, stopped short and threw the syringes at the man's face instead.

With a shout of surprise, Clean covered his face reflexively at the incoming needles.

Vincent DaCosta swept in from behind and dropped to his knees. He wrapped his arms over his head, forming himself into a small ball and braced against the short lip that ran around the edge of the deep dish.

Though only the water boy on the high school football team, Ricky used his weight as effectively as any offensive tackle. Ducking low, he plowed his head into the man's belly.

Clean gave an almost comedic "Oof!" and then stumbled backwards over Vincent DaCosta. A shout of panic escaped his mouth as he found himself tumbling back into the large depression in the floor. His head slammed into the side of the dish with a loud crack, and he slid unconscious down the slick metallic surface to the bottom.

Vincent pulled his hands from over his head and looked down into the dish. He'd assumed a 'duck and cover' position behind Mr. Clean as if he were hiding underneath his school desk as part of a nuclear bomb drill back in elementary school. With wide eyes, he said, "Holy shit! It worked!"

Ricky moved next to Vincent and looked down at the unconscious man lying spread-eagle at the bottom of the dish. There looked to be no way up as the metal was smooth as glass all the way around its circumference. At least it didn't appear like the man would be destroying anyone else's computers anytime soon. He nodded at DaCosta's, saying, "Let's just hope he doesn't gum up the works."

CHAPTER FORTY-THREE

December 31st, 1981 0000 hours

Still needing to take care of unfinished business with his father, Lively approached the main doors to the ballroom, with Selene on his arm and Simon trailing at their backs.

"What are you going to do?" Selene asked.

"Why, try to appeal to his better nature, of course."

From behind, Simon said, "I don't think he has one."

The single doorman guarding the entrance was still wearing his white face mask, his gaze unfocused as he stared into space. Lively wondered about the man beneath. Perhaps he could be swayed to come over to their side somehow? He reasoned that if the original Simon 'Sonny' Wright could become disaffected enough by the whole thing to want to be done with it all, then maybe this man might as well. Well, he thought, there's only one way to find out.

"Hey, my man! How's it going?" Lively inquired.

Like one of the Queen's Guard at Buckingham Palace, the man was implacable in his silence and didn't respond, continuing to stare straight ahead into space.

"Haven't you had enough of this? I mean, the same night over and over and over. Wouldn't you like to be done with all of this after all these years? Don't you want to return to your world and live again?"

The man's eyes flicked toward Lively for a moment as if considering the question, then looked away into space as before.

Seeing that wasn't going to get him anywhere, Lively changed his tactics and simply said, "We'd like to enter the ballroom, please."

The doorman remained mute, his eyes returned to Lively for a moment, seeming to drill into him, but he remained unmoving and then looked away again.

From over Lively's shoulder, Simon said, "He's not going to listen to you. He's bought into everything here bigtime." Then he added, "Like I said, he's from a subfrequency," as if that explained everything.

"All right, I guess we'll do it your way." Lively stepped aside with Selene to allow the big man to do his thing.

Simon moved to his alternate reality double and said, "You need to move aside, brother."

The masked man didn't respond to Simon but instead folded his arms in defiance and increased his stance slightly as if to show he wouldn't be easily moved.

"It doesn't have to be this way," Simon said one final time. He grasped the man's lapels and pulled him forward. Though his facemask was still impassive, the eyes behind it suddenly went wide with anger, and the doorman tried to wrench Simon's hands free. Nodding toward the doors, Simon said,

"Do you mind, Mr. DeMille?"

Lively shook his head and said, "Not in the least. He stepped forward and pulled the right-hand door open at the doorman's back.

Simon yanked his twin even closer for a brief moment, then suddenly thrust his arms out and pushed the man back into the room, where he landed with a bone-jarring thud.

Across the ballroom, the band was in full swing, and everyone seemed up on their feet, dancing to the music with very few noticing the battle of the titans taking place in the background.

Not breaking rhythm, several couples getting down on the periphery of the group parted like the Red Sea as the doorman joined the festivities, sliding several feet along the polished hardwood and into the midst of their melodic manoeuvres.

The boulder of a man lay on his back momentarily, seeming stunned about what had just happened to him. Giving his head a shake, he gathered himself up and climbed to his feet again, seeming ready for round two. Lively wondered if the man had wrestling experience like Simon, 'Sonny' Wright. As he watched the OG Simon enter the ballroom, he figured he was about to find out.

Shaking his head, Simon strode toward the other man. Like two rams ready to butt heads, the men charged at each other and began grappling. With a grunt, Simon pulled the other man's hands from his body and spun him to the ground, causing the man's mask to fly off from the impact. His face beneath was horribly scarred, as if from close contact with a windshield in an automobile accident many years before. Still not speaking, the doorman grabbed his mask from the floor and slipped it back on as he stood again.

Lively wondered if the man was self-conscious about his

appearance or just used to having the mask on his face after so many years now that it just seemed habit. About to turn to Selene and suggest she move to a safe spot while the fight was going on, a big, beefy hand suddenly dropped onto Lively's shoulder.

Grabbing the hand and spinning one hundred and eighty degrees, Lively wrenched back the beefy arm attached to the beefy hand until he heard tendons pop. It was the other subfrequency Simon who'd been guarding the service entrance. The man growled and shook his arm out, then charged at Lively, a crazy look in his eyes.

Off to one side, Simon and the other doorman were engaged in another muscle-bulging grapple, looking equally matched.

The second doorman charged like he was a bull and Lively held a red cape. With cat-like grace, Lively stepped aside, dodging out of the man's path at the last moment. As he moved, he grabbed a cloth from a nearby table and pulled it off, leaving the dishware, bottles, glasses and centrepiece upright. Pleased at that surprising outcome, he couldn't resist saying in his best Bill Murray, "And the flowers are still standing!"

Momentum propelled the large man forward, and he was unable to stop before crashing into an unoccupied table. Glasses, plates, bottles of wine and champagne flew everywhere. The dining table's legs snapped, and together with the man, they all crashed to the floor.

When the doorman landed, Selene had shuffled back out of the way to avoid being hit by an errant bottle or body. The man rolled over and began to stand with a grunt. In one fluid movement, Selene picked up an unopened bottle of champagne that had survived the table's collapse, then swung it in an almost perfect parabolic arc which ended just at the large man's temple. The bottle rang out a melodic clunk but didn't smash, and the man went back down, hard, temporarily stunned.

"Thanks, Mom!" Lively said. With the tablecloth now in hand, he grabbed the large man's arms and began to wrap it in a figure-eight pattern around both wrists, then tied it tightly as he pressed his knee into the man's back. Just as he finished, another crash came, and he turned to see that Selene had attempted his manoeuvre with a tablecloth of her own. Unfortunately, she'd had much less success than he, and all the plates, bottles and glasses had crashed to the floor. Seeming somewhat embarrassed, she handed the cloth to her son, saying, "That didn't quite work the way I'd planned."

Lively took the cloth, then said, "Maybe I can help you practice someday." He proceeded to tie the tablecloth around the man's legs and then tied it to the cloth already around his wrists so that the aggressive doorman was now effectively hog-tied.

A couple of tables away, Simon had his short-haired subfrequency double on the floor in a chokehold. The man thrashed and clawed at Simon, but eventually, his agitated motions began to lessen and lessen as he blacked out and then grew still.

Lively deftly pulled another cloth from a nearby table and tossed it to Simon, nodding to the other, already trussed doorman, saying, "You might want to make sure he doesn't get up and go on walkabout."

With a nod, Simon began tying the man's arms behind his back.

Selene had moved to another table and, having watched Lively perform the action an additional time, tried the trick again. This time, she succeeded, mostly, and only two plates half-filled with food crashed to the polished hardwood floor.

Lively grinned and nodded, saying, "Now you're getting it!"

Selene flashed a smile back to her son, pleased at his encouragement. She balled the cloth up and tossed it to Simon so that he could tie the other doorman's feet together as well.

Just about to tell his mother they needed to search for Edward, Kandi popped out of the crowd at Selene's back and dragged her into the sea of gyrating bodies.

"Mom!" Lively called as he moved into the undulating crowd. Behind him, Simon was just finishing the hog-tie of his other-worldly double.

Masked patrons whirled and twirled around Lively, a sea of white faces, the men's plain, the women's adorned with feathers and jewels. He looked rapidly about, panicked, but there was no sign of Selene.

A slender blonde-haired woman in a green silk dress appeared out of the crowd at Lively's side and grabbed his hand. She looked very familiar for some reason, but he couldn't quite place her at the moment. She guided him through the throng and out to the other side near the bar, where he discovered Edward now stood holding Selene, with Kandi at his side.

The woman in green released Lively's hand, and he turned to thank her, but when he did, she'd disappeared into the crowd once more.

Sinclair held Selene's shoulders tightly with one hand; the other pressed a gleaming syringe filled with pale liquid to her slender throat. A wicked grin crept over Edward's handsome face, exposing the true nature of the man beneath.

CHAPTER FORTY-FOUR

December 31ˢᵗ, 2021 2245 hours

Lying on the bartop next to the ebony box, the obsidian gemstones glinted darkly in the jaundiced light of the single chandelier above. John Harder slowly pulled the antiquated chain through the handles of the mysterious box, and the aged lock dropped to the bartop with a muted thump. He paused and looked to Amanda and then Minerva.

Minerva nodded to John, saying quietly, "Go ahead, open it."

Though temporarily forgotten, the polar bear was most certainly not gone from the other side of the ballroom doors. Almost as if it heard Minerva's hushed voice, it began scratching furiously at the thick oak, trying to gouge its way inside.

In an apparent act of caution, Minerva picked up her sword from where she'd propped it against the bar, then leaned on the hilt almost casually as she watched John work.

Seeing Minerva's actions, Amanda reached into her shoulder bag and brought out her .38 once more. She held the revolver toward the ground, her free hand folded overtop, index finger ready at the side of the trigger.

Harder reached for one of the small handles on the front of the cabinet and tentatively touched it. He wore his winter gloves but still felt the cold emanating from the dark cabinet. With a deep breath, he slowly pulled the cabinet doors open, recalling his vision from forty years before at the same time. But this time, he wasn't dazzled into unconsciousness like back then. No, this time, he was shocked into stunned silence by what lay inside.

Lining the interior space of the ebony cabinet were dozens upon dozens of obsidian gemstones. Row after row lined the cabinet's red-hued back wall and doors, each nestled tightly next to the other in what appeared to be dark red velveteen. John leaned closer and squinted into the box's dim interior, almost sure he saw the velveteen material quiver slightly as if flesh instead of fabric. The stones themselves appeared faintly luminous, though it was hard to tell; unless they were to turn off all the lights, but that wasn't something he felt willing to try in order to find out.

Though it had felt cold around the box before being opened, the chill was worse than ever now. Their breath came in great plumes as if the group had suddenly taken a stroll into a gigantic walk-in freezer.

All were speechless as they took in the strangeness of the box and the stones within. Next to it, the obsidian stones that Amanda and John had brought looked innocuous enough on their own. But the faint glow of the stones inside the box and the bone-chilling cold belayed their true nature, making them seem infinitely more dangerous and powerful.

With a start, Amanda said, "Oh my God!"

"What is it?" John asked, concerned.

"All around this box, that pearly-white trim. I just realised it's made up of human teeth!"

"Yes," Minerva said, shaking her head sadly, "That's just one of those things you have to pick up on your own around here."

"Good lord! I never noticed that." John said. As he stared at the grisly detail, he wondered how many other things he just 'never noticed' around this resort in his time here.

Amanda glanced down to the two gems on the bartop and then to John, saying, "Looks like we found where those go." Inside the cabinet, just near the top level in the centre at the back, only two spaces were not currently occupied by obsidian stones.

Harder nodded and picked up the stone that Amanda had brought. Though it wasn't much bigger than a one-dollar loonie coin, it seemed surprisingly heavy, heavier than his, in fact. He gingerly placed the dark gem into its waiting velvet nest. With that done, he picked up his own stone and discovered that it wasn't just Amanda's gem that had more weight to it; his own also seemed to weigh substantially more than ever before.

Taking great care and feeling his fingers numbing through his thick leather gloves, John slid the final stone home into its spot next to Amanda's. All at once, the gems throughout the box surged in brightness and began pulsating gently in their velveteen nests as if each now contained its own beating heart.

"That definitely done something," Amanda said, her breath steaming from her mouth. At her back, the polar bear's renewed scratching at the ballroom doors seemed to agree with her assessment of the situation.

Nodding, Minerva said, "It does seem to be a positive sign."

John asked, "Should I close the box?"

Minerva said, "I think so. The power needs to be contained."

Pushing the doors closed, John noted that the intense cold lessened almost immediately. He breathed a sigh of relief and watched his breath puff out slightly in the residual cold remaining in the air.

***

The trio stood at the bar, looking at the ebony box. The chain was back through the handles, and the lock reengaged, just in case that would somehow affect the box's abilities.

"So, what's the plan?" Amanda asked.

Minerva stood looking at the ballroom doors. There was no more scratching sound from the other side, but it didn't mean that the bear wasn't still out there. She turned to Jansen and said, "You saw just as I did that the box looks like its power has been restored. Those missing stones have to be what was stopping things from working before, and I need to try and run that program again." She looked at her watch and added, "And we don't have much time left. It's almost eleven o'clock."

Reaching into Lively's courier bag, Minerva removed the two-way radios and handed one to John, verifying the switch was still set to VOX as she did.

John did the same with his, said, "Test, test," into it, and Minerva's radio immediately crackled to life with his voice.

Satisfied it was working, Minerva said, "I'll let you know on the radio when I'm ready to try again and then you can brace yourselves."

"Brace ourselves? For what?" John wondered.

"I don't know," Minerva replied. "I've been thinking about that and believe we need to be prepared. I read the reports of some of the witnesses you interviewed, John. And if what they said is anything to go by, I don't think either of you wants to be standing inside this room when the programme is run. Stepping out into the corridor when that time comes might be a great idea, just in case, since we don't know for sure what's going to happen."

Amanda asked, "What are your concerns?"

"From everything we know, when the mainframe's programme is run, anyone in this room might be at risk of freezing to death at the very least, or perhaps worse."

The bear renewed clawing at the door again, and Minerva said, "I think I'm going to take the service passage to avoid our furry friend." Just as she turned toward the door, a resounding crash came from the room's far end near the main entrance. At first, she thought the bear may have burst through, but the heavy oak doors remained firmly closed. And then she saw what had happened. A dining table near the doors had collapsed for some reason.

John remained at the bar near the box. "What caused that?" he wondered aloud.

"I'm almost certain it's not termites," Minerva said as she moved toward the table, her sword at the ready. "And I don't think it's the entity that Lively and I call Thumper because we would have heard it approaching the room. That thing never moves silently around here."

Amanda was close behind, her Smith and Wesson at the ready. "I've experienced something like that in this room before, and you're right; I heard it approaching well before it got here."

At first, Minerva thought something might have fallen onto the table, but then she saw that there was nothing on that may have impacted its hardwood surface, and the chandelier still looked to be attached to the ceiling. The table was a sturdy piece of wood; for it to collapse like it had would have required a great weight to be thrown onto it all at once. The centrepiece and empty wine bottles lay nearby in thousands of glistening shards. Had it been a poltergeist? No, she thought, shaking her head almost immediately. There hadn't been any presence nearby before the table collapsed, and she knew she usually got quite a tingle when a poltergeist was in the vicinity. And then she wondered, perhaps something had happened in Lively's reality, and it had manifested itself here in hers. Was the membrane that separated their worlds really that thin now?

Outside the main doors, the bear renewed its scratching as if it had heard the ruckus inside the ballroom and wanted desperately to get inside to where the action was.

Tilting her head toward the entrance, Amanda said, "Let's hope you make this quick, cause I don't know how much more those doors can take."

John added, "And we'll have to stay near the box until the last minute, in case it gets through."

"I agree," Amanda said, then looked to Minerva and added, "If that creature gets past us and moves the box before you can run the programme..." She trailed off, leaving the rest unsaid.

Minerva hustled toward the service corridor, saying, "I'll try my best." She rested her sword on her shoulder, opened the door and peeked into the passageway. With nothing threatening in sight, she stepped from the room. Turning back, she tried to give an encouraging smile and held up her radio, saying, "I'll talk to you soon," then shut the door.

Unable to return Minerva's smile, Amanda looked to the closed door and said quietly, "I really hope so."

Now left standing in the passageway, Minerva listened intently for a moment. She could hear no other sound save the intermittent scratching of the polar bear outside the ballroom doors. With a determined sigh, she moved to the staircase near the service elevator, hoping any further obstacles the hotel threw at them would be of the minor and non-life-threatening variety. However, she wasn't about to hold her breath.

CHAPTER FORTY-FIVE

December 31st, 1981 0000 hours

Sinclair backed against the bar, holding Selene tightly about the waist. "Stay back, or I'll fill her with this." He pressed the syringe a little harder, the tip of the needle dimpling Selene's skin, a small drop of blood forming in the depression where the surgical steel met her pale throat.

Edward didn't say what 'this' was, Lively noted, but the pink-hued liquid was no doubt something that would knock his mother out at the very least, or at the very worst, overdose and kill her. At Edward's side, Kandi grinned at Lively in cruel contempt.

Selene saw this out of the corner of her eye, and her expression of fear changed to one of anger. She'd been holding both of her slender hands to Edward's arm that was about her shoulders, trying weakly to pry it from her body. One of her hands suddenly dropped away and groped along the bar at her back until it latched onto a stubby brown beer bottle near the edge, a bottle of Moosehead, according to the label. Her fingers wrapped around it, and she rotated her arm upward and outward, catching Kandi squarely in the side of her head, erasing her heartless smile in a flash of breaking glass.

Kandi crumpled to the floor next to the bar, and Edward squeezed Selene harder, saying, "You bitch! I should press the plunger right now just for that!" He reaffirmed his grip on Selene and began dragging her toward the stage, the needle still pressed close to her neck.

The band stopped playing as Edward stepped onto the low platform with his captive, and silence now filled the room. All the dancers stood motionless, unsure what to do. The eyes behind their masks appeared blank and emotionless as if the band's music had somehow kept them energised, and without it, they had no direction, guidance, or will of their own.

Lively moved slightly toward his parents, hands up in a non-threatening manner. He didn't want to do anything to alarm his father since he was more than sure that the man would follow up on his threat with the syringe if pressed. As all signs seemed to indicate, the man had no capacity for empathy or anything like it. No, Edward was about as far from caring or considerate as a person could get. Lively wondered if his father had ever truly cared for his mother, or had she merely been another small cog in his father's grand plan to dominate the universe?

Keeping his hands out in plain sight where Edward could see them, Lively asked, "What is it you want?"

Sinclair appeared to be considering Lively's question for a moment. The low platform on which the band was located was near the door to the service corridor, and Lively wondered if the man might be preparing to make a break for it. Edward adjusted his grip on Selene, the tip of the needle still dimpling the side of her neck. "What is it I want? Isn't it obvious? I want you to resync the frequencies and return things as they were!"

But Lively knew there was more to it than that. Edward no doubt still coveted his life force and, if given the opportunity, would most likely attempt to siphon it off again at some point in the future, so he knew he couldn't trust the man. However, he could see that his father was correct; things needed to be either restarted or ended. Right now, he was pinning his hopes that Minerva was able to work out something on her end, and he prayed to God that was the case. With the worsening conditions, it now appeared Ricky and Vincent hadn't had any luck with the mainframe.

All around them, the hotel continued its monochromatic misalignment. The people, the food on the smorg, and the room itself now looked to only contain the slightest hints of colour. Selene's red satin dress seemed to be one of the few things spared this process, at least for now, and she stood out like a lighthouse beacon on a dark and stormy night.

Sudden movement caught both Edward and Lively off-guard. In a blur, Vincent DaCosta popped up behind Edward, whisked the needle from Selene's throat, and pulled the syringe from Edward's grasp. Lively took the opportunity to rush forward and sweep Selene safely away from Sinclair's side.

As Lively had suspected, Edward attempted a dash for the door, but he encountered a roadblock before he'd hardly even started off the stage.

Ricky Rosenstein stood in the doorway to the service passage, an angry look in his eyes, his legs spread wide as if not to be easily moved.

Vincent appeared suddenly at Sinclair's back, grabbed him in his wiry arms, and then pressed the syringe closely to his throat.

Edward's wide eyes looked from their corners at the man holding the needle to his jugular vein and said, "You? How is that possible?"

"Your son found me and brought me back," DaCosta said in his gravelly voice. He nodded to Ricky and back, saying, "We just helped put down one of your bodyguards in the basement and came back up here to see if we could help out. Turns out, we could." He pressed the needle's tip into Edward's throat a little further.

"Careful with that!" Edward said, alarmed.

"Careful? Oh, trust me, I'll be careful now that I've finally got you right where I want you." DaCosta readjusted his grip and added, "Do you have any idea how long I've waited for this day?"

Edward said in a petulant voice, "If something isn't done to put right what you people have broken, there won't be any more days!"

"Maybe that's for the best," Vincent said gravely.

Ricky Rosenstein moved further into the room from the service corridor. He shook his head as he approached Lively, saying, "I can't fix this day, Mr. DeMille, even if we wanted to. The computer has locked us out completely."

"You mean you've locked us out!" Edward snapped, still being careful not to move and get jabbed with the syringe.

"Hey, I was only trying to stop this horror show you have going on here!" Ricky said, anger flashing in his eyes.

Before things spiraled out of control, Lively figured he needed to do something about the situation. First, he needed to address the syringe to his father's throat. It wasn't because he cared if the man lived or died, but Lively felt that Edward needed to be accountable for what he, and posthumously, Max Schreck, had done to all of the people at this party. He turned slowly and surveyed the group around them. They still stood like zombies, blank expressions behind most of their masks. It was as if the further out of sync the frequency got, the less life they had. If the frequencies were to become misaligned enough, would everyone eventually just fade away, him and his mother along with them? Whatever ultimately happened, that was the outcome he wanted to avoid at all costs.

"Vincent," Lively said, "I feel your pain. Trust me, I know what it's like to be used." He nodded his head toward the syringe and added, "But you can't do that." Out of the corner of his eye, he saw Simon casually moving off through the crowd and hoped the man was going to circle around behind Vincent and Edward.

"For what I've done?" Edward squawked. "I should get a Nobel for what I've done to advance science and our understanding of the universe!"

Next to Lively, Selene shook her head in disgust. "A prize for what? Kidnapping more than a hundred people and holding them captive for forty years?"

Now approaching the bandstand, Ricky added, "And it's not like you shared any of your discoveries with the world. You used all of them for your own benefit."

"It would have ultimately been shared," Edward said defiantly.

"Of course it would," Lively said in agreement. He looked to DaCosta and said, "We might need his assistance. Don't do anything rash, Vincent."

Unfortunately, DaCosta seemed to be done taking advice and looked ready to seek the justice he had so desired as payment for the years he had endured in the wastelands. As his thumb readied to press the plunger, Simon moved silently in from the back of the bandstand, grabbed the needle in his oversized, iron grip and pulled it from DaCosta's grasp.

Vincent said, "What the—,"

"Sorry, little buddy," Simon said. "Need to have him alive for now."

DaCosta's shoulders slumped in defeat. He let go of Sinclair, who was immediately secured by Simon, the large man holding him in a painful-looking bear hug.

Lively was going to tell Vincent about getting a chance to see Edward answer for his crimes when, suddenly, the lights went out.

CHAPTER FORTY-SIX

December 31ˢᵗ, 2021 2352 hours

Minerva descended the service staircase as silently as she could. Trying her best not to attract the attention of anything in the hotel, it had taken much longer than anticipated to get to the gold room. With every lethal thing the resort had at its disposal now seeming out to stop them, she was being exceedingly cautious.

She'd taken to thinking that she and Lively, along with the police inspectors, were like pathogens infecting a host body, or in this case, the Sinclair Resort Hotel, and in effect, trying to kill it. The reflexive nature of what was occurring was as if the hotel's autoimmune system was waging war with them to keep itself alive and well and enjoying the sentience it had achieved over the decades. If they couldn't stop what was happening on the mainframe, she worried that she, along with her brother and everyone else, might never leave this building alive.

The storage room door was standing open. Minerva flicked the lights on as she entered the long, narrow room and was relieved to find it unoccupied. Moving past the rows of cardboard cartons toward the hidden door, she thought of her benevolent companions whom she'd met in her journey through this hotel's guts. Where had Charlie the spider and Doppelively gotten to? She hadn't seen either of them in a while now. Was the hotel's power becoming so strong that they could no longer influence anything within its walls?

The hidden door was lying open, and the shelving was pushed aside. Minerva peered cautiously into the gloomy, red-lit passage. Nothing appeared to be in the immediate vicinity, and she moved forward, feeling more and more confident the closer she got to the gold room.

Rounding the corner of the final stretch of passage, one of the subjects of her most recent musings appeared in front of her eyes. Minerva held her hand to her chest in surprise, saying, "Oh, it's you! You gave me a fright."

Just slightly above eye level, her eight-legged tour guide clung to some pipes that ran along the wall near one of the light fixtures. Charlie, the spider, studied Minerva, the dim red of the corridor's lights sparkling slightly in its numerous, expressionless black eyes.

"I'm afraid I can't visit right now." She nodded down the corridor to the door at the far end, saying, "I'm on my way to the gold room. Big things are afoot."

The spider waggled a couple legs at her as if attempting to wave her away from her intended destination.

"What's the matter?" She asked, not expecting a response.

Her expectations were rewarded, and in lieu of any further leg signals, the creature scuttled rapidly into the dimness toward the polished aluminum door at the end of the passageway.

Minerva shook her head and followed the arachnid. When she arrived at the end of the corridor, it appeared the spider had been busy. Several layers of silk were draped across the doorway. Due to the amount of webbing, her web-slinging friend looked to have been working on it well before she arrived. If the spider had done it in the time it took her to make her way down the lengthy passage, it was a quick worker indeed.

"What is this, a 'Danger! Do-Not-Cross' barrier?'" Minerva wondered at the spider. The door behind the web lay partly open, the light of the golden room beyond glinting through the shimmering silk and dazzling her eyes after the passage's dimness.

Charlie was now perched in the corner of the wall near the ceiling, regarding her once more. He wiggled two legs alternately on each side again in what she thought was a 'warding off' gesture.

Shaking her head, Minerva said, "Sorry again, Charlie, but I need to get inside there." With the tip of her sword, she swept away the silken barrier, careful not to touch the large spider. Moving slowly through the doorway, her eyes were glued on Charlie the whole time. Though the creature had never shown any aggressive tendencies toward her, she was still leary of it, especially in light of everything else currently happening in the hotel.

It had been more than just a little terrifying and surprising when the stuffies started moving of their own volition in real-time. Now, she wouldn't have been surprised to have a trusted ally suddenly betray that trust and attack her. With that in mind, sword at the ready, she pushed the door open the rest of the way and stepped inside the gold room.

Once she was through the door, Minerva paused and glanced about the vast, shining room. It was just as bright glaring as ever, and she shielded her eyes. But something felt off, and she proceeded with caution. She took a quick detour and popped into the control room to check on things but saw nothing untoward inside. The mainframe was still whirring and clicking happily away.

Minerva knew there wasn't anything that she could do in the main control room that she couldn't do on the remote terminal out in the gold room. Soon, she was approaching the hidden door. However, it was not currently hidden, and instead stood open.

As she drew closer, she finally saw the reason for her feeling of unease. Just inside the doorway sat the Siberian tiger, its luminous green eyes piercing her with their intensity and intelligence, as if now made real.

Minerva froze, saying, "Nice kitty," then began backing away from the door at a slight angle until she was finally out of sight of the cat. If the door opened outward, she could have simply pushed it closed with the sword's tip. Unfortunately, this door opened inward, and to imprison the creature in the small room, she'd have to lean in with her hand to swing the door closed. This would mean she'd be right next to the striped terror as she reached for the recessed handle and felt unwilling to risk such a thing since she'd be completely vulnerable at that moment.

Backing toward the main control room, Minerva's eyes were locked onto the hidden door. But focusing on all things cat as she'd angled away, she hadn't realised how close she'd come to the edge of the collector dish. When she glanced back, her heart skipped a beat. The dish's shining depths now yawned wide at her back, only inches from her boot heels.

A sound Minerva didn't want to hear suddenly came to her ears. The sound of razor-like claws on metal as the tiger jerked and janked its way out of the secondary control room, then paused. With a creak and a crack, it turned its attention toward her and locked her in its predatory vision. Wiry muscles bunched in its shoulders and haunches as it lowered itself toward the ground and continued stalking toward her as if sneaking through tall grass that only it could see.

Minerva held the sword out defensively as she backed toward the main control room, her eyes again unwavering on the cat. A sudden movement from above caught her eye, and she watched as Charlie dropped down from a cable conduit snaking across the golden ceiling and landed directly on the tiger's face. It roared and tried to shake the spider from its head, but the oversized arachnid clung tight.

Seeing this as her moment to act, Minerva thrust her weapon directly at the animal's chest and pushed it back, the sharp steel piercing into the cat's tanned hide. The slick surface of the aluminum floor proved impossible for the cat to grip with its claws, and it gave another guttural hiss as it slid back several feet.

Despite the tiger shaking its head fiercely, like a Band-Aid, Charlie still clung tight.

Minerva thrust the sword at the beast again, and this time, she felt the sword's tip connect solidly with the beast's wooden armature beneath, and then she pushed as hard as she could.

The cat's claws skidded with a squeal on the smooth metal as it reached the edge of the small lip that ran around the dish's rim. One of its legs dropped into the depression, causing it to lose its balance, and it began to tumble inside. At the last moment, the beast raked out one of its claw-tipped paws, snagged ahold of the lip, and then clung there precariously. Hissing again, it attempted to hook the claws of its other paw onto the rim as well, while its hind legs scratched and scrabbled, trying to propel itself back up the dish's smooth side.

"No, you don't. You're one cat that won't come back." She raised the sword high and flashed the steel blade downward, slicing through and amputating the cat's paw. The beast shrieked, sounding almost human, then tumbled down inside, spinning and sliding along the silver surface until it was at the bottom of the collector dish. It hissed and spat as it limped upright, trying to scramble back up the side of the dish to get to her, but the smooth surface proved too much for its now-limited mobility, and it could only scratch at the metal ineffectively with its single remaining set of front claws.

Charlie, however, had no issue climbing back up the side of the dish, and soon it stood on the shining aluminum floor next to Minerva.

"Thank you, my eight-legged friend. I will never view big hairy spiders the same from now on."

Seemingly satisfied with her answer, now that its work was done, the creature waggled a single leg in farewell, then scuttled out the aluminum door and disappeared into the dimly lit passageway once again.

The severed paw of the cat clung to the lip of the dish by one of its wickedly sharp claws, flexing slightly as if still trying to rend Minerva's flesh without success. Using the blade's tip, she flicked the paw down to where the cat paced agitatedly at the bottom. As its amputated foot bumped against the creature, it paused and looked up at Minerva with a hiss and a growl, then tried to paw at the dish's slick silver sides, again with no effect.

Shaking her head, Minerva said, "Although Sigmund Freud said, 'Time with cats is never wasted', I think in this case, I'll make a special exception and let you waste some time down at the bottom of that dish." She walked away from the growling beast into the control room and closed the door, just in case the beast somehow magically learned to climb bare metal. With a slight sigh, she sat in the leather office chair and looked at the monitors. The cat still stalked back and forth at the dish's bottom, but everything else seemed quiet at the moment.

Turning her attention to the CRT monitor, Minerva examined the possibilities on the screen before her.

Initiate Aggregation - 1'
'Dissipate Aggregation - 2'
'Initiate Translocation - 3'
'Reverse Translocation – 4'
'System Reset - 5'
'Execute Subroutine Break - 6'
'Enter choice?'

Option six was ghosted and unavailable; she wondered if someone else had already utilised it. Ricky Rosenstein, perhaps? Minerva decided to stick with her original guess, pressed #2 and hit return. The prompt appeared, saying, 'Dissipate Aggregation? Are you sure?'

Before she pressed the letter Y, she pulled the radio from her pocket and said somewhat musically, "Breaker, breaker. Come in, John and Amanda. Over."

***

Amanda Jansen paced back and forth near the bar, waiting to hear from Minerva. She'd noticed the first signs of something happening in the room around them as they'd waited but was unsure if it was a result of what Minerva was doing or something happening with the hotel itself as the time drew near. Whatever it was, things seemed dirtier and dustier in the room around them all of a sudden. She looked to her watch; 11:58 P.M.— less than two minutes to go.

John sat at a table near the service door. He hadn't spoken for several minutes and stared off into space, seeming lost in his own thoughts. Amanda hoped he wasn't suffering from another fugue state like he had so many years before. She was about to ask him how he was doing when the Cobra two-way suddenly sprang to life with Minerva's melodic voice.

The radio stood upright near the ebony box at the end of the bar. Amanda sprinted toward it and snatched it up, saying, "We hear you loud and clear, Minerva. Are you almost ready?"

"Yes, I think I'm ready to roll. I had an encounter with our furry striped friend down here."

Amanda's eyes widened at this news, and she said, "I hope you're all right!"

After a brief crackle, Minerva came back, saying, "Yes, I had some eight-legged help."

"What?"

"I'll tell you about it soon. But for now, I think we should proceed."

Furious scratching came from the other side of the ballroom's entrance. Brief flashes of ebony-coloured claws were now visible as the beast tore strips of wood from the bottom of the oak door where it gapped near the floor.

With relief in her voice, Amanda said, "That works for us because it sounds like the entrance doors are getting pretty thin. That bear is very persistent."

"Okay, copy that. Like I said before, I think you need to get out of that room while this thing runs. So, you might want to head into the service corridor now."

"Roger that." Jansen moved to the chief inspector, noticing he still seemed in a trance, and said, "John! We need to go."

There was no response from Harder.

She placed the radio on the table just as Minerva said, "I'll start a countdown to initiate the procedure now. Standby."

Amanda gave John a small shake, and he came around with a sudden gasp.

"John, thank God. I wasn't sure if you heard Minerva on the radio. We have to get out of the room right now!"

Looking slightly disoriented, the inspector shook his head, saying, "I didn't hear anything. I suddenly saw everybody dancing around me." His eyes were moist as he added, "And I think I saw Helen."

Amanda began helping Harder to his feet, saying, "Let's hope that comes true."

John stood with a small groan of pain, grabbed his cane, and they moved toward the service passage. When they were almost there, the scratching outside the main doors stopped. Amanda noted this and said, "I wonder where the bear's going?"

"Hopefully, it hasn't figured out how to open the door to the service passage," John said with a shake of his head.

Back on the table, Minerva's voice said from the radio, "Beginning the procedure."

Now in the service corridor, Amanda was about to close the door to the ballroom when she glanced back inside. Standing in the centre of the room, where the balloons and streamers had fallen, looking so young and handsome again, was Danny Harder. Amanda called out his name, and the young man looked at her and gave her his crooked but winning smile. He held his arms out to her invitingly, welcoming her embrace.

"Ten, nine, eight..."

Amanda smiled broadly in return, and suddenly, all

thoughts of self-preservation flew from her mind as she called out his name. Her face beatific, she started to move back into the room.

John placed his hand on her shoulder, saying, "Amanda, you know we can't be inside the ballroom."

Jansen pulled free of John's hand as she rushed back into the vast room toward Danny. Her breath plumed from her mouth as she called over her shoulder, "I don't care anymore! I have to see him again!"

Harder was about to follow her back inside when the chandeliers around the room suddenly blinked out. Without warning, the door handle was ripped from his grasp, and the door slammed shut. He tried the handle, but it wouldn't budge. Intense cold leached through his gloved hands, and he pulled them away with a grimace of pain.

From the radio on the dining table inside the ballroom, John could hear Minerva's voice faintly saying, "Five, four, three..."

CHAPTER FORTY-SEVEN

December 31st, 1981 0000 hours

Lively spun around, trying to look in every direction at once. On all sides, nothing but smothering blackness surrounded him. It felt like he'd had a black velvet hood draped over his head, so deep was the darkness.

After several long moments, the partygoers began to gradually appear around him once more. All were motionless. Some had removed their masks, but all stood with their eyes closed, the blank look on their faces now one of tranquillity.

Strangely, none of the pale light came from the chandeliers overhead as all were dark, yet he could see everyone nearby quite clearly now. And then he realised why; they were glowing from within as if an internal fire had suddenly ignited within the core of their very being.

All around, things grew brighter and brighter, the glow within the party guests increasing as if energy long gone from their souls was now being restored. Lively looked to Selene with concern, but her eyes were also closed, the surging power coursing through her body in cascading waves of dazzling brightness. He called to her, "Mom, are you all right?" She didn't reply. Whatever was happening had put her into the same trance-like state as the others in the room.

Nearby, Ricky, Vincent and Simon all seemed to be experiencing the same thing, their eyes closed and a peaceful look on their faces. Edward, still held loosely by Simon, glared at Lively, his eyes burning with an internal fire quite different from those around him. But why was he different from the rest? Perhaps it was because of the harmonic bracelet he still wore, just like Lively, one of the select few with the gilded letter S on the front.

The low-level hum from beneath the gold room had returned, and Lively felt a tingling grow throughout his body. He looked to his hands and saw that he, too, glowed from within. Veins, arteries and muscles were now visible as if his epidermis had been rendered transparent, and he felt like he was being held in a warm embrace as the glow continued to increase.

Scanning the people around him once again, Lively saw that Edward was no longer held captive in Simon's arms. His attention on what he'd been doing had been compromised by the phenomena, and Sinclair had used the chance to burst free.

After a brief panic, Lively located his father over at the end of the bar. Kandi stood next to him, holding the side of her head where Selene had battered it with the beer bottle. She wore a harmonic bracelet on her wrist once again, so it appeared that Edward had only removed it in the basement for show upon learning of her treachery with Max. Lively wondered if there was more to their relationship than he'd previously realised.

Kandi wasn't the only reason for Sinclair's interest in the bar. On its end sat the ebony box. It hadn't been there before; Lively knew that for a fact. It had been bare save for a few glasses and beer bottles. Was this phenomenon around them a result of them aligning with where the box existed in the reality of 2021? The ebony cabinet seemed to glow from within yet was still transparent, like it hadn't yet synced completely with their reality.

Max Schreck had said there was 'but one box', and for the realignment to proceed each night, it needed to be where it was within the model. Now, it was on the bar, and Lively's hope swelled in his chest as he realised that Minerva must have been successful in its relocation. Light from within the box grew brighter and brighter, just like the people around it, and it now appeared as if seen through thick layers of gauze behind which a supernova had just ignited.

"Edward!" Lively called out, or tried to. Though he thought he'd spoken loudly, he wasn't sure if any sound had actually come from his mouth. The low-level thrumming had ramped up, and it was now louder than ever in the room. At the same time, the warmth grew within Lively as well. With great effort, he forced his legs to work and began struggling toward his father.

His back to the room, Edward didn't see Lively approaching, his attention solely on the ebony box. Together with Kandi, he tried to grasp at the box, perhaps trying to move it from its spot on the end of the bar to somewhere else, perhaps anywhere else. Unfortunately, they couldn't seem to make contact due to the transitory state in which the black box currently existed, and their hands only passed through it.

Struggling to put one foot in front of the other, Lively approached the bar. If Edward were successful in moving the ebony box, then everything they'd worked so hard to achieve might suddenly be for nought, and he knew he had to do something.

Now that he was closer, Lively called again, saying, "Dad!" This time, it seemed his voice could carry over the hum, and Edward turned toward him. But as he did, Lively stepped back in horror.

CHAPTER FORTY-EIGHT

December 31st, 2021 2359 hours

"Two, one, zero..." Minerva pressed the return key on the terminal keyboard and looked at her wristwatch—it was precisely midnight. Forty years ago, at this very moment, everyone in the ballroom had disappeared.

The CRT monitors above the console started to flicker with static as the mainframe's programming began to execute, and the humming deep within the hotel's bowels ramped up again. Within a few seconds, the monitor's picture had gone supernova, and then it blanked out completely, and she couldn't see into the gold room any longer.

Safety concerns aside, Minerva wanted to get a better view of what was going on outside the windowless control room. She reasoned it must be safe enough for a person to be outside the room during the process, judging by the sunglasses sitting next to the remote terminal's floppy disk drive. They were tinted dark blue, like welding goggles.

Stepping into the gold room, everything around her seemed to glow an electric blue. Like Lively had initially noted, between the ballroom above and the gold room below, the two were acting like a gigantic Faraday cage. Overtop the collector dish, white-hot arcs of electricity jumped through various coils and conductors that sprouted from the Universal Studios-looking aggregator. She was glad of the sunglasses as she looked about in awe.

Taking care as she moved forward, she looked down to the bottom of the collector dish, wondering what was happening to the Siberian tiger. Her heart skipped a beat when she saw it gone at first. But then it was there again all of a sudden. Had it been obscured by a surge of electricity, she wondered.

The glasses were working, but it was still difficult to see clearly, and she knew she couldn't look directly at whatever was occurring for too long despite their protection. She placed her fingers across the glasses and squinted through them as if trying to look at the sun.

One moment the cat was there, the next it was gone, suddenly replaced by a huge bald man. And then, just as quickly, he was gone, and the cat reappeared. Were the tiger and man phasing in and out of their respective realities as the past rejoined the present? Whatever it was, this cycling between the two became more and more frequent as the sound of the thrumming vibration from below became louder and louder and filled the room.

A huge energy pulse surged through the aggregator as it came to full power. Now feeling uncomfortable, just in case she was somehow sucked into the dish and another universe, Minerva moved quickly to the door through which the spider had departed earlier. She'd done everything she could think of down here and knew she needed to get back up to the ballroom as soon as possible.

Sword resting on her shoulder, she rushed down the dimly lit corridor, trying the two-way radio as she went. "Breaker-breaker! Amanda? John? Anyone?" Whether it was interference from the concrete of the tunnel she was in or the aggregator itself, for whatever reason, she couldn't get through to the inspectors, and that probably wasn't a good sign.

Minerva came out of the revolving door on the dogleg landing and took the remaining stairs two at a time. She hurtled across the lobby, her bootheels cracking against the marble floor. As she came out of the short annex leading to the ballrooms, she was suddenly reminded that she'd forgotten to be cautious.

***

At first, Amanda had felt overwhelmed by the cold. But as she'd drawn closer to Danny, she'd hardly felt it anymore. Warming her instead was the love they shared. Standing before her was the man who had been cut down in the prime of his life, denying both of them the future they'd dreamt of having. The man who'd promised her they would be together forever and never to part. But part they had.

And yet, here he was, once again, standing in front of her and looking the same as the day they'd met—tall, dark-haired and handsome in his uniform, sporting his crooked yet winning smile. Just being in his presence had always been enough to intoxicate her and make her feel as giddy as a schoolgirl. And she felt that way now. It didn't matter if she died here, in this moment. As long as she was with Danny, nothing else mattered.

Danny didn't speak and only smiled again and spread his arms wide. She stepped into his embrace, and everything she loved about him, and he of her, came flooding into her mind all at once. The room grew darker and darker around her as the humming noise filled her ears.

Part of Amanda Jansen faintly recalled she shouldn't be here and that she might perish in this moment, but the rest of her didn't care. She was with the light of her life once again, and from now on, nothing would keep them apart, not even death.

Danny Harder's love was all she ever needed, all she ever wanted, and soon, it was all she knew.

**

John briefly tried the service door handle into the ballroom, but it was still immovable and exceedingly cold. Even that had been almost too much, the biting chill penetrating the thick leather of his gloves almost instantly. He was sure there was no lock on the other side, but for whatever reason, the door wouldn't budge. Either the hotel was keeping it closed, or it had frozen shut.

After Minerva's countdown had reached zero, a low hum from below had begun to build and build, and it reverberated throughout the hotel as it reached its apogee. He needed to get to Amanda somehow and hoped to try the main entrance to the ballroom, although he was almost sure it was already too late.

Just as he turned away from the door, he caught movement at the opposite end of the corridor. Approaching him on unsteady feet was a man. As he grew closer and closer, John's eyes widened further and further.

Shambling from the opposite end of the passage was none other than Eric Eggelson. Except it wasn't the Eric Eggelson he remembered. His uniform cap was missing, and his tuft of Tintin hair stuck up on top of his head as it always had. But beneath the hair, things had changed and not for the better. His skin had an unhealthy pallor, sagging as though made of plastic exposed to intense heat. His sunken eyes peered from dark sockets, a small spark of blue fire burning deep within their core. Eric shuffled eagerly down the corridor toward him. The constable's arms were held out as if to grab John and bundle him off into the hotel's depths, eager to show what had happened to him and perhaps let John experience the same for himself.

Moving as fast as his hip would allow, John began tapping his cane down the corridor in the opposite direction. The door to the public hallway was just ahead, the one they'd made sure to close against the polar bear. Now, John prayed he'd be able to open it before the abomination that was Eric Eggelson wrapped him in its corrupt arms.

John's leather gloves slipped at first as he tried to turn the doorknob and sweat began to trickle from his temples as he prepared to try again. The sound of scuffling feet at his back came closer and closer, but he didn't look back, knowing if he did, Eric's disfigured face would be the last thing he ever saw in this hotel from hell.

Thankfully, his gloves didn't slip the second time. He ripped the door open and moved into the public corridor with speed that surprised even himself. As he turned back to pull the door firmly shut, Eggelson's deformed face leered at him from the gap, reaching toward him to stop that from happening.

John leaned back with his full weight and slammed the door shut, holding the knob for a moment, expecting to feel it turn beneath his gloved fingers.

Another jolt of fear ran through his being as he realised he hadn't checked to see if the bear had actually been gone before entering the passage. He looked over his shoulder to the ballroom doors. They were now untended by the polar predator, and he breathed a sigh of relief.

The vibrating hum from below wound down as he continued to hold the doorknob. Nothing had happened, and he presumed Eggelson had only been a hallucination. At least, that's what he was going to tell himself—not that he intended to open the service passage door again to find out for sure. He released the knob and the breath he'd held at the same time.

Making his way slowly toward the ballroom's doors, John glanced over his shoulder several times, expecting to see the doorknob turn and Eggelson shamble out.

The damage to the thick oak was horrendous, with large chunks missing near the bottom of both doors. If the polar bear hadn't stopped when it had, John felt fairly sure it would have burrowed its way into the room with them, and he shuddered at the thought. But where had the beast gone, he wondered. Why had it given up all of a sudden like that? Had someone or something distracted it?

Taking a breath, he reached for the door handles to the grand ballroom and prepared to go inside.

***

The arctic beast stood halfway down the ballroom corridor, facing directly toward Minerva. She froze and stared at the creature unblinkingly. Had it given up trying to get inside the ballroom and been on its way to stop her from doing what needed to be done, she wondered. Or had it just finished slaughtering the inspectors and was still hungry for her? Either way, the point was moot. It was here now, and it was deadly. The monstrous white bear stood completely immobile. Was it also capable of moving in real-time like the gorilla and tiger, or was it still only semi-sentient? Backing slowly in the direction she'd come, Minerva prayed it was the latter possibility. However, her hopes were shattered as the bear suddenly gave a guttural roar and began to stalk down the corridor toward her on its four thick, muscular legs.

Minerva turned and fled. She'd momentarily considered swiping at the bear with her sword, but the creature was even larger than the cat or the ape and even more dangerous, thanks to its longer limbs and sharper claws. Also, she didn't have the assistance of Amanda's firearm to blow chunks from its body, so she knew another course of action would be required.

Not slowing pace, Minerva burst into the lobby and rushed toward the grand staircase. Her eyes widened in surprise as she looked upward at the mezzanine.

Her brother stood there, gesturing toward the massive landscape painting of the hotel.

Shouting breathlessly, Minerva said, "Lively, you're back! I need help! I've got company!" He didn't respond but merely gestured toward the painting again.

The clack and crack of claws across Italian marble told Minerva the bear was in hot pursuit, and as it drew closer, she could hear the creak and squeak of its wooden armature beneath its tanned pelt.

Sprinting up the stairs to the mezzanine, Minerva turned to confront her pursuer.

The enormous white bear arrived at the bottom of the grand staircase. Seeing her stopped, it slowed its pace and began creaking its way up the stairs toward her, a low bass rumble coming from deep within its chest.

Minerva readied herself with the sword and looked briefly over her shoulder to her brother but discovered she was now alone. "Lively! Where are you, Big Brother?" she called, but he seemed to have vanished completely, and she realised it must have been her brother's double, Doppelively. In a flash of cognition, she knew he'd been trying to help her out one last time with the directions he'd been giving. Being unable to speak, she wondered if his connection to this reality was now being severed, the mainframe computer and humming machinery in the depths below doing their job. She felt brief sadness at the prospect of not saying goodbye to him but knew she had more pressing matters at the moment and turned her attention back to the bear, her eyes growing wide.

The polar beast had just reached the top of the stairs and was now less than a dozen feet from her. It grumbled again, locking her in its gaze, and then it tensed as it prepared to charge.

Angling backwards across the mezzanine, Minerva now stood next to the massive painting and glanced briefly to where Doppelively had pointed. It came to her in a flash what he'd been trying to tell her to do.

Minerva spun in a pirouette of panic, and with all her might, hacked the sword into the cable that held the enormous landscape to the Sinclair's wall. The sharp steel once again did its job, and the taut cable snapped with a 'twang'. The massive painting dropped to the floor with a tooth-rattling thud, then balanced upright for a brief moment.

At first, Minerva was afraid it would merely stay there on its edge or perhaps fall back and lean against the wall. Fortunately, gravity was in her favour, and the massive painting tilted forward, pounding down on top of her ursine pursuer.

With nerves like livewires, Minerva edged around the huge painting, her eyes still on the bear. The landscape was heavy, the ornate, gilded frame around it no doubt weighing close to a ton. The bear had been two-thirds of the way across the mezzanine when the painting landed on top of it, the thick angular frame slicing through it like a guillotine. Apart from its front paws, only one other part of the bear now lay outside the frame's edge, its decapitated head, now forever frozen in the middle of a soundless roar.

CHAPTER FORTY-NINE

Edward Sinclair's face appeared to be melting. At least, that's how it seemed at first. However, when Lively recovered from his initial shock, he realised both his father and Kandi were, in fact, ageing quite rapidly. Their hair greyed, eyes glazing over with cataracts. Their skin and muscles beneath withered like plant leaves in an August heatwave. Processes that would have normally taken years were now taking mere seconds as the natural effects of time, gravity, and bodily degeneration caught up with them all at once, their youthful appearance soon only a fond memory.

Although the pair had initially been trying to move the ebony box from its spot with little success, things had now changed, and it seemed they couldn't take their hands from it, though they tried desperately to do so. The flesh of their palms looked to have merged with it, and they were now as one.

The black box pulsed with energy, and Lively felt a surge within himself as it did. All around the room, the faint luminescence of the partygoers became amplified in that instant, and just like him, they grew brighter and brighter with each subsequent oscillation. But in the brief dimness between pulses, Edward and Kandi lost more and more of their essence, appearing less defined and more ethereal with each cycle.

With a quick glance about, Lively saw that the other revellers weren't having this problem and were becoming more solid with each subsequent pulse. The glow from the box had begun to abate, and the room resolved around them once again, their monochromatic world becoming colour-filled, like spotting the first spray of spring's flowers on a sun-dappled afternoon, blooming brilliantly against winter's drab demise.

***

John Harder looked about in disbelief as he entered the ballroom. There was no sign of Amanda, but everywhere he looked, people were beginning to appear out of thin air. At his back came a resounding crash as if a wall had collapsed somewhere in the hotel.

Near the end of the bar, John caught a faint glimpse of a man and woman fused to the dark wood of the ebony box, their mouths open and screaming in agony. But unlike the people resolving around him, this pair appeared to be dissipating into nothingness and seemed to feel the pain. Nearby, a man in a black tux with dark blonde hair had begun to appear from nowhere.

Now in the middle of the ballroom, John stared in stunned silence at the people materialising, and soon he was in the midst of a large group. Something in his guts told him there was someone behind him, and he began to turn as quickly as his aged body would allow.

A voice spoke a single word, his name. It was said with longing, compassion and boundless love. Now completely turned, his heart started to slam in his chest, and he forgot how to breathe.

Standing behind him was what had kept him going all those lonely years; the reason he'd truly never forgotten what had happened here at this hotel and the reason that gave him hope when he rose each and every day.

In a voice heavy with emotion, Helen Harder repeated his name, saying, "John?" A small, hopeful smile played across her lips as if she were unsure the elderly man standing before her might actually be her husband.

John could hardly hear her speak because of the noise from his blood surging through his veins. It was his Helen, wearing a green silk gown, her long blonde hair as lustrous as ever, looking the same youthful forty-two as the day she'd disappeared. A look of joy filled her face, and her grey-green eyes welled with tears.

Barely able to see through his own tears, John wiped the back of his hand across his eyes and reached into his parka pocket for the other thing that had kept him going for all those years.

Helen's small, hopeful smile broke into a full-blown grin of delight as John unfurled the chain and placed her silver locket with Danny's photo around her slender throat once more. Then, hoping it wasn't all just a dream, he pulled her into his arms and held her close, smelling her hair's clean, fresh scent. And then he kissed her again and again and again, and never, ever wanted to stop.

***

Fearing that her brother might suffer the same fate as Doppelively, Minerva rocketed down the corridor toward the grand ballroom. Despite her fear, there was something else: a growing sense of optimism that things might be working out. The day she and Lively had first walked down this corridor and opened the ballroom doors came flooding back to her.

The thought of finding everyone alive had just been a pipedream back then. But now, it looked like that day had finally arrived.

Slowing her sprint to a walk, Minerva entered the ballroom, her eyes wide in amazement. All around, men and women coalesced out of thin air, dressed in tuxedos and evening gowns as if ready for a party. Most were already whole, while a few stragglers were still appearing, fading from nothingness to solidity as she watched. Near the middle of the room, John Harder stood with a younger, blonde-haired woman, embracing and kissing as if they would never let each other part.

Over at the mahogany bar, Minerva saw her hopes were not being dashed this time but fulfilled instead. Now in the final stages of transparency, Lively had begun to solidify, looking as if a maladjusted camera was having its focus adjusted. Then, all of a sudden, everything seemed to lock in, and he appeared corporeal once more.

"Lively!" Minerva shouted, delight in her voice. She dropped her sword to the floor with a resounding clang and rushed forward.

"Hey, Sis! Long time no see!" Lively exclaimed as Minerva wrapped her arms around him. He returned her embrace with a big bear hug.

"I wasn't sure if I'd ever see you again, Big Brother!" Minerva said breathlessly.

"Well, you know how I don't like to disappoint you." They pulled apart and stood looking at each other, just happy to be in the same room and the same universe once again.

The Glenn Millers were standing and placing their instruments upon their chairs. They moved out onto the ballroom floor to mingle with the other newly restored.

Everyone blinked and stared at each other as if unsure what had just happened, but their faces all showed how they felt inside, and broad smiles abounded. The ballroom curtains had been pushed aside, and a small group stood at the tall windows. The storm had abated for the moment, and they looked with wonder onto the crisp cold night, admiring the clarity of the crescent moon that could be seen behind the high clouds that drifted past.

About to ask Lively a million questions, Minerva watched as a woman wearing a red satin gown approached from over near the bandstand, a woman that looked remarkably like her. Was she an other-worldly double, Minerva wondered.

The beautiful woman arrived at Lively's side, and he looked from Minerva to the woman in red and said, "Sis, I'd like you to meet your mother, Selene Hammond."

Selene shook her head, saying, "No, it's Selene Deadmarsh."

"But how?" Minerva questioned, her hands fluttering to her chest as her mind and heart overloaded with emotions.

"It's a long story," Selene said with a sad smile, then added, "About forty years too long."

Minerva regarded the woman standing before her a moment longer, and then they both reached forward at once and embraced. Like Lively, she had longed to meet her mother. Over the years, she'd even held several seances to try and speak to the woman. But now she knew why she'd always failed in that task, because her mother was alive! Her vision blurred as she hugged Selene harder than anyone she'd ever hugged, except maybe Lively.

After a moment, an incongruous group approach their location. A blonde behemoth lumbered along on the left, next to a rotund little man with a fringe of carrot-red hair. Their companion was an individual who appeared to have recently served hard time in a French penal colony.

***

Gesturing toward the ragtag trio, Lively said, "Minerva, I'd like you to meet Simon Wright, Ricky Rosenstein and Vincent DaCosta, three new friends of mine who have been instrumental in helping this day come to pass."

The group of men smiled the best they could and nodded as they were introduced. Minerva smiled back as she looked to each man, and then said, "Though I've only chatted online with Ricky, I feel as though I know you all." Ricky smiled and blushed slightly. Minerva continued, "Speaking for myself and I'm sure the families of everyone in this room, thank you for helping make this day a reality and bring everybody home."

"Not quite everybody," Lively said, looking to the ebony box where Edward and Kandi had disappeared.

John approached with Helen on his arm. After briefly introducing his wife, he looked about the room, a worried expression on his face, then said to Minerva, "I haven't seen Amanda yet. She ran into the ballroom just as you started the countdown."

"Oh no! Why would she do that?" Minerva asked, surprised.

"She saw Danny and needed to be with him," John explained.

Lively shook his head. If this were true, then he held little hope of seeing the woman alive ever again and said, "That decision may have cost her her life."

Minerva said, "I agree. After reading how others described this room during the initial disappearance and its sub-zero temperatures, the odds are slim she would have survived being caught in the middle of the transition."

John looked to Helen, his expression pained. "She'd been like a daughter to me since Danny was killed, and then after you disappeared..." He trailed off, his voice breaking, and he grabbed Helen once again and hugged her close as if believing he might still be in a dream.

Looking around the room at the throng of people, Lively said, "I think I'd better contact the authorities to get some trauma specialists up here, amongst other things. Some of these people might have a few problems dealing with their new reality."

"That's putting it mildly," Selene said.

Lively pulled out his iPhone and looked at its screen. "Hey! Someone turned on my satellite hotspot. I've got four bars!"

"That would be me," Minerva said with a small nod.

"You have your own satellite?" Ricky asked, his eyes very large.

"Well, I suppose you could say I rent the use of one on a monthly basis." Lively tapped the phone's screen a few times, then handed it to Ricky, saying, "Now that we're back to the present, I was thinking my new communications specialist might want to do the honours and call emergency services."

"Sure thing, Mr. DeMille," Ricky said reverentially, taking the phone in both hands.

Minerva looked to Lively and said, "Mr. DeMille?"

Lively replied, "Kind of a long story."

"You'll have to tell me over a bottle of Moosehead

sometime," Minerva said.

Lively nodded with a grin, then said to Ricky, "I already punched in the number for EMS. Just press the big green phone button near the bottom of the screen. And when you're done, come and see me, and I'll do a reset on that phone. Then it's yours to keep, as promised."

Ricky's eyes now seemed ready to pop from his skull, and he said, "Gosh, thanks so much, Mr. DeMille!"

"I told you, it's Lively."

Nodding, Rosenstein smiled and said, "Lively." He took a deep breath and pressed the screen. After a brief moment, a voice could be heard saying, "Emergency Services. Police, Ambulance or Fire?"

As Ricky put the phone to his ear, he looked to Lively, who gave a small shrug of his shoulders, and Ricky said, "All three, I guess." He then walked a slight distance away from the group to let the dispatcher ask their questions uninterrupted.

Lively glanced about the room again. The recent returnees to the present looked dazed and bewildered, and he was sure it would be a while before some of them could come to terms with what had happened and begin reintegrating themselves into society again. His eyes came to rest on the group closest to him, and his heart swelled as he watched his sister chatting with Selene like they were old friends already.

Vincent and Simon stood near the ebony box, presumably discussing what their next move might be now that they were both free. Thinking of the duplicates of the ex-wrestler, Lively looked to where he'd placed the Simon he'd tangled with and then to the one that Simon had bundled up. Both men were now gone, and only a couple of harmonic bracelets remained amongst the table clothes that had bound them.

John and Helen were holding hands, looking like a couple of teenagers, except for the forty-year gap in their respective ages.

A sense of satisfaction rested comfortably inside Lively's chest at the moment. The object of their quest had been accomplished, the return of what had been stolen by Edward Sinclair, the very lives of the people he'd invited to his party. In the course of this investigation, the Sinclair hotel had divulged some of its secrets; Lively knew that. But he also knew many more still remained hidden, the least of which being, who else amongst this group of people had been in on the kidnapping? During their conversations, Edward had mentioned there were some who had paid handsomely to be here, and he wondered to what depths their involvement went.

Continuing to stand apart from everyone else for a moment, Lively felt suddenly overwhelmed by everything that had just happened. While he took a breath, he watched his mother and sister talking. They were almost identical twins, the resemblance so uncanny. Both had the same lustrous auburn hair, slender physiques and modelesque height. And they both grinned like their faces had frozen in the expression, as had his.

Minerva and Selene walked over and joined Lively, waking him from his reverie. Both women put their arms around him and pulled him into their circle of love. They all hugged, not parting for several long seconds.

Lively looked to Minerva and saw the elation and wholeness he felt inside himself reflected back in her eyes. They'd both long dreamt of seeing their mother, and now, that dream had become a reality. Twins who were once orphans were orphans no longer, and a woman who suffered the tragic loss of her babies at childbirth four decades before now had them in her life once again.

They stood together, grateful, happy, and content to be with each other; all now something that none had ever expected to be, or ever be part of, a family.

EPILOGUE

June 22nd, 2022 2031 hours

The setting sun painted the top of Overseer Mountain with golden light but provided little warmth on this, the first evening of summer. Thanks to its elevation, things were quite cool and refreshing at the top of the hill, the daytime high had been a balmy seventy-two degrees Fahrenheit, and tonight they expected lows to be in the mid-forties.

Minerva stood next to Lively in the turret's model room, looking out at the dwindling daylight and the work done to the property so far this year. The red clay of the roque court far below contrasted starkly against the riot of green from the grounds and forest beyond. High above, fluffy golden-white clouds scudded across the cerulean sky.

After the craziness of 'The Return', as the media had called it, things had gradually calmed down. The circus that Lively and Minerva's lives had been now approached something normal, or as close to that as their lives ever got.

The holding company that had managed the resort

property revealed it had also held Edward's last will and testament. The family fortune hidden away offshore had been left to any remaining heirs, should Edward Sinclair's death be proven. That hadn't been a problem with numerous people witnessing Edward and Kandi's demise. And as it turned out, Lively and Minerva were the last remaining heirs. So, after selling off most of the stock Edward had squirrelled away, Lively and Minerva had been able to aid the victims of the ballroom kidnapping and give each of them a sizeable sum of money.

And now, they had to decide what to do with the Sinclair Resort Hotel. They still weren't one hundred percent sure that the paranormal aspects of the building had been fully resolved or if they would ever be completely contained. However, since the Return, it seemed that most of the phenomena occurring around the resort had subsided and, in most cases ceased altogether.

With the taxidermied terrors now more or less in pieces, they were fairly confident that was one phenomenon that would now be over. The remains of the great ape had been removed and burned. They'd considered doing the same to the bear, but since it was already pressed partially flat by the painting, Minerva had thought they might as well take things to the next logical extension, and she smiled now as she stood looking out the tall, narrow window. Instead of threatening her any longer, the polar predator now kept her sandal-clad feet warm, its thick pelt insulating her from the cold stone of the turret's floor.

The tiger in the gold room collector dish was one of the stranger things they'd discovered in the aftermath. Minerva had told Lively what she'd witnessed inside the Aggregator's collector dish and that she hadn't stuck around to see how things turned out.

Afterwards, instead of finding one or the other at the bottom of the dish, they discovered a strange hybrid of the two that resembled a man but with a tiger's fur, claws and fangs. Thinking they might have a body to report to the authorities, they had been greatly relieved to discover nothing beneath the strange creature's fur except a wire and wood armature, just like the other stuffies.

It had been a busy six months for Lively and Minerva, both having numerous other demands on their hands with other clients in need of their unique services. Though they had toyed with the thought of reopening the hotel in a limited fashion, they'd decided to put the project on the back burner for the moment. But in the meantime, they'd had a bit of basic maintenance done to the exterior and a general cleaning up of the grounds around it, but that was as far as they had gone so far. The last thing they wanted to do was reopen and have someone else disappear, not that they had any intention of ever using the Harmonic Universal Alignment Aggregator in the gold room again.

However, that had been another pleasant surprise. They'd expected the gold lining the room's ceiling to be rather thin since a single ounce could be pounded into a sheet of almost one hundred square feet, but things proved otherwise. It was nearly a half-inch thick and, according to Lively's calculations, must have weighed several tons at least. At current gold rates, it would be worth over six hundred million dollars Canadian. He'd joked to Minerva that if they were ever in need of some quick cash, they only had to come to the Sinclair and peel off a little bit of the ceiling.

Ricky Rosenstein had immersed himself in the sea of changes in the electronics world since his incarceration at the Sinclair. Thanks to his ability to quickly pick things up, he'd had little trouble integrating himself back into the world of electronics. He'd been so enamoured with his iPhone's abilities that he'd started up a small software company to make apps for the device. And it turned out, he didn't need to worry about money ever again, thanks to the two thousand shares of Apple stock he'd purchased a year before he disappeared. The shares had multiplied like bunnies over the last four decades and split five separate times. And though Lively and Minerva had offered him his share of the money from the stocks they'd sold, he passed, saying he really didn't need it since the last he'd looked, those shares were now worth close to three-quarters of a billion dollars.

So instead, Minerva donated Ricky's share to the BCSPCA in honour of the poor tortured stuffies. Despite whatever they had become through the Sinclair's influence, she'd wanted to give something back in honour of the wild animals they had been before their grisly fate had befallen them.

Some of Vincent DaCosta's time in the wastelands had been put to good use, and he'd had plenty of time to practice his writing. Just recently, he'd sold the rights to his life story for a considerable sum of money, and a major publishing company was releasing his book at Christmas time. According to what he'd recently told Lively, he already had over two million pre-orders and was working on a screenplay for Paramount.

Thanks to his newfound celebrity, Simon Wright had gotten back into the wrestling business. He was now grappling under the name of 'The Vanisher' and making a killing at it, monetarily speaking, of course. His wife, Isabelle, had passed away several years before at the Sunnybrae Mental Institution. A little while ago, Livey had asked Simon what Isabelle had seen in that suite that had driven her beyond reason. With a shake of his head, he admitted he didn't know. And although he had definitely roughed up Rob Ruby, he hadn't murdered the man as was commonly believed. No, whatever had happened to Isabelle in that suite had happened after he'd been abducted.

At first, Selene had stayed at Minerva's condo in Vancouver for a little while, and after that, she'd stayed with Lively. While there, she'd had to insist on cooking him fresh food each day of her stay rather than eating the MREs of which Lively was so unhealthily fond. After catching up with her children, she'd returned some of the calls she'd been fending off. Several studios were looking to have her star in projects they had planned, including Paramount, which had contacted her to star in the film adaptation of Vincent DaCosta's upcoming novel.

John and Helen Harder were still living in the small condo that John had bought after selling their house, and they couldn't be happier. They'd spent very little time living in it so far this year, at least judging from the postcards Lively and Minerva had both been receiving for the last month. The couple was currently on a Caribbean cruise. Though John's hip still pained him on occasion, his health was quite exceptional for a man of eighty-eight. Once they returned from the Caribbean, they were heading back out on another cruise at the end of August, this one of the world, and were not expected back till November. And so, the twins were preparing themselves for a flood of postcards in the near future.

The exterior maintenance had ended at the hotel just the week before, and they were preparing to seal the resort up again. On-site security was newly situated in a guardhouse near the front gate, and a high, electrified perimeter fence now ran around the whole property. With the addition of dozens of security cameras outside and guards at the front gate, they figured the hotel would be safe from vandals and looky-loos and wouldn't need all of its windows boarded up as before. Instead, reinforced shutters had been attached to all the first-floor windows, including the tall windows of the ballroom.

"I think we may need to revisit this place in the next year or so. Even though things seem calm here at the moment, I think we should give this place a little while to stew in its own juices, so to speak, and see what comes out in the wash," Lively said.

Still looking out the window next to her brother, Minerva added, "That's a good idea. And like you mentioned, we still don't know how many of the partygoers were involved in things up here."

When everything was said and done, almost a dozen of the Returned had rematerialised in the ballroom wearing harmonic bracelets. And all of them claimed they had no idea why they were wearing them. Lively suspected a few might honestly be suffering some sort of amnesiac effect, and of course, others might just be outright lying. Apart from stabilising other-worldly travellers, the bracelets also defrayed the memory loss from the constant realignment of the frequencies over the years, so he knew some of the bracelet wearers must be far more aware of things than they were letting on.

Lively said, "I need to do some digging around. Maybe we'll invite some of the prime suspects up here some New Year's Eve, bring out the ebony box, and see what happens."

"That would be quite a party," Minerva agreed.

Between the two of them, they'd moved the black box to a secure and hidden location in the hotel's guts. And that was where it would stay until further research could be done on its origins, along with the ebony gemstones that lined its interior. But that would have to be the stuff of future investigations.

Thinking of the future, lively rubbed his hands together and said, "But in the meantime, we could catch up on some of the new contracts that we've both amassed from all that coverage from the media."

With a nod, Minerva said, "We both have enough new clients to keep us busy for the next decade or more, that's for sure." Like Lively, she had received numerous calls to appear on talk shows and undergo interviews for various news outlets. This had resulted in a renewed interest in her modelling career as well as further work utilising her psychic abilities for those in need of someone with her exceptional talents.

"I think this place has real potential."

"Agreed," Minerva said with a small smile. "Let's hope we find the time to make something happen up here."

Shortly, they were on the ground floor, the hotel's main doors standing open at their backs. After surveying the empty lobby in silence one last time, Lively turned and flipped off the bank of light switches, recalling the first day he'd stood here in this exact same spot and turned them on.

Minerva stepped out first, and Lively reached in to pull the door closed. The setting sun bathed everything in its honey-coloured light, the lobby now looking as if lined with gold from the hidden room below.

Giving the things a final glance, Lively paused suddenly as he pulled the door closed. Across the lobby, toward the ballroom annex, a tall, handsome RCMP officer stood in full dress uniform, a crooked grin on his face. At his side was another officer, petite, young and pretty, a corporal, according to the insignia on her uniform jacket.

His face one of joy tinged with sadness, Lively nodded at them both as he pulled the door shut. They smiled radiantly in return, smiles of those finally at peace with themselves and the world. Two souls now able to make up for lost time and lost love, not only today but each and every day from now into eternity.

Katie Berry

FIN

AFTERWORD

Thank you, dear reader, for coming along on this little carnival funhouse of a story. Though this is the final book in the introductory series to Lively and Minerva Deadmarsh's adventures, it is not their last trip up the hill. There are still a few things that go bump and thump in the night at the Sinclair and there are tales yet untold. So, a return to the resort is definitely in order in the future.

For those of you following the CLAW series, the first book in the three-novel prequel, CLAW Emergence should be coming your way sometime this fall, with the second hopefully by Christmas and the final book in the trilogy in the spring of 2023.

And if you're curious where Lively will go next, it's actually a place he's been, which I referred to at the beginning of Book 1, the ocean cruise. In this novel, entitled BESIEGED, the cruise is not in any way relaxing or enjoyable for anyone involved, at least not by the end of it. But that is something for you to read and enjoy in the future, and I will keep you updated on its progress.

For now, I must run and continue work on the tale of Caleb Cantrill and Kitty Welch, two people very much involved in the founding of Lawless BC. Their adventure is just beginning and trust me when I say it will be quite a ride. Until then, take good care, my friends.

Good health and great reads to you all,

-Katie Berry

FINAL WORDS

Reviews are critical to a book's success. The more honest reviews a book has, the better it is for everybody because then, we all win. Engaged readers like yourself can help introduce new readers to the series and allow them to share in the fun.

And so, if this novel entertained you and you would like to share your thoughts with others, please leave a review. Below is a direct link to the Amazon review page for ABANDONED Book 4, so you can leave a few thoughts while everything is fresh in your memory:

http://www.amazon.com/review/create-review?&asin=B0B6RTHXSM

In order to stay on top of all these exciting developments and other surprises, please make sure to join my newsletter, The Katie Berry Books Insider, for further novel updates, free short stories, chapter previews and giveaways. To join, click here:

https://katieberry.ca/become-a-katie-berry-books-insider-and-win/

CURRENT AND UPCOMING RELEASES

CLAW: A Canadian Thriller (November 28th, 2019)

CLAW Emergence Novelette – Caleb Cantrill (September 13th, 2020)

CLAW Emergence Novelette – Kitty Welch - (November 26th, 2020)

CLAW Resurgence (September 30th, 2021)

CLAW Emergence Book 1 (December 24th. 2022)

CLAW Emergence Book 2 (July 1st, 2023)

CLAW Emergence Book 3 (December 24th, 2023)

CLAW Resurrection (Spring 2024)

ABANDONED: A Lively Deadmarsh Novel Book 1 (February 26th, 2021)

ABANDONED: A Lively Deadmarsh Novel Book 2 (May 31st, 2021)

ABANDONED: A Lively Deadmarsh Novel Book 3 (December 23rd, 2021)

ABANDONED: A Lively Deadmarsh Novel Book 4 (July 15th, 2022)

BESIEGED: A Lively Deadmarsh Novel (Fall 2024)

CONNECTIONS
Email: katie@katieberry.ca
Website: https://katieberry.ca

SHOPPING LINKS

CLAW: A Canadian Thriller:
Amazon eBook: https://amzn.to/31QCw7x
Paperback Version: https://amzn.to/31RYPK7
Amazon Audible Audiobook: https://amzn.to/2Gj3j45
(Also available on all other major audiobook platforms)

CLAW Resurgence:
Amazon eBook: https://amzn.to/2YeDdZt
Paperback Version: https://amzn.to/31RYPK7
Amazon Audible Audiobook: https://amzn.to/36nLSgk
(Also available on all other major audiobook platforms)

CLAW Emergence: Tales from Lawless – Kitty Welch:
Amazon eBook: https://amzn.to/37aSnAn
Large Print Paperback Version: https://amzn.to/3tTsoa9
Audiobook on Audible: https://amzn.to/3szAmXM

CLAW Emergence: Tales from Lawless – Caleb Cantrill:
Amazon eBook: https://amzn.to/3ldYoC3
Large Print Paperback Version: https://amzn.to/3meDVg9
Audiobook on Audible: https://amzn.to/3qkKvUe

CLAW Emergence Book 1: From the Shadows:
Amazon eBook: https://amzn.to/3VnB6di
Paperback Version: https://amzn.to/3Xjv5Q1
Audiobook: https://amzn.to/3TSvDyh
(Also available on all other major audiobook platforms)

CLAW Emergence Book 2: Into Daylight:

Amazon eBook: https://amzn.to/3JEC9Tf
Paperback Version: https://amzn.to/3NwKfhG
Audiobook Version: https://amzn.to/41y2lGR
(Also available on all other major audiobook platforms)

CLAW Emergence Book 3: Return to Darkness:
Amazon eBook: https://amzn.to/3GUVe1B
Paperback Version: https://amzn.to/47mrhCn
Audiobook Version: Coming Soon
(Also available on all other major audiobook platforms)

ABANDONED: A Lively Deadmarsh Novel Book 1 – Arrivals
and Awakenings:
Amazon eBook: https://amzn.to/3jM3GDX
Paperback: https://amzn.to/3yruNLL
Audiobook: https://amzn.to/3yNot0o
(Also available on all other major audiobook platforms)

ABANDONED: A Lively Deadmarsh Novel Book 2 –
Beginnings and Betrayals:
Amazon eBook: https://amzn.to/3BTn4a9
Paperback: https://amzn.to/3BTneyh
Audiobook: https://amzn.to/3FrwcVF
(Also available on all other major audiobook platforms)

ABANDONED: A Lively Deadmarsh Novel Book 3 – Chaos
and Corruption:
Amazon eBook: https://amzn.to/3HpBNMM
Paperback: https://amzn.to/3IOGTE7
Audiobook: https://amzn.to/3PtVyqr
(Also available on all other major audiobook platforms)

ABANDONED: A Lively Deadmarsh Novel Book 4 –
Deception and Deliverance:
Amazon eBook: https://amzn.to/3wo6XqF
Paperback: https://amzn.to/3Qh5t3m
Audiobook: https://amzn.to/3NVOdC9
(Also available on all other major audiobook platforms)

Made in the USA
Monee, IL
02 February 2024

52846752R00236